New York
Nocturne

① 11-2016
06-2021

New York
Nocturne

The Return of
MISS LIZZIE

Walter Satterthwait

MYSTERIOUSPRESS.COM

OPEN ROAD
INTEGRATED MEDIA
NEW YORK

Copyright © 2016 by Walter Satterthwait

Cover design by Michael Vrana

978-1-5040-2812-7

Published in 2016 by MysteriousPress.com/Open Road Integrated Media, Inc.
180 Maiden Lane
New York, NY 10038
www.openroadmedia.com

New York
Nocturne

Readers of my earlier recollection, *Miss Lizzie*, will perhaps recollect that at the end of the volume, I stated that I never again met with the person who served as the book's main character. This statement was not entirely true. It was, in fact, a bald-faced lie, one for which I now offer this volume as a kind of apology. The reason for the lie will, I believe, become obvious.

BOOK ONE

Chapter One

For a brief while there, before things began to fall apart, it was truly a glorious time.

I was sixteen years old and I was free, personally free, in a way that I had never been before, and possibly never would be again. And I was free in the city of New York, which was situated, as New Yorkers have always known, in the exact geographical center of the universe.

My father and my stepmother, Susan, had finally left Boston and set off on the journey they had been promising to each other for three years: an expedition that would take them halfway around the world, to Tibet and Lhasa and a trek through the Himalayas. Back then, in 1924, before international air travel and international telephone lines, and the escalating horrors of international tourism, this was truly an adventure.

It was an adventure, however, that neither I nor my older brother, William, wished to share. William refused it because he had fallen in love with yet another ethereal literature major in a black pullover. I, because I saw no virtue in wild, windy mountains and yak butter tea at the time. (I have since changed my mind about the mountains.)

After a certain amount of discussion, Father and Susan had finally agreed to let me spend the summer in New York. While the two of them were frolicking with Sherpas and yetis, I would be staying with my father's younger brother, John Burton, in a famous apartment building near Central Park called the Dakota.

William, four years older than I, would remain in Boston,

within wooing distance of the literature major. He had been to New York once, he told me, and it had shown him nothing at all. William was the older brother *par excellence*—endearing but mistaken about nearly everything.

Father and Susan left on June the second. On the sixth, at seven o'clock in the morning, William drove me to the station where I boarded the train. Six hours later, after rattling through southern New England and southeast New York State; crossing the Harlem River into Manhattan; plunging beneath the exotic streets of busy Harlem; and swaying and clanking along a gloomy, dank, and seemingly endless tunnel, the train arrived at the lower level of the Grand Central Terminal.

Between them, my uncle and Susan had arranged that John and I meet at the information booth on the main floor. A bit dazed, my suitcase dangling from my right hand, my purse dangling from my left shoulder, I stepped gingerly off the car and began treading down the platform, tilted slightly to my suitcase side.

The tunnel was still dank, but it was illuminated now with flickering yellow lights set in little wire cages along the concrete columns. Scuttling around me were hundreds of other passengers in business suits and smart summer dresses, all of them rushing toward enterprises of vast and immediate importance. I felt diminished, made suddenly inadequate and trivial by their zeal.

I followed the crowd, was swept along with it, nudged forward, jostled sideways. Not that anyone actually touched me, of course, but New Yorkers have learned how to make mere momentum contagious. Surrounded by them and their hurry, I stalked into the station and lugged my luggage up the broad, bright white stairway into the main concourse.

It was a revelation. Today—and I have not been to Grand Central Station for decades now—I can still recall precisely how I felt the first time I stepped out onto that flat expanse of marble, beneath that vast, vaulted blue ceiling sparkling with golden stars. Sunlight toppled down through the towering arched windows and splashed across the enormous room and the eager humanity who scurried across it. Men and women and children, singly and in groups, dashed this way and that. Behind clattering wooden carts piled high with baggage, red-capped porters hurried to and fro.

Awed and excited, I felt as though I had stumbled into a cathedral, the seat of the Archdiocese of Hustle and Bustle. As I stood there, still panting from the journey to the surface of the earth, the air around me seemed to shimmer and hum.

I was here! I was in New York!

I hauled the suitcase over to the information booth: a squat, upright cylinder of gleaming brass and glass huddled in the center of the concourse. On its four quadrants, travelers were arrayed in uneven, impatient lines, waiting to commune, one on one, with the earnest blue-uniformed dignitaries inside.

I looked up at the big round clock atop the booth.

Fifteen minutes after one.

I was late.

Had my uncle come and gone?

I noticed that I was perspiring—demurely, of course, as one does. My sleeves were damp.

"Ah," said a voice behind me. "Amanda?"

I turned.

Two men stood there, both in their early thirties. One of them was short and wore a black three-piece suit at least two sizes too small for his square, broad body. His black hair was slicked back from his square, broad forehead. His entire face, too, was square and broad, and it was flattened in front, as though someone had recently slammed something against it—a cruise ship, perhaps.

I recognized the other man from a photograph Father had once shown me. But this man was slightly older and impossibly better looking than the man in the photograph. With the exception of my first husband, my uncle John was the most handsome man I have ever met.

Tall, slim, and clean-shaven, he smelled faintly of some astringent, terribly masculine cologne. His thick hair was black, his nose was straight, and his teeth were white. His eyes were a soft incandescent blue—the precise color of robins' eggs, but flecked with tiny dancing sparkles of gold.

He wore a cream-colored two-piece linen suit, a blue silk shirt with a white collar, a red silk tie, a pair of tan silk socks, and a pair of serenely polished two-tone brown wing-tip shoes. Jauntily, down at his left thigh, between thumb and forefinger, he held the brim of a bone-white Panama hat.

Smiling politely, he offered his right hand to me, and I took it. He shook my hand formally once, twice, and then released it.

"This is Albert," he said, and then grinned proudly, like an inventor showing off a recent triumph. "A good friend of mine," he said, and slapped the other man on his thick shoulder.

Albert nodded his big square head. "Very pleased to meet you," he said and held out his hand.

"How do you do?" I reached for his lumpy hand, which seemed to be constructed entirely of knuckles. The thick fingers enclosed themselves around mine with an unexpected gentleness. He grinned at me, too, and said, "I am perfectly well, thank you. And yourself, miss?"

"Very well," I said. "Thank you."

"Albert'll take your suitcase," said my uncle.

"Sure I will," said Albert. He released my hand and reached out for the bag. I handed it to him, and he plucked it lightly away as though it held a mere handful of feathers and not my entire summer wardrobe. I half-expected him to tuck it under his arm, like a portfolio.

"Now," said my uncle, "have you eaten?"

"I had some crackers on the train."

"Crackers aren't food. They're *passatempi*. Time passers."

"I understand the word," I said, perhaps a shade more curtly than necessary.

He raised an eyebrow. "You speak Italian?"

"I studied Latin." Even without Latin, the word wouldn't have been that difficult to puzzle out.

He looked at me for a moment, and then he laughed. It was

quite a nice laugh, full and quick and easy. He shook his head. He ran his hand back through his hair, held it there, cupping the back of his neck, and then looked down at me aslant. "Of course you did. And I'm being a horse's ass, aren't I?"

I laughed then myself, in surprise and relief.

"Look," he said, "this is a big deal for me. Isn't it, Albert? Didn't I say it was a big deal?"

Albert had been following our conversation gravely, his big square head slowly swaying back and forth. Now he nodded again. "An extremely big deal," he assured me.

"I meet my niece for the first time," said my uncle, "and I'm expecting a little girl." He held his hand out at waist level. "Like this. And wearing God knows what—what do little girls wear?" He turned to Albert. "Dirndls?"

Albert shrugged massively, as though to say that he could not even begin to guess what it was that little girls wore.

My uncle turned back to me. "And instead I find a beautiful young woman wearing a beautiful French frock—it is French, isn't it?"

"Yes." My eyelids fluttered, as they often did back then. It was my way of briefly shuttering out the world when it suddenly became too awkward or too close.

I knew that I was not a beautiful young woman. I knew that my eyes were too far apart, my neck was too long, and my mouth too wide. But I had learned that sometimes, occasionally, if I were wearing just the right sort of finery, if I were standing exactly right in exactly the right sort of lighting, I could maybe hoodwink people into believing that I was at least pretty.

It was generous of him to permit himself to be hoodwinked, or to pretend he was, and unexpected generosity always made the world around me suddenly too awkward. Or too close.

I told him, "Susan—my stepmother—she bought it for me last month."

"I'd say that you and Susan have excellent taste."

"Thank you." It *was* a lovely cotton frock: sleeveless, summery lemon-yellow, drop-waisted, with a light and almost gauzy matching jacket—a very *chic* jacket, even if its sleeves at the moment were a trifle damp.

"Anyway," he said, "you caught me off guard. And I acted like a jerk. I apologize."

"No, no," I said. "You don't have to apologize."

"When you act like a jerk, you apologize. Am I right, Albert?"

Albert firmly nodded. "It is the done thing."

My uncle smiled. "All right, look. How do you feel about sea-food?"

"I love it," I told him honestly.

"Good. Here's what I suggest. Albert here takes your suitcase up to the apartment. Is there anything in it you need right now?"

"Not really, no. I don't think so."

"Okay. There's a seafood place here in the station. Nice place. An oyster bar. You and I can grab a bite to eat, get to know each other. And then, if you're up to it, we can explore some of the city before we head home. That sound all right?"

"It sounds really wonderful," I said.

"Good." Another smile. "But not so much enthusiasm. Every-one will know you're from out of town."

I nodded seriously. "And that's very bad."

He grinned. "The worst." He turned to Albert. "We'll be back by six, probably," he told him.

Albert nodded. "You want I should prepare some supper? Maybe a nice nourishing soufflé? Maybe a small green salad? With that escarole?"

"No, Albert, thanks. There's plenty of food in the icebox. You take off. We'll see you on Monday." He slapped him on the shoulder again, then turned back to me. "Let's go."

Albert and I said our goodbyes, and then he lumbered away with the suitcase.

"This way," said my uncle, pointing his Panama like an Amazon explorer, and together we set off through the jungle of passengers.

Looking straight ahead, he leaned slightly toward me. "Can I ask you one small favor?"

"Of course."

Still looking straight ahead, he said, "I call you Amanda, right?"

"Yes, of course."

"Well, you can call me anything you want. John. Jack. Millard."
He turned to me, smiling. "But I'd be very grateful if you didn't call
me 'Uncle John.'"

"Okay," I said. "Sure."

"Would that be okay?" he asked me as we started down a gently
inclined marble corridor. "Do you mind?"

Flattered by his asking, I shook my head. "No. Not at all. Millard?"

He grinned. "My sergeant, in the army. An idiot."

He was really quite extraordinarily handsome. And it was really
quite amazing the way those golden flecks floated in that blue of
iris.

Cocking his head, he said, "It's just that 'Uncle John' . . . well, it
makes me feel . . . a tiny bit ossified."

"Which would you prefer?" I asked him.

"John, I suppose. John would be fine." He smiled again. "You
know *ossified*?"

"Like a bone. Old. Inflexible, rigid."

He laughed. "So John's okay?"

"John is fine." I had never called an adult by his first name before.

He smiled, and read my mind. "Don't worry," he said. "You'll
get used to it."

I blushed.

And I wondered whether I would ever truly get used to it. With
an uncle. Especially an uncle like this one.

We ate at the Oyster Bar—which, on that day, became the first of
my favorite restaurants in New York.

John and I were still somewhat wary of each other. We were total
strangers, after all, passersby connected only by the mysterious accident of blood. If either of us were a disappointment to the other, might
that not suggest some inherited flaw in ourselves as well?

After we ordered our food, he sipped at his coffee and studied me. "You look a lot like your mother," he said.

Running down the exact center of his square chin was a sculpted cleft, the sort of cleft that a fully grown woman suddenly might find herself wishing to examine more closely, perhaps with the thoughtful tip of a stroking finger. Or so I imagined.

"I never knew her," I told him.

"I know. It was a tragedy. A real tragedy. William was a wreck."

It took me a moment to realize that he meant my father, not my brother.

He put down his coffee cup. "I liked her. She was smart, very smart. And very beautiful."

"When did you meet her?"

"At the wedding. Just that once."

"I've seen pictures. Do you really think I look like her?"

"Yes." He smiled. "Are you fishing?"

Once again I felt my cheeks redden. "For what?"

"Ah. Your face gives you away."

"Yes," I said, "well, I'm from out of town."

He laughed. "Smart, too. Like your mother."

I fluttered my lashes and carefully examined the tablecloth, which had suddenly become a still center point around which the awkward, lovely world revolved.

It was a wonderful meal: oysters on the half shell, fleshy gray Belons from Maine; a rich, savory, sea-scented oyster stew as well; then a sumptuous baked stuffed lobster; and finally a sinfully dense cheesecake heaped high with slick sweet strawberries.

Afterward, in the intersection of corridors directly opposite the restaurant's entrance, John showed me the whispering corners. If a person stood facing one stone corner of the square, and another person stood facing the corner diagonally opposite, each could speak to the other in a whisper and still be heard perfectly, despite the crowd churning and chattering between them and behind their backs.

Delighted, I glanced up at the low gray arches overhead. I whispered, "The sound travels along the ceiling!"

"Exactly," whispered the stones.

"Is this a big secret?" I asked them.

"Well," they said, "there are still two people in Brooklyn who don't know about it."

I laughed.

"Come on," said the stones. "We'll do the town."

We left the terminal at the Vanderbilt Avenue exit, walked beneath the dark sweep of the bridge above Park Avenue, turned right at Forty-Second Street, and headed west. It was a fabulously sunny day. John's unbuttoned coat flapped and fluttered heroically in the breeze.

We walked past Madison to Fifth Avenue, just north of the wonderful white sprawl of the New York Public Library and its wonderful sprawling lions. We turned right and marched along Fifth up through the Forties. As we walked, John pointed out the sights: the Shepard and the Goelet brownstones, the Church of St. Nicholas, the Vanderbilt mansions, St. Patrick's Cathedral. By then we were in the Fifties, passing all the sparkling storefronts—Steuben Glass, Cartier, Bergdorf Goodman.

It was in the window of Bergdorf Goodman, among an elaborate display of mannequins—slick young papier-mâché men and women frozen in a tableau around a gleaming black Stutz Bearcat automobile—that I saw the hat. I stopped walking.

One of the figures was wearing it. She stood with her left foot on the car's shiny running board, her right arm on the doorframe, as she stared, unblinking, into the unblinking eyes of the resolutely jaunty driver.

"What is it?" asked John.

"Oh, nothing. Just looking."

"Nice car," he said.

"I like the hat." I nodded toward the mannequin.

"Ah," he said. "Iris Storm."

I should not have been surprised—although I was, a bit—that

he knew of Michael Arlen's novel *The Green Hat*. But of course everyone knew of it that year, even those (very few) who had not read it. Sermons had been preached against the "decadence" of its characters, especially its beautiful and doomed young heroine, Iris Storm. A woman of independent means, Iris spends her time slinking about Europe, striking poses and breaking hearts. She loves. She suffers. She wears the hat in question, a green cloche. In the end, she deliberately runs her huge yellow Hispano-Suiza touring car into a very large tree, very quickly. In the context of the novel, this is presented—and at the time we readers happily accepted it— as an act of great nobility.

"Come along," said John, tipping off his Panama. "Let's investigate."

I followed him into the building, into that lovely great welcoming bubble of department store fragrances, of perfumes and colognes and powders. In the millinery department, arranged along a stepped mahogany counter, were cloche hats of every size and color. Several of them were green, and one of those seemed to be my size. I touched it tentatively.

"Try it on," said John.

"Oh, no," I said. "I couldn't."

Casually, he dropped his Panama onto the counter, picked up the cloche, and held it out. "Please. As a favor."

At that moment, a saleswoman swept down upon us, possibly from the rafters. Tall and sheathed in black, she was at least ten years older than I and at least thirty years more sophisticated. Her bobbed black hair was as sleek and seamless as patent leather. Her long, beautiful face was white against her florid cosmetics— the cheekbones bluntly rouged, the lips brightly painted. Her dark Egyptian eyes were huge. She radiated Chanel No. 5.

The eyes glanced down at the hat in my hands. "It's our most popular color," she announced. She looked at John, and her eyes flickered once—a quick, avid flicker, immediately disguised as a glance of polite interest. Over the next week, I would see similar flickers and disguises in the eyes of many other women.

I eased the hat on, looked at John, looked at myself in the mirror, adjusted the hat, adjusted the tilt of my head. I imagined how I should feel wearing the hat, if I stood in a pose that was at once sophisticated and louche. I attempted to stand in such a pose. I failed and glanced at John.

He was fiddling with the rest of the display, lifting hats, casually examining their interior, not looking at me at all.

The saleswoman pronounced, "It suits you."

Still fiddling, still not looking at me, John said, "May I say something?"

I looked at him.

"Did you notice," he asked, idly fiddling away, "how many women were wearing that hat? Out on the street?" Looking over at me, he nodded toward the cloche on my head. "Exactly that color hat?"

I hadn't; I had been too busy observing the lengths of the hems on the smart skirts and stylish dresses and determining, unhappily, that my own yellow frock was perhaps not as utterly soigné as I had believed.

The saleswoman had been watching him, her lips slightly parted. "It's our most popular color," she announced.

"Exactly," said John. "Here," he said, holding out another cloche, this one a tawny yellow. "Try this?"

I removed the green one, set it down, and took the yellow. I put it on, eased it into place, and turned to look at myself in the mirror. The hat's color, naturally, went much better with my frock and the jacket.

"The lining is green," said John and smiled.

I knew instantly what he meant—that I could pretend to be Iris Storm in secret with no one the wiser.

I blushed again. Found out.

"Do you like it?" he asked me.

"Yes, but—"

"No buts. Here, let me see something." He reached forward, put a hand on either side of my face, and gently adjusted the hat.

Over the years, I have noticed a curious phenomenon. Whenever anyone presents to me a physical act of kindness, I experience a peculiar physical response.

I first noticed it, fittingly, in the first grade. We were using watercolors, and on my virgin sheet of paper I had accomplished a plump red apple. The girl who sat beside me—Nancy Warbuton—leaned over, looked at my production, and said, "That's really good. Can I show you something?"

"Sure."

She dabbed her brush into her palette, leaned over again, and then, judiciously, with precise pink strokes, created a small casement window on the side of my apple, a reflection lovingly distorted by the plump red roundness of the fruit. As she took the time—her time—to demonstrate this, I felt a distinct and agreeable flush that began at the back of my neck and then fanned out across my back and shoulders—a delicious, hidden flush of pleasure unfolding slowly along my skin.

It is not, I believe, at all sexual. Over the years, it has appeared whether the kindness was from a man or a woman or from someone in whom I have any interest. In Borneo once, years later, it showed up when a map, carefully hand-drawn in the sand, was provided by a man I suspected—accurately, as it happened—of being a pederast and a murderer.

And it happened now, in Bergdorf Goodman, as John Burton fine-tuned the altitude and attitude of my new hat.

"If you have to say anything," he said, "you can say 'thank you.'"

"Thank you."

"You're welcome," he said and smiled. In his blue eyes, those flecks of gold danced.

We walked to his apartment: past the Plaza Hotel, west on Central Park South, north into the park, and along West Drive through the Playground and the Green, and then out across Central Park West onto Seventy-Second Street.

The Dakota was a gorgeous pile of old yellow brick, gabled, dormered, and pinnacled like something from a fairy tale. It was not tall, but it took up an entire block, and John's apartment, on the fourth floor, facing the park, took up a large chunk of the building's side.

It was the first apartment I had ever seen decorated in what was then called "moderne" or "contemporanian" style, which is now called art deco, painted and stained in shades of brown—sienna, umber, and tan. The furniture—richly lacquered wood, light and dark, inlaid with tortoiseshell and mother of pearl—was smooth and streamlined as though it were all planning to take flight.

He led me on a tour: a huge kitchen that held a sit-down circular mahogany table and smoothly sculpted mahogany chairs; a formal dining room; a bi-level living room with a broad fieldstone fireplace, its mantle a thick ledge of bright stainless steel, and a sweeping picture window that overlooked the luminous green park; a library, three walls stacked with beautiful old leather books, the fourth sporting another fireplace, this of onyx and polished chrome; and three bedrooms, each exquisitely appointed, each with its own bath. One of these, he told me, belonged to Albert, who used it during the week. On weekends, John said, Albert stayed with a friend in Queens—a lady friend, he added.

"What does Albert do?" I asked him.

John smiled. "About what?"

"What does he do for you?"

He shrugged. "This and that. He helps out. He's a friend."

Not an especially helpful answer, but I was too polite to press the issue.

The third bedroom was mine, and my suitcase stood upright beside the white sprawl of my king-size bed. Stretching across the hardwood floor was something I had never seen before: a wide Greek flokati rug, as white and shaggy as a polar bear.

The promised food was in the icebox, and before we went out again, we had "a little snack." For the first time in my life, I ate Beluga caviar on buttered toast points. This was accompanied by another agreeable novelty: a half glass of Dom Perignon champagne.

Afterward, we took a taxicab down to Broadway, where we saw the Marx Brothers in a play called *I'll Say She Is*. Perhaps the champagne was partly responsible, but I have never laughed so hard in my life, before or since. I would have been embarrassed had John, beside me, not been laughing equally as hard.

By the time I went to bed that night, I had begun to feel that I was, myself, something from a fairy tale.

I was very much looking forward to the rest of my summer with John Burton.

Unfortunately, we would have only one week together.

Chapter Two

It was a busy week.

I had arrived on a Friday. Over the weekend, John took me all around the city: to Ferrara's on Grand Street, the Empire Room at the Waldorf Astoria, the Oak Room at the Plaza, the Café Julien on University Place, around the corner from Washington Square. On Saturday night, we watched Douglas Fairbanks, the Thief of Baghdad, zoom about Arabia on a rather wobbly magic carpet. At a Sunday matinee at the Earl Carroll Theater, we watched Eddie Cantor flash his banjo eyes and prance through Ziegfeld's *Kid Boots*.

That evening, we took a taxi down to a speakeasy on East Fourth Street called the Red Head. John knew the owners, a Mr. Berns and a Mr. Kreindler—Charlie and Jack—and, as we ate thick rare steaks and crispy fried potatoes, they joined us at our table. Mr. Kreindler told me that at the beginning of 1919, when alcohol was last legally served in New York, there had been fifteen thousand bars in the city. Now, five years after the start of Prohibition, when they had all been outlawed, there were thirty thousand of them. Mr. Kreindler was clearly quite tickled by this.

John Burton knew almost everyone, it seemed, and everyone knew him. Restaurant owners, headwaiters, maître d's, hostesses, they all greeted him by name. He introduced me as "my niece, Amanda," and they looked at me with a kind of smiling, bland politeness that masked, I was certain, a roiling curiosity. John was invariably the most handsome and the best dressed man in any restaurant, café, or club—why was he hauling this gawky young albatross from place to place?

I was still feeling as though I had wandered into a fairy tale.

On Sunday night before I went to bed, John told me that he would be leaving for work early in the morning. (Like my father, he did mysterious things with stocks and bonds.) We were in the kitchen sitting at the table, John with a King's Ransom Scotch and soda in front of him, me with a Coca-Cola. John had loosened the knot of his tie, and he sat back in his chair, easy and relaxed.

He reminded me that Albert would be there when I awoke.

"I still don't understand what Albert does," I said.

"He helps out with things," said John. "Cooking, housecleaning, whatever."

"Sort of like a butler."

"Sort of. And he's a friend. He helps out if I need something. And if *you* need something tomorrow, while I'm gone, you just ask him."

The next morning, when I woke up and looked at the clock on the nightstand, I saw that it was nearly nine o'clock. I took a quick shower and threw on some clothing, ending up in another light-weight summer dress, this one of pale blue cotton.

Albert was in the kitchen. He sat in John's chair, studying the *New York Times*, his square face still looking as though it had been run into, or over.

Opposite him, the table had been set for one: a white linen placemat, a white linen napkin folded into a triangle, silverware, a porcelain plate, a butter dish, a porcelain cup and saucer, and a cut crystal glass filled with orange juice.

"Good morning," I said.

He turned to me and lowered the paper. "Oh, hey, miss," he said, and standing up, he set the paper on the table. He wore a white shirt, a black tie, and black slacks. Around his thick waist, reaching to just below his knees, was a spotless white apron imprinted with delicate little daisies. He grabbed a shiny metal spatula from the table, raised it up, and swung it in a kind of circular salute beside his head. "What is your pleasure, if I may ask?"

"Pardon me?"

He lowered the spatula. "Food-wise, I mean. What I am thinking, see, is along the lines of flapjacks. In certain circles, my flapjacks are very highly regarded, if I do say so myself." He said this with a perfectly straight face. As I was to learn, Albert said almost everything with a perfectly straight face.

"Flapjacks would be wonderful," I said. "If they're not too much trouble."

"No trouble whatsoever," he said. "In point of fact, these I make already. Also, there is orange juice, and this I squoze only five minutes ago. Scientifically speaking, according to those in the know, fresh orange juice is one of the most healthful beverages known to man."

"Thank you. Can I help with anything?"

"Nothing whatsoever. You just sit yourself down, miss."

I did.

"Now," he said, "tell me this." He put his hands together over his beefy chest, palms joined and fingers straight as though praying and cocked his big square head. "Are you the sort of individual who enjoys a nice hot cup of coffee in the morning?"

"Yes. Very much."

"Right-o." He lowered his hands, turned, and walked to the stove. "The thing of it is, see, I do not number among my acquaintances many individuals of the youthful sort." He lifted a percolator from the stove and a small tray from the nearby counter, turned, and walked back. His movements were precise, almost dainty. "So I am not exactly in the know as to their preferences, eat- and drink-wise."

"Sure," I said. "Of course not."

He set the tray on the table. A small pitcher of cream, a small bowl of sugar. He poured some coffee into my cup. "There is a message for you," he said. "From your uncle. Right there. On the book."

To my right on the table, a folded sheet of paper lay atop a small book. I took the sheet and opened it.

Dear Amanda,
   Good morning.
   I'm leaving you a guide to the city. If you need anything, ask Albert. I'll be back at six tonight. See you then.

Regards,
John

I picked up the book. *New York City and Its Environs.* Sticking out from the center of the pages, at the top, like a bookmark, was the crisp tip of a twenty-dollar bill.

Twenty dollars, back then, was rather a lot of money. And every day for the next four days, even after I protested to John about it, another twenty would await me at the kitchen table. By the end of the week, I still had change left from the second twenty and another sixty dollars. My plan was to return the money to John at some point. For reasons that will soon become clear, this I was unable to do.

Albert had set the tray on the counter, opened the door to the oven, and removed a platter wrapped in aluminum foil. He set the platter on the table beside my plate along with a small white porcelain pitcher of maple syrup. He peeled away the foil to reveal a steaming stack of golden brown pancakes. The air in the room grew dense with their rich, moist scent.

Albert said, "What I am thinking, see, as an accompaniment, is maybe some nice fried eggs. This morning, on my way over, I obtained the eggs from a source known to me personally. I can vouch for their freshness, totally."

"Eggs would be great," I said.

"And your preference here would be what? Over easy? Sunny-side up?"

"Over easy, please."

"The yolk still in a runny condition, am I correct?"

"Correct. Yes."

"An ace? A deuce?"

"Um—a deuce, please."

"You go ahead," he said and fluttered his fingers twice at the food in front of me. "Please. Eat, miss."

I forked some pancakes onto my plate, buttered them, and poured on some syrup.

At the stove, Albert held a lighted match to the burner. The gas lit with a small *thump.*

"Your uncle tells me," he said as he put a frying pan onto the burner, "that you will probably wish to see more of the city, this being your first occasion to visit here. I would be pleased to volunteer my assistance, in any way, shape, or form whatsoever. What I mean is, I can act as a guide, like. If you want me to, I mean to say."

"Thank you," I said. "That's very kind."

"Not at all, miss. The thing of it is this: Any person who is a friend of your uncle, that person is a friend of mine also."

The frying pan was sizzling. He turned down the gas and plucked a large brown egg from a bowl on the counter. Nimbly, he cracked it against the edge of the counter, held it over the pan, separated the halves of shell with a twist of his fingers, and then deftly raised his hand. The yolk and the white slipped smoothly out and crackled merrily in the hot fat.

"If you don't mind," I told him, "I think I'd like to look around on my own."

He nodded. "Right-o. I totally understand." He plucked another egg from the bowl and expertly cracked it into the frying pan.

I took another bite of pancake. "How long have you known John?"

"Since the Great War." He gave the pan a little shake and picked up his spatula.

"You met him in the army?"

He was examining the eggs. "Correct."

"And you work with him now?"

"Correct."

"What kind of things do you do?"

He looked at me. "That would depend, miss, on what needs doing. A little bit of this, a little bit of that."

This was almost exactly what John had said, and almost exactly as helpful.

For that week, this became the pattern of my days. First, I would breakfast with Albert. Sometimes we talked about the sights and sounds of New York. Sometimes Albert would make suggestions— where to go, what to see, what to avoid.

After breakfast, I would set out on an expedition around the city. Sometimes I took the subway, sometimes the elevated train along Sixth Avenue, but usually I walked. All that week the weather was perfect: bright and sunny and warm. With the tour book as my Virgil, I journeyed everywhere, from Battery Park to Columbus Circle, from the East River to the Hudson.

I admired the Woolworth Building at Broadway and Park Place, the tallest building in the world. I admired the expansive Roman bath magnificence of Pennsylvania Station on Seventh Avenue. I admired the Flatiron Building at Madison Square, that thin preposterous wedge of stone and steel that rose twenty stories high.

Every day I ate some new, delicious food: knishes, soft pretzels, bagels and lox, hot dogs with sauerkraut on a steamed bun, Horn & Hardart apple pie.

I loved New York, loved everything about it. Larger and brighter than Boston, it was glib and flashy and magnificently loud. Horns honked, whistles shrieked, autos grumbled and growled, people shouted and bellowed. It was the Land of More, and sometimes, when I stepped out onto the sidewalk, I could feel the concrete throbbing beneath my feet as the entire city roared, cometlike, toward the center, the wild unguessable heart, of the Roaring Twenties. It was, for a sixteen-year-old girl, really quite breathtaking.

All that it lacked—or I lacked—was someone with whom to share it. Sometimes I would see a couple, a man and a woman not much older than I, strolling along the sidewalk, their fingers inter-laced, their heads inclining toward each other, and I would feel a tart pang of envy, and then a long, slow, cheerless breath would sigh through my empty chest, and I would wonder whether someone would ever hold my hand in just that way, or incline his head at just that tilt toward mine.

In the evenings, John and I would go out. We saw Paul Robeson in *All God's Chillun Got Wings* at the Provincetown Playhouse in Greenwich Village. On Broadway, we saw Sophie Tucker's stage review, and Buster Keaton's latest movie, *Sherlock Jr.* We saw Fletcher Henderson and his band at Roseland, accompanied by an amazing young trumpet player named Louis Armstrong.

So it went, all week—dinner at some charming restaurant, then a play or a review or a film, then a nightcap (Cherry Coke for me) at some club or speakeasy.

That Friday, Friday the thirteenth, was no exception.

But, unlike the other nights, it ended very badly.

Chapter Three

"So," said John. He ran his hand back through his thick black hair. "Where to tonight?"

It was six thirty in the evening. Both John and Albert had been in the apartment when I arrived back from my expedition about half an hour earlier, but Albert had since left for Queens. Sitting at the kitchen table, John and I were now plotting our evening.

He wore an opened pinstripe black vest, a white shirt with its sleeves folded back along his forearm, and a gray silk tie, its knot loosened at his collar. He sat slumped in the chair, relaxed, his right ankle hooked over his left knee. His left hand, resting on his lap, lightly clasped another King's Ransom Scotch and soda.

"Harlem," I said.

"Harlem?"

"I've never been there. I'd like to see the Cotton Club."

He smiled. "And how do we know about the Cotton Club?"

"From Albert. He said it was a totally swank destination."

"Did he indeed? I shall have to speak with Albert."

"Is there something wrong with the Cotton Club?"

"Wrong? Well, we'll go there tonight, and you can tell me what you think. But it doesn't really get interesting until later. Let's go downtown first. Okay?"

"Okay."

He smiled. "It's Friday night. Shall we dress up a bit?"

I had brought one formal evening dress—supple black silk, sleeveless—from Boston, and so far I had not worn it. "Yes!" I said.

"In that case," he said, "I've got something for you."

"For me?"

He smiled again, stood up, put his glass on the table, and walked over to the icebox. He opened it, reached inside, and pulled out a small square box of shiny golden cardboard, about six by six inches, tied with glossy black ribbon. He crossed the floor and handed it to me.

"What is it?" I asked him, taking it.

"Open it."

Inside, lying amid whispering white tissue paper, was an extravagant velvety orchid corsage, creamy yellow and brilliant scarlet against a feathery spray of green.

I looked up at him.

He said, "Is it all right?"

No one had ever given me an orchid before. Along the rims of my eyes I felt the faint sting of a swelling gratitude. "It's gorgeous," I told him. I cleared my throat, which had unaccountably gone a bit croupy. "It's really beautiful."

I looked away and blinked, once, twice, three times, very quickly.

"Good," he said heartily. Perhaps too heartily—perhaps my gratitude had made him as self-conscious as his generosity had made me. "Good," he said again. He picked up his drink and finished it.

I braved a look upward. He grinned down at me, heartily. "Shall we get ready?"

Forty-five minutes later, we were in a taxi, heading south along Fifth Avenue.

With the dress, I wore a black silk jacket and a black velvet cloche I had bought only two days before at Wanamaker's on lower Broadway. The orchid was pinned to the jacket's front.

John was, as usual, magnificent. He wore a single-breasted midnight-blue dinner jacket with peaked satin lapels, matching trousers, a softly pleated white shirt, a black silk bow tie, a red silk cummerbund, black silk socks, and black patent-leather formal pumps with grosgrain ribbon bows. He wore all this, as he wore everything, with an effortless ease and sophistication. Several years would pass before I met someone—the dancer Fred Astaire—who appeared as casually comfortable in formal wear.

We ate dinner at a speakeasy called Chumley's, which had a discreet entrance in a small courtyard on Barrow Street. John told me that the place also had an inconspicuous exit at 86 Bedford Street. On the rare occasions that federal agents conducted a raid, the waiters advised the customers to "eighty-six it," and then all of them—customers and waiters alike—went merrily scrambling out that back door. The speakeasy, John said, was famous now, and so was the catch phrase—waiters in other restaurants, all over the city, were using it among themselves. Whenever a particular menu item was no longer available, that item was said to be "eighty-sixed."

It was a cozy bohemian place: sawdust and peanut shells on the floor, wooden walls lined with framed photographs and drawings, banners of blue cigarette smoke slowly streaming beneath the low wooden ceiling. Like most of the bars and cafés in the Village, it held a mixed crowd: intense young students in rumpled suits and wire-rimmed Lenin glasses; bearded men in long conspiratorial overcoats; handsome young couples, fingers locked together as they huddled over the tiny tables and inhaled from the same two cubic inches of air.

John ordered the sautéed filet of sole, and I ordered the grilled steak.

We were halfway through dinner when a woman suddenly appeared at our table. John stood up, laying his napkin on the table. Several times during the past week, while we were eating, people had approached him and asked for a moment of his time. But until now, all of these had been men and, so he told me, clients.

"Daphne," he said. It seemed to me that he was deliberately keeping his voice neutral.

She was one of those beautiful women absolutely certain of the effects she had on the people around her. (It is the certainty, of

course, as much as the beauty that creates the effect.) She looked to
be perhaps thirty-five years old, and although only five feet and two
or three inches tall, she was slender and perfectly proportioned.

Until she arrived, I had been extremely pleased with my silk
dress. It draped well; it shivered and shone. But now I realized that
I had clearly been out-silked. There was a fringed black silk shawl
on her angular smooth shoulders below a tumble of bright blonde
ringlets. There was a short, shimmering silver-gray dress, cut on
the bias, that clung to the elegant curves and hollows of her small,
perfect body. There was still more silk, sleek and sheer, in the black
stockings that sheathed her thin legs and glistened from the top of
her cunning round knees to the glossy silver-gray leather of her
high-heeled shoes.

A moment before, I had been as unaware of her existence as she
had been of mine. Now a small part of me, flickering away at the back
of my thoughts, wondered whether she wanted to stamp mine out.

She smiled at John. "Johnny," she said in a sulky southern drawl.
She raised her right hand and lightly placed the tips of her splayed
fingers on his chest. "How *are* you? It's been ever so long."

Johnny?

She turned to me, a half smile on her scarlet Cupid's bow of a
mouth. Inquisitively, she arched her sculpted eyebrows and batted
her long eyelashes, signaling that I should explain myself.

"Daphne," said John, "this is my niece, Amanda. Amanda, this
is Daphne Dale."

"Hello," I said.

Ignoring me, she turned back to him, her mouth pursed now
into a mock half pout. "Why, Johnny, you devil. You never told me
you had a niece."

He smiled faintly. "You never asked."

Ignoring him, she turned back to me. "Such a pretty little thing.
Aren't you just *darling*."

I was four or five inches taller than she. And considerably less
irritating.

"Daphne's a writer," John said to me, as though that explained something. Perhaps, to those who knew more about writers than I, it did.

She cupped her hand to the side of her mouth, leaned slightly forward, and spoke to me in a stage whisper that was audible across the room and probably in the building next door: "You do know," she said, "that you're the envy of just about every girl in the room." She looked back at John and flashed a sweet smile up at him. "Including me, of course."

He smiled bleakly. "Is there something I can do for you, Daphne?"

She cocked her small, perfect head. Her ringlets trembled. She leaned toward him, as though his gravity was drawing her closer. "Could we talk for just a little bit, sugar? In private?"

He looked at her for a moment, neutrally, and then looked down at me and smiled. "Excuse me for a minute?"

"Sure," I said. "Of course."

Sugar?

Daphne swung the right end of her shawl up over her left shoulder, regally turned, and then swished off toward the bar, her hips swinging. I could almost hear them ticking, *click-clack*, like a metronome. John followed her.

I picked at my food as I watched them. She sat down on a stool and ordered a drink, something pink and frothy. She sipped at it daintily while she talked. John stood beside her, facing forward across the bar, not looking at her, his elbows on the top of the bar, his hands clasped, his lowered head nodding from time to time. She chattered away.

Then John turned to her and said something.

Daphne slammed her drink down onto the bar. Some pink swirled out and spattered onto the counter. Along the bar, on either side of them, heads swiveled in their direction. She swung herself around, away from John, stepped down off her stool, flipped the shawl up over her shoulder again, and marched across the room, her head raised. She disappeared into the entryway.

John had turned and watched her as she stomped off. Now

he glanced over at me. I lowered my head and became extremely industrious, sawing away at my steak.

A moment later, he sat down opposite me. "Sorry for the interruption," he said.

I looked up from my steak. "No, that's okay." In my most cheerful voice, I asked, "What does she write, Miss Dale?"

He had ordered white wine to go with his fish, and his glass was still half-full. He reached out, lifted it to his mouth, and drained it. He set down the glass, stared into it for a moment, then looked up and smiled. "She wrote a book. A novel. *Seekers of the Flesh.*"

"Is it any good?"

"I don't think so." The smile turned wry. "But then I'm biased, I suppose. I'm in it."

"Really? She put you in a book?"

"Yes. Disguised, but not terribly well."

"Is that legal? Couldn't you sue her?"

"She makes me out to be fairly disreputable. If I sued her, I'd be admitting that I *was* fairly disreputable, wouldn't I?"

I realized that somehow, as soon as possible, I must obtain a copy of that book. "She seemed pretty upset—when she left, I mean."

"Daphne gets upset with a certain frequency. The world seldom lives up to her expectations."

"What was it you said to her?"

He smiled faintly.

I said, "Am I being too nosy?"

He grinned. "Not *too* nosy, I suppose."

I frowned and looked away. "That's okay," I said. "You don't have to tell me."

John laughed. "And you don't have to game me, Amanda."

I turned to him. He was still grinning.

I startled myself by giggling, and then I looked away, blinking very quickly.

He laughed again.

(Some time later I realized that, despite the giggles and the blinks, this was actually the first adult conversation with a man I had ever been a part of.)

"I told her," said John, leaning toward me, "that she should lower her expectations. She clearly disagreed." He nodded toward my plate. "You're not eating. Are you finished?"

I looked down. What remained of the meat lay pink and tattered in a congealing pool of streaky red.

"I think I am," I said.

"Shall we go to a nightclub?"

"The Cotton Club?"

He glanced at his wristwatch. "It's still too early. Let's go to El Fay. They've got a dancer there who's supposed to be good."

"Okay. Sure."

He nodded his head once toward the front door, where Daphne had disappeared. "I'm sorry about the scene with Daphne."

"It wasn't your fault."

"Maybe not. But I want you to have a good time."

"This is great," I told him. "Honestly. The best time ever."

He smiled. "Okay. Good. Let's hit the road."

During the rest of that evening, two more people asked to speak with John. I mention this now because later it seemed possible that these conversations had a bearing on what happened.

The first approached him at El Fay, an enormous glittering dance hall on West Forty-Fifth Street.

We were sitting at a table opposite the bandstand at the very edge of the dance floor. The "Mistress of Ceremonies" was an opulent blonde woman named Texas Guinan, big and bold, slung with pearls, sparkly with sequins. She wore a colossal hat, very belle epoque, which she ripped off at random moments and waved in the air, as a cowgirl might. She was pleased as punch to be there, and so was the audience, despite her addressing them, collectively, as "suckers."

She introduced the next act, a fellow named George Raft. She waved her hat again. "*Give a big hand*," she bellowed, "*to the dancing man!*"

The audience applauded wildly. From a side door, a short, slender form darted out onto the shiny wooden floor, legs and arms pumping. But just as the orchestra struck up "The Charleston," a heavyset man stepped up to our table, put his hand on John's shoulder, leaned down toward him, and whispered in his ear.

John nodded, then turned to the man. "Larry," he said, raising his voice to be heard over the sound of the band, "this is my niece, Amanda. Amanda, this is Larry Fay. He owns the place." With his raised hand, he made a small circle, indicating the whole room.

"Hello," I said to the man.

"Hey," he said. "How ya doin'?" Beneath thinning black hair, his broad face was gray, as though it had seldom seen the sun. His mouth was wide and thin. He wore a black suit, a black shirt, a purple tie skewered with a stickpin of diamond and gold. The diamond was the size of a tangerine.

John told me, "I'll be right back."

"Okay."

As he and Mr. Fay walked back through the tables, I watched the other customers watching them—or watching John, rather, because it was upon him that everyone's stare was focused. Perhaps I imagined it, but the men seemed either resentful or envious; the women seemed speculative, or simply lost in yearning.

But perhaps I was projecting.

When I turned back to look at the stage, the dancer was in the midst of his routine.

He was extraordinary. Wearing a tight black suit, black shoes, and bright white spats, with his shiny black hair slicked back over his skull, he was slim, nimble, and remarkably fast. Swinging his arms to the right, he kicked his right leg wildly to the left; swinging his arms to the left, he kicked his left leg wildly to the right. Effortlessly, he twirled across the floor, kicking and swinging. As the music sped up, he spun more swiftly, swirling down into a crouch, legs flailing out, one after the other—left, right, left, like a Cossack dance, without any pause between kicks. Sometimes, impossibly, it seemed that both feet were off the ground at the same time. It was inevitable that he fall.

But he did not fall. He spun and he twirled and then, as the band finished off the music with a triumphant clash of cymbals and a brassy blare of horns, he leaped into the air, spinning still, flung out his arms and swung out his legs—right leg in front, left leg behind, both legs parallel to the floor. He plunged earthward and landed in a perfect split, his arms upraised now, his head back, his face broadly smiling, ecstatic.

The audience went wild. They applauded, they whistled, they hooted and whooped and stamped their feet against the floor.

With infinite grace, his arms held out lightly, parallel to the floor, using only the strength of his legs, the dancer rose magically from the split. Dropping his arms to his sides, he suddenly gave us a huge, toothy smile. He bowed to the center of the room, then to the left, and then the right.

Miss Guinan stormed up, grabbed his right hand in hers, and raised both their hands overhead, like a referee hoisting the fist of a victorious boxer. She bellowed: "*Howzabout that, you suckers?*"

As the crowd exploded again, I felt a hand on my shoulder. It was John. He bent toward me. "Ready for the Cotton Club?" he asked.

"Sure!"

It was impossible to miss. Located on the corner of Lenox Avenue and 142nd Street, it blared its name in gigantic electric lights across the marquee out front, and for good measure, on an ornately blinking neon sign above that.

It was nearly midnight, and the sidewalks were aswarm with people. All of them, I was surprised to see, were white. Our taxicab had driven us here on Lenox, north from Central Park, and once we passed 125th Street, everyone on the street was black. In the glare of the streetlamps, we saw men, women, couples, entire families bustling happily along the pavement, all of them looking exactly like the folks who lived south of 125th, except perhaps for the color of their skin. (And except, perhaps, for a certain exuberance of style that was, so it seemed to me, somewhat lacking in the white souls to the south.)

Yet, as we left the taxi, we stepped into a throng of well-dressed white people, young and old, male and female. Milling about, shuffling from foot to foot as they stood in line, murmuring, whispering, giggling, giving off the giddy scent of money, cigars, perfume, and cologne, they were alight with excitement.

When John led me to the head of the line, I heard some angry mutters behind us. Someone called out "Hey!" but John ignored it all and so did the very large white man in a black dinner jacket who was guarding the door. His mouth opened in an enormous grin. One of his upper front teeth was missing.

"Hey, Mr. Burton," he said. He raised his big fists and pretended to throw a punch at John. Beaming back at him, John pretended to block it and then pretended to throw a punch back. I confess that I was a tad surprised, and perhaps a tad disappointed, to see my elegant uncle stoop to such adolescent silliness. (But I have noticed over the years that nearly all men, especially those who have never fathered children, remain partly adolescent. This is almost always less endearing than they believe it to be.)

Stepping back easily from John's punch, the large man grinned. "You got the moves, Mr. Burton."

"Not like you, champ," said John. He turned to me. "Amanda, this is Bobby Minton." He held up his right hand, finger and thumb separated by a quarter of an inch. "He came this close to being the heavyweight champion of the world."

Mr. Minton grinned. "Close don't count," he said. He leaned toward me and held out a hand the size of a hubcap. "Put 'er there, sweetheart."

I took his hand. Like Albert's, his grip was surprisingly gentle.

He released me, stood back up, grabbed the long brass doorpull, and tugged open the big wooden door. Music had piled up behind it like a torrent behind a dam—guitars and drums and horns—and now it all came rumbling out onto the sidewalk.

"Thanks, Bobby," said John. He reached into his pants pocket, pulled out a bill, and handed it to the man. And then we slipped into that surge of pounding sound.

Inside at the reception desk, another large man in a dinner jacket smiled at John, shook his hand, smiled at me, said something that I couldn't hear over the clamor of the music, and led us to our seats.

The place was huge. The dining area was arranged around the cavernous space in a two-level horseshoe shape, each floor packed with tiny tables and chairs and scattered artificial palm trees that looked bravely tropical.

There must have been nearly a thousand people, all of them, it seemed, bobbing their heads to the throb of music. At the far end there was a proscenium stage on which a small orchestra of neatly tuxedoed men was somehow producing this marvelous din. Beneath the stage, on the polished wooden dance floor, a line of slender young women in skimpy costumes shimmied and swayed. Behind them, acting almost as the backdrop, a line of men danced, tall and graceful.

All the customers, without exception, were white. All the performers were black.

Not black, exactly—at least not all of them. While *black* might describe most of the musicians and the male dancers, it is not really the proper word for those women. Lithe and young (none of them over twenty-one, I later learned), their smooth, unsullied skin was every possible shade of pale brown: cinnamon and mocha and milk chocolate and café au lait.

They pranced through the blaze of the spotlights, flashing their long satiny arms and long satiny legs. Their teeth sparkled, and their sleek black hair shone. The men behind them were handsome, but the women were extraordinary. They were vibrant. They were spectacular.

First Daphne Dale and now these glistening marvels. I felt dim and gray and hopeless, and thought that I should be giving serious consideration to a nunnery.

The man led us to a table near the stage that was, inexplicably, empty. We sat down, and the man leaned forward and murmured something into John's ear. John nodded and the man left.

The music built to a crescendo, drums rumbling, and then it

crashed to a dramatic stop. The audience erupted as the chorus girls flounced off the dance floor.

John leaned toward me again, grinning, but another man in yet another dinner jacket appeared at his side. In his late forties, this man was even taller than the former boxer at the front door—but rounder, more heavyset. His face was lumpy and sad-looking, the loose flesh sagging away from big brown eyes, like the flesh of a basset hound. He glanced at me, nodded, bent forward, and whispered into John's ear.

John looked up at the man, nodded, and turned to smile at me. "I've got to go for a minute. Amanda, this is Frenchy DeMange, the manager. Frenchy, my niece, Amanda."

Mr. DeMange smiled, and his rumpled face lit up abruptly with an unexpected and radiant charm. "Very pleased to meet you," he said, taking my hand.

"I'll be right back," John told me, standing up.

Mr. DeMange asked me, "Get you something, Amanda? A Coca-Cola? A cherry phosphate?"

"No, thank you," I said. "I'll wait."

"Okee-dokee," he said. He touched John on the back, as though guiding him, and the two of them slipped away.

I looked around.

The room held an edgy sort of excitement. Even after arriving inside, these people were still keyed up. Their faces were shiny, their features animated, their movements abrupt, impatient. They were all awaiting something, expecting something, something exotic and perhaps dangerous. I had no idea what it was, and it was possible they had no idea either.

I sat there for perhaps ten minutes, admiring the outfits, speculating on their costs, when suddenly John was at my side. "Come on, Amanda," he said. "We're going."

I looked up at him. His face was closed, his mouth grim.

"What's the matter?" I asked.

"Stomach," he said and touched his side. "Coming down with something, I think."

This seemed unlikely to me, and it was certainly unfair, but I stood up. Together we walked toward the entrance.

We had nearly reached it when I noticed a couple standing against the wall, watching us. The woman was blonde and short, like Daphne Dale but voluptuous rather than slender. Her petite white hand rested on the man's arm. She wore a white dress that clung more closely to her body than was fashionable in that year—or, really, in just about any year of the twentieth century. But she wore it, I thought, with a loose, languid, lovely bravado.

The man, perhaps six inches taller than she, his hair black, wore a brilliantly white dinner jacket and black slacks. He was quite handsome, his face craggy and brooding, his shoulders square, his back held straight. His brown eyes were sleepy, the eyelids half-shut against the smoke from the cigarette that dangled from his lips.

As we approached, he used his right hand to pluck away the cigarette, and he took a step toward John and me. Without changing his pace, John looked at him and said, very distinctly, "*No*."

The man stopped moving, and an expression flitted across his face, cold and hard, and then, in an instant, it was gone. John and I passed him by and went out the front door.

As we headed south in the taxicab, back toward the apartment, John stared out the window.

"Do you think it was the fish?" I asked him.

He turned to me. "What, sweetie?"

He had never called me *sweetie* before. I pretended not to notice. "The fish you ate," I said. "Maybe it was bad?"

He nodded. "Yes," he said. "It was probably the fish."

He turned and looked out the window again, like someone who did not wish to speak about fish, or about anything else.

By the time we got home, it was nearly one o'clock. John told me that he was going to bed. I asked him how his stomach was. Better, he said, and added that he would see me in the morning. I placed my orchid back in its cardboard container, put the container into the icebox, and went off to my room. I carefully changed into my nightgown, brushed my teeth, and finally lay down in bed.

If this were a novel rather than a kind of memoir, just about now I would be describing my difficult sleep, my troubled dreams, my feverish premonitions. But in fact, I slipped almost instantly into sleep, and I had no dreams that I can recall. Certainly I had no premonitions.

When I awoke, it was nearly nine. I threw on my robe, stepped into my slippers, and wandered out to see if John was awake.

The door to his bedroom was opened, and the bed was made.

I expected to find him in the kitchen, sipping his coffee. But the kitchen was empty. No smell of coffee, no sign of John.

The living room, too, was empty. But the door to the library was closed.

I knocked. No answer.

I turned the knob, pushed open the door, and stepped in. In the air was a sour, coppery odor. It was oppressive—bullying and sharp—an odor that, distantly, I remembered from some other place, some other time.

Across the room, in the brown leather chair illuminated by a tall, futuristic brass floor lamp, something sat unmoving. I had a sense that at some point in the past, years ago, I had once seen a somewhat similar thing, and for a moment I did not understand what this was exactly. Part of it was dressed as John had been dressed last night, in black trousers and a pleated white shirt. But part of it, the upper part, was draped with a wild confusion of strips and stripes and splotches of some dark, tarry substance.

And then I realized that the tarry substance was blood, John's blood, and that there was ever so much of it—pints of it, quarts of it—splattered across the chair and across the shelves of books behind it; and I realized that John's face had been smashed and shattered; and I realized, as my stomach cramped and began to betray me, that the short wooden rod poking impossibly from the side of John's skull was the smoothly worked handle of a hatchet.

Chapter Four

"And how did ya know it was a hatchet?"

"I've seen hatchets before."

Balding, red-faced, thick-bodied, wearing a white shirt, a narrow black tie, and a funereal black gabardine suit that was shiny at the elbows and knees, Detective Daniel O'Deere leaned toward me. His breath came in little gusts of darkness, the smell of a cave where damp things moldered and died. "And where would a girl like yourself see such a thing?" he asked.

He seemed to be a kind man. But he was not terribly appealing, physically or mentally. And he was not, I suspected, terribly competent.

We were in the living room. I was sitting on the sofa, Detective O'Deere on a chair he had wrestled from the side of the room. He held a fountain pen in his right hand. In his left hand, he held a small notebook, opened.

Other police officers wandered about the house, some in uniform, some in civilian suits like O'Deere's. They seemed very casual to me, ambling here and there, picking things up, putting them down, all of them moving with a sort of blasé, easily satisfied curiosity, like bored tourists.

"At our house in Boston," I told him, "we have a hatchet there. We use it to chop the kindling. For the fire, in the winter."

"'We'?" said the detective. He smiled in a manner that he probably believed to be avuncular. His teeth were gray. "That would be you, would it, miss?"

"My father. My brother. They use it."

He nodded. "Right, then. Tell me again how it was ya happened to find him."

"But I've already told you."

He nodded amiably. "'Course ya have. And look, I know you've had yourself a terrible shock and all, but this is the way we do things. We get all the details down just so. We dot all the *i*'s and cross all the *t*'s. You follow me?"

"Yes."

"So suppose you just tell me the way of it again, how it all happened."

I told him again.

I had been standing at the opened door into the library when I realized that the battered thing in the chair was John. I had doubled over, clutching at the outside of my stomach as its insides came mushrooming up through my center, exploding out of me and splashing against the wooden floor.

I reeled away from the door, out of that horrible room, and slumped back against the hallway wall, panting. My throat was raw and bitter, scorched with bile, and I could not catch my breath—I sucked in air, again and again, but for a time there was not enough of it, and it seemed to me that there would never be enough of it, ever again. I could feel a thick thread of spittle swaying from my lower lip. With the back of my hand, gracelessly, I wiped it away.

It suddenly occurred to me that this had happened while I slept only a few feet down the hall.

Whomever John had let into the house, that person had done *that* to him, spent that enormous fury and hatred in killing him—and, all the while, I had been blithely sleeping away in my room.

Breathing heavily, moving on legs packed with sawdust, I shambled back down the hall into the living room, over to the sofa, and sank down into it. I turned to the end table and reached for the telephone. It was English, a fat chrome base and a black Bakelite cradle and handset. My reflection in the shiny, spotless metal was distorted, my forehead swollen, my chin shrunken.

I picked up the handset and listened to it, hearing the banal, indifferent dial tone. I stuck my finger into the last opening of the dial and spun it all the way around.

It took forever for the dial to spin back into place, the earpiece clicking remotely against my ear. It took another forever for the telephone at the opposite end to start ringing. It rang once, twice, three times, four times . . .

"Operator," came a woman's flat, nasal voice. "How may I help you?"

"The police," I said. "I need the police."

She seemed not at all alarmed. This was, after all, New York City. Calmly she asked me, "It's an emergency?"

"Yes. No . . . Yes."

She sighed impatiently. "Which is it? An emergency or not?"

"It's an emergency. Yes. Please."

"One moment."

At the other end, another telephone rang. Once, twice . . .

"Twentieth precinct. Sergeant Halloran."

"There's been . . . There's been a murder."

He was as calm as the operator—even calmer, perhaps. "And who am I talking to?"

"Amanda Burton."

"And where are you, Miss Burton?"

"The Dakota apartment building. It's on—"

"We know where it is. What apartment number?"

I gave it to him. "It's my uncle's apartment. John Burton. He's the one who's—I came into the room, the library, and he was dead. He got hit with a hatchet, and there's blood all—"

"Miss Burton?"

I took a long, wavering breath. "Yes?"

"Is there anyone else in the apartment?"

"No. No, just me and my uncle."

But then I realized—I couldn't know that for sure. I hadn't checked. There were bedrooms, bathrooms, closets that could be hiding the person who had done that to my uncle.

"I think so," I said. "I think just me and my uncle."

He heard the quaver in my voice. "Don't you worry, Miss Burton, we're sending someone right away."

"Yes. Yes. Thank you."

"And you're sure your uncle's dead?"

"Yes, of course I'm sure. There's . . . blood everywhere."

Abruptly he seemed to sound a bit kinder. "Are you hurt? Have you been hurt yourself?"

"No. I just got up, a few minutes ago. I was sleeping."

"And how old are you, miss?"

I took another deep breath. "Sixteen. I'm sixteen."

As the words left my mouth, I had the sudden dreadful notion that the man would simply hang up, refusing to talk to anyone so young.

"All right," he said. "Now listen to me. What was your first name again?"

"Amanda."

"Amanda. Here's what's going to happen, Amanda. First of all, you don't touch anything. Anything at all. You clear on that?"

"Yes."

"Right. I'm going to send some police officers over there. You stand by the front door. There's a peephole? In the door? A little—"

"Yes, there's a peephole."

"When they come, they'll ring the bell. Before—"

"I need to get dressed."

"What?"

"I just got up. I need to get dressed."

"No. I don't want you wandering around that place. You—"

"I'm wearing my bathrobe. I *need* to get dressed." I could hear a faint, thin ribbon of hysteria running through my voice.

The sergeant no doubt heard it, too. He took a breath and then slowly exhaled. "Right," he said. "Right. You get yourself dressed. When the officers arrive, you ask for their identification. You ask through the door, *before* you let them in. Understand me? They'll hold their badges up to the peephole."

"I understand."

"They'll be there as soon as they can."

"Yes," I said. "Thank you."

"You go get ready, Amanda."

I made one other telephone call, very brief, and then I left the living room. Quietly and warily I padded down the hallway to the kitchen. It was as silent as an empty ballroom, and it was impossibly sad. I knew where the kitchen knives were kept, and I tugged open the drawer, found the big chef's knife, and wrapped my fingers around the comforting wooden handle. Carrying the knife with its blade pointed straight down, in stabbing position, I padded warily back to my room.

I left the knife on the bed within easy reach as I dressed. Panties, a bra, a silk slip, a white cotton blouse, a flouncy white cotton skirt, white cotton socks. It seemed somehow absurd to be going through such mundane, everyday motions, putting on the same sort of mundane, everyday clothing that I had worn yesterday, pretending that the world hadn't drastically changed since then, that it hadn't become an altogether different sort of place.

When I was finished, I picked up the knife again and walked to the entryway of the apartment. I checked to see if the front door was locked. It was.

But it was only slam-locked. The dead bolt had not been shot into the jamb; the security chain had not been snapped into the brass slider on the door.

I tried to remember if John had fully locked the door last night.

And then I did remember; he had. The two of us had been talking about his upset stomach at the time.

He had definitely turned the dead bolt and latched the security chain, which meant that later that night, John had opened the door for whomever it was that came into the apartment and killed him.

Detective O'Deere and his partner, Detective Cohan, along with two uniformed policemen, were the first to arrive. The others trickled in slowly, four or five of them, individually or in pairs, looking like idle passersby with time on their hands. It seemed to me a peculiar way to run a murder investigation, but at that point, my experience of murder investigations was limited to only two: this one and one other, some three years previous.

Detective Cohan was still in the library with the body.

Detective O'Deere asked me, "Did you touch him?"

"Who?" I said. "John? No."

"Did you go up to him, to the body?"

"No. I didn't even cross the room. I couldn't. I was . . . sick."

"You called him by *John*, did ya?"

"Yes. He asked me to call him that." I could hear it in my voice: I sounded defensive. In my experience, the police always make you sound defensive, whether they intend to or not. Usually they intend to.

He nodded. "You touch anything at all in the room?"

"No. Nothing."

"Anything in the apartment?"

"No. He told me not to. The man I spoke to on the phone. Sergeant Halloran."

He glanced down at his notebook then looked back up at me. "Right. Now tell me about this Albert fella, will ya? Over in Queens."

I told him, once again, what I knew about Albert.

O'Deere said, "He was what, then? Like an assistant?"

"And a friend. My uncle said he was a friend."

"You don't have an address for him?"

"No. He lives here during the week, but I don't know where he stays in Queens."

He took another look at his notebook then looked back to me. "He wasn't here last night?"

"No. I told you. He left around five thirty."

"He—"

O'Deere looked to his right and then abruptly stood up, his hands held stiffly at his sides as though he were standing at attention.

A man had entered the living room, a fedora in his hand. Perhaps forty years old, he was tall, well over six feet. Under his expensive and well-tailored gray suit coat, his shoulders were broad and square. His dense blond hair was parted on the left. The features of his face were handsome in a rugged, outdoorsy way, but they were utterly empty, no expression in them at all. His gray eyes were blank and his mouth was set.

"Lieutenant," said Detective O'Deere, his voice snapping.

The man nodded at O'Deere and then looked me over with a cold, cursory glance, up and down. It took barely three seconds. But for some reason, the thought went through my head that thirty years from that moment, even if he had never thought about me once in all that time, he would be able to describe me exactly, down to the color of my shoes.

He looked back at O'Deere. "Where is it?" he asked him.

"In the library, sir. Cohan's in there."

"The medical examiner?"

"On his way, sir."

The big man nodded. He glanced at me once more, his eyes still blank, and then turned and walked from the room. His shoulders nearly filled the doorway. Despite his size, he moved lightly on his feet.

O'Deere sat down, still staring at the door through which the man had gone. He puffed up his cheeks and blew out a small, quick *whoof*.

"Who was that?" I asked him.

"Lieutenant Becker," he said. He turned to me. "One of the big brass. From headquarters."

"The big brass?"

"A very important fella, Lieutenant Becker." He looked down at his notebook as though he had forgotten it and flipped over a sheet. "Right, then." He glanced at the door then turned back to me. "Suppose you tell me about last night."

Once again, I told him about the night before. I had reached the point at which John and I were eating at Chumley's, just before Daphne Dale had materialized in her silk, when the big man, Lieutenant Becker, returned to the room.

"That's enough," he told O'Deere.

For an instant, O'Deere looked like he was about to say something. But then he shut his mouth, and his face went vacant.

Becker said, "Get rid of everyone but Cohan. And don't let anyone else come in, except the ME."

"Yes, sir."

"No one," Becker repeated. "Especially not the press."

"Yes, sir."

Becker turned to me. "You have a purse?"

"Yes." The clinical directness of his stare had tightened my throat. I cleared it.

"Get it," he said. "We're going downtown." He shoved the fedora onto his head.

I turned to Detective O'Deere.

He nodded. "You go along now," he said, and then he smiled. "Everything will be just fine."

He was, as it happened, entirely wrong.

I sat alone in the wide rear seat of Lieutenant Becker's car, a long black Packard. The lieutenant sat up front with his driver, a short, swarthy man wearing a patrolman's uniform and cap.

For the entire trip, Becker never turned back to me, never said anything to me or to his driver. He simply sat there, looking straight ahead as the big, expensive car hummed along the streets.

Drained and limp, I simply stared out the window and watched the city unfold around me. What glided past us, as the big car sailed down Broadway, was a surreal kind of summary of what I had seen and where I had been during the previous week—Times Square, Madison Square, Union Square, Wanamaker's department store. But everything—the trees, the buildings, the pavement, the crowd—was different this morning. What had been thrilling and genial was bleak and alien now. Even the sky had changed; it had become morose and overcast, the color of lead.

We drove farther south, past Houston and Prince and Spring streets, and then turned left at Broome Street. Three blocks later we turned right, onto Centre Street. We slid past the broad, arched entrance of an enormous stone building where four or five men in shoddy suits lounged along the broad set of stairs, sucking on cigars and cigarettes. Another hundred feet on, we came to a stop beside a smaller door in the same building.

Becker turned to me. "Here."

He opened his door, and I opened mine. We stepped out onto the sidewalk.

I looked up. The structure was as imposing as the Dakota, but it was darker and more somber and much, much longer. Four gray stories tall, festooned with grim Baroque columns and pilasters, it seemed to stretch off, left and right, into infinity.

"This way," said Becker.

I followed him up the narrow stone steps and through the door. Inside, the tight corridor was painted a pale green. The air smelled of disinfectant and acrid old cigar smoke.

We tramped down this corridor, then another, and then through another door and up a cramped wooden stairway. The dark green steps were scuffed, their centers worn down to the bare wood. The air held more smells: varnish, dust, hair oil. We saw no one.

One flight up, we passed through yet another door, out into yet another corridor, this one broader and carpeted. Like all the others, its walls were pale green, the air spiked with the stink of old cigars. Men strode along the carpet as though they knew exactly where they were going and planned to get there very soon. Some wore uniforms, some did not. Most of them, passing us, nodded respectfully to Becker and glanced at me, but none of them said anything.

By this point, I had no idea which direction was north or south or east or west. I had no idea where in the building we might be, or where we might be going.

We arrived at another door. Becker came to a halt and held up a hand, signaling me to stop. He reached into the right pocket of his trousers, pulled out a small ring of keys, searched through it until he found the one he wanted, and then used it to unlock the door. After pushing the door open, he stepped in, flicked a wall switch, and waved me forward.

It was a small room, windowless, smelling even more strongly than the hallways of pine disinfectant. The walls were, once again, pale green. The floor was dark green linoleum, in the center of which was a screened circular drain, about six inches wide, like a wider version of the drain in a standard shower.

I wondered about that drain. Why install a drain in a room like this?

On the far wall was a wooden table that held a dented metal pitcher and a flimsy-looking metal cup. On one side of the table was a single wooden swivel chair, and on the other side were two more.

Becker said, "Take a seat." He nodded to the single chair.

I walked over to the table then turned back to him.

He was watching me, his face still expressionless.

He shrugged, lightly, almost invisibly. He said, "Breaks of the game, kid." His voice was flat.

It might have been an explanation; it might have been an apology. But as an explanation, it left a lot to be desired. And as an apology—well, I did not believe that Lieutenant Becker was capable of apology, to anyone, and least of all to me.

He turned, walked out, and drew the door shut. I heard the key click in the lock, the sound punctuating the moment like the period at the end of a sentence.

Chapter Five

I discovered that all three chairs were bolted to the floor. So was the desk.

I swiveled the single chair around and sat down. I placed my purse on the table. I checked the metal pitcher. It held about a quart of water. I poured some into the cup and tasted it: warm, flat, and rusty.

I had nothing to read, nothing to look at but the empty room around me; nothing to do but to wonder what Lieutenant Becker had meant—the breaks of the game?—and to remember my morning, remember the sight of my uncle, bloodied and battered on the far side of the library.

My hands and feet were cold. I realized I was shaking very faintly. I wrapped my hands around my upper arms and held onto myself, as though I were afraid I might shatter into pieces that would go spinning across the room.

Very soon, perhaps only five or ten minutes after I arrived in that room, I began to cry.

I cried for John, so handsome and so elegant and so wickedly brutalized. I cried for my parents, so good, so compassionate, so far away.

And then, of course, as in the end we all do, I cried for myself. Cried long, quivering sobs, choking on loneliness and loss.

I was leaning forward, my head resting on both my arms, which were folded along the table. A key clicked in the lock, and I jerked upright. My eyes were dry; I had cried myself out. But my nose was still stuffy and red.

The door opened, and Lieutenant Becker stepped into the room, big and craggy and grim, his fedora gone, his hands in his pockets.

He was followed by a jolly, heavyset man in his fifties. Like Becker, the man wore an expensive gray suit, but his was vested, and a thick gold chain hung across the vest's smug round belly. Except for gray muttonchops and a few thin gray hairs that seemed to be shellacked across his shiny pink scalp, he was bald. As though to make up for this, his eyebrows were bushy and his mustache was thick and carefully brushed. His puffy cheeks and bulbous nose were curlicued with the broken veins of a serious drinker. He was grinning at me happily, and behind a pair of gold wire-rimmed glasses, his warm brown eyes sparkled with good cheer.

Lieutenant Becker said to him, "This is Amanda Burton." He turned to me, his face still blank. "This is Police Commissioner Vandervalk."

Mr. Vandervalk smiled heartily and held out his plump red hand. "Hello there, Amanda," he said enthusiastically. "How are you doing?"

I shook his hand. His was dry, but mine wasn't. "I'm all right," I said. "Thank you."

He nodded as though he had expected no less. "Sorry we couldn't get to you before this, but it's been a madhouse here today." He grinned cheerfully at Lieutenant Becker. "Run, run, run, eh, Lieutenant? No rest for the weary."

Becker just stood there, watching me.

Commissioner Vandervalk turned back to me. Behind the wire rims, his eyebrows rose. "Is there anything you need, anything we can get for you?"

"May I use the bathroom, please?"

"What? Oh. Of course, of course. Come along."

I glanced at Becker. He still stood there with his hands in his pockets, watching me.

Outside the door, leaning against the wall with her arms crossed, stood a thin, middle-aged woman in a starched black uniform. She was rather alarming, with pinched eyes and a bitter mouth. Behind her narrow, corded neck, her gray hair was clenched into a ball as tight as a fist.

"Mrs. Hadley," said Mr. Vandervalk, "take young Amanda down to the WC, would you?"

Without a word, the woman led me down the hallway. She smelled of talcum powder and peppery old perspiration, and she jangled as she walked—attached to her thin black belt was a short chain and a ring of keys. When we came to a wooden door, she knocked on it and waited. Nothing happened. She opened it and gestured for me to go inside. I entered into the reek of old cigars and older urine.

It was a men's toilet, and I had never before seen a wide porcelain trough like the one that ran along the entire wall. I would be happy, I decided, if I never saw one again.

Before I left the room, I rinsed the salt from my face and tried to wash the red from my eyes. I looked around. The towels hanging on the wooden racks were grimy, streaked with black. I shook my hands in the air, then dried them, or attempted to, along the back of my dress.

I looked at my watch: one o'clock.

Silently, Mrs. Hadley led me back to the room, knocked on the door, pushed it open, and looked down at me. After I stepped into the room, she pulled the door shut behind me.

Mr. Vandervalk and Lieutenant Becker were sitting in the two adjoining chairs. In front of Mr. Vandervalk was a large notebook and a fountain pen. He nodded to me. "All right now," he said. "You just take a seat over there, Amanda, and we'll get this over with as soon as we can, eh?"

I walked around the table and sat down in the single chair, opposite them.

Lieutenant Becker's hands were on the table, his long, thick fingers interlaced. Blond hair, like bristles of thin white wire, grew on the skin between the knuckles. He looked at me now as he had looked at me from the very first, without even the tiniest flicker of interest.

Mr. Vandervalk had uncapped the pen and opened the notebook. He smiled at me again and adjusted his glasses. "Now, Amanda," he said. "First of all, why don't you tell us where your mom and dad are right now. Are they here in the city with you?"

"Tibet," I told him. "They're in Tibet."

"Tibet?" he said merrily. "My goodness! What are they doing in Tibet?"

"They're traveling. They've always wanted to go there."

"Well, good for them," he said. "Well, travel is broadening, I always say." He looked down to write something in the notebook. I thought it was the single word *Tibet*. He looked up at me. "And when will they be getting back to the USA? Do you know?"

"In September or October. It's a long trip."

"It is, indeed," he said and smiled again. "It is, indeed." He wrote something in the notebook—*September*, probably—and then adjusted his glasses. "Now. Tell me. Do you have any other relatives?"

"My brother. In Boston."

"Here in the city, I meant. Here in New York."

"No."

"No." He nodded. "All right. Fine, thank you." He wrote something else in the notebook. Then he sat back and clasped his hands together on his lap. He made his face go serious. "Now suppose you tell us just exactly what happened."

I had nothing to gain by pointing out that I had already told my story to Detective O'Deere. Lieutenant Becker knew this, and so, probably, did Mr. Vandervalk. The police were still dotting their *i*'s and crossing their *t*'s.

"Where should I start?" I asked him.

"Why don't you just start with last night? You and your uncle went out to dinner, I understand."

The only way he could have known about that was from Detective O'Deere. If he had heard that much from O'Deere, then presumably he had heard the rest of it, too. But he wanted to hear it again, so I recounted it all—Chumley's, El Fay, the Cotton Club—and then the events of this morning.

Neither Mr. Vandervalk nor Becker asked questions. Mr. Vandervalk occasionally scribbled something into his notebook.

When I finished, Mr. Vandervalk smiled at me again. "Very good. Thank you, Amanda." He turned to Becker. "Lieutenant?" he said.

Becker looked at me, and for the first time, he produced a smile. It was brief and bleak. "We've been in touch," he said, "with the police in Boston."

"Yes?" I said politely, and I felt the skin of my back prickle, as though a chilly breeze had curled across it.

Becker said, "This isn't the first time you've bumped into a dead body, is it?"

I wondered who among the Boston police had told him. It didn't matter, of course. Any of them could have known, and any of them could have told Becker. Although the murder had been committed outside of Boston, in a small town along the shore, for a time it had been Big News in all the city newspapers.

"No," I said. "It isn't."

"Your mother," he said.

"My stepmother," I corrected him.

"And she was killed with a hatchet, wasn't she?"

"That's right. Yes." I glanced at Mr. Vandervalk. He sat there with his arms crossed over his chest, his lower lip pushed out. He was looking at me with concern. He narrowed his eyes and nodded.

Becker said, "No one ever did figure out who did it."

I corrected him again: "No one was ever arrested." In the end, the local police did actually know who had done it. But for various reasons, the identity of the murderer had been kept secret.

I turned to Vandervalk, my one ally in the room, my one ally in the city of New York. "You don't really think I killed my uncle."

He smiled again, a friendly, kind smile. "Amanda, all we're trying to do here is get to the truth."

"But I've told you the truth. I don't know who killed him."

Becker said, "It's an amazing coincidence, isn't it? One little girl finds two dead people. Both of them killed with a hatchet."

"I was only thirteen years old then."

"Old enough to hold a hatchet. Old enough to use it."

"Yes, but I didn't."

Mr. Vandervalk waved Becker gently away. "Now, Amanda," he said softly. "Listen to me, dear. We're not ogres here. Lieutenant Becker and I are trying to help you." He leaned toward me, his smile friendly beneath his mustache. "You know what? I'll bet you had a good reason. An excellent reason."

"Excuse me?"

"It happens all the time. We know that. A good-looking young girl. An older man living alone. There's an attraction. Perhaps, at first, it's even mutual. We can understand that. Believe me, we can. But then the older man, well, he takes things a little bit too far. He demands more from the girl than she's prepared to give. He reaches out, and he touches—"

"*'Touches'*?"

"If your uncle touched you, if he—"

"*'Touched' me*?"

"If your uncle touched you, if he—"

"That's *crazy*," I said.

But I knew that it wasn't, not entirely.

In a sense, Mr. Vandervalk was right. Mutual or not, there *had* been an attraction. I remembered the way I had looked at John while he was reading or writing or sitting beside me watching a show; I remembered the way my glance—tentative, always ready to dart away—had caressed the clean lean lines of his face. I remembered the flecks of gold floating in the blue of his eyes. . . .

"It's natural, of course," said Mr. Vandervalk. "It's inevitable. But then one night, things went a little too far—"

"Things never went *anywhere*."

"Maybe he *didn't* touch you," said Becker. For the first time, he smiled at me. Slyly. "Is that it? That's why you hated him? That's why you killed him?"

I shook my head, not so much to deny the idea as to shake it away, to shake away the nightmare that was beginning to settle around my shoulders. "This is . . . crazy. This is absolutely crazy. I didn't hate my uncle. I admired him."

"Of course you did," said Vandervalk, nodding again, encouraging me. He smiled, and all at once I realized that his smile and his concern were both utterly false. He was as convinced as Becker that I was responsible for John's death. Or convinced that I should be.

"Of course you did," he said. "You admired him. You respected him. And then he did something that frightened you. Something you could never forgive. One night when you were sleeping, he came to you and—"

"That is just not true," I said. I turned to Becker. Of the two men, he had suddenly become the less unpleasant. His hostility, at least, was open. I said, "I'd like to talk to a lawyer, please. I have a right to talk to a lawyer."

I sounded enormously grave to myself, but clearly I amused Lieutenant Becker. "Where'd you hear that?" he asked me.

"It's in the Constitution of the United States."

"Yeah?" he said. "The Constitution of the United States? Does that say anything about minors? Because that's what you are, *little girl.*"

The words were spoken with such easy contempt that for a moment I was stunned. My throat clamped shut, and I felt a swelling behind my eyes. I blinked, swallowed painfully, and took a deep breath. I would not cry in front of this man. I would not cry in front of either man.

Sensing my vulnerability, I believe, Vandervalk leaned forward. "Look, Amanda," he said, sincerity purring in his voice, "we're trying to help you. Believe me, no jury in the world would convict you if they knew the truth."

"But that *isn't* the truth."

He sat back, sighed, and shook his head, vastly disappointed in me.

Becker attempted another approach. He said, "Did your uncle lock the door when you two came back last night?"

"Yes."

"How many keys are there?"

"Pardon me?" I said.

"Was that a complicated question? How many keys to the apartment?"

"I don't know. I'm not sure. I had one. Albert had one."

Becker turned to Vandervalk. "Albert Cooper. The butler. We talked to him, he's alibied."

I realized that until that moment, I had never heard Albert's last name. I wondered how Becker had learned it.

Becker said to me, "And your uncle's key—it was in his pocket. That makes three."

"There could've been more," I said. "Someone else could have come in last night. Anyone."

"Who?" said Becker.

"I don't know. But—"

"The door was chained shut," he said.

"Pardon?" I said.

"The front door to the apartment. When the detectives got there, they heard you unchain it."

I glanced at Vandervalk. His arms were crossed, and his head was cocked.

"Yes," I said, "but I chained it shut myself. This morning, after I called the police."

"And why do that?"

"To stop—to keep out whoever did that to . . . my uncle."

"Little late, wasn't it?"

"I wasn't—"

"You know what defensive wounds are?"

"No."

"Wounds on the hands and arms. They happen when someone's trying to stop someone else from cutting him. With a knife. Or a hatchet. Your uncle didn't have any."

"So?" The single word was so adolescent that, hearing myself speak it, I nearly cringed.

"*So*," said Becker, smiling his wintry smile, "that means he knew the killer. He knew *you*. You walked right up to him, and he never knew what you were planning. You—"

"Wait a minute, wait a minute," I said. "How could I walk up to him with a hatchet in my hand?"

"You hid it. Behind your back." He shrugged his broad shoulders. "Maybe you wrapped it up in some clothes. Or maybe he was nodding off. It was late. He'd probably put away a fair amount of booze last night."

"If he was nodding off," I said, "then *anybody* could have killed him."

"There wasn't anybody else in the apartment."

"There *had* to be."

"Here's what happened," said Becker. "Something went on between the two of you. Maybe he *did* do something he shouldn't have. Maybe, like Mr. Vandervalk says, he went over the line and he deserved to be punished for it. We can take that into consideration. But last night you went and you got the hatchet—"

"I didn't even know there *was* a hatchet."

"In the kitchen pantry, in the wood box. You had to know that."

"I've never seen the wood box. I've never been inside the pantry. We haven't used any wood since I got here. It's *summertime*." My voice was reedy, and I could hear the panic crackling in it. They could hear it, too, I knew, and that shamed me.

Another thought occurred to me. "What about fingerprints?" I said to Becker. "You didn't find my fingerprints in there. You couldn't have."

"You wiped them off," he said. "Obviously, you know about fingerprints. For a little girl, you've had a lot of experience."

I looked from him to Mr. Vandervalk. "But this is crazy! I didn't kill him. I didn't kill anyone. It's crazy for me even to have to say that."

Mr. Vandervalk unwrapped his arms, leaned forward, and put his hands on the table. "Now listen to me, Amanda," he said earnestly. "We can't help you if you won't help yourself."

"But I didn't kill him!"

He smiled sadly. "Sweetheart," he said, "come on. Do your-self a favor. All you've got to do is tell us how it happened—how your uncle, you know, *touched* you. It upset you. Naturally it did. It frightened you. And you were all alone in the big city. You had nowhere to go, no one to talk to. Anybody in the world could understand that. So last night—"

"But it's not *true*."

"This'll all be over, Amanda. We can get you out of here. Get you a nice big meal, eh? Find you a nice comfortable place to stay."

The notion that I would betray my uncle for a "nice big meal" was so infuriating that I threw myself back in the chair. "No," I said. I folded my arms, locking them across my chest. "I won't. My uncle was a good man. He didn't do what you said. He didn't and he never would have."

I raised my chin in a defiance that seemed feeble even to me. But it was all I had. "And I didn't kill him," I said.

He looked at me for a moment. Then, shaking his head, he sighed. He turned to Becker. "Tell Mrs. Hadley to take her downstairs."

Chapter Six

The cell was perhaps seven feet by eight and it stank, like just about everything else in the building, of pine disinfectant. Overhead, a single lightbulb dimly glowed behind metal screening. The floor was bare concrete. Two of the walls were cinder block, painted a flat dull gray; the other two consisted of long black metal bars, running vertically. Along the two cinder-block walls were narrow cots, each holding a swaybacked mattress, a threadbare cotton sheet, a flat pillow in a shabby cotton case, and a stiff brown woolen blanket. In the corner, about four feet from the floor, hung a small metal sink with a single faucet. A metal cup, identical to the one in the room upstairs, rested on the sink's ledge. Underneath the sink was a single small metal bucket. Next to that, upright on the floor, someone had carefully placed a thin roll of brown toilet paper.

No other cells were nearby. Mrs. Hadley had led me down three flights of stairs, along a cinder-block corridor, and into a small basement area. The cell took up half of it. The rest was stuffed with a jumble of old furniture—desks, chairs, stools, tables—hastily thrown together and thickly layered in dust.

"What is this place?" I asked Mrs. Hadley. I meant: Where are the other cells? Where are the other prisoners? Surely a building the size of police headquarters would hold more prisoners than a single sixteen-year-old girl.

Until that moment, she had not spoken to me. Now she smiled sweetly and said, "This is where we put the little girls who don't tell the truth."

Her voice was much softer than I expected. But the softness and the sweetness of her smile made the words themselves sound patronizing and spiteful—as they were meant to, of course.

I flushed. Spite is something with which I have never dealt well. It is simple naked cruelty, and even now, years later, I am always startled when someone actually *wishes* to be seen as cruel.

"I *am* telling the truth," I said.

"If you were," she said with the absolute conviction of a minor functionary, "you wouldn't be here."

She reached for the chain hanging from her belt, lifted the ring of keys, immediately found the one she wanted, and unlocked the barred door to the cell. She swung the door open and then turned to me, holding out her hand. "Purse," she said.

I handed it over. She clamped it under her arm, and once again I smelled the sharp aggressive tang of old, dried sweat. She held out her hand again and nodded to my wrist. "Watch," she said.

I hesitated. Susan, my stepmother, had given me the watch on my sixteenth birthday, a lovely Bulova with a narrow rectangular gold case and four small emeralds notched into each corner. It was my very first wristwatch.

Impatiently, the woman twitched her fingers. "Watch."

I would not beg. I unfastened the band and handed it over. The time then was two thirty.

I felt bereft, as though a good friend had abandoned me.

Indifferently, Mrs. Hadley shoved the watch down into the pocket of her uniform. She jerked her head. "Inside," she said.

I swallowed, took a deep breath, and stepped into the cell.

With that single step, everything changed. I went from being one kind of person, in one kind of life, to someone entirely different, with an entirely different and uncertain set of ragged possibilities.

I was abruptly weak and frail. My breath left me, sighed itself hopelessly away, and, beneath my blouse, a droplet of perspiration wormed down my side like a small sinister snake.

Mrs. Hadley shut the door. It clanged loudly. She locked it—

click click—and then without another word she walked away, her heavy shoes snapping against the cement.

Breathing quickly now, hyperventilating, I glanced around. Everything was horrid and menacing. But that thin brown roll of toilet paper, standing at attention beside the drab gray bucket, seemed especially ominous. Someone had used it before I arrived, perhaps more than one person—what had happened to them? Where were they now?

I could still hear the distant brittle snap of Mrs. Hadley's shoes. I did not start crying until it had faded into silence.

Without a timepiece to contain it, time expanded like vapor, thinning, dissipating, until finally it vanished altogether.

After I had cried myself dry once again, I lay there on one of the cots, staring up at the ceiling.

I remembered things I had not thought about for years. My father laughing at the shore, knee-deep in a foamy surge, his sunbrowned arms held out to me as he cheered at my awkward, lumbering splash through the water. My grieving brother in our living room, wailing because he and his new slingshot had actually killed a small sparrow. My first day at a new school, second grade, walking in line outside beside a stunning young boy named Adam whose blond hair caught and held the sunlight.

I thought about my uncle. Who had killed him, and why? Who had come up to the apartment last night to take his life? Why would he—or she—risk coming up there? People lived in the building. They were moving in and out of it all day and all night. Any one of them could have seen the killer.

I could have seen him. Why enter an apartment where you might be seen?

And why were the police so convinced that I was responsible?

Well, the hatchet, of course. As Becker suggested, I had a history with hatchets.

But why had the killer used such a weapon? Certainly there were guns available in New York City, probably an endless supply of them. And there were knives and explosives and a thousand other means by which to take a life.

Why a hatchet?

But who? Who would *want* to kill John?

Daphne Dale? That man at the Cotton Club, the man in the white dinner jacket?

Someone else? Someone I had never met, a person I could never imagine?

I harried myself with these questions, but sooner or later, inevitably, I would sink back into self-pity: How *could* they put a sixteen-year-old girl in jail? How could they do this to *me*?

At some point, much later, I heard footsteps coming toward me, and the jingle-jangle of keys. Mrs. Hadley. I sat up, swung my legs from the cot, and straightened my dress.

She held a small metal plate.

I stood up. Between the bars was a small horizontal opening. Without a word, Mrs. Hadley shoved the plate through and held it there. I stepped forward and took it from her. The plate was heaped with some thick substance the color of rust, and lying atop the heap was a worn metal spoon.

"Thank you," I said.

She crossed her arms and said, "They want to know. Upstairs. If you're ready to tell the truth."

"I've already told the truth."

She nodded, as though this were exactly the mulish answer she had expected. She pointed a bony finger toward the food. "Either eat it or give it back. I'm waiting right here."

I sat back down on the cot.

The rust-colored substance was beans, boiled nearly beyond recognition but cold now.

Although I had not eaten since last night, I believed that I owed it to John to spurn whatever food these people offered me. I hated beans, and my good intentions should have prevailed. But, like most of my good intentions, they failed me. I started scooping up the beans and shoveling them down. The body, as we learn over time, does not really care much about our good intentions.

Mrs. Hadley had been watching me. I placed the spoon in the empty plate, stood up, walked to the door, and slid the plate back through the opening in the door.

"When can I see a lawyer?" I asked her.

She sniffed. "When you start telling the truth," she said.

She lifted the plate and then walked away, her shoes clapping at the floor, her keys jangling. I stepped back to the cot.

Once again, her footsteps ebbed into the distance. And then, just as the sound stopped, all the lights went out.

My heart slammed against my chest.

At home, in hotels, in John's apartment, everywhere I had ever slept, in all of my life, there had always been some residual light seeping into the room from somewhere. From beneath the door, from between the curtain and the wall. Even starlight, sifting through the draperies, can soften the darkness.

But there were no windows down here. The darkness in that cell was absolute. I could see nothing at all; it was as though the cell, the city, the world had ceased to exist. Or I had.

I sat there, listening to my heartbeat, willing it to slow.

It would not.

I was alone, utterly alone, in the utter blackness. Around me there was only the silence and the stink of disinfectant.

But worse than being alone in the darkness, of course, is the realization that you are not alone.

And, very soon, over the thumping of my heart, I began to hear other sounds.

A low mechanical mutter, as of some distant machinery.

A faint scratching sound, not so far away. Someone in another cell?

A scrabbling sound, much closer, of tiny claws scratching on stone. And then again, closer still. Something scuttling along the concrete nearby.

Rats.

Once again my heart juddered.

The scrabbling sound came again, nearer this time.

I tried to quell fear with reason. They were only rats.

What, then, did I know about rats?

They were mammals, yes. They were filthy, sodden with sewage, and once upon a time they had carried the plague. I recalled stories from the war, of men in trenches falling into exhausted slumber and awakening to find their fingers gnawed away.

Reason was not doing an especially good job of quelling. It seldom does.

Another scrabbling sound. Even closer.

I knew that they were in the cell with me, scurrying along the floor, thirsty, hungry.

I swung my feet up onto the cot and held my breath.

I have no idea how long I stayed awake. Today I cannot reckon how long it might have taken a rather spoiled young girl, frazzled by the events of the day, to overcome her fears—or be overcome by them—and finally fall asleep.

Possibly by that point in the night I was so weary that I simply surrendered, reaching a point at which I decided that the rats could have me.

But fall asleep I did. I know this because, sometime later, I was suddenly awakened.

The lights were on, seemingly brighter than before, and footsteps were rattling toward me. More than one set of footsteps.

It was Mrs. Hadley once again, but this time she was not alone. With her was a girl, perhaps eighteen years old, an inch or two shorter than I but much broader through the torso. She wore a frayed white cotton shirt, gray at the collar; a pair of denim overalls; and heavy black lace-up boots, scuffed and scratched. Beneath her straight black hair, cut in the shape of a large inverted soup bowl, her dark face was broad and heavy—small hooded brown eyes, a snub nose, and a plump narrow mouth that was turned down at the corners in a permanent, sullen frown.

Mrs. Hadley smiled at me. Sweetly. "We brought you a little friend. This is Ramona. Ramona, say hello to Amanda."

From beneath her fringe of black hair, the girl merely glowered at me.

Mrs. Hadley plucked the keys from her belt, unlocked the door, swung it open, and turned to Ramona. The girl entered, looked coldly down at me on my cot, and then turned to face the door. Mrs. Hadley pushed it shut, locked it, and went off, her shoes *clip-clopping.*

This time the lights stayed on. I wasn't sure whether this was a good or a bad thing.

When the sound of Mrs. Hadley had died away, the girl turned back to me. She glanced down at my pumps, which I had set beside the cot. She glanced over at the other cot. Then she looked directly at me.

"That's my bed," she said. "Get out."

For a second or two I was baffled. I could see no reason for anyone to prefer one cot over the other.

Then I realized that the cots were not her real concern. Her real concern was establishing the dynamics of power in that cramped gray room.

One might think that a sixteen-year-old girl such as myself would know nothing of the dynamics of power. But there are few places better to learn about it than a Boston finishing school like the one I had been attending for the past few years.

Carefully, I eased back the covers. I sat up and put my stocking feet onto the cold concrete floor. I stood.

Ramona looked me over, up and down. Then she smiled—a small, cunning smile. "Real pretty," she said.

She took a step closer to me. "We're gonna get along just fine, aren't we, pretty?" She put out her hand to touch my face.

I backed away.

Her plump lips turned down again. "Maybe I gotta teach ya how," she said, moving toward me.

Three years before, during the investigation of my first step-mother's murder, I had spent time with a squat, balding Pinkerton detective named Harry Boyle. We had talked about many things as we drove around that small seaside town, and one of them had been self-defense.

"*When you know someone wants to hurt you,*" he said, *looking out at the road,* "*what you got to do is hit him first, and hit him as hard as you can.*"

He had explained the technique: a knee to the groin, a grab of the hair, then a dash toward the nearest wall, smacking the head into it: *klonk.*

"*What about a girl?*" *I asked him.*

The car hit a pothole, and the steering wheel bucked lightly in his hand. He swung it gently back to center and looked at me. "*If it's a girl wants to hurt you?*"

"*Yes.*"

Another nod. "*A stomach punch. Right below the rib cage. You don't aim for the stomach, see. You aim for a few inches behind it. You aim for the spine, and you put all your weight behind it. Everything you got. That'll double her right up. Then you do the same thing with the hair.*" *He looked at me.* "*Straight into the wall.*"

"*I don't think I could do that.*"

"*Yeah,*" *he said, nodding.* "*It's hard. Hurting people is hard. But if you don't do it, you're the one gonna get hurt.*"

Now, as Ramona came closer, I remembered Harry Boyle.

I had never in my life hit a human being, had never hit even an animal.

But I had been through a difficult day. And now this big, sullen, dangerous person wanted to hurt me.

She took another step. "Hey," she said. "You ain't goin' nowhere, pretty. You're mine now."

I said, "What about her?" And with my left hand I pointed over Ramona's shoulder.

It had been, of course, a schoolyard trick since antiquity. But perhaps Ramona had never been on a schoolyard. Or perhaps she simply did not expect a trick of any sort from someone so clearly helpless as I. She turned.

I believe that she realized, even before she reached the apex of her turn, that it had been a mistake. She was reversing herself, swiftly, but I had cocked back my arm already, and then, just as she faced me again, I swung my fist forward and slammed it as hard as I could, with every single ounce of my bodyweight behind it, smack into her broad, round stomach.

Chapter Seven

With a great *whoosh* of air, arms flying to her belly, Ramona folded forward.

After this promising beginning, however, I am afraid that I rather let Harry Boyle down.

I did in fact grab Ramona's hair and run her toward the cinder block wall—she was limp and unresisting—but at the last moment, I hesitated. I abruptly saw myself as though from above, looking down upon the two of us, seeing what I was doing to another human being.

Self-consciousness is not always a good thing. (I speak not morally here but tactically.)

Yet I had established so much momentum that I could not stop my rush. Ramona's head did indeed hit the wall but not with the force that Mr. Boyle had (very wisely) recommended. Still, it produced a kind of sickening *smack*, and, as I released her, she bounced away from the wall and collapsed to the floor onto her back. Her arms flapped against the concrete.

I was horrified.

On the floor, Ramona moaned unhappily and then her hand reached up to touch her head. She gasped, almost a cough. When her hand came away, it was dripping red.

She blinked again, looked left and right, then blinked some more. Tentatively, she touched her stomach. She exhaled dramatically.

Then, ever so slowly, she rolled over.

Many years later, someone suggested to me that it was exactly at this moment that I should have sprinted forward and kicked Ramona with as much enthusiasm as possible, directly in the face.

This I failed to do.

Slowly, slowly, she raised herself onto hands and knees. She shook her head, and I was reminded of a dog shaking off water. She looked around the cell again, and this time she saw me. Her small eyes narrowed. "*Kill* you," she said.

She pushed herself to her feet. Blood was trickling from behind her bangs and down along the right side of her face. She wiped it away. She wavered slightly. With visible effort, wincing, she forced herself upright. "*Kill* you, bitch," she said.

I readied myself.

For what, precisely, I did not know. I did know that I would not be permitted any more tricks. Not that I possessed any; my bag was empty.

Just as she made a lumbering move toward me, hurried footsteps came clattering down the corridor.

"*Disgraceful*," I heard a male voice say. "*Outrageous!*"

Then, through the bars, I saw him: a short and balding middle-aged man in a gray wool suit who held a derby hat in his left hand and, surprisingly, my purse in his right. Mrs. Hadley stood beside him, looking more cowed than I would have believed possible. She was fumbling with her keys.

"*Open it up!*" said the man. "*Right now*, madam, or I'll slap a suit against the city so fast your nose will bleed." He was splendidly splenetic—his wide eyes were glaring, his face was bright red against the white of his handlebar mustache.

Mrs. Hadley slipped the key into the lock, turned it, and pulled the door open. She stepped back, looking down.

The man rushed in and leaned toward me. "You all right, kiddo?" Lightly, he tapped the crown of his derby against my shoulder. "You okay?"

"Yes," I said. "Yes."

He turned to Ramona. She had backed up against the wall, and now she was wiping more blood from her face. He said, "What happened to you?"

She glanced at Mrs. Hadley, looked back at the man, and lifted her chin. Her defiance was as flimsy as mine had been with Becker and Vandervalk, and I actually felt a sputter of sympathy. She said, "I slipped."

The man looked at Mrs. Hadley, looked at Ramona, then looked at me. The redness drained from his face. He grinned at me. "Okay. I'm Morrie Lipkind. You're Amanda Burton. We're leaving." He looked down at my feet. "You got shoes?"

"Yes."

"Terrific. Put 'em on."

I sat down on the bed and picked up a shoe. As I slipped it on, he turned back to Mrs. Hadley.

He said, "This is low. This is about as goddamn low as it gets."

Mrs. Hadley said, "It wasn't my—"

"Save it. You tell that little pig Vandervalk that he'll hear from me in the morning."

I stood up.

Mr. Lipkind said, "Ready?"

"Yes."

He handed me the purse. "They got anything else of yours?"

"My watch," I said.

He turned to Mrs. Hadley, whose hand was already fumbling in the pocket of her uniform.

I noticed, with surprise, that her face was a vivid scarlet, and I felt a kind of horrible gloating satisfaction, one that I had never felt before, and one that I did not much care for.

Mr. Lipkind stepped over, snatched away the watch, stepped back, handed it to me, and placed his arm around my shoulder. "Let's go. You can put it on in the car."

I glanced at the time.

Nine thirty. That seemed impossible. I had been certain that it was two or three in the morning.

Mr. Lipkind looked at Ramona then looked back at me. "What about her?" He nodded toward the girl.

She frowned and glanced away, blinking very quickly.

It was the blinking that did it.

I turned to Mr. Lipkind. "Can you get her out?"

"I can do anything," he said. Then he turned to Ramona. "You want out?"

Her eyes darted back and forth as she looked from Mr. Lipkind to me to Mrs. Hadley. She looked back up at Mr. Lipkind. "Uh huh."

"Outside the front door," he told her. "No farther."

She nodded. "Uh huh."

Mrs. Hadley's voice was querulous. "You can't do that, your papers say—"

"Madam," said Mr. Lipkind, "please shut it."

As soon as we stepped outside into the summer night, through a small door onto Centre Street, Ramona started running. Without a glance back, her boots clomping on the asphalt, she sprinted across the street.

"You're welcome," Mr. Lipkind muttered. He stroked his hand down his handlebar mustache.

She slipped like a ghost into an alleyway.

I did see her once again, some ten years later, on a cruise ship heading for Havana. She was sailing in first class, and I was working undercover, traveling in steerage. By then we were both professionals, and we each let the other do her job.

Mr. Lipkind's car was a glossy black Cadillac that came with its own livery driver, a large black man named Robert. As Mr. Lipkind and I settled down on the leather backseat, he introduced me to the man.

In the glow of the car's overhead light I could see Robert nod his big handsome head. "Miss," he said. Deep and resonant, his voice reminded me of Paul Robeson's.

Mr. Lipkind pulled the door shut, and the light went out. "Okay," he said to me. "Tell me about it."

The car moved forward.

I said, "My uncle, you mean?"

"You can tell me that part later. Tell me about the cops. When did they turn up?"

And so, as the big car purred through the nighttime city, streamers of bright lights flickering by on either side of us, red and white and green, I told him.

Now and then he interrupted with a question.

"So when did Becker make an entrance?" "They feed you?" "That Ramona babe. She hurt you?"

When I told him what Becker and Vandervalk had wanted me to say—that my uncle had in some way interfered with me—he shook his head. "Bottom of the barrel stuff. They're desperate. They got no one else for this."

When, finally, I finished, he shook his head again. "Cossacks," he said. "Filthy Cossacks. Putting the frame on a kid. You want to, Amanda, we can sue 'em blind. Personally, tell the truth, I'd love to shiv that Vandervalk."

"But how did you know where I was?" I asked him.

"I—hold on, we're here." He leaned toward the driver. "Robert, let us off across the street, okay? Then, you don't mind, you could zip over to the apartment and grab the stuff. 'Kay?"

"Okay," came the deep bass voice.

We were in Midtown, somewhere in the Forties. The Cadillac swung over to the right and came to a smooth stop. Mr. Lipkind opened the door, stepped out onto the curb, and held the door for me. After I clambered out of the car, he slammed the door shut.

We walked around the Cadillac. He looked left and right, waited for a few cars to pass, then said, "Okay, kiddo."

We were heading across the asphalt toward an expensive-looking hotel called the Algonquin. I followed him through the big brass-and-glass door into the carpeted lobby, and then across it, between elegant pillars of polished wood. Mr. Lipkind waved his derby at a man behind the front desk and the man nodded. When we arrived at a pair of elevators, Mr. Lipkind pushed the UP button.

"You were going to tell me," I said, "how you knew about me."

One of the elevator doors smoothly rumbled open.

He grinned at me. "Tell you in a minute. In you go."

It was all very mysterious, but the man had arrived in my life as a wonderful deus ex machina. He had plucked me away from that frightful little cell, plucked me away from Mrs. Hadley and Lieutenant Becker and Mr. Vandervalk. I stepped into the elevator. It smelled of perfume, a huge improvement over the various bouquets available at police headquarters.

The elevator rose three floors and then stopped. The door opened, and Mr. Lipkind held it back with his hand while I stepped into the corridor. He followed me out and the door rumbled shut behind him.

"This way," he said.

We padded along the thick red runner of the hallway floor until we came to room 311. He knocked on the door.

After a moment, it was opened by an attractive woman in her early thirties. She was tiny—not quite five feet tall. Her shiny, short black hair was parted on the right, and she wore a smart green dress that showed off her excellent legs and her black patent leather pumps. I could smell her perfume, laced with the woodsy fragrance of chypre.

She looked from Mr. Lipkind to me and then back at Mr. Lipkind. She smiled. "Hail the conquering hero." Her voice was soft, and she spoke with the expensive drawl taught in East Coast finishing schools. When she turned to me, the smile widened into something dazzling. "Hey, Amanda. Get your ass in here."

I blinked. No adult had ever used that word in front of me before.

She stood aside. With his derby, Mr. Lipkind gestured for me to proceed.

I went in. A miniature black-and-white Boston terrier capered around me on the carpet, panting elaborately, its stubby tail frantically twitching.

I was in the living room of a brightly lighted expensive suite furnished with overstuffed chairs and a big overstuffed sofa. The long drapes at the window were drawn together. A large upright radio was softly playing Chopin. And opposite me, beyond a coffee table, pushing herself up from the sofa with a black Malacca walking stick, its crook held in both hands, was a woman I had not seen in three years. Wearing a long, black silk dress identical to the dresses I remembered her wearing back then, back when all those appalling things had happened at the shore, back when my stepmother had been murdered, was my good friend Miss Lizzie Borden.

BOOK TWO

Chapter Eight

As we embraced, I inhaled the sweet scent of cinnamon and oranges and cloves that, all at once, I remembered with astonishing clarity. It was as though no time, not a single second of it, had passed since I had seen her last.

"Amanda," she said. "How are you?"

I stepped back. "I'm okay. I'm fine, Miss Lizzie. How are you?"

In truth, looking at her more closely, I could see that the three years had changed her. Her hair was still silver-white, and it was still drawn back behind her small ears, but she was thinner now, and her face seemed strained. The gold pince-nez that had once looked like an afterthought, an ornament to set off her large, luminous gray eyes, now looked like what they were: an optical device.

And back then, she had never used a walking stick.

But the three years had changed me, as well. I was now a full head taller than she.

The Boston terrier was still at my feet, sniffing frantically at my shoes—intoxicated, possibly, by the police headquarters bouquet.

"I'm quite well, thank you," Miss Lizzie said. "It's very good to see you, dear. You look lovely. And, goodness, you must have grown at least a foot taller."

"It's great to see *you*, Miss Lizzie. But how did you get here? How did—"

"All in good time," she said. "First, the introductions. You've already met Mr. Lipkind. This is Mrs. Parker, a friend. I met her last year, here at the hotel."

Mrs. Parker stepped forward and held out her delicate white hand, as casually as a man might. I shook it. "A pleasure," she said and then smiled as she released me.

The terrier romped around the room, paws pattering at the carpet, its eager head swiveling back and forth.

Miss Lizzie glanced down at the dog, smiled vaguely, and then looked back at me. "It was Mrs. Parker," she said, "who suggested that I engage Mr. Lipkind."

"The best damned shyster in the city," said Mrs. Parker, in that languorous drawl.

"The country," said Mr. Lipkind.

"But how—" I started to say to Miss Lizzie.

"Have a seat, dear," she said and glanced around the room. "Let's all sit, shall we?"

She lowered herself, right hand on the arm of the sofa, left hand using the walking stick to help her. I came around the coffee table and sat at the other end of the sofa. Mr. Lipkind and Mrs. Parker each took one of the chairs. On the small end table beside Mrs. Parker's chair was an ashtray in which a cigarette burned, pale white smoke slowly spiraling toward the ceiling.

As soon as Mrs. Parker sat down, the dog scampered across the carpet and leaped onto her lap. Mrs. Parker bent forward, wrapped her tiny hands around its tiny head, and kissed it on the nose.

Watching this, Miss Lizzie blinked. Then she turned to me. "Are you hungry, dear? Mrs. Parker brought a sandwich. It's there on the end table."

"Yes," I said. "Thank you." I turned to Mrs. Parker. "Thank you." She smiled. "It was Lizbeth's idea."

I had thought of my friend for so long as "Miss Lizzie," hearing her real name came almost as a jolt.

I ignored it, however. I was ravenous. On the table to my left were two paper napkins, a bottle of Coca-Cola, and a sandwich wrapped in aluminum foil. I put the napkins on my lap and then laid the sandwich atop them.

"Here," said Mr. Lipkind. He stood up, reached into his pocket, pulled out a Churchkey opener, stepped across the carpet, lifted the bottle of cola, opened it, and set it back down. "There you go."

"Thank you."

"You bet." Slipping the opener back into his pocket, he went back to his chair.

I unfolded the aluminum foil. Inside was a fat sandwich of roast beef on dark rye bread. I raised it to my mouth and took a demure bite—I was in public. The meat was rare and tender, spread with pungent mustard; the bread was dense and chewy. Apart from a fresh swordfish steak that I shared, many years later, with my second husband on the island of Lamu, off the coast of Kenya, this was the best meal I ever ate in all of my life.

Miss Lizzie waited for me to swallow and then said, "It was very clever of you to call your brother."

That had been the other telephone call I made this morning, after I spoke with the police.

"I couldn't think of anyone else. But I thought that if William could talk to Mr. Slocum, then Mr. Slocum might be able to help," I explained.

Darryl Slocum was the lawyer who had represented Miss Lizzie and me during the investigation of my stepmother's death. Except for Mr. Lipkind, tonight, Mr. Slocum was the only lawyer I had ever met. I think I had some notion that if my brother got in touch with him, Mr. Slocum would swirl on a cape and come dashing to my rescue. Back then, during the investigation, I had had a terrible crush on the man— one from which, perhaps, I had not yet fully recovered.

"And he *was* able to help," said Miss Lizzie. "He's very busy just now, and he knows no one here in New York, but he knows that I do."

"How did he know that?" I asked. "Have you seen him since . . . that time at the shore?" I took another bite of the sandwich. My stomach gurgled. I wondered if everyone had heard.

"Once or twice," she said. "He's helped me with a few minor things." She fluttered her fingers to show how minor they were. "In any event, he telephoned me. I told him that I'd take care of it. I telephoned Mrs. Parker and then went to the station and purchased a ticket for the first available train."

I pushed aside the thought that Mr. Slocum had been too busy to purchase a ticket for the first available train, and I swallowed some more roast beef.

"Meanwhile," said Mrs. Parker, inhaling her cigarette, then exhaling smoke with her words, "back at the ranch, I was going through my list of ambulance chasers. Clarence Darrow was busy, so I called Lipkind here." Lightly, with her left hand, she stroked the dog, which was now lying across her thighs.

"Darrow's a piker," said Mr. Lipkind, and he stroked his luxuriant mustache.

I took a sip of Coca-Cola. It was warm but absolutely delicious.

"Mr. Lipkind, Mrs. Parker, and I," continued Miss Lizzie, "met at the Plaza Hotel for . . . well, I suppose you could call it a council of war. Mr. Lipkind has friends in the police department—"

"*Friends* is putting it kind of strong," said Mr. Lipkind.

"Lawyers don't have friends," Mrs. Parker explained to me, stubbing out her cigarette. "They have torts." She turned to Mr. Lipkind. "Or is that tarts?"

Miss Lizzie smiled brightly at them both. "May I finish, please?"

I had once seen her lose her temper, and she had been terrifying. Even now, with only that bright, controlled smile, she was formidable.

"Sorry about that," said Mrs. Parker. "Sometimes I get carried away." She smiled wryly. "Sometimes I think I should be."

Miss Lizzie looked at Mr. Lipkind.

"Absolutely," he said. "You got it."

She turned back to me. "Mr. Lipkind's *acquaintances*," she said, "were able to determine where you were being held. Mr. Lipkind knew of a judge who was able to provide the papers necessary to secure your release. Once he had them, Mr. Lipkind proceeded to police headquarters. He has done, I think, an excellent job." She turned to him. "For which I sincerely thank him."

"Hey," said Mr. Lipkind. "It's what I do."

I swallowed the last bite of sandwich and asked Miss Lizzie, "Why didn't you come down there yourself?"

"Mrs. Parker suggested that, all things considered, it might be best for me to remain in the background. I believe she was right."

I looked at Mrs. Parker, who was bending forward, whispering to the dog. She looked up at me and again she smiled that dazzling smile.

Miss Lizzie said to me, "Knowing something of how the police operate, I imagine that you've explained several thousand times what happened today. But perhaps, if you're able, you could explain it one more time, for us."

"Okay." I dabbed at my mouth with a paper napkin, took another sip of the Coca-Cola.

Slowly, I explained it one more time.

Now and then Mr. Lipkind asked questions.

"Daphne Dale?" he said. "The writer?"

Mrs. Parker's dog was following all this closely, his small, square head turning from one speaker to the next.

"That's what John told me," I said. "He said he put him in her book."

"Really?" said Mrs. Parker. "*The Flesh Seekers*? He was Jerry Brandon? Well, of course he was. John Burton, Jerry Brandon." She turned to Miss Lizzie. "She calls herself Sophie Hill in the book. Daphne doesn't go very far for her names." She smiled. "Just over the hill and down the dale."

"I wouldn't know," I said. "I haven't read the book."

"Consider yourself lucky," she said. "But if you want a copy, I can lend you mine. It's propping up a bookcase in my apartment."

"Okay," said Mr. Lipkind. "What next?"

I continued on to El Fay.

"Larry Fay," said Mr. Lipkind. "And your uncle went off with him?"

"Yes. For about fifteen minutes."

"Interesting."

"In what way?" Miss Lizzie asked him.

"He's a hoodlum. A rumrunner." He turned back to me. "How is it your uncle knew him? Did he say?"

"No."

Still stroking the dog, Mrs. Parker asked me, "Did you get to see George Raft?"

The dog looked up at her, its tiny tongue lolling.

"Yes," I said. "He was amazing."

She smiled. "Amazing in a way that makes you wonder how amazing he might be in other ways."

"Yes," said Miss Lizzie. "All right, Amanda. What happened next?"

"We went to the Cotton Club," I said. "In Harlem." I mentioned the man in the white dinner jacket.

"Good-looking guy?" Mr. Lipkind asked me. "English accent?"

"He was good-looking, yes. But I don't know about the accent. I didn't talk to him."

"Black hair, brown eyes, smokes cigarettes? Stands real straight?"

"That's him, yes."

"Owney Madden."

"And who might he be?" Miss Lizzie asked.

"He owns the place. Also a couple of breweries. Another hood. A Brit. Got sent up for killing a guy about seven years ago. He got sprung last year. Smooth as silk these days, but very definitely a hood."

Miss Lizzie turned to me. "Your uncle, it seems, knew some rather colorful characters."

"But he was a stockbroker," I said. "Maybe they had investments."

"Guys like Owney and Larry," said Mr. Lipkind, "they don't need investments. They *are* investments."

"You're on a first-name basis?" Mrs. Parker asked him.

"I get around." He shrugged. "Part of the job."

"Go ahead, Amanda," said Miss Lizzie. "What happened next?"

I told them about coming home, going to sleep, and finding John's body.

"Yes, dear," said Miss Lizzie—wishing, I believe, to hurry me past that horror. "I know it must have been dreadful. So you called the police?"

I continued with the story. When I came to Lieutenant Becker, Miss Lizzie turned to Mr. Lipkind and asked him, "Who is he, this Becker person?"

"A big deal at headquarters. Got a lot of juice."

"By 'juice' you mean power? Influence?"

"Right. Word is, he's the bagman between the mob and the cops."

"Bagman?"

"According to the grapevine, Becker's the guy who carries cash from your criminal element—folks like Madden and Fay and Arnold Rothstein—to the department. Down at headquarters, it's divvied up among the troops."

"Arnold Rothstein?"

"Big gambler. Runs the richest floating crap game in the city."

"The name is familiar. Isn't he somehow connected to the sports world?"

Mr. Lipkind smiled. "Kind of. He's the man who fixed the World Series back in 1919."

She nodded. "We are talking, then, about bribes."

"Contributions, the police like to call them."

"And the police can get away with this?"

Mr. Lipkind shrugged. "New York City. They can get away with whatever they want."

"The New York City cops," said Mrs. Parker, "are notorious assholes."

The word, coming out of that tiny frame, spoken in that elegant accent, startled me. I glanced at Miss Lizzie. If she were startled, she didn't show it. She simply nodded and then turned to Mr. Lipkind.

"But if Mr. Becker is such a powerful figure," she asked, "why should he involve himself in this particular investigation?"

"Good question," said Mr. Lipkind. He shrugged. "I dunno. Unless maybe the cops want to keep Madden and Fay out of it."

"But Mr. Becker couldn't have known, before he arrived at John Burton's, what Amanda's testimony might be. He couldn't have known that she'd mention Mr. Madden and Mr. Fay."

"Maybe Madden or Fay heard that Burton got nailed, and they decided to be included out. All it would take is a call to Becker."

"Why should they care?"

"Dunno. Something we've got to find out, I guess."

She turned to me. "All right, Amanda. Mr. Becker brought you down to police headquarters. What then?"

I told them about Vandervalk and Becker.

Once again Miss Lizzie turned to Mr. Lipkind. "They can't really believe that Amanda's uncle tried to . . . harm her?"

"Nah. Like I told the kid—"

"Amanda," corrected Miss Lizzie.

"Right. Like I told her, they're up against it. They got no one else. She's handy, right? An out-of-towner. No family, no friends, no connections. They tie the can to her; they can close out the case."

"That's despicable."

"Yeah. Cossacks. They had her in a little holding cell they got downstairs. Wanted to spook her. Even brought in some bull—" Lightly, he covered his mouth with his fist and cleared his throat. "They even brought in some hard-nosed babe from the streets, stuck her in there with her."

He grinned. "Turns out the babe got decked." He turned to me. "What'd you hit her with? The sink?"

"The wall," I said. "Sort of." I turned to Miss Lizzie. "She was going to—"

"I'm sure you did exactly what needed to be done," she said.

I looked over at the lawyer. "Mr. Lipkind?"

"Yeah?"

"The room I was in, with Becker and Vandervalk. There was a big drain in the floor. What was that for?"

"For when they rinse the room down. Afterward." He turned to Miss Lizzie. "Sometimes, the cops, they get a little carried away when they ask people questions."

"Charming," she said. "All right. Where, exactly, do we go from here?"

Before he could answer, someone knocked at the door to the suite.

Miss Lizzie said, "Who on Earth . . ."

Mrs. Parker set the dog on the carpet and stood. The dog looked up at her, expectant. "Let's find out," said Mrs. Parker.

His tail twitching, the dog followed her to the door.

Chapter Nine

It was Mr. Lipkind's chauffeur, Robert. He strode into the room, holding his cap in his left hand and carrying a suitcase in his right. I recognized the suitcase as my own.

Panting, the Boston terrier danced around him.

Mr. Lipkind rose from his chair. "Okay, Robert, thanks. You can just set that down."

Robert lowered the suitcase, placed it against the wall, and stood straight up, waiting. Taller than he had seemed in the car, he was broad-shouldered and narrow-waisted. And still very handsome in his well-cut gray uniform.

Mr. Lipkind turned to Miss Lizzie. "This is my right-hand guy, Robert Jenkins. Robert, this is Miss Borden."

Miss Lizzie smiled. "How do you do?"

"Ma'am," said Robert in his smooth, rolling baritone, and he nodded politely.

"And this is Mrs. Parker," said Mr. Lipkind.

"Dorothy," said Mrs. Parker.

"Ma'am," said Robert.

"Dorothy," said Mrs. Parker and smiled.

"Grab a seat, Robert," said Mr. Lipkind. He looked to Miss Lizzie. "That okay?"

"Of course," she said.

Only one more seat was available, a small upholstered chair pushed up against the wall. With a dancer's grace, Robert lifted it, swung it out into the room, set it back on the floor, and sat down in it. He held himself upright, holding his cap in his lap with both hands, the terrier sniffing and snuffling at his shiny black brogues. Robert leaned forward and used his right hand to scratch the dog behind the ear. The terrier jumped up into his lap. Robert grinned and scratched it some more.

"Mrs. Parker," said Miss Lizzie, "perhaps your dog would be happier somewhere else."

"That's okay," said Robert, and he grinned as he scratched at the dog's ear.

Mrs. Parker said, "*Woodrow*," and the terrier looked at her, looked up regretfully at Robert, then jumped from his lap, bounced across the floor, and bounded up into Mrs. Parker's lap. Once again she kissed him on the nose.

Once again, Miss Lizzie blinked.

Mr. Lipkind sat back down. "I sent Robert over to the Dakota to get the kid's stuff."

"Amanda's," said Miss Lizzie.

"Right." He turned to the chauffeur. "Any problem?"

"No," said Robert. "As soon as he saw the papers from the judge, the superintendent let me into the apartment."

I glanced at Mrs. Parker. She was studying him while she absently stroked the dog's back.

"Terrific," said Mr. Lipkind, and he turned back to Miss Lizzie. "'Kay. You want to know where we go?"

"Indeed," she said.

"Time being," he said, "we're copasetic. The cops'll lay off the kid"—he held up his hand—"Amanda. They'll lay off Amanda for a while. But if they can't finger someone else, pretty soon they'll get back to her. What we got to do is start nosing around on our own, find out who else looks good for this. I know a guy, Carl Liebowitz, a very good snooper, done a lot of work for me. You want, I can put him onto this."

"Can he be here tomorrow morning?" Miss Lizzie asked him.

"What time?"

"Nine."

"I'll call him. Meanwhile"—he turned to Robert—"you know one of the dancers at the Cotton Club, right?"

The corner of his mouth edged upward in a half smile. "Pardon me?"

Mr. Lipkind told him about my visit there. "Sounds like Amanda's uncle knew Owney Madden. Maybe that's important, maybe it's not. You ask around, could be you dig up something."

Robert nodded. "I can do that."

"Terrific," said Mr. Lipkind. He stood. Off to the side, Robert stood as well. "'Kay," Mr. Lipkind said to Miss Lizzie. "That's it for now, I think. You need me, give me a jingle."

"I will, yes," she said. "And again, I thank you very much for your help today."

He shrugged. "Like I said, all part of the job."

Mrs. Parker set down the dog and stood. "It's time for me to go, too," she said to Miss Lizzie. She turned to me. "Great to meet you, Amanda."

"Thank you," I said. "You, too. And thank you very much for the sandwich. And the Coke."

"My pleasure," said Mrs. Parker. She looked at Miss Lizzie. "Would it be all right if I sat in tomorrow morning? While you talked to the"—she smiled—"to the snooper?"

"Of course, dear," said Miss Lizzie. "I'm in your debt."

"No, no, not at all. But that's swell. Thanks. I'll see you at nine, then." She turned to Mr. Lipkind and Robert. "I'll share the elevator. I live one floor down."

After the three of them left the suite accompanied by the prancing Boston terrier, Miss Lizzie turned to me.

"Now," she said, "truly. How are you, Amanda?"

"I'm okay," I said. "Honestly. But I'm really glad I got out of there. That cell at police headquarters—it was awful."

"I'm sure it was. But tell me, dear. What have you been doing for the past three years?" She smiled. "Are you still working with the cards?"

I beamed at her. "Want to see my Mystic Seven?"

"I'd like that very much. But are you sure you wouldn't rather get some rest? The room next door is yours."

"No, no," I said. "Really. I'm fine. Want to see it?"

Smiling, her hands on the knob of her walking stick, she leaned slightly toward me. "More than anything in the world."

Three years ago, before the murder, when Miss Lizzie had been my next-door neighbor, she had taught me how to manipulate cards. Since then, practicing a few times a week, sometimes more often, I had become fairly proficient. But I would never be as accomplished as she. Over the years, I have seen the best in the business—Dai Vernon, Al Baker, Leslie Guest, Theo Annemann, John Scarne—and Miss Lizzie was at least as good as any of them.

Back then, I had decided that she became so adept because she had studied and used the cards to fill up the hollows in what had probably been a very lonely life. For me, every trick she performed was, by its very expertise, invisibly bracketed by a framework of sadness. Sometimes I wonder whether this isn't true of all magicians, even the ones who work with words or paint rather than with playing cards.

I went over to the suitcase and opened it. Everything seemed to be there. All the clothes, including my underwear, had been carefully folded and neatly arranged. I thought of handsome Robert—sitting gracefully on my bed, perhaps, or standing gracefully beside it—meticulously packing the case, one frilly pair of panties after another, one filmy pair of hose after another. I blushed—the sort of furious all-over blush that makes you fear you might implode. My back was turned to her, so Miss Lizzie did not see.

The deck was in one of the pockets of the divider. I slipped it out and carried it back.

She asked me, "Have you heard from your parents?"

"Not yet," I said. "You know they're in Tibet, right?"

"Yes, Mr. Slocum told me."

"It takes a while for mail to get here from over there." I set the deck on the coffee table, walked over to the chair in which Robert had been sitting, and moved it, less gracefully than he had, over to the table. I sat down, picked up the cardboard box, slid the deck from it, and started shuffling.

Miss Lizzie sat there, her gray eyes watchful behind the pince-nez.

"Okay," I said, handing her the deck. "Divide it up into seven piles. You don't have to deal them out. Just cut them."

She knew all this, probably better than I ever would, but she said nothing. Smiling faintly, she did as I had directed, leaning forward and positioning the piles along the coffee table with her right hand.

"Okay," I said. "Pick a pile and look at the top card."

She did, lifting back a corner of the top card on the leftmost pile, peering at it for a moment through her pince-nez, and then lightly snapping the card back into place.

"Okay," I said. "Just to show that there's no trickery involved"— Miss Lizzie smiled, for whenever you hear this from a card handler, you know that the trickery is already well advanced—"I'll put three of these piles on top of that pile." I did this. "And three on the bottom." I shuffled the deck and then handed it to her.

"Cut," I said.

She set the deck on the table and cut it once. I lifted it and then, one by one, faceup, I dealt the cards out along the table in four vertical rows.

"Okay," I said, "I'm going to turn around. You pick up your card and keep it and push all the others to the side." I turned away, shielding my face with my hand so I couldn't see what she was doing.

"Ready," she said.

I turned back to her. "Okay. Put the card facedown on the table and cover it with both of your hands. And *concentrate* on the card."

Miss Lizzie laid the card down, leaned forward, put her hands atop it, and then suddenly she sat back, laughing, and clapped her hands together.

"That was wonderful," she said. "Really wonderful. You did an excellent slight, dear, and a really lovely false shuffle. If I hadn't known, I should never have seen them."

"Really?"

"Really. The key card was the four of clubs."

"Yes."

She nodded, smiling broadly. "*Wonderful*, Amanda."

It was not an especially elaborate trick—it's quite simple, really—but I was immensely gratified by her reaction to it.

Neither of us bothered to turn over the isolated card that lay facedown on the table, the card that Miss Lizzie had selected. Both of us knew that it was the king of spades.

We spent a few more hours talking and manipulating the cards. She showed me some variations on the Mystic Seven and then a few rather intricate card-spelling tricks. As deft as ever, she performed slights that were totally undetectable, despite my knowing that they were coming, despite my intense study of her hands.

It was sometime after one o'clock in the morning when I carted my suitcase into the adjoining suite. I brushed my teeth, climbed into my nightgown, and then climbed into bed. I turned off the light, waited a moment for the streetlight seeping around the curtains to become visible, and then finally—it seemed for the first time in years—I relaxed.

I thought that I might have a difficult time falling asleep, that visions of my uncle would flash out at me from the darkness, but I was unconscious almost immediately.

Chapter Ten

At five minutes to nine the next morning, Miss Lizzie and I were back in the living room of her suite. We had finished the room-service breakfast—bacon and eggs, fried potatoes, buttered toast with jam—and we were both sipping our tea.

Someone knocked at the door.

"I'll get it," I told her and set my cup in its saucer.

The man who stood outside the door was extraordinary. He was quite short, about five foot two or three. He was wearing a beautifully tailored gray silk suit, a white shirt, a gray tie, and small black patent-leather shoes. In his left hand, he held a gray fedora. He was good-looking in an almost classical way—large, brown oval eyes; a strong, sculpted nose; a square jaw.

What made him extraordinary was that he was virtually without hair—none on his chin, none on his upper lip, none on his eyebrows or eyelids, none at all on his shiny white scalp.

I was staring at his scalp, contemplating it, and he smiled. "No," he said, "none anywhere."

I blushed superlatively but tried to pretend my way out. "Excuse me?"

"*Alopecia universalis,*" he said. "From the Greek. *Alopékia.* Hairlessness. It happened when I was twelve. An attack of scarlet fever."

He seemed so comfortable with it, spoke of it so matter-of-factly, that I said, "All at once?"

"Overnight." He smiled again, showing two rows of white even teeth.

"Wow," I said.

"I'm Carl Liebowitz. May I come in?"

"Oh, sure, of course. I'm sorry."

"Don't be," he said and stepped into the room. "Amanda?"

"Yes," I said, pushing the door shut.

He held out a small perfect hand. "Delighted."

I shook it. "And this is Miss Borden," I told him.

After the introductions, we organized ourselves. Mr. Liebowitz sat down in the same chair in which Mr. Lipkind had sat last night, and he placed his small fedora on his lap. I came around and sat once again at the end of the sofa, opposite Miss Lizzie.

She said, "Mr. Lipkind has explained the situation to you?"

"Yes." He turned to me, his face serious. "I'm very sorry for your loss."

"Oh," I said. "Thank you."

Miss Lizzie asked him, "How do you think we should proceed?"

Sitting upright, his elbows on the arms of the chair, his fingers tented above the fedora, he said, "Morrie believes that in the circumstances, it's imperative that we discover who actually killed Mr. Burton." His speech was slow and precise, almost pedantic. "If the real killer goes undetected, the police will continue to perceive Amanda as a suspect—even knowing that she had nothing to do with it."

She frowned. "Why on earth should they do that?"

"From what Morrie told me," he said, "Mr. Burton had at least a passing acquaintance with Owney Madden and Larry Fay. These are important men in New York City. Criminals, but important. They're among the people who make large clandestine payoffs to the police and the politicians. Morrie told you about the payoffs?"

"Yes. 'Contributions,' he said."

"And he told you about Lieutenant Becker?"

"Yes."

He turned to me. "And you told Morrie that Vandervalk sat in on your interrogation?"

"Um. Yes." I was still dazzled by his gleaming bald head.

He turned it toward Miss Lizzie. "With Becker and Vandervalk involved, it's likely that the police are trying to steer the investigation away from Madden and Fay. If Mr. Burton was in any way complicit with those two, the police will want to wrap up the case as soon as they can. And Amanda, unfortunately, makes a convenient scapegoat."

"He wasn't a criminal," I said. "My uncle."

He turned to me and flashed that brilliant white smile. "I'm sure he wasn't," he said. "But in my experience, the most successful way to operate is to begin with no assumptions at all, including that one."

"Begin," said Miss Lizzie, "in what manner, precisely?"

"With what we know," he said, "and with whom we know."

He reached into his inner coat pocket and slid out a small notebook. He opened it, flipped through a few pages, and looked up at Miss Lizzie. "Albert Cooper. Daphne Dale. Mr. Burton's business colleagues. And then Fay and Madden."

"Who is Albert Cooper?" Miss Lizzie asked.

"Albert," I said. "He works—he worked for my uncle." I realized that I had barely thought of the man since Friday. "I hope he's okay."

"We need to start at Mr. Burton's apartment," Mr. Liebowitz said to Miss Lizzie. "Morrie could obtain legal papers to get me entrance, but it would be faster by far, and more convenient"—he turned to me—"if you could come along, Amanda. You have a legal right to be there and to bring anyone you'd like with you. Would you be willing to do that? Are you up to it?"

An image of John flashed across my mind. I saw him as I had last seen him, sitting there battered beyond recognition in the library. All that blood. Blood everywhere. . . .

I swallowed. "Yes," I said.

Miss Lizzie said, "Are you quite sure, Amanda?"

"Yes, I'm sure."

"Very well, then," she said and reached for the Malacca cane, propped up against the sofa's arm. "We're off."

Mr. Liebowitz coughed politely into his balled fist. "Um," he said.

"Yes?" said Miss Lizzie.

"Miss Borden, I think that given your, um—I think that in the circumstances, it might be better if you remained here." It was the first time he had seemed even slightly uncertain about anything.

"Nonsense," said Miss Lizzie. "I am not going to have young Amanda wandering around New York City on her own."

"She won't be on her own," said Mr. Liebowitz. "She'll be with me."

"*Quis custodiet ipsos custodes?*"

"Juvenal," said Mr. Liebowitz. "Who will guard the guards themselves?"

Miss Lizzie gave him a small measured nod, like an approving schoolteacher, and then put both her hands in her lap, one primly atop the other. She said, "I'm quite certain, Mr. Liebowitz, that you are an entirely honorable man. But if I've learned one thing over the years, it is that the perception of reality is at least as important as the reality itself. In some cases, it can actually become the reality. I will, therefore, accompany the two of you."

Looking down, Mr. Liebowitz ran his small hand back along his slick, shiny scalp. He looked up and smiled again. "A chaperone."

"For want of a better word."

"But Miss Borden, when people hear your name—"

"They won't," she said, raising her head. "I shall assume a nom de guerre."

"Miss Borden—"

"My aunt," I said. "You could be my aunt."

Mr. Liebowitz looked over at me, frowning. He probably felt like we were ganging up on him. We probably were.

"Excellent," said Miss Lizzie. "Yes, Aunt Elizabeth." She smiled at me. "Lovely. I haven't been an aunt before."

She turned back to Mr. Liebowitz. "Very few people in New York know me. Only Mrs. Parker, downstairs, and a few others. And no one in this city has seen a recent photograph of me. None exists." With something that might have been pride, she added, "I have seen to that."

"Where is Mrs. Parker?" I asked. I looked at my watch. "It's almost nine thirty. She was supposed to be here."

Miss Lizzie said, "We'll check with her on our way out."

Mr. Liebowitz smiled wearily. "Is she coming, too?"

"If she so wishes," said Miss Lizzie.

As it happened, Mrs. Parker did not so wish.

The three of us stood outside her apartment on the second floor as Miss Lizzie knocked at the door. Nothing happened. Miss Lizzie knocked again.

There was some rattling behind the door, chains being unlatched, and then, slowly, the door crept open, and a corner of Mrs. Parker's head poked around it. Her hair was disheveled, and her face was pale. "Oh," she said. "Jesus wept. I went out last night, and I believe I caught pneumonia. I tend to catch it a lot. I'm extremely susceptible."

Miss Lizzie smiled. "Perhaps some aspirin will help."

"Yes," said Mrs. Parker, "or an undertaker. I really am sorry."

"There's no need. This is Mr. Liebowitz."

Mrs. Parker's gaze fell from Miss Lizzie and found Mr. Liebowitz. She blinked, and then her eyes moved up and down his short, slim form, from shiny black shoes to shiny white scalp. "Hello," she said.

"Mrs. Parker," he said.

Narrowing her eyes, she asked very seriously, "You wouldn't be in disguise, would you?"

Mr. Liebowitz smiled wanly. "No," he said.

Miss Lizzie told her, "Perhaps you could join us later, for lunch."

"That would be swell. Could you ring me?"

"I could, and I shall. Take some aspirin, dear. And go back to bed."

"My pleasure," said Mrs. Parker. "G'bye." She looked at me. "'Bye, Amanda. See you later."

"Goodbye."

"Mr. Liebowitz."

"Mrs. Parker."

She closed the door.

As we walked toward the elevator, Mr. Liebowitz said to Miss Lizzie, "Mrs. Parker has an entertaining way with a phrase."

"She is a writer," said Miss Lizzie.

"And a drinker."

"Yes," she said.

"Then why—"

I am not certain what he had been about to ask. Whatever it might have been, Miss Lizzie interrupted it.

"She is my friend," she said.

The day was summery bright. Beyond the terraces and pinnacles of the gray towering buildings, the blue sky was cloudless. We took a taxicab to the Dakota and arrived there at a little before ten thirty. After we rode the elevator up to my uncle's floor, I used my key to open the front door of the apartment.

As soon as the door swung back, I could smell the piercing stink of disinfectant. The place reeked of it. I remembered Mrs. Hadley at police headquarters, that cramped little cell, Ramona shuffling toward me . . .

We filed in and I turned, shut the door, and locked it again.

I looked around the hallway. For a week, the apartment had been a home to me; I had grown accustomed to its surfaces and its spaces, the textures of its sounds and smells. Now, in the stillness that surrounded us, it seemed like a museum diorama, a re-creation of the life in some vanished, ordered past.

"Right, then," said Mr. Liebowitz. "If you're prepared for it, Amanda, I need to see where it was you found him."

"In the library," I said. "Just up—"

From the library door, Albert stepped out into the hallway. "Oh, miss," he said. "This is wonderful! Are you okay?"

Once again, a white apron was wrapped around his broad middle. His tie was loosened, and the sleeves of his white cotton shirt were rolled back along his thick upper arms. He was wearing a pair of enormous yellow rubber household gloves, their gauntlets reaching nearly to his elbow.

"Yes," I said. "I'm fine. And you?"

He raised his right arm, turned his head to the right, and

dabbed the upper sleeve of his shirt at his big square forehead. I noticed then that his eyes were rimmed in bright red. "As well as can be expected, thank you, miss, in such a totally rotten situation." His brow furrowed. "But if you do not mind my asking—during all this time, where are you, miss? Yesterday, I make inquiries of the cops, but as per usual, they are not forthcoming."

"I'm sorry, Albert," I said. "I've been with my aunt. This is she, Miss Elizabeth Cabot. And this is Mr. Liebowitz. He's a private detective."

Albert looked at Miss Lizzie and Mr. Liebowitz as though he had just realized they were there. He stripped the glove from one hand—*snap*—stripped the glove from the other—*snap*—wiped the palm of his big right hand against the broad chest of the apron, and then stepped forward, his hand outstretched.

Miss Lizzie shook it. Albert said, "Very pleased to make your acquaintance, Miss Cabot."

"How do you do?" she said.

Albert turned to Mr. Liebowitz, looked down on him somberly, and gave him his hand. "And you, too, of course, Mr. Liebowitz. A private detective, is it?"

"That's right, Mr. Cooper. I'm investigating Mr. Burton's death. I wonder if I might ask you a few questions."

"Naturally. What do you say we retire to the parlor?"

"An excellent idea," said Mr. Liebowitz.

We trooped into the living room. Albert sat down in one of the padded brown leather chairs, laying his rubber gloves on the floor beside it, and the rest of us sat on the long brown leather sofa. Even sitting forward on the couch, Mr. Liebowitz's feet only barely met the floor.

He plucked his notebook from inside his jacket, opened it, slid a pen from his shirt pocket, unscrewed the cap, and slipped it onto the pen's barrel. He crossed his legs, right over left, and said, "Mr. Cooper, when exactly did the police inform you of Mr. Burton's death?"

Albert nodded. "I am informed of this yesterday at approximately eleven o'clock in the morning. Yesterday. Saturday, that is.

At that point in time I am in Queens, on Long Island, visiting with a friend."

"They sent someone out there?"

"Correct. They send two detectives from the twentieth precinct: Detective O'Deere and Detective Cohan."

"How did they find you?"

"I am very cooperative with them, I believe."

Mr. Liebowitz smiled. "I meant, how did they locate you?"

"Oh sure," said Albert and nodded. "The superintendent of the building, Mr. Bryant—"

"The superintendent of this building? The Dakota?"

"Yes, sir. What he does is he notifies them of my whereabouts. I always make certain that Mr. Bryant knows of my current whereabouts in the event of an accident occurring."

"Did they bring you back into Manhattan?"

"Yes, sir. To the precinct house, on Seventieth Street. After I assist them with their inquiries, I ask for permission to return here. To the apartment, I mean to say. They inform me that I cannot return until today. So I spend the night in a hotel that is owned by an acquaintance of mine, downtown, a very nice place I know of, and I come up here this morning."

"The name of the hotel?"

"The Broadway Inn. Situated at Sixth and Broadway."

"Why return to the apartment?" Mr. Liebowitz asked him.

"To assure myself that everything is in order."

"And was it?"

"No, sir, not in the least. The moment I get here, I discover it is a terrible mess. Everything is out of place. Everything is totally covered with powder."

"Powder?" said Miss Lizzie.

"Fingerprint powder, miss."

She nodded.

"And, naturally," he said, "the library . . ." His voice trailed off as he looked down. He stared at the floor for a moment then looked up at me. His bloodshot eyes were shiny. He shook his head. "I am so sorry, miss. I know that you and him, Mr. Burton, the two of you are getting along real well, like birds of a feather." He swallowed and then turned to Mr. Liebowitz. "It is a terrible thing, sir." He cleared his throat.

Mr. Liebowitz nodded. "Yes, it is. Was anything missing?"

Albert inhaled deeply then shook his head again. "No, sir. Not that I can determine, as of yet. But I have very little faith in the police of this city. I will not be surprised to discover they are purloining things."

"But nothing of which you're aware. So far."

He nodded. "Nothing of which I am aware so far. That is correct."

"What's the name of your friend in Queens?"

"Mrs. Hannesty. Mrs. Madge Hannesty."

"And how do you know her, Mr. Cooper?"

"We are friends now for many years. Many years ago, see, I work with her late husband. Before the war, that is."

"May I have her address?"

"Naturally." He gave it.

Mr. Liebowitz wrote it down. "And when did you go over to Queens?"

"I leave here at approximately five thirty on Friday evening." He looked at me. "Correct, miss?"

"Yes," I said to Mr. Liebowitz.

"The trip takes approximately one and a half hours," said Albert. "So I arrive at Mrs. Hannesty's residence, I would say, at approximately seven o'clock."

"And you spent the entire time with her?"

"Correct. At nine o'clock p.m., approximately, we go out to a dance hall—she is extremely fond of the dancing life, Mrs. Hannesty is. We stay there, I would estimate, until approximately one in the a.m., and then we return to her residence."

"The name of the dance hall?"

"The Jolly Roger."

"Who do you think killed him, Mr. Cooper?"

Albert blinked in surprise. "I got absolutely no idea, sir. I am totally in the dark. Like I tell the police, I cannot conceive of anyone wishing to cause harm to Mr. Burton. He has no enemies whatsoever, that I know of."

"Are you aware that he knew Owney Madden and Larry Fay?"

"I know of those names, sir, but I never hear them from Mr. Burton."

"Do you know who they are?"

"They are gangster types, I believe. And they are the owners of nightclubs. On occasion, I see them mentioned in the various newspapers."

"How do you suppose he knew the men?"

"I could not say, sir. Maybe from the nightclubs? Mr. Burton, he enjoys his evening out."

"Do you know a woman named Daphne Dale?"

"Yes, sir. The writer lady. At one time, she is an acquaintance of Mr. Burton's."

"What was their relationship?"

Albert glanced at me, almost furtively.

"Mr. Cooper," said Mr. Liebowitz, "I'm hoping that you want to help us apprehend whoever killed Mr. Burton."

"Yes, sir. I want that totally."

"Then I think you ought to tell us whatever you can. Mr. Burton is beyond embarrassment at this point."

Albert glanced at me again, then looked back to Mr. Liebowitz. "Yes, sir."

"Their relationship?"

"It is no longer current, sir."

"And when was it current?"

"Approximately two years ago, I would estimate."

"They were intimate?"

"Yes, sir." Once more, he glanced quickly at me and then back to Mr. Liebowitz. "For a period of time," he said.

"For how long?"

"For five months or so, I would say. Approximately."

"Did she have a key to this apartment?"

"Yes, sir."

"And did she ever return it to Mr. Burton?"

"I could not say."

"Who ended the relationship?"

"Mr. Burton, I believe."

"Do you know why?"

"No, sir. Mr. Burton and me, see, we do not discuss his personal affairs."

"Has Miss Dale been to the apartment recently?"

"No, sir. Not that I am aware of."

"I've heard it said that Miss Dale used Mr. Burton as a character in one of her novels. Do you know anything about that?"

"Yes, sir. At one point, Mr. Burton informs me of this."

"At what point?"

"Shortly after the book comes into circulation. Approximately one year ago, that is. He is here in the library at that point, Mr. Burton is, and he is sitting in that . . . chair. The same chair, I mean to say, as when he is . . . discovered yesterday." He turned to me. "I am so sorry, miss, that it is you who discovers him. What a totally rotten situation."

Once again I felt a stinging at my eyelids. "Thank you, Albert."

Mr. Liebowitz said, "He informed you . . ."

Albert nodded. "In the course of that evening, I am passing in the hallway when I hear him laugh. At that point, I step in to see if he needs anything. He has the book in his lap, and he says to me, 'Albert, that silly piece of fluff, she puts me into her book.' I ask who he means, and he says 'Daphne. Daphne Dale. She makes me into something out of *Jane Eyre*.' That's a book, he tells me."

"Did he say anything else?"

"No, sir. He laughs again. He is very amused. I ask him if he is in need of anything, and he tells me no. So I leave."

"Did you ever read Miss Dale's novel?"

"No, sir."

"Albert?" I said.

"Yes, miss?"

"Is the book still here? Miss Dale's book?" Sometime soon, I knew, I would read that book.

"No, miss, it is not. Mr. Burton, the very next day, he deposits it into the garbage."

Mr. Liebowitz nodded. "All right, Mr. Cooper. How did you meet Mr. Burton?"

"In the war, sir. At that point, he is a lieutenant, and I am his assistant. I am a corporal at that point, sir."

"Which branch of the service?"

"The army, sir. The infantry."

"And you've been with him ever since?"

"Yes, sir."

"Doing what, exactly?"

"A little of this, a little of that. I cook, I shop, I run the errands. I keep the house tidy until Mrs. Norman arrives."

"Mrs. Norman?"

"The cleaning woman, sir. Mrs. Jeanelle Norman. She comes twice a month. On every other Saturday afternoon, just like clock-work. A very nice Negro woman, very respectable."

"She wasn't there last Saturday," I said.

"No, miss. Mr. Burton, he tells her she can skip a day. Yesterday, she is supposed to come. But after I talk to the police, I telephone her and I give her the bad news. She is very distressed. She has a great fondness for Mr. Burton. We all do."

Mr. Liebowitz said, "Do you know where she lives?"

"Yes, sir, I do. In Harlem." He gave him another address and a telephone number, and Mr. Liebowitz wrote them down.

Mr. Liebowitz nodded. "Since the time of Miss Dale, has Mr. Burton been seeing any other women?"

"For the most part," said Albert, "no. Until recently, I mean to say."

"And who would that be?"

"A Miss Sybil Cartwright, sir. A very nice young woman, in the show business."

"In show business where?"

"At the El Fay Club, sir. She is a dancer there."

Mr. Liebowitz turned to me. "You were there. Did you meet her?"

"No," I said. I felt an absurd flicker of resentment at John for hiding something from me. "I've never heard of her."

Mr. Liebowitz looked back at Albert. "For how long had Mr. Burton been seeing Miss Cartwright?"

"For two months, I would estimate. Over that period, she comes here several times. That I personally know of, I mean to say. This is during the week, see. On the weekends, like I say, I am in Queens."

"Does Miss Cartwright have a key to the apartment?"

"I could not say. I have never seen her use one."

"Do you know her address?"

"The Broadmore Hotel on Forty-Fourth Street. Mr. Burton, he mentions it to me once."

Mr. Liebowitz wrote in his notebook then looked up at Albert. "Do the police know about Miss Cartwright?"

"Yes, sir. They ask me is Mr. Burton seeing any women? I mention her name."

Mr. Liebowitz nodded. "Did Mr. Burton have a lawyer?"

"Yes, sir. Mr. James McCready, of McCready, McCready, and Porter."

Mr. Liebowitz wrote again then looked up. "Did Mr. Burton use an address book?"

"No, sir. Not here at his residence. As for his business addresses and such, it may be they are located at his office. I could not say."

"Did he keep a diary? A journal?"

"No, sir. Mr. Burton, he keeps everything in his head. Phone numbers and the like. Addresses. He has got a remarkable memory for such items, Mr. Burton has."

"What about his records? His valuables? Did he keep them here in the apartment? Did he have a safe?"

For a moment, Albert looked at him without answering. Then he said, "When they are here, I inform the police that no such a thing exists."

"And was that, strictly speaking, the truth?"

For the first time, Albert smiled. It was not much of a smile, but it was there. "Not speaking strictly, sir," he said. "In point of fact, there *is* what you call a safe."

"But you didn't mention it to the police."

"Like I say, sir, I have very little faith in the police. Mr. Burton, he usually keeps large sums of money in the safe, see. Cash money. My belief is that if the police examine the safe, the money will have occasion to disappear."

"Do you know the safe's combination?"

"No, sir."

"Does anyone else? Miss Dale, for example? Miss Cartwright?"

"Not to my knowledge, sir. Only Mr. Burton."

Mr. Liebowitz stood up. "Show me," he said.

Chapter Eleven

The smell of disinfectant was stronger in the library, strong enough to make my eyes water.

I glanced over to the chair that had held John. It was empty now, of course, and the dark horrid splatters were gone from the books behind it. But on the parquet floor beneath the chair, there was a faint irregular gray patch, like a shadow. Beside it sat a galvanized metal bucket.

I felt my stomach shift slightly to the side.

Miss Lizzie put her hand on my shoulder for a moment and gently squeezed it. I looked at her and smiled weakly.

"Over here," said Albert, walking to the left side of the room. He reached into one of the bookcases, removed some books, set them on the floor, then reached into the shelf below and removed another batch. These he put on the floor beside the others. He placed his hand along the right side of the adjoining bookcase, pulled gently, and two of the shelves came away from the case together, as though they were both connected to a single long hinge at the case's left side. Behind the shelves, set into the wall, was a black metal safe, perhaps two feet high and a foot and a half wide. Its dial was black too, and at its center was a silver-colored knob. To the left of that was a vertical handle.

Mr. Liebowitz stepped forward. "A Mosler," he said. "Prewar. Quite a good safe."

Albert said, "According to Mr. Burton, sir, it is totally uncrackable."

He nodded. "*Totally* is a big word, Mr. Cooper. Let's see for ourselves, shall we?"

He put his small left hand, fingers splayed, along the handle and leaned toward the safe, holding his shiny white head close to the dial. Gripping the knob of the dial lightly between the finger and thumb of his right hand, he slowly turned it.

I looked again at Miss Lizzie. She looked at me and then, very faintly, nearly invisibly, she shrugged. Beyond the lens of her pince-nez, her eyes flicked back toward Mr. Liebowitz.

He slowly spun the dial some more, reversed the direction of the spin, and then stepped back, letting his hands fall to his sides.

"Like I say, sir," said Albert. "Totally uncrackable."

Mr. Liebowitz reached forward with his left hand, placed two fingers against the handle, and tapped it to the right. Silently, the door to the safe swung open.

I looked at Miss Lizzie. She was smiling at the detective. "Mr. Liebowitz," she said, "you are showing off."

He looked at her over his shoulder and grinned. "Let's see what we have."

The three of us gathered around behind him. The safe held three metal drawers and, in the open space below them, a small black metal box.

He slid open the first drawer and looked inside. "Nothing," he said. He pushed the drawer back in.

The second drawer. "Nothing." He pushed it back in.

The third drawer. "Nothing." He pushed it back in and turned to Albert. "Does that seem right to you, Mr. Cooper?"

"No, sir, it does not. Just last week I observe Mr. Burton deposit some papers into the bottom drawer. At that point in time, all the drawers are full."

"How do you know?"

"He attempts to deposit them in the other two drawers first. They are both full."

"What sort of papers were they?"

"I got no idea. Mr. Burton and me, we never discuss his business affairs."

"What *did* you discuss, you and Mr. Burton?"

"The events of the day, sir. Politics and the like. Mr. Burton, see, he is a very up-to-date person, insofar as the events of the day are concerned."

Mr. Liebowitz nodded. Leaning toward the safe again, he angled his head to look at the drawers from the side. "No fingerprints, except the ones I've put there. It's been wiped clean."

"And the box?" said Miss Lizzie.

Mr. Liebowitz reached in, lifted the box by its handle on the lid, and drew it from the safe. As he moved it, something softly thumped inside. He stepped over to a small circular wooden table, set down the box, and once again put his head at an angle to examine it. "No prints," he said. "Wiped again."

He flicked open the latch at the lip of the lid, flipped back the lid, and dipped his right hand inside. When the hand emerged, it held two packets of hundred-dollar bills, each neatly wrapped with a strip of paper. He dropped one of the packets to the table and then, using his thumb, he flipped through the other.

"Bank packets," he said. "Five thousand each. Ten thousand dollars, all told."

"Why on earth," said Miss Lizzie, "would he keep so much cash on hand?"

"An excellent question," said Mr. Liebowitz. "And one that suggests another."

"Why is the money still there?" she said. "Why would whoever took the papers not take the money, too?"

He smiled at her, looking now like an approving schoolteacher himself. "Well done, Miss Cabot."

"You're assuming," she said, "that someone did, in fact, take the papers."

Mr. Liebowitz looked to Albert. "Mr. Cooper, to the best of your knowledge, those drawers were full when you saw them last?"

"Yes, sir. To the best of my knowledge."

"And was it usual for Mr. Burton to keep so much cash on hand?"

"Like I said, sir, Mr. Burton, he often keeps large sums available."

"This large a sum?"

"I could not say, sir."

"Are you surprised to see this much cash here?"

"No, sir. I cannot say I am."

"What did Mr. Burton use it for?"

"I could not say, sir. Possibly for investment purposes."

"And to the best of your knowledge, no one else knew of the safe?"

"Yes, sir. To the best of my knowledge."

Mr. Liebowitz nodded. He picked up the other packet and was about to put both back into the box when Albert interrupted him.

"Excuse me, sir."

"Yes?"

"Is this such a good way to proceed, do you think? The police can come back here, if you follow me, and they can conduct another search. They locate the safe and they open it, I am certain the money is going to evaporate totally."

"What do you suggest we do with it, Mr. Cooper?"

"I believe, personally, that it should go to Miss Amanda here. She is Mr. Burton's closest relative."

"No, I'm not," I said. "My father is. And then my brother."

"But I know for a fact," said Albert, "that Mr. Burton, he is extremely fond of Miss Amanda."

Once again, an image of John flashed through my mind. I saw him as he was early on Friday evening, so dashing and charming in his dinner jacket, so handsome . . .

"Well, Mr. Cooper," said Mr. Liebowitz, "the suggestion does you credit. But I don't believe that, legally, we can simply hand the money over to Amanda."

"I don't want it," I said. "It's not mine."

"If you hand it over to the police," Albert told Mr. Liebowitz, "then it will totally evaporate. I can promise you that."

"I suspect you're right." He turned to Miss Lizzie and me. "Let's say I do this. I have a safe at my office." He smiled. "Rather a better safe than this one. With your permission, and yours, Amanda, I'll put the money there. I can assure you that it'll be secure and that no one will touch it."

"It isn't for me to say," said Miss Lizzie. "The decision is Amanda's."

Mr. Liebowitz and Albert looked at me.

"Okay," I said. "Fine."

"But a receipt," said Miss Lizzie, "would not be amiss, I feel."

Mr. Liebowitz smiled. "I agree." He set down the packets, plucked his notebook and pen from his inner left coat pocket, and opened the notebook. Quickly he scribbled something inside then tore off the sheet of paper and handed it to me.

It read, *$10,000 in cash owed to Miss Amanda Burton by Carl Liebowitz, removed from the personal safe of Mr. John Burton in the Dakota Apartments on 15 June, 1924. Due upon demand.* He had signed it at the bottom.

Mr. Liebowitz said, "Satisfactory, Miss Cabot?"

On my right, Miss Lizzie had been reading along with me. She looked over at him. "Entirely," she said.

"Right, then," he said. He returned his notebook and pen to his pocket then slipped one of the packets in behind them. He slid the second packet into another interior pocket, on the right side of the jacket. He patted himself, as though to make sure the packets were comfortable, and then, from the breast pocket of the jacket, he pulled out a white silk handkerchief. He flipped the lid of the box shut, wiped it all over with the handkerchief, closed the latch, then used the handkerchief to carry the box back to the safe. After it was stowed away, he wiped the front of the three drawers. He shut the safe and wiped down the handle and the dial.

Tucking the handkerchief back into his pocket, he turned to us. "Now," he said, "we need to go over the entire apartment."

Miss Lizzie had removed a gold pocket watch from the front pocket of her dress. She looked up from the watch and said, "I wonder, Mr. Liebowitz, if you have a telephone number for Daphne Dale."

"Yes, I do," he said. "Why?"

"I propose a division of labor. You search Mr. Burton's apartment. In the meantime, Amanda and I shall meet with Miss Dale. It is nearly twelve now. We can invite her to lunch. And then, afterward, perhaps we can speak with this Miss Cartwright. It may be that with just Amanda and me there—a young girl and a senile old biddy—these two women will be more likely to provide information."

He smiled. "*Senile old biddy* is rather good. But Miss Cabot, you *are* paying me to conduct the investigation."

"If you feel it necessary," she said, "you can always speak with them later. But we're operating here, as you yourself pointed out, within the pressing constraints of time. If the police don't locate another suspect, they may very well return to Amanda. I'm simply trying to expedite matters."

He nodded. "As you wish." He took out his notebook and pen, scribbled another something inside, and tore off another sheet. "Miss Dale's number," he said and handed it to her.

"Thank you," she told him.

"Don't forget," he said, "to ask her about the key. Miss Cartwright, too."

She smiled. "I'm very good at remembering things, Mr. Liebowitz."

He smiled. "Yes, ma'am. I'm sure you are."

Chapter Twelve

Six stories tall, the Hotel Brevoort stretched along the east side of Fifth Avenue, taking up the entire block between Eighth and Ninth Streets, a few hundred feet north of the stately white arch that led into the greenery of Washington Square Park.

The hotel's main dining room was an elaborate space of high molded ceilings and serene linen draperies, of white damask and gleaming porcelain and brightly polished silver. Sunlight spilled through the tall windows. Black-coated waiters sailed silently between the tables.

When we arrived at a quarter to one that Sunday, the room was nearly full, the customers being mostly families and couples dressed in their churchgoing best. An urbane buzz of conversation floated in the air, punctuated by the discreet clatter of cutlery. The maître d', whose French accent seemed genuine and whose eyebrows seemed permanently arched, led us to a corner table for four, handed each of us a large pasteboard menu, nodded once, and then sailed impressively away.

"Should we wait for Miss Dale?" I asked Miss Lizzie.

"From what you tell me, I suspect that Miss Dale does not number promptness among her virtues." She smiled. "And besides, I confess to feeling somewhat peckish at the moment."

We studied the menu for a few minutes. Miss Lizzie decided on the onion soup and the squab casserole. I chose the soup as well, and the coq au vin. As soon as we lowered our menus, a tall and very thin waiter suddenly loomed between us.

"Wee, maydahms?" His accent was considerably less successful. Miss Lizzie gave him our order.

"Somezing to drink, perhaps?" he asked. "Zee water? Zee soda pop for mamzell?"

"A glass of water, please," said Miss Lizzie.

I ordered the same.

"Tray bone," he said and then sailed off toward the kitchen.

Once the waiter had disappeared, I turned to Miss Lizzie. "Why do you think John had so much money in the safe?" I asked her.

"I can't imagine," she said. "He was, to all appearances, a very successful business man. I should think that anyone—anyone legitimate—would be happy to accept his personal check."

"Do you think that maybe he was involved with someone who wasn't legitimate?"

She smiled. "I think that Mr. Liebowitz is right," she said. "I think we must make no assumptions until we have some evidence to support them."

We had finished our soup and were nearly finished with our main course when Daphne Dale arrived. She swept up to the table in another symphony of silk—white this time: a rakish beret, a finely wrought lace shawl, a slim ivory shift, a pair of creamy white hose, and white patent leather pumps. She still seemed tiny, almost elfin.

"I am *so* sorry," she said in her magnolia drawl. "I was just leaving my apartment when I received a telephone call. Long distance, from Los Angeles. In California?" She had the southern habit of ending some of her sentences with a question mark.

"It was a movie offer, to tell the truth," she said, "for my last book, and I simply couldn't get off the line. Those people *refuse* to understand that we have lives to lead." Rounding her cheeks slightly to blow out a faint feminine puff of distaste, she fanned her delicate face with the fingers of her delicate right hand. "I positively *ran* over here."

"That's quite all right," said Miss Lizzie. "I am Elizabeth Cabot. You know Amanda, of course. Please do sit down."

Miss Dale sat beside me, placed her white leather purse in the empty chair to her left, leaned toward me, and put her hand atop mine, entrapping it. "You poor little thing." Her eyes narrowed, and her red cupid's bow of a mouth turned tragically downward. She fluttered her long eyelashes. "This must be simply *awful* for you, sweetie. If I were in your position, I'd be utterly *devastated*."

"Yes," I said. "Thank you."

She released me, adjusted the shawl at her shoulders, and smiled at Miss Lizzie. "One of *those* Cabots?" she said. "The Boston Cabots?"

Miss Lizzie smiled. "For my sins, alas."

Miss Dale laughed, a light chime of a laugh that reminded me of small coins tinkling into a cup.

Our waiter once again materialized at the table and bowed to Miss Dale. "A menu, mamzell?"

"I don't think so," she said. "Do you have any of that lovely caviar? The Russian?"

"Wee, mamzell. Zee Beluga?"

"The Beluga, yes. That would be yummy. Is it very cold? I can't eat it unless it's very, very cold."

"Wee, mamzell. It is on zee ice."

"Lovely," she said. "And a glass of seltzer."

"Tray bone, mamzell."

As he sailed away, Miss Dale turned to Miss Lizzie. "Aren't they *darling*? I just adore that accent. The French have such fabulous style, don't you think?"

"Fabulous," agreed Miss Lizzie, and adjusted her pince-nez.

"Now," said Miss Dale, putting her tiny hands together on the table and interlocking her fingers, "how can I help you all?"

"What we're attempting to do," said Miss Lizzie, "is learn as much about John Burton as possible."

Miss Dale frowned. "You know," she said, "Johnny never mentioned having an aunt."

"I'm Amanda's aunt, actually. Her great aunt, on her mother's side. No blood relation to John."

Miss Dale glanced at me with new respect. I had abruptly become a Cabot.

"I liked John very much," said Miss Lizzie, "but we were not, I confess, very close. As you may know, the police have no idea who killed him. They have even gone so far as to suspect Amanda."

"Well now," said Miss Dale, "that's positively *silly*, isn't it?" She turned to me and smiled.

"But it is also potentially dangerous," said Miss Lizzie. "In order to protect Amanda, we need to discover if there's anything in John's past that might have led to his death."

"Couldn't you just hire one of those private detective people? I mean, from what I hear, they're all dreadful little men, not the kind you'd want to see *socially*, but they'd probably be useful in a situation like this."

"Before I take that step, I should prefer to see what I can learn on my own."

"But Miss Cabot—is it Miss or Mrs.?"

"Miss," she announced.

"Miss Cabot, honestly, there simply wasn't *anything*. The women all adored Johnny, and the men, all of them, they just envied him to pieces."

"But envy," said Miss Lizzie, "can grow bitter."

"Yes, surely, but everyone *loved* him."

"Someone clearly did not. And you have no notion who that might be?"

She sat back. "Absolutely none. I was completely flabbergasted when I heard. The idea that anyone would want to hurt Johnny just positively boggles the mind."

"Do you know of a man named Larry Fay?"

"Surely. He owns El Fay uptown." She leaned forward, smiling. "It's a marvelous place, but I hear that Mr. Fay has an *unusual* personal history. He's a bit of a rogue?"

"What have you heard?"

"I love this story. Well, apparently, before he owned El Fay, he owned a small taxicab company. The way I heard it, what happened was, one day he drove one of his taxis clear up to the Canadian border—this is all the way from New York City?—and he filled his trunk with liquor. When he got back to New York and he realized how much *money* he could make from bootlegging, he just never looked back. And now he owns one of the biggest clubs in New York." She smiled. "Isn't that a *fantastic* story?"

"Extraordinary. Did you know that John knew him?"

"I'm not surprised. Johnny knew *everyone*."

"Did he ever mention Mr. Fay?"

"No. And I'd remember if he had, I definitely would. As a writer, that's the kind of mind I have? I just can't help it, no matter what I do. Information," she said, narrowing her eyes, "virtually any information, just *sticks* right here." She tapped at the side of her head, to pinpoint the location.

Miss Lizzie said, "What about a man named Owney Madden?"

"Well now, I know for a fact that Johnny *did* know Mr. Madden. He introduced me to him, up at the Cotton Club. That's this wonderful big speakeasy in Harlem? Very *chic*. Lovely young darkie girls, a *fantastic* jazz band."

Just then, the waiter arrived with Miss Dale's caviar. It came heaped in a small crystal bowl nestled inside another crystal bowl, the second packed with shaved ice. Lying alongside the caviar was a small spoon made of horn. Next to the bowl, the man set a platter of buttered toast points, and, beside this, three small plates, one filled with lemon wedges, one with chopped hard-boiled eggs, and one with chopped onion.

He put her glass of seltzer beside the plates and said, "Would mamzell perhaps wish for some crème fraîche?"

"No," she said. "This is just absolutely perfect."

"Tray bone," said the waiter and then glided away.

Miss Dale leaned toward Miss Lizzie again. "A single ounce of crème fraîche and I turn into a *balloon*."

Miss Lizzie smiled politely.

Ignoring the onion, the lemon, and the chopped egg, Miss Dale used the caviar spoon to scoop up a large dollop of translucent gray eggs. She dabbed them onto a toast point and spread them carefully along the surface, meticulously nudging a few reluctant eggs along the sides and into the corners, then neatly poked the spoon back into the bowl. Holding the toast with her pinky extended, she took a dainty bite, closed her eyes, and thoughtfully chewed on it.

She opened her eyes and smiled dreamily. "Scrumptious."

"I am so glad," said Miss Lizzie. "But tell me, Miss Dale. What do you know about Mr. Madden?"

"Hardly anything at all, really. Well, I know that he's had a checkered past, of course, like Mr. Fay. They say he actually *killed* a man once. But honestly, you'd never ever suspect that, to talk to him. He's so soft-spoken and so gracious, and so *enormously* charming." She took another bite of toast.

"What was John's relationship with him?" Miss Lizzie asked.

Miss Dale delicately swallowed. "I assumed that Johnny knew him because, like I said, Johnny knew virtually *everyone*. It was just one of the things he did."

Miss Lizzie nodded. "I understand that you and John were intimate for a time."

Miss Dale fluttered her eyelashes. She carefully set down her toast point, wiped her hands on her napkin, and then put her right hand between her breasts in an impersonation of surprise that might have been more persuasive if she had taken less time to prepare it. "Wher*ever* did you hear *that*?" she said.

"From Albert Cooper. You know Albert, I expect. John's majordomo."

Miss Dale took a sip of her seltzer. "Albert, yes, of course. I could never understand why Johnny kept that awful man around. He has this horrible *lumbering* quality, don't you think?" She shivered theatrically. "He gives me the heebie-jeebies."

"You did have an intimate relationship with John, did you not?"

She dabbed at her mouth with her napkin. "Well, yes, briefly, but that was *years* ago. Literally *ages*. We decided, mutually, that we got along ever so much better as friends than we did as lovers." She leaned slightly forward again, smiling. "I do hope I haven't shocked you."

"Not as yet," said Miss Lizzie, who smiled back. "Amanda tells me that you and John had an argument on Friday night."

"Oh no," said Miss Dale. "Not an argument. Not really." She glanced over at me then looked back at Miss Lizzie. "I did explain all this to the police." She picked up her toast point and took another, less dainty bite.

"Perhaps you could explain it to us," said Miss Lizzie.

Miss Dale swallowed. "Well," she said, "frankly, it was a financial matter, of sorts."

"Of what sort?"

Miss Dale was spreading caviar on another toast point. "A friend of mine had let me know, *very* confidentially, about a truly marvelous business opportunity. It required an investment on my part, naturally." She looked at Miss Lizzie. "My books have been doing very well, of course, thank goodness for that, but just at the moment, what with one thing or another, my resources have been stretched just the *tiniest* bit thin."

"And you asked John for money?"

Miss Dale took a bite of her toast, chewed again, and swallowed. "A loan. A small one."

"How small?"

She set down her toast, picked up her glass, and sipped at her seltzer. "A thousand dollars."

"And what did John say?"

"Well, he explained that his own resources were stretched a bit thin, too, at the moment." She shrugged her small square shoulders. "And that was that."

"From what Amanda tells me, you didn't take his refusal quite that calmly."

"Ha, ha, ha," she said, as she turned to me, smiling. "Were you *spying* on me, sweetie?"

"You were just across the room," I pointed out. "Twenty feet away."

"Of course I was," she said. "And in a way, of course, you're absolutely right." She turned back to Miss Lizzie. "I was a *bit* out of sorts on Friday. It was, well, it was my time of the month?" She turned to me and gave me a saccharine smile. "You wouldn't know about that, sweetie. You lucky thing."

She turned again to Miss Lizzie. "And I suppose," she said, "that I overreacted a tiny bit when Johnny turned me down. I honestly did regret it later. Almost immediately. And as soon as I got home, I telephoned him to apologize. But he wasn't there."

"What time was that?" asked Miss Lizzie.

"At ten o'clock. I tried again, later, around eleven, but it was the same thing."

Miss Lizzie nodded.

At ten o'clock, John and I had been at El Fay. By eleven, we were on our way to the Cotton Club.

"I tried again the next day," said Miss Dale. "Saturday. In the morning. And some horrible policeman picked up the telephone. He told me about poor Johnny. And that was how I learned about it—over the telephone, from a stranger."

She looked down, her eyelids fluttering again, and she sighed loudly. She looked up bravely. "And now, of course, it's too late for me to apologize."

I glanced at Miss Lizzie. Her face was politely blank. She asked Miss Dale, "Did the policeman identify himself by name?"

She thought for a moment. "O'Deere? Was that it? Yes, O'Deere. I remember, because it seemed such an awfully *silly* name for a policeman."

"And the police spoke with you again?" asked Miss Lizzie.

"Yes. A Lieutenant Becker. He came to my apartment on Saturday evening."

She glanced over at me then looked away. I had been, of course, as she knew, the reason for Lieutenant Becker's visit.

"Did he ask you," said Miss Lizzie, "about the key to John's apartment?"

"The key?"

"Yes. At one point, when you were involved with John, you did have a key to the apartment?"

Miss Dale nodded. "Albert," she said flatly.

"You *did* have a key?"

"Well, yes. At one time I did. And Becker—the lieutenant—he did ask me about it. Whether I still had it or not? And, you know, I *truly* thought I did. I looked all over for it, all over my apartment, while the lieutenant was there." Once again, she shrugged. "But I must've lost it somewhere. Misplaced it?"

"When might that have been?"

"I've no idea. You know how it is. You put something away, for safekeeping, and then it just goes and disappears on you? I mean, it's been *years* since I used the thing."

"Hi," said a woman to my left. "Sorry I'm late."

It was Mrs. Parker. Suddenly the smell of chypre was heavy in the air.

"Mrs. Parker," said Miss Lizzie. "Do you know Miss Dale?"

"Sure I do," she said. "We're old friends, aren't we, Daphne? Of course, *old* is a word we'd both probably want to avoid."

"What a lovely dress," said Miss Dale sweetly. "Did you make it yourself?"

Chapter Thirteen

"Not at all," said Mrs. Parker, just as sweetly. "I had one of my slaves run it off."

The dress in question was a pink cotton affair, low-waisted, nicely cut, but nowhere near as elaborate as Miss Dale's silk number.

"Mrs. Parker," said Miss Lizzie, "won't you join us?"

"Love to," she said. She tugged out the chair beside Miss Dale's and hooked the strap of her purse onto the chair's back.

Miss Dale's purse was lying on the seat of the chair. She leaned over, her blonde ringlets swaying, and snatched it up as though afraid that Mrs. Parker would sit on it, or pilfer it. She set it on her lap and put both her hands atop it, protectively.

Mrs. Parker sat down.

"I didn't realize," said Miss Dale to Miss Lizzie, "that you knew Dorothy."

"Mrs. Parker is an old friend," said Miss Lizzie.

"What a nice surprise," said Miss Dale. She looked again at Mrs. Parker and produced a smile.

"Daphne and I," said Mrs. Parker, removing a white cloth glove from her left hand, "haven't gotten along all that terribly well since I reviewed a novel of hers. What was it called again, dear? *The Flesh Pokers? The Flush Strokers?*"

"*The Flesh Seekers.* You know perfectly well what it was called. And your review was—well, Dorothy, you *know* it was a good deal less than kind."

Laying the glove on the table, Mrs. Parker cocked her head. "I honestly don't understand how you can say that, Daphne. Nearly the entire review consisted of direct quotations from the book."

It was a duel of drawls—Mrs. Parker's Northern Finishing School against Miss Dale's Sunny Southern Maid.

"You took everything completely out of context," said Miss Dale. "And you did it deliberately. Just to make me look silly."

Removing the glove from her right hand, Mrs. Parker said, "So far as I could see, Daphne, you certainly didn't require any help from me to look—"

"Mrs. Parker?" said Miss Lizzie. She was smiling her bright, controlled smile.

"Yes?" Eyebrows innocently raised, she dropped the second glove beside the first.

"Miss Dale has been kind enough to come here and answer my questions. I wonder if you'd mind if we finished with that?"

"No, of course not. Sorry. I'll just sit here and be as quiet as a little bird." Putting her hands on her lap, scrunching her thin shoulders together, she smiled and settled more deeply into the chair. "Chirp," she said.

"Thank you. Now, Miss Dale—"

She was interrupted by our waiter, who sailed up to Mrs. Parker and said, "Mamzell? Somezing to eat?"

She let her little bird pose fall away, sat up straight, batted her eyelashes, and smiled at him. "No, thanks, Pierre. I'm trying to quit. But you know what I *would* like?"

"What is zat, mamzell?"

"I'd like a big water glass, half-filled with water. You can throw some ice cubes in there, too."

"Tray bone, mamzell."

She batted her eyelashes again. "*Merci beaucoup.*"

He nodded once and then floated away.

"He's about as French," said Mrs. Parker, "as a fucking hotdog."

Miss Dale turned to her. "Must you *always* be such a horrible *potty* mouth?"

"Well, Daphne, coming from someone who's famous for sucking the chrome off a fender—"

"Miss Dale?" said Miss Lizzie.

Miss Dale turned away from Mrs. Parker. Mrs. Parker looked at me, waggled her eyebrows, and smiled.

"Yes?" said Miss Dale.

"You have no idea when the key to John's apartment might have gone missing?"

"No," she said, sullenly. "None." She reached toward the bowl of caviar and then, as though deciding against this, moved her hand to the glass of seltzer and lifted it.

"Did you know," said Miss Lizzie, "that there was a safe in John's apartment?"

She had raised the glass perhaps six inches off the table. "Pardon me?"

"A safe. A place to store valuables."

"No." She raised the glass to her mouth and drained it. "I didn't." She placed the glass on the table.

Miss Lizzie said, "Do you know of a woman named Sybil Cartwright?"

"No," she said. "Who's she?"

"A friend of John's, apparently."

"No."

The waiter reappeared at that moment, carrying Mrs. Parker's tumbler of water. He set it in front of her. "Nozing else, mamzell?"

"This is fine," she said. "Thank you, Marcel."

"Tray bone," he said, and sailed away once more. As soon as his back was turned, Mrs. Parker turned, reached into her purse, and plucked out a small silver flask. She unscrewed the cap.

"Miss Dale," said Miss Lizzie. "What—"

Miss Dale was looking at the gold watch on her left wrist. "Oh my," she said. "I've *got* to go. I'm supposed to meet somebody in fifteen minutes."

Mrs. Parker, smiling, was pouring liquor into her glass of water.

"But your lunch," said Miss Lizzie. "You've barely touched it."

Miss Dale lightly brushed her fingertips against her stomach. "I seem to have lost my appetite."

"What a shame," said Mrs. Parker. She reached in front of the woman with both hands, lifted the bowl of caviar, and set it down beside her tumbler.

"I'm sorry," said Miss Lizzie. "If you do think of anything else, could you telephone me? I'm at the Algonquin. Room three eleven."

Mrs. Parker returned the flask to her purse.

"If I think of anything," said Miss Dale, standing up. "Well. Goodbye, then."

"Goodbye," said Miss Lizzie. "And thank you for coming."

"Goodbye," I said.

Mrs. Parker had picked up the caviar spoon and scooped up some caviar. Sitting back, she raised the spoon in a salute toward Miss Dale, "*Au revoir*, Daphne."

"Dorothy," said Miss Dale curtly, and then she turned and walked away.

Holding out the spoon toward Miss Lizzie and me, Mrs. Parker said, "Anyone else want some?"

"No, thanks," I said.

"No, thank you," said Miss Lizzie. "You certainly have an enlivening effect on the conversation, dear."

Mrs. Parker stuck the caviar spoon into her mouth. Her cheeks hollowed for a moment, and then she plucked out the spoon and swallowed. "I know," she said. "I'm the death of the party."

"It's probably a good thing that you didn't arrive any earlier."

"I'm sorry. Honestly. But I can't stand the bitch. She's as phony as a Park Avenue hooker." She licked the back of the spoon then suddenly said, "But speak of the devil." She turned to me. "I brought you something."

She stabbed the spoon back into the caviar, swiveled around in the chair, and snagged the strap of her purse with one finger. She swung the purse onto her lap, opened it, reached inside, and took out a slim book. She handed it to me.

The Flesh Seekers.

On the cover, a tall dark man in a smoking jacket dominated the foreground. The New York City skyline stretched out behind him, backlit with a lurid sunset that oozed orange and red across a purple sky. In the man's right hand, he held an empty champagne goblet. His left hand was wrapped around the waist of a young blonde woman in a silver satin evening gown whose slender body was arched backward, her long hair trailing, her long, bare arms dangling. She was either swooning or dead. The man was studying her throat as though mulling over the merits of taking a large bite from it.

"If you finish the thing," said Mrs. Parker, "'you're a better man than I am, Gunga Din.'"

I showed the book to Miss Lizzie.

She adjusted her pince-nez and peered at the cover. "Yes. When you're done, you must let me borrow it."

I laughed. I realize now, looking back, that this was the first time I had laughed since John's death.

Mrs. Parker asked her, "Did you actually learn anything from Daphne?" She stuck the spoon in her mouth.

Briefly, Miss Lizzie summarized what Miss Dale had said.

"And how much of that," said Mrs. Parker, "do you think is true?"

"Very little, I expect. Over the years, I've noticed that when people are telling something less than the truth, they will use certain specific words. Words like *frankly* and *truly*." She smiled. "Words like *honestly*."

Mrs. Parker said, "Honestly, I really am truly and deeply and frankly sorry that I was such a horrible nasty bitch to Daphne Dale."

And, for the first time since we had been together in New York, Miss Lizzie laughed. I had forgotten what a good laugh she had, deep and relaxed and up from the diaphragm.

I asked her, "What don't you believe?"

"For one thing," she said, "I'm a bit dubious about movie people conducting business on a Sunday."

"Really?" said Mrs. Parker and licked at the caviar spoon. "She knows movie people?" She turned to me. "The only movie people I know are ushers."

Miss Lizzie looked to me. "And I wonder about her reason for speaking to your uncle. From what you told us, John was very cool to her. He wasn't someone, I suspect, to whom she'd have gone for a loan. And, from her clothes, the way she comports herself, she's used to having money. No matter how well or badly her books might be doing, I can't believe that she'd find it difficult to raise a thousand dollars."

"She could make it in a week," said Mrs. Parker, "working Park Avenue. Of course, she'd have to put in a couple of shifts a day."

"In any event," said Miss Lizzie, "I believe that the argument between them was about something else."

"She was telling the truth," I said, "about talking to the police on Saturday morning. She knew Detective O'Deere's name."

"Yes. And she was probably telling the truth about Lieutenant Becker's visit."

"What about that key?" said Mrs. Parker, scooping up some more caviar. "The key to John's apartment. Do you think she actually lost it?"

"Perhaps. Keys are rather like virtue, aren't they? They are notoriously easy to lose."

Mrs. Parker smiled. "Yeah," she said, "and notoriously difficult to find again."

Our taxicab arrived at the Broadmore Hotel a little before three. Miss Lizzie led the way across the sidewalk, her handbag dangling like a large padlock from her left arm, the rubber tip of her walking stick tapping quietly at the pavement. Mrs. Parker and I followed behind.

The hotel was a smallish brick building between Ninth and Tenth Avenues, five stories tall. No doorman stood outside, and when we entered the small, stuffy lobby, we discovered that no one stood behind the desk at the moment.

We walked over to the single gray elevator.

Miss Lizzie pressed the UP button. The door bumbled open, we stepped in, Miss Lizzie pushed the button for the fifth floor, and the door bumbled shut.

On the fifth floor, we followed Miss Lizzie as she stepped out into the hallway and turned to the right.

The carpet runner beneath us, vaguely Persian, was frayed and worn, red patterns scuffed down to pink. When we came to room 505, Miss Lizzie knocked on the door.

Nothing.

Miss Lizzie knocked again.

Still nothing.

She switched the walking stick to her left hand and took out her watch. "Three o'clock. She promised me she'd be here." She had telephoned the woman from John's apartment.

She knocked again, harder this time.

Nothing.

"How aggravating," she said.

Mrs. Parker leaned forward and turned the doorknob. When she pushed the door, it swung silently inward. Inside, the room was quite dark.

Mrs. Parker cleared her throat. "That can't be a good thing," she said.

Miss Lizzie took the cane into her right hand, stepped into the room, moved her left hand off to the side, found a light switch, and flicked it on.

We followed her in.

It was a small room, floral wallpaper all around, cheap pine furniture—a dresser, a writing desk, a pair of upholstered chairs. The place was very neat, everything carefully ordered. The bed was made.

But the bedspread was soaked in blood, so dark it was almost black, and lying limply in the midst of it, like a rag doll flung there, was a pale, young, dark-haired woman in a filmy black gown. Her throat had been cut, flesh and muscle sliced down to the pink windpipe, and the horrible red wound gaped up at us, a tortured, lunatic mouth.

For a moment, I tottered. My lungs would not work.

I heard Mrs. Parker suck in her breath. "I think," she said, "we should get out of here."

"One moment," said Miss Lizzie. She turned to me. "Amanda?"

"I'm okay," I said reflexively.

"Why don't you wait in the hall, dear. I'll be right out."

I could smell it now, the same dense, coppery smell that had hung in the air of the library when I found John. "Why . . ." I said. I did not know then, I do not know now, what I was about to ask.

"Hey," said Mrs. Parker softly. She touched my arm. "Come on."

I shuffled alongside her out into the hallway, and a moment later, Miss Lizzie joined us, a white handkerchief in her hand. She used it to pull the door shut and carefully wipe down the knob, and then she tucked it into her purse.

"We'll go down the stairway, I think," she said. She turned to me. "Can you manage that?"

"Yes."

We took the dimly lit stairway all the way down, the three of us hushed, the soles of our heels clicking softly against the steps. When we reached the lobby, it was still deserted.

"You two go on," said Miss Lizzie, and Mrs. Parker and I walked toward the door.

I turned back. Miss Lizzie limped around to the side of the front desk, looked down, adjusted her pince-nez, and frowned. She took a very large breath, her shoulders rising with it, and then came limping after us.

Outside, on Forty-Fourth Street, she said, "Keep walking." Her voice was tight.

"What is it?" said Mrs. Parker.

"The desk clerk. Behind the counter. His throat was cut."

"*Shit*," said Mrs. Parker. She opened her purse and took out her flask.

Chapter Fourteen

"How long did you stay in Cartwright's room?" Mr. Lipkind asked.

"No more than a minute," said Miss Lizzie.

We were back in her suite at the Algonquin—Miss Lizzie, Mrs. Parker, and I—where Mr. Lipkind and the diminutive Mr. Liebowitz joined us. It was now six thirty. Earlier today, before leaving John's apartment, Miss Lizzie had made arrangements to meet the private detective here at six, and shortly before we arrived back at the hotel, she had telephoned the lawyer from a pay phone and asked him to come over.

We were also joined by Mrs. Parker's Boston terrier. She had picked him up from her apartment, and now he sat on her lap, his small rectangular head turreting left and right as we talked. With her left hand, Mrs. Parker stroked his neck; in her right, she held a cigarette. On the table beside her, next to the ashtray, sat a glass of Scotch and water.

"Why stay that long?" Mr. Lipkind asked Miss Lizzie. Under his gray sport coat, he was wearing a colorful print shirt, the broad collar points lolling out across the coat's lapels.

"I wished," she said, "to determine when she might have died."

"You're not a medical doctor."

"I am not a doctor of any kind. But I can tell the difference between fresh blood and dried blood."

"And hers was which?"

"No longer fresh."

Mr. Lipkind was stroking his handlebar mustache. "So a couple of hours," he said.

Mr. Liebowitz ran his hand back over his shiny skull. "And you telephoned her at twelve." He had been there, of course, at John's apartment, when she made the call. "Obviously, then, she died not long afterward."

Exhaling smoke, Mrs. Parker asked, "But who would've wanted her dead?" The dog looked up at her, panting happily.

"Someone, possibly, who didn't want her to talk to you," said Mr. Liebowitz to Miss Lizzie. "Who knew you were going to Miss Cartwright's room?"

"Albert Cooper," she said.

"But if Albert didn't want her to talk to us, he could've just kept her name to himself," I replied.

"That is quite true," agreed Miss Lizzie. "And we've no idea to whom *she* might have spoken. She could have telephoned anyone. And anyone to whom she spoke could have decided to silence her."

"Damn," said Mr. Lipkind.

Mr. Liebowitz turned to him. "I'll talk to the desk clerk. At the Broadmore. He might remember her outgoing calls."

"I am afraid," said Miss Lizzie, "that that will not be possible."

"Why not?" asked Mr. Lipkind.

"You're going to love this," said Mrs. Parker flatly. She took a sip of her drink.

Looking at Miss Lizzie, Mr. Liebowitz said, "He's dead."

Miss Lizzie nodded. "He was behind the counter, on the floor. His throat had been cut."

Mr. Lipkind said, "Wait a minute. This guy snuffed the desk clerk, *too*? This was in broad daylight?"

"Yes," said Miss Lizzie.

"See?" said Mrs. Parker and inhaled on her cigarette.

"Presumably," said Mr. Liebowitz, "because the clerk *did* know the identity of whomever Miss Cartwright telephoned. Or he saw whomever it was that visited her."

"Terrific," said Mr. Lipkind. "That's just terrific. He walks into a hotel in Midtown Manhattan, in broad daylight, half a million people walking by, and he aces two people. Cuts their throats, *zip, zip*. One of them right in the *lobby*. And then he just walks away."

"I told you," said Mrs. Parker, exhaling smoke.

Mr. Liebowitz again turned to Miss Lizzie. "You didn't leave any fingerprints at the scene?"

"I wiped them away. From the doorknob, from the light switch."

"You probably wiped away the killer's, too," said Mr. Lipkind.

"In the circumstances, I felt that I had no choice. And it seemed likely to me that he had already wiped them away himself. None were left, you will recall, at John Burton's apartment."

"Same guy, you figure?" said Mr. Lipkind.

"I expect so, yes."

"Did anyone," asked Mr. Liebowitz, "see you enter or leave the hotel?"

"No. I don't believe so."

He turned to Mrs. Parker. "There was no one around?"

"No one who paid us any attention," she said, exhaling smoke. She ran her hand along the dog's back. The dog preened. "But we're used to that," said Mrs. Parker. "Aren't we, Woodrow?"

"Amanda?" said Liebowitz.

"I didn't see anyone," I told him.

He nodded. "How are you holding up?" he asked me.

"I'm okay."

"Three murders in three days. You're sure you're all right?"

"I think so, yes."

"I'm all right, too," said Mrs. Parker and took a sip of her drink. She smiled wryly. "Thanks for asking."

He smiled at her bleakly. "I'm glad to hear it, of course, Mrs. Parker." He turned back to Miss Lizzie. "Have you reported Miss Cartwright's death?"

"I thought it best to speak with you first. But having done so, I really *should* report it. The woman will have friends, relatives. They must be told."

"By now," said Mr. Lipkind, "someone's stumbled onto the desk clerk."

"No doubt," she said. "But possibly no one has found Miss Cartwright."

"I'll call it in to the cops," said Mr. Lipkind. "Anonymously. When I leave."

Mr. Liebowitz turned back to Miss Lizzie. "You said earlier that you gave your room number to Daphne Dale. Was that wise? Suppose she phones here and asks for Miss Cabot?"

Miss Lizzie nodded. "Before we left the Brevoort, I telephoned here myself and spoke with the manager. He'll arrange to send up any calls for a Miss Cabot and for any messages to be taken. He understands the need for discretion."

"Have there been any messages? Did you check?"

"I checked, yes. There were none."

He nodded. "And you think Miss Dale was lying about her argument with Mr. Burton on Friday night."

"I suspect she was, yes, but I've no proof."

"Well," he said, "I believe there's one thing we can safely assume about her."

"Yes. That Miss Dale does not know whatever it was that Miss Cartwright knew. Or that someone believes she doesn't."

"Right," said Mrs. Parker. "She's still alive." She stubbed out her cigarette. "This is getting extremely creepy."

"It is possible, of course," said Miss Lizzie to Mr. Liebowitz, "that whoever killed Miss Cartwright is unaware of Miss Dale. It's also possible that Miss Cartwright's death has nothing to do with John Burton's."

"A hatchet," said Mr. Lipkind. "A knife. A knife twice. Sounds like the same guy to me." He shook his head. "Extremely creepy is right. This is turning into a first-class rat's nest."

Miss Lizzie turned to him, a bit stiffly. "If you would rather," she said coolly, "I will make arrangements to employ another lawyer."

"Hey," he said and raised his hand. "I was handing in an opinion. Not a resignation. Don't worry. I'm here for the long haul."

"Very good," she said. "You said something the other day about talking to the police commissioner?"

"Vandervalk. Yeah. Talked to him this morning. Read him the riot act. I'm pretty sure the cops'll leave us alone for a while."

"Excellent. Thank you." She turned to the private detective. "What about you, Mr. Liebowitz? Did you learn anything from your search of the Burton apartment?"

"Nothing useful," he said. "But I did find this." He reached into his inner coat pocket. "It was in the top drawer of his dresser, in the bedroom."

He took out a worn passport and handed it to Miss Lizzie.

As she leafed through it, he said, "Since the war, he's been all over the world."

"Indeed he has," she said. "Germany. England. France. My goodness—China. Last year. For a month. And then, more recently, Europe again. He was in Germany in February, and he returned to the states on . . ."—she peered through her pince-nez—". . . the fifteenth of March."

"Maybe," said Mrs. Parker to Mr. Liebowitz, "it was business travel. Can't you ask at his office?" She finished off her drink and put the glass on the table.

"I can," said Mr. Liebowitz, "and tomorrow morning, I will."

"And what shall we do in the meantime?" Miss Lizzie asked.

"'We,' Miss Borden?"

"We, Mr. Liebowitz. Although that would depend upon Amanda, naturally."

"What would?" I said.

She turned to me. "I believe it very likely that the person who killed your uncle is the same person who killed Miss Cartwright and that poor man in the hotel. And I believe that he killed Miss Cartwright because she might have revealed something to us. If I'm right, she mentioned my telephone call to someone else. One way or another, I believe, this led to her death."

"We don't know that," said Mr. Liebowitz, "to be a certainty."

"We don't, no. But I feel that our wisest course, just now, would be to act as though it were. If we're wrong, nothing is lost. If we're right, however, then Amanda is possibly in jeopardy."

"Me?" I said. "Why?"

"Because of what you might know."

"But I don't know anything."

"The person who killed your uncle can't be certain of that. You spent a week with John, the last week of his life. You were the last person to see him alive, apart from the murderer. And you were there, in the apartment, when he died."

"But if I'd known something, I would've told the police."

"Perhaps you know something without being aware of it. Perhaps you saw something, or heard something, that might reveal his identity. I'm not saying, Amanda, that you actually did. I am saying only that the killer may believe it to be true."

"So what should we do?" I asked her.

"We have two alternatives," she said. "We can go to Boston, the two of us. Once we are there, I can arrange for you to be protected."

"A good plan," said Mrs. Parker. "Can I come along?" Using a gold lighter, she lit another cigarette.

"Cops won't like it," said Mr. Lipkind. "Amanda scramming like that."

Miss Lizzie smiled. "I believe," she said, "that I have sufficient resources in Massachusetts to deal with the New York City Police Department."

"If we leave," I said, "the police probably won't find out who killed John."

She nodded. "I am not sanguine about their prospects, no."

"They don't have any," said Mrs. Parker, exhaling smoke.

"What's the alternative?" I asked Miss Lizzie.

"We continue to do what we've been doing. We attempt, on our own, to learn the identity of the murderer."

"A good plan," said Mrs. Parker. "Can I still go to Boston?"

"But Miss Borden," said Mr. Liebowitz, "you said it yourself. If Amanda stays here, she may be in jeopardy."

"Yes. If we stay, we shall still need to see about some sort of protection."

"Robert," said Mr. Lipkind and stroked his big mustache.

Mr. Liebowitz turned to him, frowning.

"I beg your pardon?" said Miss Lizzie.

"Robert. My chauffeur. You met him yesterday. He's good. He's smart, he's tough, and he's got a carry permit. He packs a rod."

"I'll bet he does," said Mrs. Parker.

Mr. Lipkind turned to her.

Innocently, she said, "I mean, you'd expect him to carry a gun, wouldn't you?" She took the dog's head in her left hand and spoke down to him. "Right, Woodrow?"

"There are places in New York City," said Mr. Liebowitz to Miss Lizzie, "that Robert won't be able to go."

"Why not?" I asked him.

"Because he's a Negro," he said.

"I know a guy," said Mr. Lipkind. "White guy. He can fill in when you need him."

Mr. Liebowitz frowned again. "You mean Cutter."

"He's very good."

"He's dangerous."

"Some situations, that's very good."

"Does he pack a rod?" asked Mrs. Parker.

"Yeah," said Mr. Lipkind. "He does, as a matter of fact."

"Oh good," she said, stroking the dog.

Mr. Liebowitz turned back to Miss Lizzie. "Miss Borden—"

"It is not my decision to make," she said. She turned to me. "Whoever he is, Amanda, this person is ruthless. He has probably murdered three people, all of them brutally. If we stay here, you may be in danger. Even if Mr. Lipkind can provide us with some level of protection, we'll have no absolute guarantee of safety. I am perfectly happy to leave with you for Boston. Tonight, if you wish."

I looked around the room, at Mrs. Parker, Mr. Liebowitz, Mr. Lipkind. I looked back at Miss Lizzie.

"It is," she said, "entirely up to you."

I thought of John, sprawled in that library chair. Alone. Abandoned there like a piece of rubbish.

"I want to stay," I said.

Chapter Fifteen

At twenty minutes to ten that night, Mr. Lipkind's shiny black Cadillac drew up in front of the Algonquin, where Miss Lizzie and I stood waiting.

Robert opened the driver's door. Moving with his dancer's grace, he stepped out, walked around the back of the car, took off his cap, opened the door to the passenger compartment, and held it open with one large brown hand. "Miss Borden," he said, his deep bass voice rumbling. He smiled down at me. "Miss Amanda."

"Good evening," said Miss Lizzie. "Thank you, Robert."

"Hi, Robert," I said.

Miss Lizzie stepped into the car first and then, using the walking stick to help her, she shifted over to the far side of the seat. I got in and Robert shut the door. He strode around the car again, slid inside, and pulled the door shut.

He looked up into his rearview mirror. "El Fay, Miss Borden?"

"Yes, please," said Miss Lizzie. "Mr. Lipkind has explained our situation?"

"Yes, ma'am. He said you might need my help for a few days."

"We won't be imposing on you?"

"No, ma'am." He turned his broad shoulders and smiled back at her. "Be an interesting change."

"You do realize," she said, "that it could be dangerous?"

"Yes, ma'am." He smiled again. "But I've been dodging New York City traffic for four years now. Anything else will be easy."

"I do hope so."

"Yes, ma'am. You comfortable back there?"

"I'm fine, thank you."

"Miss Amanda? Comfortable?"

"Yes. Thank you, Robert."

"Then here we go," he said and turned to face the front.

Earlier, after a bit more arguing with Mr. Liebowitz, Miss Lizzie and I had made our plans. She wanted to retrace the route that John and I had taken on Friday night. Except for the appearance of Daphne Dale, to whom we had already spoken, nothing of note had happened at Chumley's, where John and I had eaten dinner. Miss Lizzie, therefore, felt that we should begin at El Fay, the big dance club on West Forty-Fifth Street. Mr. Liebowitz would join us there at ten o'clock.

Mrs. Parker wanted to be there as well. ("If Robert's coming, I figure we'll be safe. He packs a rod, you know.") She asked whether she, too, could join us at ten, after she met some people for dinner. Miss Lizzie told her that she would be most welcome.

El Fay was only one block north of the hotel. We could easily have walked the distance, but Mr. Lipkind and Mr. Liebowitz had both insisted that Robert drive us for the entire evening.

"Robert?" said Miss Lizzie as we eased away from the Algonquin's awning.

"Yes?"

"You mentioned that you had a friend at the Cotton Club?"

"That's right, ma'am."

"Have the two of you spoken?"

"Not yet, ma'am. I'll try again tonight. We'll be going up there afterward, Mr. Lipkind said. Is that right?"

"Yes," she said. "If there's time. When you see your friend, I wonder if you could find out something for me."

"Yes, ma'am?"

"Mr. Lipkind said that Mr. Madden, the owner, was in prison until last year. From the sound of it, the Cotton Club would be an expensive proposition, both to purchase and to provision. I'd like to know where Mr. Madden obtained the money."

"Yes, ma'am. I'll ask about that."

Within minutes, we were at El Fay. As he steered the big car toward the curb in front of it, Robert tilted his head slightly back and to the side. Over his shoulder he said, "You understand, Miss Borden, that I won't be going inside?"

The car stopped.

"Yes," she said. "We understand."

He turned around. "Mr. Lipkind said to tell you he's got someone in there."

"Mr. Cutter?" I said. Naturally, I was curious about the man.

"That's right, miss."

"So we'll be meeting him?"

"Only if he wants you to."

"Why is that?"

He smiled. "If you meet him, miss, you'll find out."

Mr. Cutter was sounding increasingly more mysterious.

Robert got out of the car and came around to open the passenger door. I stepped out; Miss Lizzie followed. After he shut the door, Robert said to her, "I'll be around, Miss Borden. When you come back out, just look for me."

"Thank you, Robert."

Mr. Lipkind had made reservations for us, and the hostess, a tall blond woman in a red satin dress, led us to a table for five. We were obviously between shows; the house lights were up, and beneath the sallow haze of cigarette smoke, the crowd was murmuring complacently to itself.

Mr. Liebowitz was already at the table, wearing a black two-piece suit. I confess, seeing him out in public like this, I was once again shocked by the glistening scalp and shiny brows. His small, round face seemed naked, unprotected, stripped as it was of the standard defenses with which most faces came supplied.

He stood up as we approached, greeted us, and then sat down when we did.

"Would you like dinner menus?" asked the hostess.

"No, thank you," said Miss Lizzie. We had eaten in the Algonquin's dining room. "Unless, Amanda, you'd like something?"

"No. Thanks." I had not been able to eat much, only a few sips of soup. The dead Miss Cartwright had been sitting invisibly beside me, and she was still hovering nearby now.

"Mr. Liebowitz?" said Miss Lizzie.

"No, thank you."

"I'll send a waiter over for your drink order," the hostess said.

Miss Lizzie thanked her.

As she walked away, Mr. Liebowitz said to Miss Lizzie, "Your friend Mrs. Parker hasn't arrived yet."

"It is early yet. She will be here. I am sure of it."

"If she can manage to find the place."

"Pardon me?"

"Well, Miss Borden, you do have to admit that this afternoon she'd already had a fair amount to drink."

She frowned. "Mr. Liebowitz, earlier in the day, she had walked into a room that held a woman whose throat had been cut. It seems to me that Mrs. Parker can be forgiven for having a drink or two."

He smiled faintly. "I'm not entirely sure," he said, "that Mrs. Parker actually requires a dead woman."

Miss Lizzie nodded. "You do not drink yourself, do you, Mr. Liebowitz?"

I noticed then that the glass in front of him held only a clear liquid, probably water.

"No," he said. "It doesn't agree with me."

"And neither, I am afraid, do I. If Mrs. Parker drinks perhaps a bit too much, she may very well have good reason for doing so."

He shrugged. "Whatever you say, Miss Borden."

She nodded once and then smiled. "Thank you so much for humoring me."

He grinned. "My pleasure."

The waiter arrived then, an overweight young man in black slacks, a ruffled white shirt, a black bow tie, and an elastic black garter snugged around his upper left sleeve. He asked Miss Lizzie if she would like anything to drink.

"I should very much like," she said, slowly, deliberately, "a Ramos gin fizz." She said it without looking at Mr. Liebowitz. I looked at him, and I saw that he was watching her, another smile on his lips.

When the waiter asked me, I said that I wanted nothing. Mr. Liebowitz told him the same.

As the waiter tucked his order book into his garter, Miss Lizzie said, "Excuse me."

"Yes, ma'am?"

"Is Mr. Fay in the club at the moment?"

"And who's asking, ma'am?" he said.

"I am."

He smiled uneasily. "Yes, but—"

"You may tell him," she said, "that a relative of John Burton wishes to speak with him."

"John Burton," he said. He nodded easily. And then, all at once, his face tightened. "Okay. I'll see if he's here."

"Thank you."

After he walked away, Mr. Liebowitz said, "He knows the name."

"Yes," said Miss Lizzie. "But we already knew that John was a regular customer here."

After ten minutes or so, the waiter returned with Miss Lizzie's drink balanced on a round metal tray. He set the tall glass in front of her. It was filled with what looked like a vanilla milk shake, a red paper straw speared through its white froth. He stood back and said to her, "Mr. Fay is busy right now, but he'll see you in a few minutes."

"Thank you," she said. Bending forward, she took the straw between her fingers and deftly tucked the end of it into her mouth.

It took half an hour—and Mrs. Parker still had not arrived—but at last the waiter returned. The band was playing a slow tune, and couples were swaying across the polished wooden floor, each of them tightly knotted together. The waiter leaned toward Miss Lizzie and said, "Mr. Fay will see you now."

"Thank you," she said and stood up. So did Mr. Liebowitz and I.

The waiter looked around the table. "All of you?" he said.

Miss Lizzie nodded toward me. "She is the relative. I am her guardian. This gentleman is my friend and consultant."

"Well," said the waiter, "I don't know. . . . I thought it was just gonna be one of you."

Miss Lizzie smiled. "Perhaps Mr. Fay should decide."

"Yeah, well, okay. Follow me."

Miss Lizzie and I picked up our purses and, with Mr. Liebowitz beside us, we followed the waiter around the dance floor, out into the entryway, and down a narrow, dimly lit corridor. Outside an expensive-looking mahogany door stood a man whose shoulders appeared to be three feet wide. Stuffed into a dark suit, he stood there immobile, his thick arms crossed over his thick chest. Running across his left cheek was a wide pink scar.

The waiter told him, "They all wanna go in."

The other man studied us, one by one, and then jerked his head toward the door. "Ask 'im," he told the waiter.

The waiter knocked on the door, then opened it, stepped in, and pushed the door shut behind him.

The man said nothing more, merely looked down at the floor, ignoring us, waiting. We waited with him.

After a few moments, the door opened, and the waiter stepped out, pulling the door shut. "He says it's okay."

"Right," said the man. "Take off."

The waiter left, and the man let his arms fall from his chest and turned to look down at Mr. Liebowitz. "You packing, shorty?"

Mr. Liebowitz reached into the left side of his coat, eased out a small semiautomatic pistol, and handed it over.

The man bounced it twice on his broad palm then said to Mr. Liebowitz, "A twenty-five caliber. A sissy gun."

Mr. Liebowitz nodded. "I shoot a lot of sissies."

I giggled; I could not stop myself.

The man glanced at me, his eyes hooded above that impressive scar. He looked back at Mr. Liebowitz. "Yeah," he said. "Funny." He slipped the pistol into his coat pocket and turned to Miss Lizzie.

"I have only this," she said, holding up the walking stick. "Without it, alas, I tend to be quite useless."

"The bag," he said. "Open it."

Miss Lizzie's face went pink, and she pressed her lips together. "Please," she said.

"Come again?" said the man.

"Open the purse, please," said Miss Lizzie.

The man looked at Mr. Liebowitz, at me, and then back at Miss Lizzie. "Huh?"

"Open the purse, *please*," said Miss Lizzie.

"Oh, right," said the man. He grinned. "Right. Sure. *Please.*"

She nodded, slipped the purse off her arm, opened it, and held it out for him to look inside.

He peered down into it, nodded, and then turned to me. "Okay, kid. The bag." He glanced at Miss Lizzie, looked back to me, and grinned again. "Please," he said.

I held open my purse, wishing, ridiculously, that my crumpled handkerchief were not lying there, as I knew it was, curled up in one corner like a dead mouse.

He looked in, leaned back, crossed his arms, then jerked his head toward the door. "Go ahead."

Smiling, Mr. Liebowitz opened the door and waved his arm toward it, gesturing for Miss Lizzie to go ahead. She did, and I followed her, and Mr. Liebowitz followed me.

Chapter Sixteen

It was a big office, brightly lit, lavishly appointed, richly carpeted. Each of the walls held twenty or thirty framed photographs. Every one of them, as far as I could see, was a picture of Mr. Fay being chummy with someone presumably famous.

Mr. Fay himself was leaning back in a swivel chair behind a huge wooden desk, the heels of his large black shoes perched on the dark green blotter. His face was still gray, but tonight he wore another black suit, this one double-breasted. The jacket was open, and beneath it he wore a dark blue shirt, a white tie, and a different stick pin, one that held a large blue star sapphire in a silver setting.

A second man sat to the left of Mr. Fay's desk. A short, very fat man in a gray suit. Gray-haired and as gray-faced as Mr. Fay, he was likely about fifty years old. His blunt elbows were propped against the chair's arms, his plump hands locked together over his wide, soft stomach.

Mr. Fay pointed a finger at me. "You, I know," he said. "Sorry about your uncle. A real tragedy. Amanda, right?"

"Yes."

He looked at Mr. Liebowitz and Miss Lizzie then back at Mr. Liebowitz.

"Liebowitz, right?" he said.

"Yes."

"You did that bank thing. The investigation. For Morrie Lipkind."

"That's right."

His thin lips slid into a thin smile. "Don't it slow you down some, being such a little guy? And bald and all? You kind of stick out in a crowd."

Mr. Liebowitz smiled. "I'm a master of disguise."

Mr. Fay turned to the fat man. "Snoopers. Ask a question, get a wiseass answer."

The fat man said nothing.

Mr. Fay looked at Miss Lizzie. "And you?"

"Elizabeth Cabot. I am Amanda's aunt."

"Okay," he said. He nodded toward the fat man. "This here is Mr. Greene. He's what you call my legal adviser."

The fat man nodded, his glance moving easily from me to Miss Lizzie to Mr. Liebowitz.

Miss Lizzie asked Mr. Fay, "May we sit down?"

He waved a hand impatiently. "Yeah, yeah. Grab a pew."

Apparently, Mr. Fay used the room as a meeting place; arranged along the thick carpet in front of his desk were five chairs. We took three of them.

"The chair all right?" said Mr. Fay to Miss Lizzie.

"Splendid," said Miss Lizzie.

"Okay. What's your beef? You got five minutes."

"Who killed John Burton?" she asked him.

He turned to the fat man. "Right to the point. Direct."

"And perhaps," said Miss Lizzie, "you could provide a direct answer?"

He looked back at her. "Who says I got to provide anything?"

"But why shouldn't you?"

"An old lady. A kid." He looked at Mr. Liebowitz. "A billiard ball." He turned back to Miss Lizzie. "Not a whole lot of leverage."

"I should've thought," she said, "that you'd want to help us resolve the issue."

"Why?"

"Simple civic duty."

He turned again, smiling, to the fat man.

The fat man said nothing.

"I'm sure," said Miss Lizzie to Mr. Fay, "that you personally have nothing to hide."

He looked at her. "Nothin."

"So. Do you have any idea who killed him?"

"Not a one."

"You knew Mr. Burton."

"I knew him. A customer."

"You spent some fifteen or twenty minutes with him on Friday night."

He looked at me. "That would be you. You talked to the cops."

"I had to," I said.

He nodded, as though that were an answer he understood. He turned to Miss Lizzie. "We were talking investments, Burton and me. He gave me some advice."

"What advice?"

"Come again?"

"What advice did he give you?"

"Commodities. Commodities are very good right now, he said."

"Which particular commodities?"

He frowned. "What difference does it make?"

"I'd simply like to know," she said.

"Peanuts," he told her.

"You spent fifteen minutes discussing peanuts?"

"You know. The ins and outs." He raised his left hand then glanced down at the gold watch on his wrist.

"There's a woman who works for you," said Miss Lizzie. "A Miss Sybil Cartwright."

He pointed a finger at her. "Right there, see, you got what you call the wrong tense."

"How so?"

"Sybil Cartwright, she don't work here no more. She got herself killed today."

Blinking behind her pince-nez, Miss Lizzie put her hand to her breast. It was a better performance than Daphne Dale had given at the Hotel Brevoort this afternoon. "How horrible," she said. "How on earth did it happen?"

"Someone cut her throat," said Mr. Fay.

Miss Lizzie winced. "My goodness."

"Yeah. Nice kid, I hear."

"You hear? She was an employee of yours."

"I didn't know her close. Dancers are a dime a dozen in this town."

"Do the police have a suspect?"

"The police and me, generally, we're incommunicado, know what I mean?"

"Perfectly. But don't you find it interesting?"

"What? What's interesting?"

"You knew, of course, that John Burton and Miss Cartwright were seeing each other?"

"Anything goes on in this place, I know about it."

"John Burton was killed on Friday, with a hatchet. Miss Cartwright was killed today, with a knife."

"Yeah. And?"

"Might there be a connection?"

"Who knows? Life is complicated. What did you want with Cartwright?"

"To speak with her."

"I guess you can forget about that." He looked at the fat man and smiled.

"So it seems," said Miss Lizzie. "Do you have—"

Someone knocked at the door.

Mr. Fay called out, "*What*?"

The door opened and the big man poked his head around it. In the brightness of the room, the scar on his face seemed darker. "We got another one," he said.

"Who?" said Mr. Fay.

"A broad. Says she's with them."

"Let her in." He turned to the fat man. "We got a bus station here."

It was Mrs. Parker, wearing a smart black evening dress, black gloves, and a small toque, shiny with black feathers. She stepped into the office, stopped, then looked around the room. She said, "Ain't this the Ritz."

"You want to buy it," said Mr. Fay, "or you want to take a seat?"

Mrs. Parker smiled brightly. "I think take a seat."

"And you are who?"

"I'm Mrs. Parker," she said. "Wonderful to meet you." She moved to the empty chair beside Miss Lizzie's. "Sorry I'm late," she said to her softly, sitting down.

Mr. Fay looked at his watch again then at Miss Lizzie. "I figure like I'm being very reasonable here. Your five minutes, they're up already."

"Have you any theories," said Miss Lizzie, "as to who might have killed John Burton?"

"Yeah, I got a theory. It was a guy with a hatchet." Smiling, he turned to the fat man. Then he turned to me. "No offense, kid."

Mr. Liebowitz said, "Mr. Burton did a lot of traveling."

Mr. Fay looked at him. So did the fat man. "That right?" said Mr. Fay.

"Europe, several times a year. France, Germany. Last year, he went to China."

"China. No kidding."

It seemed to me that the fat man was watching Mr. Liebowitz very closely.

"Do you know why?" said Mr. Liebowitz.

"What am I, a travel agent?" said Mr. Fay. "Maybe he likes noodles." He glanced at his watch again then turned to Miss Lizzie. "That about it?"

"Yes." She rose from her chair. "Thank you very much."

The rest of us stood.

"Don't mention it," said Mr. Fay. "Tell the waiter I said to put your drinks on the cuff." He looked at me. "The least I can do, your uncle and all."

"Thank you," I said.

"Don't mention it."

We were nearly at the door when he said, "Hey. One thing."

We all turned back to look at him.

"Yes?" said Miss Lizzie.

"A lot of people getting popped around here. Burton. The Cartwright broad. Maybe it ain't such a hot idea to go pokin' around."

"Perhaps not," said Miss Lizzie. "But I do thank you for your concern."

After Mr. Liebowitz retrieved his pistol from the man outside the door, we returned to the table. Our bill was waiting there. Despite Mr. Fay's instructions, Miss Lizzie lifted it, looked at it, set it back down, opened her handbag, and pulled out a five-dollar bill. She lay that on the table, and then we all went outside to find Robert.

Within a minute or so, he cruised up to the curb. Mr. Liebowitz, Miss Lizzie, and I sat in the backseat, me in the middle, and Mrs. Parker in the front, across the bench seat from Robert.

"Hello, Robert," she said.

"Evening, ma'am."

"Dorothy," she said.

The car moved out into the street.

Mr. Liebowitz said to Miss Lizzie, "He didn't much care for that question about John Burton's traveling."

"No," said Miss Lizzie. "He didn't. And he seemed altogether uninterested in the death of Miss Cartwright."

"Yes. But it's possible that he *did* know her only as a dancer. As he said, in New York, dancers are a dime a dozen."

"Do you dance, Robert?" said Mrs. Parker.

"No, ma'am."

I said, "He told us five minutes, and he let us stay a lot longer than that."

"Yes, he did," said Miss Lizzie. "I suspect that he wished to determine how much we knew."

"Which is approximately nothing," said Mr. Liebowitz.

"We do know," she said, "that he was lying about his conversation with John Burton."

"Do we actually know that?" said Mr. Liebowitz.

"As it happens," she said, "I follow the commodities market. There's a glut of peanuts just now, worldwide. No one in his right mind would invest in their future, or advise anyone else to invest in them."

"Did you know, Robert," said Mrs. Parker, "that George Washington Carver has invented over three hundred different uses for peanuts?"

"Yes, ma'am, I did."

"Well, yes, of course you did."

"Perhaps," said Mr. Liebowitz to Miss Lizzie, "Mr. Burton was attempting to put something over on Fay."

"Would *you* attempt to put something over on Mr. Fay?"

Mr. Liebowitz put his hand on his bald scalp, rubbed it softly, and smiled. "Not without a very large gun in my hand."

"Yes," she said. "There you are."

Chapter Seventeen

We arrived at the Cotton Club at a little after eleven. Dropping us off, Robert told Miss Lizzie that he would park the car, enter the club through the rear, and attempt to find his friend.

"The game is afoot, Robert," said Mrs. Parker.

He grinned at her. "Yes, ma'am."

It was a Sunday night, but the people gathered outside the club had evidently not been informed of this. There were as many of them in line as there had been on Friday, and they were just as impatient and just as excited. I saw Mr. Minton, the former prize-fighter, standing at the front door in his dinner jacket, and I led the others toward him.

Tonight's crowd disliked the breach of etiquette as much as the crowd on Friday. "Get in line!" a man hollered.

Mr. Minton looked down at me grimly for a moment, and then his face opened in recognition. He smiled, showing the gap in his upper front teeth. "Hey, sweetheart," he said.

"Hello, Mr. Minton."

He moved down into a crouch, knuckling his left hand against the pavement, and his face grew serious. "Listen," he said, "I'm real sorry about your uncle. He was a top-notch guy."

Unlike Mr. Fay, he seemed genuinely sorry.

"Thank you," I told him. "Mr. Minton, we need to talk to Mr. Madden. Is he here tonight?"

He glanced up at Miss Lizzie, Mr. Liebowitz, and Mrs. Parker.

"These are friends of mine," I said.

He nodded at them, then looked back at me. "I gotta tell ya, sweetheart, Mr. Madden's a busy guy. Is it something really important?"

"Yes, it is. Honestly."

He nodded again. "Okay. You go inside with your friends, and you talk to Mr. DeMange. You know who he is?"

"The manager. I met him."

"Right. He'll let you know if it's okay. Deal?" He held out his big hand.

I took it. "Yes. Thanks a lot, Mr. Minton."

"You bet." He stood up from the crouch, moving with more effort now. He turned and tugged at the brass door-pull. Once again, the blare of music billowed out onto the pavement.

At the reception desk stood another large man, one I didn't recognize. Like the man who had been here on Friday, he wore a black dinner jacket. He smiled at Mr. Liebowitz and then asked over the music, "You have a reservation, sir?"

Mr. Liebowitz nodded toward me. "We're with her."

The man looked down at me.

"May I talk," I said, raising my voice to be heard, "to Mr. DeMange?"

He smiled, as though amused to discover that I was capable of speech. "And who are you, little lady?

"My name is Amanda Burton," I said, "and I'd like to talk to Mr. DeMange."

The man looked at Mr. Liebowitz.

Mr. Liebowitz smiled. "She'd like to talk to Mr. DeMange."

The man looked at Mrs. Parker.

Mrs. Parker said, "Must I say it, too?"

He looked back at me. "What was the name again?"

"Amanda Burton. John Burton's niece."

This time, at the mention of John's name, there was a flicker of recognition. He nodded. "Wait here," he said and then glided smoothly away.

Inside, the band suddenly stopped playing. The audience applauded wildly, whooping and hollering. From the entryway, the noise sounded like the howl of single large, ecstatic beast.

After a minute or two, Mr. DeMange came looming around the corner, tall and bulky, his long, basset-hound face still looking rumpled. He took in Miss Lizzie and the others, then glanced down at me. When he had first met me, two nights ago, his sad face had abruptly lit up. This did not happen tonight.

"Amanda," he said. "How you doing?"

"I'm okay, thank you."

"A tough break what happened to your uncle."

"Yes."

"We all liked him here." He looked again at the others then back at me. "What can I do for you?"

"These are my friends," I told him. "We'd like to talk to Mr. Madden."

"And who are your friends?"

I introduced them.

He nodded. "Okee-dokee. What I'm gonna do is get you folks a table, and then I'm gonna talk to Mr. Madden. See if maybe he can spare some time. No promises, right?"

"Fine," I said. "Thank you."

"Come on in."

We followed him into the cavernous room, into the smells of cigars and cigarettes, perfume and cologne, hair spray and perspiration. He led us to a large circular table on the second level of seating, at the arch of the horseshoe-shaped dining area, opposite the stage. Once again, the crowd was entirely white. Like the crowd two nights before, they seemed restive yet energized by some secret feverish expectation. All around us, people leaned toward one another, gaily chattering.

As we sat down, Mr. DeMange said to me, "I'll send over the waiter."

I thanked him, and off he went, his big ungainly body moving easily through the clutter of customers.

"Shit," said Mrs. Parker. She had taken off her gloves, and now she put a cigarette between her lips. "We missed the show."

"We didn't actually come for the show," said Mr. Liebowitz.

She searched through her purse. "I wanted to see Robert's friend." The tip of the cigarette bobbed as she spoke. "She's one of the dancers, he said."

"And how would you know which of them was Robert's friend?"

She had found her lighter. "Easy," she said, lighting the cigarette. "She'd be the one with the big smile on her face."

A waiter, a thin black man, came weaving through the tables, a tray tucked under his left arm, an order book in his right hand. "Evenin', folks," he said and turned to Mr. Liebowitz. "What kin I getcha?"

"Nothing for me, thanks," he said.

Miss Lizzie ordered another Ramos gin fizz, Mrs. Parker a Scotch and water. I ordered a Coca-Cola.

"Got it," he said and then weaved his way back.

Miss Lizzie was looking around the room. "An extraordinary place," she said.

Mr. Liebowitz smiled. "Nothing like it in Fall River, Miss Borden?"

"Nothing at all."

"That's him, isn't it?" said Mrs. Parker.

I looked. Out on the empty dance floor, a man had stopped the waiter, his hand resting lightly on the waiter's arm, and now he leaned toward him and whispered in his ear. It was the same man I had seen two nights ago, the short, dark-haired, broodingly handsome man who stood very straight. Tonight, he wore another white dinner jacket, as trimly tailored as the first, and beside him stood the woman who had been with him on Friday. Her small, voluptuous body was tightly sheathed in a glistening black silk gown that left her arms and her pale round shoulders bare. It also left bare a large percentage of her chest, which itself took up a large percentage of her body.

"Yes," I said to Mrs. Parker.

As the waiter stalked off, the man and the woman approached our table.

Mr. Liebowitz stood.

"Good evening," said the man. His accent was British, his voice low and silky. He smiled pleasantly at the others. "I'm Owney Madden. Welcome to the club." He turned to me. "Amanda. We didn't meet the other night. I regret that. And I deeply regret what happened to your uncle. He was a fine man."

I thanked him, then introduced the others.

To Mrs. Parker, he said, "I've read your theatre reviews in *Vanity Fair*. They're very well done."

She smiled—surprised, I think, at the recognition. "You should tell the owner."

"I'm sure that Condé Nast is already aware."

Mrs. Parker blinked, cocked her head, and studied Mr. Madden, as though surprised that a club owner would know anything about magazines.

"Mr. Liebowitz," said Mr. Madden, putting out his hand, "you're an associate of Mr. Lipkind's, I believe?"

"On occasion," said Mr. Liebowitz as he took it and shook it.

"A gifted lawyer," said Mr. Madden. He held his hand toward the short blonde woman. "This is my friend, Miss Mae West."

"Charmed," she said. She had an accent with which I was then unfamiliar, but I later learned had originated, like Miss West herself, in Brooklyn. Hanging from her neck, dangling between her imposing breasts, was a long strand of large, opalescent pearls.

Mr. Madden turned back to me. "You wanted to speak with me?"

"If that's okay."

"Certainly. Come along. We'll use my office."

As I stood up, so did Miss Lizzie.

Mr. Madden turned to her. "You're coming as well, Miss Cabot?"

"I am Amanda's guardian."

He smiled. "Then of course you're coming."

Mr. Liebowitz started to move around the table.

"Make yourself comfortable, old man," Mr. Madden told him. "I promise I'll return these two safely."

With a brief glance at Miss Lizzie, Mr. Liebowitz nodded.

Mr. Madden asked him, "Would you mind terribly if Miss West joined you in the interim? I dislike leaving her alone."

"Of course not," said Mr. Liebowitz.

"Sure," said Mrs. Parker, without a great deal of enthusiasm. Her glance moved glumly over the woman's dress. "Join the party," she said.

Miss West smiled. "Don't mind if I do."

Mr. Madden turned to her. "I'll be back shortly, Mae."

"Take your time, sweetie," said Miss West.

Mr. Madden's office was bigger than Mr. Fay's, but it was simple and extremely white—the carpet, the walls, the two long sofas, one on either side of the room, each flanked by white oval end tables. Even the desk, a curved, sweeping piece of gleaming wood, was white. On it was a white telephone, a small white calendar, a notepad of white paper, and a long white pen in a white marble holder. Behind it hung a pair of long white curtains, drawn shut.

The only real decoration was a single oil painting on one wall, opposite the desk. Simply framed in wood, about six feet wide and four feet tall, it showed a jolly group of men and women laughing and drinking at a trestle table, green trees and a blue lake visible behind them, a lavish yellow sunlight splashing everywhere.

"Please," said Mr. Madden, gesturing toward one of the sofas, "have a seat."

We sat down as he moved around behind the desk. He lowered himself into the chair, leaned forward, clasped his hands together on the desktop, looked at me with his sleepy eyes, and said, "Now, how may I help you?"

"Maybe it would be better," I said, "if my aunt explained."

He turned to Miss Lizzie.

"As perhaps you know," she said, "the police have yet to discover who killed John Burton."

Mr. Madden nodded.

"Initially," she said, "they focused their attention on Amanda."

He smiled at me. "Must have been a bit of a bother for you."

"Yes," I said. I remembered what Miss Dale had told us. *They say he killed a man.* Like her, I found it difficult to believe.

"And we suspect," said Miss Lizzie, "that their attention will return to her unless we can discover who was actually responsible."

He nodded. "And you propose to do that how, exactly?"

"By speaking with everyone who knew him. By trying to determine if anyone had a motive for killing him."

He shook his handsome head. "Afraid I can't help you there, Miss Cabot. To the best of my knowledge, John was universally liked. Everyone thought very highly of him."

"And yet you had some sort of disagreement with him on Friday night."

Smiling, he sat back. "Who told you that?" He turned to me. "Ah. The little exchange in the entryway. Between John and me."

"It looked like you were angry with each other," I explained.

"It must have." He turned to Miss Lizzie. "Do you know anything about baseball, Miss Cabot?"

"Only a very little," she said.

"A few weeks ago, John and I made a bet with each other. The Washington Senators have a pitcher named Walter Johnson. He's quite good, and this year he's having an exceptional season. I bet John that when the Senators played the Chicago White Sox, Johnson would pitch at least a one-hitter, and possibly a no-hitter. Do you know what that means?"

"That the opposing team, I assume, would score no more than a single hit during the course of the game."

"Yes. And that's exactly what happened. A one-hitter. When I—"

Someone knocked at the door.

"Come in," Mr. Madden called out.

The door opened and a waiter entered, a black man but not the same waiter who had taken our order. He carried two drinks on his tray: my Coca-Cola and Miss Lizzie's gin fizz.

"Thank you, Paul," said Mr. Madden. "Could you set up a table for our guests?"

The waiter slipped the tray onto the end table beside Miss Lizzie, circled to the other table, slid it out, and arranged it in front of us. He then returned to his tray, put paper napkins on the table before us, and placed a glass atop each napkin. Miss Lizzie's straw, this time, was yellow.

After the waiter left, Mr. Madden nodded to the drinks. "Please," he said.

I picked up my Coke. Miss Lizzie sat forward and lifted her drink. Holding the napkin to the glass's bottom, she sat back. She lowered her head, put the straw between her lips, and took a sip.

"It's all right?" Mr. Madden asked her. "The drink?"

Her head rose. "Most refreshing," she said. "Thank you."

"You're quite welcome. Now. Where was I?"

"A one-hitter," said Miss Lizzie. "Mr. Johnson had pitched it, and John had lost his bet."

"Yes. When I saw John, I reminded him about it." He smiled. "If John had a flaw, it was his competitiveness. He hated to lose. Just absolutely hated it." He turned to me. "And that was why he was so grumpy when he left."

"I don't suppose," said Miss Lizzie, stirring her drink with the straw, "that you kept any record of the bet?"

"Come now, Miss Cabot. No one keeps a record of sports bets."

"For how much was it?"

"Five hundred dollars."

"Rather a large bet." She sipped her drink again.

"I could afford it. So could he."

"And he paid you how? By check?"

"In cash." He smiled. "You'll find that very few people are willing to accept a check for a sports bet."

"You were afraid that John might cancel his?"

"The subject never came up. As I said, bets are paid in cash. John knew that. He was carrying the cash, and he gave it to me."

"But you had to remind him of the bet, you said. So presumably he wasn't carrying the cash in order to pay you."

"John always carried quite a lot of cash. I'd warned him against it—several times, actually. New York can be a dangerous city."

"But this time his carrying it worked to your advantage."

He frowned. "I can promise you, Miss Cabot, that if my giving up the cash could somehow bring John back, I'd give it up in a second."

She nodded. "Where did you first meet John, Mr. Madden?"

"Here. In the club. As a customer."

"And the two of you became friends?" Another sip of gin fizz.

"Friends? We knew each other. I like to think that we enjoyed each other's company. We were comfortable acquaintances, let's say."

"Do you know Mr. Fay? At the El Fay club?"

"We've met."

"Do you think him a honest man?"

Another smile. "So long as honesty is in his own best interests. But to some extent, Miss Cabot, that's probably true of us all."

"Perhaps." She lowered her head and sipped at her drink.

"Why do you ask?" he said.

"John was with him on Friday night, before he came here. Mr. Fay maintains that John and he discussed peanut futures."

"That's possible, I suppose. But there is an oversupply of peanuts at the moment. John surely knew that."

"According to Mr. Fay, John advised him to invest in peanut futures."

He frowned. "That I find unlikely."

"As do I," she said. She sipped her drink, and the straw rasped as the last of the gin fizz disappeared. "Excuse me," she said.

Mr. Madden smiled.

She leaned forward and set the glass back on the table. "Do you know anything about John's travels, Mr. Madden?"

"His travels?"

"He spent quite a lot of time outside the country. France, Germany. Last year he spent a month in China."

He smiled. "I can't imagine why. I understand that the facilities there are a bit primitive."

"He never mentioned the travel to you?"

"No."

"And you can think," she said, "of no one who might have wished him harm?"

"No one." He sat back and put his arms along the arms of his chair. "But suppose I do this. Suppose I make a few telephone calls. There are people in town who may know something."

"People who knew John?"

"People who knew *of* John."

"Was John so well known, Mr. Madden?"

"He was wealthy. He was out and about on a fairly regular basis. There are individuals who make it their business to know about such people."

"Really?"

"Really. Is there some way I can get in touch with you?"

"Probably not," she said. "Amanda and I will be moving about the city for the next few days. Would you object to my getting in touch with you?"

"Not at all. I'll start telephoning right now. But I shouldn't expect any immediate answers. This may take a while."

"I understand."

"Why don't you call me in two or three days?"

"I shall."

Mr. Madden reached into the inside pocket of his white dinner jacket and pulled out a business card. He stood and walked around the desk to hand it to Miss Lizzie. "It's my private number," he told her. "If I'm not there, leave a message and I'll get back to you within ten minutes."

Miss Lizzie opened her purse and slipped the card inside. "I'll call you sometime in the next two or three days, then."

"That'll be fine."

Although we could not know it then, we did not have two or three days.

Chapter Eighteen

When we returned to the table, Mr. Liebowitz was smiling and Mrs. Parker was laughing. Miss West was sitting back in her chair, slightly sideways, her handsome legs crossed, her smooth left arm hooked casually over the chair's back. She was sipping from a tulip glass of champagne. Somehow a bottle of Dom Perignon and an ice bucket had blossomed in the center of the table.

As we sat down, Mrs. Parker leaned toward Miss Lizzie and said, "Did you know that Mr. Madden has seven bullets in him?"

"No," said Miss Lizzie. "He failed to mention that." She turned to Miss West, who had obviously been the source of this information. "He wears them very well."

"I'll say," said Miss West. Her Brooklyn drawl was slow and sultry, very different from the cramped finishing-school drawl of Mrs. Parker. "They definitely don't have any effect on his performance."

Miss Lizzie smiled. "He's a lucky man."

"Owney," she said, "makes his own luck."

"I imagine that's true. By the way, he asked me to tell you that he'd be a few more minutes."

Miss West shrugged her white shoulders. "I'll live."

"Mae's a playwright," announced Mrs. Parker.

"Indeed?" said Miss Lizzie.

"Tell her the name of your play," said Mrs. Parker.

"*The Hussy*," said Miss West. With her left hand, she gently fluffed at her bright blonde hair. "It's by way of being autobiographical."

"You do yourself a disservice, I'm sure."

Miss West smiled, a slow languorous smile. "I never do myself a disservice," she said.

"Has the play been produced?"

"I'm workin' on it. You gotta strike while the iron is hot." She looked at Mr. Liebowitz and smiled that smile again. It may have been my imagination, but it seemed to me that the private detective's shiny scalp turned slightly pink. "A hundred years from now," she said, "we're all gonna be memories."

"In the long run," said Miss Lizzie, smiling, "perhaps being a memory is not such a bad thing after all."

Miss West looked at her, and then she grinned. "You know, honey, you got something there."

"What is the play about?" Miss Lizzie asked her.

"A lady of easy virtue. She climbs up the social ladder. Wrong by wrong."

Miss Lizzie smiled again.

Mrs. Parker said, "Mae's also a singer and a dancer."

"In this town," Miss West said, "you gotta have a broad range. Even more so, naturally, when you're a broad."

Mrs. Parker said, "*Variety*—it was *Variety*, wasn't it, Mae?"

"*Variety*, that's right, yeah. I've always liked *Variety*."

"*Variety* said she did the best shimmy on Broadway."

"Not the best," corrected Miss West. "The *rawest*." She said it proudly.

"And what is a shimmy, exactly?" said Miss Lizzie.

"It's the kind of dance," said Miss West, "that separates the men from the boys. And then turns both of them, *alakazam*, into the other."

"That must be a very useful social skill."

Miss West laughed, and then she narrowed her eyes. "Say," she said, "you're all right, Liz. You mind if I call you Liz?"

I had been taking a drink from my glass of water. I nearly drowned.

"Not at all," said Miss Lizzie. "Are you all right, dear?"

"Yes," I said and coughed again into my hand. "Yes. Thank you."

"Sorry to be so long, Mae." It was Mr. Madden, suddenly standing beside my chair.

"That's okay," said Miss West, setting her glass on the table. "We've been chewin' the fat like a batch of brownies."

She stood, smoothed down her dress, stepped back from the table, and then looked around at us, smiling. "It's been swell." To Miss Lizzie she said, "I'll see you around, maybe."

"I should like that."

"Don't forget to call me," Mr. Madden told Miss Lizzie.

"I shan't."

"The drinks are on me, by the way."

"I generally prefer to pay for my own," she said.

He smiled. "Unfortunately, tonight you can't."

"Very well. Thank you."

"My pleasure. Good evening."

"Good evening," Miss Lizzie replied.

The two of them turned and moved in tandem down the steps to the dance floor, Miss West's round hips swaying, Mr. Madden's fingers resting lightly on the exposed white skin of her back.

"She's amazing," said Mrs. Parker. "I hate her." She leaned toward Miss Lizzie. "She says she speaks two languages: English and body."

"Both of them fluently, it would appear."

Mrs. Parker laughed.

I asked Mr. Liebowitz, "How does she know Mr. Madden?"

"Madden owns the hotel that Miss West's mother manages. She met him there, she says."

"He owns a hotel as well?" said Miss Lizzie. "Mr. Madden is doing very well for himself."

"If I could walk like that," said Mrs. Parker, looking off toward Miss West, "I'd never have to write another word."

"Did Madden say anything helpful?" asked Mr. Liebowitz.

Miss Lizzie recounted what Mr. Madden had told us.

As she did, Mrs. Parker seemed distracted. She looked off, looked down, and crossed her arms. She yawned once, delicately, putting her tiny stiff hand before her mouth. She lit a cigarette and let it burn, untouched, down to a fragile gray finger of ash. Several times she blinked her eyes in a quick little burst, as though trying to keep herself awake.

At the end, Mr. Liebowitz asked Miss Lizzie, "Do you believe him?"

"No," she said. "And neither does Amanda."

Mrs. Parker looked up from the tablecloth. "And neither do I," she said.

Mr. Liebowitz turned to me. "Why not?"

"Well," I said. "John liked sports. He knew about prizefighting, and he probably knew about baseball. Maybe he made bets, but I don't believe that if he made a bet, he'd be so . . . cheap about paying it."

He said, "You were with him for only a week, Amanda. People can surprise us, even after years, by what they do. By who they are."

"That's for damn sure," said Mrs. Parker. She looked off, idly, toward the bandstand.

"Yes, but I just can't see him doing that. And Mr. Madden said John was grumpy on Friday night. He was a whole lot more than grumpy. He was really upset. I don't think it was a bet."

He looked at Miss Lizzie.

"I agree," she said. "Mr. Madden was entirely too smooth."

"You know," he said, "Walter Johnson *did* pitch a one-hitter a few weeks ago. Against the White Sox."

"That does not surprise me. And it would not surprise me to learn that Mr. Madden had in fact made a wager on the game. But he did not necessarily make it with John."

Mr. Liebowitz nodded. "We're not making much progress."

"Well," she said, "we do know that Mr. Madden has excellent taste in art. He has a Renoir hanging on the wall of his office."

"Really?" I said. "That was a Renoir?"

"Yes."

"Do you think it was real?"

"More real, I expect, than Mr. Madden himself." She turned to Mr. Liebowitz. "And we know that both he and Mr. Fay are lying. We know that they're both deliberately distancing themselves from John. Each of them maintains that John was merely a customer."

"But perhaps he was."

"He had a private discussion with each of them on Friday night. How many other customers can say the same? Do you see Mr. Fay as the sort of man who mingles with his customers?"

"He mingled with you and Amanda."

"Long enough to pacify us," she said. "Or so he thought."

He sat back and looked at his watch. "Midnight," he said. "Do we quit now or should we make one more stop?"

"One more stop?" said Miss Lizzie. "Which?"

I looked at Mrs. Parker. With her head lowered, she was staring idly again at the tablecloth.

"Do you remember Mrs. Norman?" said Mr. Liebowitz. "Jeanelle Norman? Mr. Burton's cleaning woman—Albert mentioned her."

"Yes."

"I was able to reach her this afternoon. We can go talk to her if you want. She lives only a few blocks away."

"At this hour?" said Miss Lizzie.

"She'll be there," he said and smiled. "And we won't be intruding. She's having a rent party."

Mrs. Parker looked up, beaming. "A rent party," she said. "Now there's an idea."

"It's rather late," said Miss Lizzie. "Amanda?"

"I'm fine. I'd love to go."

"Very well, then." She took a deep breath and sighed then turned to Mr. Liebowitz. "Let us go meet Mrs. Norman."

When we were all back in the Cadillac, once again with Robert at the wheel and Mrs. Parker sitting beside him, Mr. Liebowitz explained what a rent party was.

At that time, rents in Harlem were higher than they were in most of Manhattan, but black people were essentially not permitted to live anywhere else in the city. In order to pay the rent, some of them organized parties in their apartments. Guests paid to get in, and they received free drinks and, at some of the parties, free entertainment.

Mr. Liebowitz leaned forward. "Have I put that accurately, Robert?"

"Yes, sir," said Robert over his shoulder.

"And white people are allowed in, Robert?" I asked.

"At some of them, miss."

"They are at this one," said Mr. Liebowitz. "I asked Mrs. Norman."

"Goody," said Mrs. Parker.

"Robert?" said Miss Lizzie.

"Yes, ma'am?"

"Did you find your friend?" Miss Lizzie asked.

"Yes, ma'am, I did. My friend didn't really know Mr. Burton. Some of the customers, the men, they like to meet with the dancers. On the side. Secretly. You understand what I mean?"

"Yes."

"Mr. Burton didn't do that."

"What about Mr. Madden? How did he acquire the club?"

"The story is that Arnold Rothstein lent him the money, ma'am, after Mr. Madden got out of prison."

"Really." She turned to Mr. Liebowitz. "I thought that Mr. Rothstein was merely a gambler."

"There's no *merely* about Arnold Rothstein," he said. "He's a gambler, yes. But he's one of the biggest and most successful gamblers in New York City. And I've heard that he does invest in businesses now and then—restaurants, nightclubs, Broadway shows."

"Robert," said Miss Lizzie, "does Mr. Rothstein have a continuing interest in the club?"

"My friend says he does, ma'am. It's common knowledge."

"He's an impressive man," said Mr. Liebowitz. "There are a thousand stories about him. Some of them may even be true."

"What sort of stories?"

"Fixing the World Series. Shooting a couple of policemen and getting away with it. Arranging the first delivery of bootleg whiskey from Scotland. Providing bail for all the bootleggers arrested in the city—at exorbitant interest rates."

Miss Lizzie smiled. "The Napoleon of Crime."

"My own favorite is the one about the pool game."

"And how does that go?"

"Back in 1909, Rothstein was one of the best pool players in the city, and he knew it. There were a number of people, gambling types, who never liked him. They brought in a fellow named Jack Conway, the champion of the Philadelphia Athletic Club, and they arranged a match between him and Rothstein. Rothstein and Conway started playing at eight o'clock on a Thursday night, at John McGraw's pool hall, south of Herald Square. Conway won the first match. Rothstein won the second. They played through Thursday night and Friday morning, straight. They played all of Friday, and they didn't stop playing until early on Saturday morning. Thirty-two hours after they started. Rothstein won four thousand dollars."

"But that makes him sound rather admirable," she said.

"It makes him sound like a good pool player."

"Certainly a pool player with stamina. And the stories of his bootlegging? Are they true?"

"Who knows? Probably."

"Mr. Fay began as a bootlegger, I understand," she said.

"You've heard about his trip to Canada in the taxicab?"

"Yes. Could there be some connection between him and Mr. Rothstein?"

"Even if there were, how would that help us?"

"I can't imagine."

"Robert," said Mrs. Parker.

"Yes, ma'am?"

"Your friend. What's her name?"

"It's Leroy, ma'am."

"Is she very—oh. Oh . . . Ah . . . And the two of you—"

"Yes, ma'am. That's right."

"Oh." Her voice sounded flat and deflated. "I'm sorry."

Robert turned to her, and I could see the flash of his teeth as he smiled. "Nothing to be sorry about, ma'am."

Mrs. Norman's apartment building was on 135th Street, a few blocks west of Lenox. Cars were parked bumper to bumper in front of it, and Robert had to drive two blocks farther to find a space for the big Cadillac.

As he parked it, Miss Lizzie said, "Robert, would you like to come in with us?"

He turned around in his seat. "Excuse me, ma'am?"

"Would it be acceptable, to the people there, if you accompanied us to this party?"

"Acceptable, ma'am? Sure it would. Mr. Liebowitz said it was an open party."

"It's up to you, of course. But it does seem rather silly for you to be waiting out here in the car."

Robert looked at Mr. Liebowitz.

In the soft light drifting in from the streetlamp, Mr. Liebowitz smiled. "You're supposed to be keeping an eye on Miss Borden and Amanda. You can't do that if they're there and you're here."

Robert grinned. "No, sir, I guess not."

"As Miss Borden says, it's up to you."

"Would it be all right with you if I change my jacket? There's another one in the trunk. It'll only take me a minute."

"Fine with me."

We waited on the sidewalk. Robert tossed his chauffeur's cap into the trunk and stripped off his uniform jacket. Strapped beneath his thick left shoulder was a leather holster that held a large automatic pistol.

"My goodness," said Mrs. Parker. "Is that loaded?"

"Yes, ma'am," said Robert.

Mrs. Parker looked him up and down, puffed out her cheeks, and then audibly sighed.

Robert laid down the uniform jacket and lifted a suit coat that matched his black pants. He slipped into it and buttoned it shut. Like the chauffeur's jacket, it had been well tailored. Unless you looked carefully, you could not see the faint swell in the fabric caused by the holster.

"Sorry to make you wait, ma'am," he said to Miss Lizzie.

"Not at all, Robert. Perhaps you should lead the way."

We could hear the music even before we reached the building—the tinkling of a piano, the thumping of drums, the earnest wail of a trumpet.

Three black men were sitting on the stoop, two of them side-by-side on the first step, the third sitting two steps up, his forearms on his knees, his right hand holding the neck of a large beer bottle. All the men wore suits, and they all had their coats opened and their ties loosened. They looked up at us without expression, their faces shuttered.

"Evening," said Robert.

The man with the beer bottle nodded. "Sure is."

"Excuse us," said Robert.

No one stood, no one changed expression, but the man sitting farthest to the left moved his knees slightly to the right.

We went up the steps, Robert leading, then Miss Lizzie and her walking stick, then me and Mrs. Parker, and finally Mr. Liebowitz. As we reached the top of the stoop, the man with the beer bottle said something, and the others laughed.

We followed the thumping of the drums up the stairs, the sound growing louder as we rose. Between the third and fourth floor, we passed a couple wrapped in a passionate embrace, their hands scrambling at each other's shoulders. They ignored us. On the fourth floor, where the music was loudest, we stepped out into the hallway.

It was crammed—men and women, black and white, everyone wearing suits and dresses, the dresses of the black women, bright reds and pinks and yellows, wildly more colorful than the dresses of their white counterparts. The people were animated, laughing or smiling as they stood there, leaning toward one another and burbling cheerfully, gesturing with paper cups and cigarettes. A cumulus of smoke hung beneath the ceiling, fogging the light from the overhead fixtures. The air was thick with the sharp smells of perfume and hectic flesh.

There was an energy there, a feeling of excitement, and it occurred to me that it was an excitement very different from the kind I had witnessed at the Cotton Club. It seemed to me then—and it still does—that the people at the club were anticipating, without any real hope of achieving, what these people were actually living. It was exactly this busy jumble of races and genders, this heated erotic bustle, that the customers of the nightclub had been seeking—without, of course, ever actually finding it.

As I wound my way through the crowd with Miss Lizzie beside me, a young black man in a green suit stepped forward and, with a gallant flourish, handed her a paper cup. "Here you go, mama."

The people around us laughed. Miss Lizzie smiled. "Why, thank you," she said and took the cup, raised it to her lips, and sipped at it. She smiled. "Delightful," she announced. The man grinned happily.

We moved on, and I turned to her. "What is it?" I asked her.

She leaned toward me. "Furniture polish."

We arrived at last at the open door of one apartment. Standing there with a cigar box under his arm was a short, thin black man in a gray suit, a large black beret slumped across his head. He said to Miss Lizzie, "How many, ma'am?"

"There are five of us," she said.

"Be ten dollahs, please."

As Miss Lizzie opened her purse, Mr. Liebowitz stepped forward and handed the man a ten-dollar bill.

"Thank you," said the man. "You go ahead in now."

And so we did, all of us, into the clash and dash of movement.

Chapter Nineteen

The room was larger than I expected, but it was even more tightly packed than the hallway.

Over in one corner, in white shirts and unknotted black ties, were the musicians: a painfully thin trumpet player, a small but determined drummer, and a jolly young mustachioed fat man who pounded at the keys of an old upright piano while he beamed back over his plump shoulder at the crowd. Perched on the pianist's head was a tiny porkpie hat that looked as though it were about to go flying off.

In front of them, on a few square feet of bare wood floor, three black couples were ardently dancing, elegant arms and legs flying, managing somehow not to slam an elbow or a knee into the crowd huddled to either side of them.

To the left was the bar, an improvised table of two-by-eight boards supported by sawhorses. Behind it, ladling out a red liquid from a galvanized metal tub, was a tall black woman in a sleeveless purple dress. More people were clustered along the length of the bar, some of them couples, laughing and grinning and chattering. Some were single men, their glances moving over the crowd, searching through it with a brittle nonchalance.

I looked around.

People were everywhere in the room—standing, sitting, shuffling about. In one overstuffed chair, amid a clutch of attentive young men, sat two young smiling black women in gorgeous matching black gowns. The sofa held three couples, men alternating with women. The last couple was white, and they were chatting merrily with the black couple to their right.

I saw Robert heading off toward another corner, followed by Mrs. Parker.

"Amanda?" said Mr. Liebowitz. "Miss Borden?"

"Yes?" said Miss Lizzie.

"Could the two of you come with me?"

"Certainly."

Miss Lizzie and I followed him over to the bar, where he edged himself between two men and leaned toward the woman in the purple dress. Using her long metal ladle, she was expertly pouring more red liquid into another paper cup. He said something to her, and she looked at me and then at Miss Lizzie.

Over the music she called out to Miss Lizzie, "You be wantin' a drink?"

"Thank you, no," said Miss Lizzie, smiling, and raised her paper cup. "I already have one. Delicious."

The woman grinned and then looked at me. "Glass of water, chil'?"

"No, thank you," I said.

In her midforties, she was big-boned and wide-hipped. Her skin was a flawless milk-chocolate brown, and her face, with its broad cheekbones and wide mouth and large solemn eyes, had the simple stoic beauty I would later admire in Olmec statuary. Clinging to the right side of her shiny marcelled hair was the spectacular white sunburst of a dahlia.

"Mr. Liebowitz?" she shouted. "Drink?"

"No. Thanks."

She called out to a woman standing on this side of the table, to her right, "Florence?" She held up the ladle.

Florence stepped around the table, took the ladle, and the woman in the purple dress edged out from behind the bar. "You all come along with me, okay?" she said to Mr. Liebowitz.

We all followed her through the crowd, down a congested hallway. I caught a whiff of another odor, sweeter than tobacco smoke, a smell that I would learn, some years later, was marijuana. We passed one door and came to another. At this second door, a threesome of guests stood talking: two middle-aged black women and a tall, distinguished-looking older black man. All of them nodded to Mrs. Norman. She nodded back, leaned between them, pounded underhanded at the door with her balled fist, and calmly shouted, "You inside! You finish up that weed and git your ass out here. People be *waitin'*."

She turned back to us. "Come along."

A few feet farther on, at the end of the hallway, we arrived at another door. Mrs. Norman reached into the pocket of her dress, found a key, and unlocked the door. She turned to Mr. Liebowitz. "Got to keep it locked or some of these folks be climbin' into my bed."

She pushed open the door, leaned in, flicked a light switch, and then gestured with her long brown arm. "Go ahead."

Miss Lizzie entered, then I, then Mr. Liebowitz. Mrs. Norman came in behind us, shut the door, slipped the key into the lock, and turned it.

I glanced around me. It was the first time I had been in the bedroom of a black person, and I suppose that I was vaguely disappointed. It seemed utterly, relentlessly normal. The walls were white, and the drawn curtains were brown. On the right was a small mirrored makeup table arrayed with tiny flat tubs of cream and squat glass bottles of perfume. A ladder-back wooden chair stood before it. On its left was a plump padded reading chair and a floor lamp, its yellow shade fringed. Beside these, a dresser and a wardrobe, both painted brown. The bed was large, and it had a lacy yellow coverlet, two oversize pillows, and a kind of headboard that incorporated a bookshelf, the shelf stuffed with books. Above the bed, on the wall, hung a small framed print of a smiling Jesus, his robe opened, the finger of his right hand serenely pointing to his disembodied, glowing, ruby-red heart.

Mr. Liebowitz introduced us, once again referring to Miss Lizzie as Miss Cabot.

Mrs. Norman looked at me. "It's an awful thing, what happened to your uncle. A cruel, terrible thing." She turned to Mr. Liebowitz. "What kind of evil person do a thing like that?"

"That," he said, "is exactly what we're trying to find out."

She looked around the room and then back at him. "I apologize," she said. "Don't have but the two chairs. I can stand."

"Of course not," he said. "I'll stand."

After a few moments, we had worked out the disposition. Miss Lizzie sat in the reading chair, I sat on the wooden chair from the makeup table, and Mr. Liebowitz stood, leaning his small body against the table. Mrs. Norman sat on the end of her bed, her back straight, her hands in her lap, her knees together, her shapely, muscular legs crossed at the ankles.

"First of all," said Mr. Liebowitz, "thank you for taking time away from your party."

Smiling, Mrs. Norman reached up and gently touched the white dahlia in her hair. "Real nice party, it turned out."

"Very nice," said Mr. Liebowitz.

"Fats—the piano player—he had him a birthday couple weeks ago, and he still be celebratin'."

"He is very good," said Miss Lizzie.

"He the best. He be big-time one day."

"How often," Miss Lizzie asked her, "do you have these parties?"

"'Bout once a month. I do any more, the neighbors git riled. But what I do, I invite 'em in, let 'em all come in for free." She smiled. "Couple glasses of punch, they git happy as clams at high tide."

"It's a lovely punch," said Miss Lizzie.

Mrs. Norman laughed. "You pullin' my leg now. It ain't poison, but it ain't no nectar of the gods. It git the job done, though. People these days, they need a little somethin' take they minds off they troubles."

"People in any days," said Miss Lizzie.

Mrs. Norman nodded. "That the truth."

"Mrs. Norman," said Mr. Liebowitz, "how well did you know John Burton?"

"Not hardly at all. I work for him. Three years now. But I don't know him, exactly."

She turned to me. "He nice, though. I know that. A real nice gentleman. He real excited you coming to town."

"Excited?" I said.

She smiled. "Like a little boy. Two weeks ago, he there, at the apartment. I knock on his bedroom door. I want to go in and give it a cleanup, and he come to the door. He wearin' one of them spiffy black coats. Dress-up coats."

"A dinner jacket," I said.

She nodded. "Dinner jacket. He say, 'What you think, Mrs. Norman?' He always real polite. He say, 'My niece I tol' you about, Amanda, she comin' in next week. You think she like this?'"

"He really asked you that?" I said.

"Sure he did. I say, 'You be looking real suave, Mr. Burton. Your niece, she be deep down impressed, for sure.'"

I thought of John trying out his dinner jacket like a high school senior, eagerly asking Mrs. Norman her opinion, and I felt a sadness sift slowly through me. When I first met him at Grand Central Station, he had said that my upcoming visit had been a big deal, but I had discounted that. I would never have imagined that he, so debonair, so self-assured, would actually be nervous about meeting a sixteen-year-old girl.

"I say to him," Mrs. Norman continued, "'You know what you do, Mr. Burton?' I say, 'You buy that young girl a great big ole flower. You buy her a corsage, a real nice one, for when the both of you go out together.'"

She smiled at me. "He do that, chil'? He buy you a flower?"

"Yes," I said, and my throat clamped shut. Until this moment, I had completely forgotten about the orchid John had given me on Friday evening. As far as I knew, it was still in the icebox at his apartment, where I carefully tucked it away when we returned that night. I imagined it lying there in its tiny cardboard coffin, limp and withered, and I lowered my head, abruptly guilty, abruptly forlorn. I felt a tear trickle down my cheek.

"Aw, honey," said Mrs. Norman softly. "Hey now. I'm sorry. I got me a big fat mouth. Don't half know what I'm sayin' sometimes."

I looked up, swallowing. "No," I said. I lowered my head again, rubbed at my eyes with my finger and thumb, and then looked back up at her. "Thank you so much for telling me."

"He a good man," she told me. She nodded and reached out and touched my arm. "He a real gentleman."

Mr. Liebowitz asked Mrs. Norman, "Did he have any enemies that you know of, Mrs. Norman?"

She turned to him. "No one I ever knew about."

"Have you met Sybil Cartwright?"

She thought a moment then shook her handsome head. "Don't recollect the name."

"What about Daphne Dale?"

She frowned. "She the writer lady?"

"Yes."

"Her, yes." Her handsome black face was serious now.

"You didn't like her," said Miss Lizzie.

Mrs. Norman shook her head. "Not my place to have feelings about Mr. Burton's friends."

"Mrs. Norman," said Miss Lizzie, "we're all very much in the dark here, Amanda and I and Mr. Liebowitz. None of us really knew John. Anything you can tell us about him, anything at all, will be helpful. Why is it that you disliked Miss Dale?"

"Didn't say that."

"You didn't need to."

"More like she be dislikin' me."

"Why?"

"She don't need no reason. She from the South. In her mind, black people still be slaves."

"How did she and John get along?"

Mrs. Norman shrugged. "They get along just fine. All lovey-dovey, mostly. Except at the end there. Then they have themselves a big ole argument."

"When was this?"

"A year past. No, more than that. Two years, almost."

"Do you know what they were arguing over?"

"Not the particulars."

"How did the argument come about?"

"The two of them, they in the library. Someone come knockin' at the door, and I be in the hallway there, sweepin' up, so I go to the door and I open it. Be a little man out there, say his name is Walters. Joe Walters. Say he need to talk to Mr. Burton. I say for him to wait, and I go to the library and tell Mr. Burton. He say for me to show the man in."

"You have an impressive memory, Mrs. Norman," said Mr. Liebowitz. "This happened nearly two years ago?"

"Near-abouts." She shrugged. "Don't know 'bout impressive. Got me a cousin married to a man name of Joe Walters. Same name exactly. That how come it stick in my mind."

"Sorry," he said. "Go ahead."

"Mr. Walters, he come in, and he go into the library, but he don't stay long, only a couple minutes. He come out, and he turn around back to the library, and he say, 'Okay. Tomorrow, at the Spyglass. Two o'clock.' He call it out, like. That how come I hear it."

"The Spyglass?" said Miss Lizzie.

"A bar downtown," said Mr. Liebowitz. "Near the Fulton Fish Market." He turned to Mrs. Norman. "You remember him saying that? The Spyglass?"

"The Spyglass." She smiled faintly. "Guess my memory, it pretty impressive after all."

Mr. Liebowitz grinned. "I guess so."

"What did Mr. Walters look like?" asked Miss Lizzie.

"He short. He be wearing real good clothes, real nice cut to 'em. He real clean."

Miss Lizzie nodded. "And what happened then?"

"Then is when they have the big ole argument. That Miss Dale, she gits real upset. Like I say, I be standing just outside the door, cleaning up, and I hear her, clear as a bell. Can't help but hear her. She be shoutin'. She be tellin' Mr. Burton that Mr. Walters, he no good. He work for that Rothstein man."

"Rothstein?" said Miss Lizzie.

"That Arnold Rothstein," said Mrs. Norman. "The gamblin' man."

"You're certain," said Miss Lizzie, "that she said *Rothstein*?"

"I be right there, standin' just outside the door. Like I say, couldn't *help* but hear her."

"Did she say just *Rothstein*, or did she say *Arnold* as well?"

"Just the *Rothstein*. But I know who she mean. Only one Rothstein be famous in New York."

"But it could have been some other Rothstein," said Mr. Liebowitz.

Mrs. Norman shrugged. "Maybe. But from the way she say it, she be talkin' 'bout the gamblin' man."

"What else did they say?" asked Miss Lizzie.

"Don't know. Just then, Mr. Burton, he come to the door, and he see me out there. He give me a little smile, embarrassed-like, and then he shut the door."

"And Miss Dale and John ended their relationship shortly after that?"

"Never saw her again. One time—this a few months later—I ask him, I say, 'What happen to that nice Miss Dale?'" She leaned a fraction of an inch toward Miss Lizzie. "I say *nice* because that the polite thing to say." She sat back. "Mr. Burton, he just smile and he say, 'We agree to disagree.'"

Miss Lizzie nodded. "Did Mr. Walters ever come to the apartment again?"

"Not when I be there."

"What about Mr. Rothstein?"

"Never saw him. Read about him. He famous. He fix that World Series back in 1919."

"Do you know Owney Madden?"

"He own the Cotton Club over on Lenox. Big gangster."

"Did he ever come to the apartment?"

"Only person I ever saw in the apartment was that Miss Dale. And that Joe Walters. And Mr. Cooper a few times. Mr. Albert. Mr. Albert, though, usually he not there. Mr. Burton, he tell me he got him a girlfriend over in Queens." She turned to me. "Mr.

Albert, he the one call me on Saturday, tell me about Mr. Burton. I ask him about you. I worried, you know. Young girl all on her own. He say you with the police, he tryin' to find you." She nodded. "Glad you okay."

"Thank you," I said.

"Mrs. Norman," said Mr. Liebowitz, "did Mr. Burton ever mention Arnold Rothstein to you?"

"No."

"Owney Madden?"

"No."

"Larry Fay?"

"No."

He turned to Miss Lizzie. "Is there anything else?"

"I don't believe so." She looked at Mrs. Norman. "If you think of anything that might be helpful, could you telephone me? I am at the Algonquin Hotel. Shall I write that down?"

Again, Mrs. Norman faintly smiled. "I reckon I kin remember."

Miss Lizzie nodded. "I thank you very much for your time."

"You welcome. I think of somethin', I give you a call."

Chapter Twenty

"So we come across Mr. Rothstein again," said Miss Lizzie.

We were in the Cadillac, south of 135th Street, heading toward Central Park on Lenox Avenue.

"Perhaps Mrs. Norman misheard the name," said Mr. Liebowitz.

"I think it very unlikely that Mrs. Norman ever misheard anything in her life. Did you notice the books in her bookshelf?"

"Yes. Spengler. DuBois. Freud. Translations of Baudelaire and Chekhov. She's obviously well-read."

"She was also most entertained when you doubted her memory," said Miss Lizzie, and I could hear the smile in her voice.

"Yes," he said. "She's smart. I'm surprised, really, that she doesn't speak better English."

"I suspect that she can speak it as well as any of us. Or better. I think she was doing us a kindness."

"What kindness?"

"Providing us with what we were expecting to hear."

"You think she lied?"

"No, no. I think she told us the truth. But she was presenting it, and herself, in a way that she believed we could understand."

"Simple old woman, fresh from the country."

"Yes, exactly."

"You'd make a good lawyer, Miss Borden."

"Miss Cabot."

"What will we do now?" I asked her.

"Now?" she said. "I think that now we should all get some sleep.

But tomorrow morning, I think that we should talk to Daphne Dale again."

"Miss Dale never mentioned Arnold Rothstein," Mr. Liebowitz pointed out.

"But neither did we. The next time, we shall."

"Mr. Liebowitz," Robert said from behind the steering wheel. His deep bass voice was soft.

"Yes?"

"I think we're being followed."

Beside Robert, Mrs. Parker's head swiveled around to face the rear of the car. I turned around and looked out the window.

"Are you sure?" said Mr. Liebowitz.

"Behind us. Two cars back. The Ford. It pulled out the same we did, on One Hundred and Thirty-Fifth Street, and it's been staying back there."

Mr. Liebowitz was silent for a moment. Then he said, "Go left on One Hundred and Twenty-Fifth."

When we reached 125th Street, the traffic light was red, so we stopped and waited. No one spoke. The light went green. Some cars passed us, heading north. Robert made the turn.

A moment passed. Mrs. Parker, still looking back through the rear window, said, "It's still there."

Mr. Liebowitz told Robert, "Make a right at Fifth."

We drove silently for a few moments. Then Robert turned onto Fifth Avenue. We waited.

"The bastard is still there," said Mrs. Parker.

Mr. Liebowitz turned to Miss Lizzie. "We have three choices: We can stop right now and see what they do, we can try to outrun them, or we can ignore them and see if they follow us all the way back."

"No," said Miss Lizzie. "I see no reason to let them know where Amanda and I are staying. And I don't like the idea of stopping. I think we ought to outrun them. Robert, can we do that?"

"Out in the country, ma'am, it'd be easy," he said. "No Model T can keep up with this car. But here in the city, it's a different story."

Mr. Liebowitz said, "Then let's go to the country."

"Pardon me?"

"Central Park. Take One Hundred and Tenth west, and head into the park opposite Lenox Avenue."

"Yes, sir," said Robert.

At 110th, with the traffic light green, Robert swerved the big car to the right. All of us in the car swung toward the left. I looked at Miss Lizzie. Silhouetted against the light from the streetlamps, she sat slightly forward, her walking stick upright between her knees, her hands wrapped around its crook. She turned to me, and I think she smiled.

"Maybe the bastard won't follow us," said Mrs. Parker, still swiveled around in her seat and peering out the rear windshield. "Maybe it's just a coincidence that—"

I turned to look and saw the Ford making the same turn onto 110th, about a hundred yards behind.

"Shit," said Mrs. Parker.

"The park entrance is coming up," said Mr. Liebowitz.

"Yes," said Robert.

"Don't signal the turn."

"No."

We were lucky. When we arrived at the entrance to the park, no cars were approaching from the other direction. Robert whipped the wheel to the left, and the Cadillac's tires chirped as the car shot across the road. We went racing into the darkness of the park.

"Now stay left up here," said Mr. Liebowitz.

"No offense, Mr. Liebowitz," said Robert, "but it'd be best now if you just let me drive."

"Right. You drive, Robert."

And drive Robert did. The big car roared south, picking up speed, its tires drumming along the pavement. To our left was the Harlem Meer, a flat black expanse of water, glossy in the moonlight.

"They've done something to that car," Robert said. "That's not a standard Ford."

The headlights of the Ford were now only seventy-five yards behind us and getting closer.

We made a long sweeping turn to our left, toward the east, tires squealing. I swayed against Miss Lizzie. Then came another squealing turn, this one to the right, and we went shooting south.

"Damn," said Robert.

I looked back. The Ford had moved closer.

It occurred to me that we had perhaps made a serious mistake by entering the park.

Possibly the same thought had occurred to Mr. Liebowitz, for he reached into his jacket and slipped out his pistol. "Robert," he said, "turn right up here." He yanked back the pistol's slide and let it snap forward.

The car shot off to the right, tires squealing once more. Again, we all swayed to the left.

"That Colt of yours, Robert," said Mr. Liebowitz, "is it cocked and locked?"

"Yes, sir."

"Okay."

Miss Lizzie said, "Are we absolutely certain that this is the right response?"

"If we're going to confront them," said Mr. Liebowitz, "I'd rather that we be the ones who pick the place and time."

"Yes," she said. "Of course."

I felt her hand squeeze my knee. I took the hand in mine.

Mr. Liebowitz said, "Robert, take the next right—"

"West Drive," said Robert.

"Right. As soon as you make the turn, pull over and stop the car. I'll get out on this side. You get out on that side and come around behind the car with me. The rest of you, all of you, get down on the floor and stay there. Miss Borden, can you do that?"

"With great dispatch," she said.

"Amanda?"

Miss Lizzie's hand tightened briefly around mine.

"Yes," I said.

"Mrs. Parker? Can you get onto the floor?"

"I can dig through the damn thing if I need to."

"Turn's coming up, sir," Robert said.

"Everyone hang on," said Mr. Liebowitz.

We swerved to the right and kept swerving, and then we roared down the road for a moment. The tires hissed and sputtered. For a moment, the Cadillac lumbered forward, its wheels bumping along the grass now, and then it jerked to a skidding stop. All of us lurched forward, and Miss Lizzie's hand was wrenched from mine.

Mr. Liebowitz threw open his door and darted out, slamming it shut behind him. From behind the steering wheel, Robert did the same, his big body moving with astonishing speed.

"Get down, Amanda," said Miss Lizzie and moved to her right, taking up Mr. Liebowitz's space. Awkwardly, she began to lower herself to the floor. I leaned forward to help her, and then the gunshots began—quick, loud *pops*, a rapid scattering of them, behind me.

I spun around and looked out the window.

In the moonlight, across the roadway, the Ford had stopped, and men were tumbling from open doors on the car's far side. In their fists, fire flashed. The blasts of their pistols blended into one long, ragged clatter—the sound of paper tearing but magnified a thousand times.

More *pops* behind me, Mr. Liebowitz and his .25, and then two loud *booms* from Robert's big pistol. One of the men went down, clutching at his side.

"*Amanda,*" said Miss Lizzie.

I shifted over and lowered my body, but I kept peering over the bottom of the window.

The men were gathered behind the Ford now, four or five of them. More flashes, more *pops* from behind the Ford. More gunfire from behind me.

Suddenly, the side window on the Cadillac's front seat exploded inward, scattering ragged chunks of glass into the car. I flinched.

"*Shit,*" said Mrs. Parker. "*Shit, shit, shit, shit, shit.*"

"*Amanda!*" said Miss Lizzie, and her hand wrapped around my calf.

I let myself be forced back a bit, and I lowered my head slightly, but still I kept watching, mesmerized.

We will never know, of course, why they decided to attack just then, why they did not remain in the relative safety of the Ford's far side. Perhaps they simply wanted to end this before the police arrived. Whatever their reason, suddenly they were swarming around the Ford on both sides, their guns flashing and crashing. One of them crumpled to the street almost at once.

And then, for only an instant, they were all brilliantly lit up, as though by a spotlight. They froze into a tableau, faces white, mouths open, stiff arms extended, and then they were hurled aside as a huge gray Lincoln swept in from the left and smashed into them with a loud and sickening *whump*. I saw bodies go spinning crazily off to the right and others go flying over the car's long hood, arms and legs outstretched, empty hands grasping at nothing. Something slammed against the front end of the Cadillac, and the car wobbled once.

I heard the squeal of brakes, off to my right, farther up the road, and then the heavy slam of a car door. A gun was fired closeup by the Ford and then another farther off. Then silence.

And then footsteps.

Mr. Liebowitz came into view from the left side of the car, Robert from the right. They stood there for a moment in the hazy moonlit darkness, their pistols held down at their sides.

From beyond Robert, a third man came down the road. He was tall, dressed entirely in black, only his hands and head visible, his face a ghostly white blur.

The three of them spoke softly among themselves. Behind me, I could hear Miss Lizzie trying to get up from the floor. I turned and helped her back onto the seat. In the front, Mrs. Parker was arranging herself, wiping at her dress. *"Shit,"* she said.

"Amanda," said Miss Lizzie, adjusting her pince-nez, "I am *very* disappointed in you."

"I wanted to *see*," I said. I was panting, and I realized that my heart was pounding like a fist against my chest.

"But you could have been *hurt*. You could have been—"

"I'm okay. Really I am."

"Yes, but—"

Someone tapped at the window behind me. I wheeled around.

Mr. Liebowitz, bending down toward us, said, "Stay in there."

He walked away. Robert and the third man were moving across the road toward the Ford.

"Who *is* that?" said Mrs. Parker.

"That, I expect," said Miss Lizzie, "is Mr. Cutter."

Chapter Twenty-One

Miss Lizzie opened her door. "I shall be back," she said and began to step from the car.

Up front, Mrs. Parker said, "Me, too." She opened her door and swung her legs out.

I opened my own door, stepped out, closed the door, and looked around me.

In the moonlight, I could see bodies everywhere, lying like bags of trash in the wide ribbon of road and along the black velvet expanse of grass. One man was slumped against the front fender of the Cadillac, his neck twisted at an impossible, sickening angle.

Mr. Liebowitz, Robert, and the third man were examining the bodies by the Ford.

The third man said something in a voice that was almost a whisper. I could not make out the words.

The air was threaded with the bitter stink of gun smoke. All at once, Miss Lizzie was beside me. She put her arm around me, and I slumped toward her, breathing in her scent of citrus, cinnamon, and cloves.

A retching noise came from my right, and then a whiff of sickness. I turned. Mrs. Parker had come around the car, and now she was bent forward, her hands on her thighs, very sick.

Mr. Liebowitz and Robert walked toward us. Both of them had returned their pistols to their holsters. The third man followed behind.

"You need to get out of here," Mr. Liebowitz said. "All of you."

"What about you?" Miss Lizzie asked.

"I'll help Cutter clean up." He turned to the third man. "This is Cutter."

An inch or two over six feet tall, he wore a pair of black slacks and a black shirt, opened at the collar, buttoned at the cuffs. A large semiautomatic pistol, like Robert's, had been jammed under his black belt, to the left of the buckle. Now that he was closer, I could see his features: a lock of black hair falling in a curl over his forehead, deeply set eyes, a sharp nose, a strong jaw, and a precisely defined and almost feminine mouth.

Dressed all in black with his eyes masked by a shadow, he seemed a part of the night himself, an elemental creature, an angel of death.

In a matter of seconds, with no hesitation, he had smashed out the lives of four or five men. But, by so doing, he had probably saved ours.

"Ma'am," he said to Miss Lizzie in a sandy, whispery voice. He nodded once, almost a bow. In the circumstances, it seemed an extravagantly courtly gesture.

"How do you do?" said Miss Lizzie. "Lizbeth Borden. This is—"

Mr. Cutter had turned to me, his eyes still in shadow. I could see, within the darkness, just the faintest faraway glimmer of light, like that from a distant star.

"No time," said Mr. Liebowitz. "Robert, get them back to the hotel."

"Yes, sir."

He turned to Miss Lizzie. "I'll call you in the morning."

I glanced at Mr. Cutter. I still could not clearly see his eyes. He nodded toward me, once.

"Well, Lizbeth," said Mrs. Parker, "I'll say this for you: you certainly know how to show a girl a good time."

We were back in Miss Lizzie's suite at the Algonquin. Mrs. Parker was sitting opposite the sofa where Miss Lizzie and I sat, and she was holding her silver flask in her hand, resting it upright on the arm of her chair.

"You were very brave," Miss Lizzie told her.

"Brave?" Mrs. Parker laughed, sounding somewhat frayed. "My sphincter was plucking buttons off the car seat." She raised the flask to her lips and sipped from it.

"You were very brave," Miss Lizzie repeated. "Are you sure, dear, that I can't get you a glass?"

Mrs. Parker shook her head. "No time," she said. "I need to replace all that classy Scotch I lost in the park." She sipped again, took the flask's cap, and screwed it on. "Anyway, I've gotta go. Poor Woodrow's been alone for hours. The apartment will look like an explosion in a shit factory." She stood up.

"Will you be all right?" Miss Lizzie asked.

"I'll survive. But I may just sit tomorrow out, if you don't mind."

"Of course. I'll speak with you in the morning."

"Assuming I'm capable of speech. Which is unlikely." She offered a tired smile. "But the change will probably improve my social life. G'night, Amanda."

"Good night, Mrs. Parker."

"Dorothy," she said automatically, and then she smiled at Miss Lizzie. "That's a bitch, isn't it? About Robert? About his being . . ." For the first time since I had met her, she appeared to be searching for a word.

"Not entirely heterosexual?" offered Miss Lizzie.

Mrs. Parker exhaled another frayed laugh. "Yeah. That."

"He was very careful not to state the gender of his friend."

Mrs. Parker frowned. "You noticed that?"

"Yes."

"Why didn't I?"

"Perhaps you didn't wish to."

She nodded. "Yeah. Perhaps." She sighed once again. "Okay. See you tomorrow."

After she left, I said to Miss Lizzie, "She's not a very happy person, is she?"

"No. Not very."

"Is there a Mr. Parker?"

"I asked her once. She said she'd misplaced him somewhere."

I smiled. "She's funny."

"Yes. But she's lived a lonely life. Her mother died when she was quite young, and she hated her stepmother."

Both statements were true of me as well. And, I realized, they were also true of Miss Lizzie, whose relationship with her stepmother had been famously unhappy.

"She's very smart, though," I said.

"She is, indeed."

"She's really not coming with us tomorrow?"

"Not where we'll be going, I'm afraid."

I frowned. "What do you mean?"

"We must leave, Amanda."

"Leave?"

"Leave the hotel. Leave New York."

"Miss Lizzie—"

"We've no choice."

"You're still angry at me," I said. "For not getting down on the floor of the car. Back in the park."

"I wasn't angry," she said. "I was frightened."

"I'm sorry. I—"

"It doesn't matter now, dear. It's over. And in any event, that isn't the reason we're leaving."

"Then why?"

"Amanda, it's no longer a question of *potential* danger. Those men wanted to kill us. They followed us from Mrs. Norman's apartment building with that purpose in mind."

"But how'd they know we were there? How *could* they know?"

"I suspect that Mr. Fay or Mr. Madden sent them. Perhaps the two of them conspired. They are evil men, Amanda. Mr. Fay may seem comical, and Mr. Madden may seem suave and civilized, but the two of them are steeped in violence. It is their milieu. They couldn't have survived within it unless they were prepared to use it themselves—immediately and ruthlessly—against anyone who threatened them. Either of them would blot us out in an instant, with no more compunction than someone swatting a horsefly."

"But why? Why would they *want* to?"

"There is clearly something about your uncle, about his death, that they wish to keep hidden."

"But if we leave now," I said, "we'll never find out what it is."

"Perhaps not. But if ignorance is the alternative to death, then I have no difficulty in opting for ignorance."

I could not have explained back then why I was so determined to stay and finish the investigation.

I felt that I owed something to John, yes. It was not right for someone to take his life so callously, so brutally, so senselessly and then be permitted to walk the world unpunished.

But today I know that there was more to it than that.

I was terrified during that battle in the park. My hands were clammy, and my heart was racing. But, along with the physical symptoms of fear, and perhaps because of them, there had been a kind of horrible fascination, a breathless excitement; there had been, God help me, almost an exultation.

Some people revel in a life lived along the borderline. They seek out what others prudently avoid: the extremes, the ends and the beginnings of things, the heights and the depths. I did not know it then, but I was becoming such a person. It would take many more years for me to become that version of myself and for me to understand who and what it was I had become. By then, of course, I could not have been anyone else.

But in Miss Lizzie's living room that early morning, I was merely petulant and willful.

"Miss Lizzie—" I said.

"Amanda, I cannot in good conscience let you remain here."

"You're not *really* my guardian, you know."

There was a sour twist of scorn in my voice. I heard it, and immediately I regretted it.

Miss Lizzie had the grace to ignore it. "No," she said. She peered at me, unblinking, through the lenses of her pince-nez. "But I like to think that I am your friend. And friendship, it seems to me, carries with it concern and responsibility. I would be an inadequate friend if I did not take you to safety."

Once again a blatant and undeserved generosity did me in. I felt the familiar pressure gathering behind my eyes.

"Okay," I said. I swallowed. "We'll go. We'll leave in the morning."

"It may be that Mr. Liebowitz and Mr. Lipkind can learn something after we leave."

"Maybe, yes. But you're right. We should get out of here."

I could not sleep.

As I lay there, the events and the characters of the night kept replaying themselves, gaudy, inescapable, along the screen at the back of my mind. The thuggish Mr. Fay warning us off. The smooth Mr. Madden promising his help. The cheerful black man in the green suit, gallantly handing a paper cup to Miss Lizzie. The stately Mrs. Norman sitting poised and upright on the bed. The race through the park, the gunfire, the moonlit grass, the bodies hurled about, the pale enigmatic face of Mr. Cutter emerging from the murk . . .

At last, I picked up the book I had set upon the nightstand. Miss Daphne Dale's *The Flesh Seekers*. I opened it and began to read.

In any other circumstances, I should have tossed the book aside or possibly hurled it out the window. It was dreadful.

The narrator, Sophie Hill, admits at the outset that she comes from the upper levels of Alabama aristocracy. She also admits, fetchingly, to an inborn brilliance and a bubbly native congeniality. That she is beautiful we know from the countless courtly swains who seek her delicate hand. All of these she spurns, driven by a fierce desire to "make it" on her own. Within a few pages, she has hied herself off to the wicked social whirlwind of New York City, where she hopes to achieve great success as a novelist. Her father, the old colonel, is furious, but her mother, with the wisdom of

mothers throughout the South, secretly sends her ribboned packets of cash.

At a party in Greenwich Village, surrounded by hirsute Bolshe-
viks, both male and female, Miss Hill meets Jerry Brandon, "a scion
of the city." Mr. Brandon is tall, dark, and, of course, handsome; a
stockbroker "with mysterious ties, rumor had it, to the powerful,
clandestine people who, behind the scenes, manipulated the politi-
cal and economic strings of Manhattan."

Miss Hill is, understandably, smitten. After only one more page she
is in the library of Mr. Brandon's luxurious apartment—in a building
called the Nebraska—girding herself for her upcoming ravishment.

*I felt his hot breath upon my neck. With one simple, powerful
movement, his strong, masculine hands ripped open the back of my
dress. It fell to the floor, a puddle of mauve silk, and he stepped back.
I stood there immobile as his burning eyes roamed over my white
nakedness. "I must have you," he declared. "I WILL have you."*

An erotic shock jolted down my spine. "Take me," I challenged.

After a demure set of ellipses and then a shared cigarette on the
carpet, the naked Mr. Brandon rolls over, gets up, and pads to the
bookcase. He removes some books and pulls out a section of the
case to reveal a large black safe. . . .

"She *lied* about it," I said. "She *knew* there was a safe in the library."

"I am not altogether astonished," said Miss Lizzie. "Miss Dale
was not exactly forthcoming. What was it that Mr. Brandon
removed from the safe?"

"An emerald necklace. A gift for Miss Dale. For Sophie Hill, I
mean."

It was ten o'clock, and we were eating our breakfast in her living
room. When she ordered it, Miss Lizzie had told the clerk at the
front desk that we would be leaving this morning.

"But why lie about the safe?" I asked her.

"For the same reason, no doubt, that Mr. Fay and Mr. Madden
lied: to distance herself from John and from his death. Is there any
mention of Arnold Rothstein in the book?"

"I flipped through the rest of it, but I couldn't find anything. Just that line about the clandestine people and the strings."

She smiled. "And a lovely line it is." She raised her cup and sipped her tea. "Well, we'll let Mr. Liebowitz know about the safe. Perhaps he can pry something loose from Miss Dale."

"I suppose we can't go down and see her," I said. "On our way out of town, I mean."

She smiled again. "Amanda."

"Okay, okay. We'll tell Mr. Liebowitz. I—"

Someone knocked at the door. Miss Lizzie and I looked at each other. She had not yet called room service to request that the breakfast things be removed.

"I'll see," I said. Wiping my mouth with my napkin, I stood.

"Ask who it is first, dear," she said.

I nodded, and, at the door, I called out, "Who is it?"

A raspy, whispery voice came back: "Cutter."

I turned to Miss Lizzie. She nodded. I opened the door.

Mr. Cutter stood there. He was wearing clothes nearly identical to those he had worn in the park—another black shirt, another pair of black slacks. (Those clothes had been somewhat rumpled when last seen; these were not.) The lock of shiny black hair still curled loosely down over his pale, square forehead. But in the light of the hallway, without a pistol thrust into his belt, he no longer looked like an angel of death. He looked like a sleek, improbably handsome young man in his midtwenties. His eyes, I saw now, were blue, nearly as blue as the eyes of my uncle.

But standing beside him was a taller, broader man who wore a gray suit and a gray fedora. It was Lieutenant Becker, the man who had taken me from John's apartment on Saturday.

Becker stepped past me, a few feet into the room. Mr. Cutter followed him. I simply stood there.

Becker looked at Miss Lizzie. "I figured it was about time," he said, "I had a little talk with the famous Lizzie Borden."

BOOK THREE

Chapter Twenty-Two

Standing behind Becker, Mr. Cutter whispered to Miss Lizzie, "I saw him downstairs. I followed him up."

Mr. Cutter must have come to the Algonquin at the suggestion of Mr. Liebowitz. For how long had he stationed himself downstairs? For how long had he gone without sleep?

"Thank you, Mr. Cutter," said Miss Lizzie.

"I'm a police officer," Becker told Miss Lizzie. "No two-bit trigger is going to keep me out."

"Evidently not," she said.

Becker turned to Mr. Cutter. "You can beat it now."

Mr. Cutter produced his hard, cold smile. "I don't think so," he said.

"You want trouble, Cutter?"

Another cold smile. "You got some?"

When Mr. Liebowitz had bantered with the big guard outside Mr. Fay's office, I had giggled, briefly but helplessly. I did not giggle now. The two men were standing only a few feet apart, glances locked, faces grim. Becker weighed perhaps forty pounds more than Mr. Cutter, but Mr. Cutter seemed unconcerned. It was obvious that neither man would back away from the other.

"Excuse me," said Miss Lizzie.

They turned to her.

"Let me remind you," she announced to Lieutenant Becker, "that Mr. Cutter is a representative of my lawyer. As such, he has a legal right to be here. And I insist upon his exercising that right."

For a moment, Becker said nothing. Then he shrugged. "Fine. I'm Becker. Lieutenant Becker."

"I had gathered that, yes."

Becker walked into the suite and looked around. "Mind if I sit down?"

"I do, actually."

He grinned and walked over to the sofa and sat anyway. I had not seen his grin before, and I did not like it. It was a bully's grin, one that showed simple, pure delight at the exercise of power.

Mr. Cutter had followed him in, and now he sat down in a chair opposite Becker, his back straight, his hands on the chair's arm.

I was still standing at the door. I shut it and walked back to the breakfast table, making a wide circuit around Becker, who sat leaning forward, watching me with the same lack of expression I remembered from Saturday. I returned to my chair.

Becker tipped off his fedora, hooked it over his outstretched index finger, and spun it casually around the finger as he glanced about the room. "Nice," he said and nodded. He turned to Miss Lizzie. "Never been in the Algonquin before."

"If you ask downstairs," she said, limping slightly as she walked to the breakfast table, "perhaps they could arrange a room for you." She lifted the teapot and turned to me. "More tea, Amanda?"

"Yes, please."

She lifted the teapot and poured some into my cup. Her hand was rock steady; she did not spill a drop.

"Mr. Cutter?" she said, holding up the pot.

Without looking away from Becker, smiling, he whispered, "No, thanks."

Miss Lizzie set down the pot and then sat down.

If Becker was disappointed by not being offered tea, he did not show it. He tossed his hat to the far end of the sofa, ran his hand through his dense blond hair, and then relaxed and swung up his right leg, hooking his ankle over his left knee. Smiling expansively, he spread his arms along the back of the sofa. "I guess you're won-dering why I'm here," he said.

"I expect you'll be telling us," said Miss Lizzie.

"Here's what *I'm* wondering," he said. "I'm wondering how the local papers'll like it when they hear that the famous Lizzie Bor-den is right here in the city. The famous ax murderer. Hanging out with a kid who's suspected of killing her uncle. Killing him with a hatchet." He grinned. "That's the best part, the hatchet."

"Yes," said Miss Lizzie. "I suppose you would think so."

"It only takes a telephone call," said Becker. "One little tele-phone call."

"Do make sure," she said, "that they get the name right. It's *Liz-beth*, not *Elizabeth*. They often make that mistake."

He smiled his brief, bleak smile. "You think I'm kidding?"

"Oh, no," she said. "You're obviously quite serious."

"You got some idea of skipping town, you and the kid? Forget it. She's a material witness. She goes anywhere, we'll get her back. You ever heard of extradition?"

"Certainly. But we love New York City, both of us. We've no plans to leave. In fact, you know, I've actually been considering the idea of talking to the newspapers myself."

"Yeah?" said Becker. "What about?"

Miss Lizzie took a sip of tea and carefully set down her cup. "About certain police officials," she said calmly, "who attempted to browbeat a frightened sixteen-year-old girl into confessing to a crime she never committed."

Becker opened his mouth. Miss Lizzie raised her arm and pointed her finger at him. Her face was flushed again, and her gray eyes, always slightly protuberant behind the pince-nez, now seemed to bulge. "*No,*" she said.

To my surprise, Becker closed his mouth and sat back.

Miss Lizzie, as I said, was formidable.

She settled back into her seat, sipped at her tea, and lowered the cup to its saucer. "About an interrogation," she continued in the same calm voice, "which lasted for hours, without legal counsel, without food, without any charge being brought against her. Your name, of course, would figure prominently in this account. Yours and that of Mr. Vandervalk, the police commissioner."

Becker shook his head. "Won't cut any ice with anyone."

"Will it not? Perhaps you, Lieutenant, are indifferent to public scrutiny, but does Mr. Vandervalk share that feeling? And there's another detail you might wish to consider. I suspect that any decent reporter would demand to know why two such stalwarts as you and Mr. Vandervalk would focus their attention on a young girl. To that, I could offer only my suspicions—that you did so at the behest of important criminal figures in this city, people like Larry Fay and Owney Madden and Arnold Rothstein."

"That's bullshit."

Miss Lizzie smiled. "Perhaps so. But, as you suggest, for good or for ill, my name is recognized. If I speak to the newspapers, they *will* quote me. I very much doubt that those three gentlemen would enjoy seeing their names associated with yours. And I very much doubt that Mr. Vandervalk would enjoy seeing *his* associated with theirs. I can do all this, Lieutenant. And I will. On the other hand . . ."

She sipped her tea again.

Becker's glance flicked to Mr. Cutter then returned to Miss Lizzie. He tilted his head slightly backward. "On the other hand what?"

"On the other hand, I can continue to do what I've been doing. That is to say, continue my effort to learn why John Burton was murdered. If I do learn anything, I shall provide the information to you, to do with as you see fit."

Another bleak smile. "What're you? Sherlock Holmes?"

"Simply a concerned citizen."

"Uh-huh. Cutter here helping you out?"

"Along with several others."

"You know he's a button man. A killer."

She nodded. "We all have our flaws, Lieutenant."

I glanced at Mr. Cutter. Without moving any other part of his body, he smiled.

Becker lowered his arms, locking his fingers together on his lap. "What've you got so far?"

"Have we an agreement?"

He shook his head. "I want to know what cards I'm holding."

She told him about the conversations with Daphne Dale, Mr. Fay, and Mr. Madden. She did not mention the death of Sybil Cartwright, the conversation with Mrs. Norman, the events of Central Park, nor the safe that Miss Dale had placed in "Jerry Brandon's" library.

When she finished, Becker said, "Not much."

"No." She smiled. "But what is mine, as they say, is yours. Have we an agreement?"

"What's your next step?"

"Sooner or later, I must speak with Arnold Rothstein."

"Rothstein?" He laughed. "*You* want to talk to Arnold Rothstein?"

"From things I've heard, I suspect that Mr. Rothstein is somehow involved in all this."

He laughed again. "What things have you heard?"

"Enough to suggest that I ought to meet with him."

Grinning again now, he said, "Rothstein will fit you with a pair of cement shoes."

"Cement shoes?"

"Before he tosses you in the river." He shook his head. "Playing around with Madden and Fay isn't a great idea. But playing around with Arnold Rothstein is just plain stupid. You'll be dead."

"Then at least one of your problems will have been solved."

He looked at her for a moment and he grinned once more. "Okay."

"An agreement, then?"

He reached for his hat and tamped it onto his head. "Yeah, sure. An agreement." He stood up. "I want one telephone call a day. You give me everything you get."

"Certainly."

"But listen. You leave town, the deal is off. We grab the kid and bring her in. Doesn't matter where you take her, I'll find her. Personally. You follow me?"

She smiled wearily. "Like a shadow," she said.

He nodded and then turned to Cutter. "Like to give you a try sometime, Cutter."

"Pick a time," Cutter whispered.

"One day, I'll do that." He turned back to Miss Lizzie. "I'll see my own way out."

"Lieutenant?" said Miss Lizzie.

"Yeah?"

"How did you learn who I was? Where I was?"

Another bleak smile. "You got your secrets, lady, I got mine."

He turned, walked across the room, and opened the door. Without looking back, he slammed it shut behind him as he left.

"Miss Lizzie," I said, "you were great. You were really fantastic."

She glanced toward the door. "The man's a poltroon."

"He came here for money, didn't he?"

"Of course. That and power are all he understands."

Mr. Cutter whispered, "Why give him Rothstein's name?"

"I had no choice, really. I had threatened him in front of two other people. It was important to provide him with a way to regain his authority. And to provide him with information he could use." She poured herself some more tea.

"He gave in pretty quickly."

She nodded. "He believes, no doubt, that if I keep him informed of our progress, he can maintain some level of control over us. And perhaps provide information to other people. Like Mr. Rothstein."

Mr. Cutter smiled. "You're not going to keep him informed."

"Not with any great accuracy, no."

I said, "Does that mean we're staying?"

She turned to me. "For a short while. I don't want that man coming after us. But we haven't much time."

"You've got five minutes," said Mr. Cutter. "By then, Rothstein will know all about you."

"I'm sure he already does."

"How?"

She raised her cup and sipped at it. "We know from the woman who cleaned John's apartment that Mr. Rothstein had some connection to John. We've spoken to at least one associate of his, Mr. Madden. To two of them if we include Mr. Fay, and I'm inclined to do so. It seems almost certain that someone has informed Mr. Rothstein of our presence."

"Becker's right about one thing," said Mr. Cutter. "Madden, Fay, and Rothstein. You don't want to fool around with any of them. Especially Rothstein."

"I do not intend," she said, "to fool around." She smiled. "But I should like to ask you a favor."

"Sure," he said.

Chapter Twenty-Three

We drove downtown in a long brown Packard, neither new nor old, faintly musty with the smell of old cigarette smoke. Mr. Cutter told us he would be using the car until his Lincoln was repaired.

At Miss Lizzie's request, he had made a phone call before we left the hotel and arranged for someone to pick up our luggage and move it to the Plaza. She had then telephoned Mr. Lipkind and told him we were moving. She had not mentioned the name of the hotel.

"Do you remember where we met?" she asked him. "There."

Miss Lizzie then called Mrs. Parker and told her that we were moving. She used a similar code to tell her where: "The place where you met the man with the amusing hat. Don't say it, but you do remember? Him, yes. There. I'll telephone you this evening."

We had then packed and gone downstairs, where Miss Lizzie settled the bill before we left with Mr. Cutter.

On our way south through the city, Mr. Cutter explained what had happened to the men in the park. Two had still been alive. Both had refused to say who sent them.

"They probably don't know," he said. "They're street soldiers."

"What happened to them?" I asked. "The ones who were alive." I sat with him in the front seat, the two of us separated by his black sport coat draped over the seat's back. Miss Lizzie was sitting in the rear.

"We filled up the car for them," he said. "They drove it away."

"Filled it with the other men, you mean?"

"Yeah."

"The police never appeared?" asked Miss Lizzie.

"No."

"Curious," she said.

"Are you in trouble now?" I asked Mr. Cutter. "For helping us, I mean."

He had faintly smiled that small cold smile of his. "No."

Later, farther south, I tried to learn more about the man himself.

"Do you have a first name, Mr. Cutter?"

"James."

"And how did you get into . . ."

"Amanda," said Miss Lizzie.

"That's okay," said Mr. Cutter to the rearview mirror. "This line of work?" he asked me.

"Yes," I said.

"I picked up some things in the army. Some skills." He turned to me. "Seemed a shame to waste them." He looked up at the rearview mirror, his forelock trembling, then looked out at the road ahead.

"What sort of skills?"

"Amanda?" said Miss Lizzie.

"Sorry," I told him.

Again, he looked at me and smiled. Then he turned back to the traffic.

Miss Daphne Dale lived in a small four-story townhouse on Morton Street in Greenwich Village. The walls were made of spotless pink brick, each brick looking so fresh that it might have been slipped from the kiln only moments before. Flowers in red window boxes trembled brightly at every ledge. A gleaming black front door held an ornate brass knocker at its center. The closely cropped grass in the tiny, tidy yard was emerald green. Enclosing the yard was a fence of black wrought iron, glistening with a coat of black enamel paint.

As we drove past it, I wondered whether Miss Dale, like her heroine, received regular packets of cash from the South.

Miss Lizzie may have wondered the same thing. "It does not

look," she said from the backseat, "like the house of someone in desperate need of a thousand dollars."

We parked about two blocks from the brownstone. Mr. Cutter reached beneath his seat and slid out his pistol. He leaned forward, stuck the muzzle behind his back into his slacks, and then lifted the sport coat from the seat and slipped his slender arms into it.

I had seen more guns in the past few days than I had seen, before this, in my entire life.

We walked back toward Miss Dale's brownstone, Mr. Cutter a few steps behind us. I noticed that his shoes made no sound as they met the sidewalk.

When we came to the house, he whispered, "I'll be out here. I hear anything, I'm coming in."

Miss Lizzie nodded. "Very good. Thank you."

She opened the gate and we stepped into the yard, went up the cement walkway, and climbed up the stoop. She lifted the big brass knocker and let it fall.

Nothing happened. I turned to look down at Mr. Cutter. He stood with his back to us, his arms loose at his sides, his head slowly turning left and right. In the sunlight, his hair was as black and glossy as a raven's wing.

Miss Lizzie lifted the knocker and let it fall again.

A few inches above the knocker was a small glass peephole circled with more gleaming brass. For a moment, the glass darkened.

"She's in there," I said.

"Yes."

She raised the knocker, smacked it down once, then again, more sharply. She raised it again and the door swung open, pulling the knocker from her hand, to reveal Miss Dale, her face flushed.

"*What?*" she said. "I'm *working*."

Her face was perfectly made up: mascara, eyeliner, lipstick, and rouge. She was wearing a pair of pink silk harem pants, red ballet slippers, and a gauzy red top with balloon sleeves and a floppy opened collar. On her head, holding in her ringlets, she wore a pink silk bandana tied behind at the nape of her neck.

"I apologize for interrupting," said Miss Lizzie. "But we need to speak with you."

"You don't understand," said Miss Dale. "I'm *hot* right now. The words are simply *pouring* out of me. This is the best thing I've ever *done*."

"Ah," said Miss Lizzie. "Good for you. I'll simply ask my lawyer to serve you with a subpoena."

I had no idea whether this was possible and neither, apparently, did Miss Dale.

"A subpoena?" she said.

"We really do need to get to the bottom of all this, Miss Dale."

She glanced at me, looked back to Miss Lizzie, then looked around her, down the front steps. "Who is that man?"

"Our driver," Miss Lizzie told her.

Miss Dale took a long deep breath and let it out. "Oh, *fiddle*," she said. "All right. Come on in."

She led us into her living room.

I did not know, back then, exactly what an Oriental bordello might look like, but I suspected that it would look rather like this. The walls were covered in glossy red silk. Round white paper lanterns dangled from the ceiling. A low red silk divan crouched against one wall. Two red silk ottomans squatted opposite. There were several small black lacquered tables. There was a squat black lacquered chest and an upright folding screen painted with cranes soaring over a mountainous landscape. In the air was the smell of sandalwood.

"Have a seat," said Miss Dale. She added, "Please." Perhaps talk of a subpoena had nudged her Southern hospitality awake.

She nodded toward the divan and sat down on one of the ottomans. Miss Lizzie, with some difficulty, lowered herself to the divan, keeping her hands on the crook of her upright walking stick. I sat beside her.

"I can get you something," said Miss Dale. "If you're thirsty? I've got some champagne. And there's water if you want."

"No, thank you," said Miss Lizzie and I repeated the same.

Miss Dale looked back and forth between us then slipped her

hands between the ottoman and her hips. She crossed her legs atop the silk and leaned forward, gaminelike. "So," she said to Miss Lizzie, "what is it?"

"Miss Dale," Miss Lizzie said, "you lied to us."

Miss Dale's eyebrows rose. "Lied?"

"You told us that you didn't know about the safe in John's library. This was a particularly foolish lie, because you included that safe in your description of John's library, in your book."

"Miss Cabot, that was a piece of fiction. A work of *imagination*."

"You described John's apartment exactly," said Miss Lizzie, "down to the bric-a-brac in the living room. You installed your fictional safe in precisely that section of the bookshelf occupied by the real safe. No, Miss Dale. You knew. My question is, why deny the knowledge?"

Miss Dale looked back and forth once more. She took another deep breath, slipped her hands free, and crossed her arms beneath her breasts. "I was in shock."

"Shock," Miss Lizzie repeated. She adjusted her pince-nez.

"At Johnny's death," said Miss Dale. "I'd seen the poor man on Friday, only two days before. We'd been close once, extremely close, as you know, and we were still the very best of friends. I was horrified to hear he was dead. Absolutely *horrified*."

"It was shock that compelled you to lie."

"I wasn't *lying*, exactly. I just didn't want to deal with it—with Johnny's death, I mean."

"You didn't wish to become involved."

Leaning forward, she placed the palms of her hand flat against the ottoman. "No, no, it wasn't that. It's just that—in a way, you know?—if I didn't think about things, didn't *linger* over them, then I wouldn't have to realize that Johnny was . . . gone." She lowered her head.

"Was that why you lied about the money?"

She looked up, confused. "What money?"

"The money you said you wanted to borrow from John."

"But that was the *truth*. I needed that money."

"For what?"

"I *told* you. An investment opportunity."

"Which investment opportunity?"

She shook her head. "I'm not at liberty to say. Honestly, I'm not. It was confidential."

Miss Lizzie looked at her for a moment then said, "Why is it, Miss Dale, that you never mentioned John's connection to Arnold Rothstein?"

She blinked. "Who?"

Miss Lizzie's face was suddenly a bright red, nearly the color of the divan. Swiftly, she raised the walking stick and slammed its rubber tip down against the floor: *thump.* Her fingers curled around its crook, and she leaned over it, her eyes narrow now, her jowls trembling. "You *silly* girl! You moronic little twit! Even *you* can't be that impossibly stupid. Do you *really* expect me to believe that you've never heard of *Arnold Rothstein?*"

Although I had seen Miss Lizzie's anger before, the outburst startled me.

It startled Miss Dale, too. She snapped back on the ottoman as though struck in the face. "I . . ." She shook her head and leaned forward again. She uncrossed her legs and put her feet on the floor with her hands on her lap. Her mouth went firm. "I don't have to sit still for this."

"No," said Miss Lizzie. "You may stand if you wish." The redness had left her face. "But you *will* hear what I have to say, Miss Dale. I am going to the police with all the information I have. Everything. I shall let them know about your argument with John, in his apartment, some time ago. The argument that concerned Mr. Joe Walters. That concerned Mr. Arnold Rothstein. And I—"

"Who *told* you that?"

"That hardly matters. I—"

"That bitch. That *bitch.* It was her, wasn't it?"

"Miss Dale, if you interrupt me one more time, I am leaving and I am going directly to the police station."

"It was the bitch, wasn't it? Mrs. Goddamn Norman."

Pushing down on her walking stick, Miss Lizzie rose from the divan. "Enough."

Miss Dale reached out. "No, wait! You can't go to the police!"

"Why not?"

"The police—they're as bad as the others!"

"What others?"

"Rothstein, those people. You'll get me killed." She shook her head quickly. "You don't understand."

Miss Lizzie lowered herself to the divan. "Explain it to me."

Miss Dale took a deep breath. "I don't know where to start."

"With Friday," said Miss Lizzie. "What did you want from John? The truth, now."

"You can't go to the police. Promise me that. Promise me you won't go to the police."

"So long as I believe what you tell me. What did you want from John?"

The woman looked at me then looked back at Miss Lizzie. She folded her arms under her breasts again. "Opium," she said.

Chapter Twenty-Four

"Opium," said Miss Lizzie, her voice flat.

"It's not that big a thing," said Miss Dale. "Honestly. Tons of people use it. You'd be surprised."

"Possibly so."

"You know that before the war, it wasn't even illegal here in the United States."

"Yes. The Harrison Narcotic Act. 1914."

"That's exactly right."

"And you and John used it."

"Once in a while." She briefly glanced at me then looked back to Miss Lizzie. "When we were together? You understand?"

"Yes, yes. You smoked it?"

"We ate it. You can eat it. A lot of people don't know that."

"How interesting."

"Johnny would roll it up into these cute little black pellets, and we'd swallow them with champagne—we liked Veuve Clicquot. After a while, about twenty minutes, you start to feel it. It's this deep, warm, wonderful . . . softness? It just slows everything down, makes everything all languid and mellow."

"Lovely. But you hadn't been involved with John for some time. Why should you ask him for opium now?"

"The thing of it is, once in a while—you know?—I still like to take it. Not every day or anything—I mean, I'm not an *addict*. I take it maybe once, twice a month at the *most*. It helps me wonderfully with my work. Relaxes me. And I had this little man who'd get it for me? But he left town a few weeks ago, and I didn't know anyone else who had it. I was high and dry, so to speak. So when I saw Johnny last Friday, I asked him if he had any."

"And he told you no."

"Yes, but I didn't believe him. Johnny *always* had it. The whole time we were together he had it. And so I got . . . upset with him. I admit it, I overreacted. It was utterly foolish of me. And I regretted it right away. I told you that."

"Where did John obtain the opium?"

"Europe. You knew that he was always going off to Europe?"

"To buy opium?"

"No, no, no. He went there on, uh, business. It's just that opium is terribly easy to find over there. They've got different laws? So whenever he went, he always brought some back. Not a lot—maybe half a pound or so? But he always brought some back."

"What sort of business was he conducting in Europe?"

Miss Dale looked to her left then back at Miss Lizzie. "I'm not exactly sure."

"You clearly have some idea."

She frowned. "I can't swear to it."

"You needn't. Just tell us what you believe."

"I think," she said, "I think he was helping Arnold Rothstein bring in liquor shipments. From Europe to here."

"Liquor shipments?"

"Scotch, gin—"

"Yes, yes, but what makes you think so?"

"That little man you mentioned? Walters. Joe Walters. He works for Rothstein. And every time Johnny came back from Europe, Walters would come around to the apartment."

"How do you know that Mr. Walters works for Mr. Rothstein?"

"I met Rothstein once. Walters was with him."

"Where was this?"

"You know Lindy's? That delicatessen thing on Broadway? In the theater district?"

"I've heard of it."

"That's where Rothstein works. I mean, he uses it as a kind of office. There's this booth, over in the corner, in the back, and he's there every night. Seven nights a week. That's what Johnny told me."

"And how did the meeting come about?"

"It just sort of happened. We were walking along Broadway once, Johnny and I, after dinner, a lovely dinner, and we came to Lindy's, and he said, 'Come on in. I want you to meet someone.' This was around ten o'clock, and the place was absolutely packed. A lot of show-business types, actors and actresses—famous people, some of them. But also a lot of these very shady characters, little men in checkered suits and big oafish-looking men who look like prizefighters. Bent noses and swollen ears and things? And prostitutes—you could tell they were prostitutes because they wore these horrible flashy clothes, black mesh stockings, *frightful* stuff."

"Yes, yes," said Miss Lizzie. "Getting back to Mr. Rothstein."

"He was sitting in the back, like I said. In his booth. There were a bunch of people standing around, waiting to talk to him, and there was a tall man, very thin but not bad-looking in a dark-ish way, with a kind of hatchet face? He was acting like a guard, keeping everyone back. Johnny knew him—the guard, I mean. He called him Jack and shook his hand, and he introduced him to me, and then Jack let us walk right through to Rothstein's booth."

"And you spoke with Mr. Rothstein."

"That's right, yes. He was sitting in the booth, him and that Joe Walters person. Walters was sitting right beside him. I'd seen him once or twice before, like I say, when Johnny came back from Europe. And there was another man sitting across the booth, some-one asking for a favor, I suppose, some *supplicant*. Anyway, Johnny shook hands with both of them, Rothstein and Walters, and then he introduced me to Rothstein. I'd heard of Rothstein, naturally—you know he's the man who fixed the World Series?"

"I'd heard that, yes."

"I didn't like him at all. Not at all. He's got these terrible obvi-ously false teeth—they look like dice or something?—and these beady little brown eyes that bore *through* you. Like they're undressing you? He was all smiley and everything, very polite, but he gave me the heebie-jeebies. I said so to John, when we left. But he only laughed at me. I said, 'John, he's just a common *criminal.*' And he laughed again, and he said, 'Arnold Rothstein is anything but common. He's the man who created the speakeasy.'"

"What did he mean by that?"

"I asked him that exact thing. He said, 'After Prohibition started, he's the one who arranged the first shipment of Scotch whiskey to the United States.' John seemed almost proud of it."

"Yes," said Miss Lizzie. "But that hardly involves John in any of Mr. Rothstein's ventures."

Miss Dale looked down again, examined the floor, then looked back up. "All right. Look. Here's what happened. A couple of weeks later, we were in the apartment, Johnny and I, in the library, and he was putting something in the safe. We were going to go out to dinner. And then the telephone rang. It's out in the living room, the telephone, so he went out there to answer it. I probably shouldn't have done this, but I mean, I'm a writer, and a writer has to find things out. That's what we *do.* You understand?"

Miss Lizzie nodded. "John had left the safe open. You looked inside."

"Just for a teeny, tiny moment. There are these drawers inside the safe—metal drawers?—and the top one was still open a bit, so I eased it out, quiet as a mouse. There was a piece of paper inside there, all folded up, and I unfolded it. It was some kind of invoice or something, some kind of record, and it listed five thousand bottles of King's Ransom Scotch, and four thousand bottles of Gordon's Gin, delivered to St. Pierre Island. That's off the coast of Canada. I looked it up."

King's Ransom Scotch, I remembered, was the Scotch that John always drank.

"Was there anything else on this record? Any names or dates?"

"No names. A date. The week before."

"And that was when, exactly?"

Miss Dale frowned then shook her head impatiently. "I don't

know. Two years ago? June, it must've been. Yes, two years ago this month."

"How is it you remember the numbers so clearly?"

"How could I forget? It was proof that John was up to something illegal."

"Did you ever mention it to John?"

"You think I'm crazy? I folded the thing back up again, lickety-split, and I shut the drawer and ran back to my chair. We went out to dinner, and I never said a thing. But it worried me. It truly did. It preyed on my mind?"

Miss Lizzie nodded. "Tell us about your argument with John."

Miss Dale took another deep breath. She glanced at me again, quickly. To Miss Lizzie she said, "Look, you promise you won't be going to the police?"

"I will not go to the police."

"You swear it?"

"Yes, Miss Dale. I swear it."

Miss Dale nodded. "Okay. What happened was like this: Johnny had just come back from England the day before. This is maybe two months later, after I found that invoice thing. Anyway, it was wonderful to see him. He'd been gone for *weeks*, and I was all excited. We were in the library again, and we were talking about where we'd be going that night, and then the doorbell rang. I started to go to the hallway, but Johnny said don't bother, Mrs. Norman would get it. It was *her*, wasn't it? The one who told you?"

"Forget that, Miss Dale. Please continue."

Miss Dale blew out a small puff of air. "Yes. Yes. All right, so a few seconds later, Mrs. Norman came to the door and said it was Walters. Johnny told her it was all right. And Walters came in. I think he was surprised to see me there. Anyway, he apologized to Johnny for bothering him and said he'd meet him the next day. At some place downtown. Some bar. Near the fish market on Fulton Street? I forget the name."

"The Spyglass?"

She frowned. "How'd you know?"

"It doesn't matter. Please continue."

"Well, after Walters left, I tried to talk to Johnny. I didn't tell him about the paper I'd found in the safe—how could I? But I said I thought it was terribly dangerous, him being involved with people like Walters and Rothstein. They were criminals, *gangsters*. And John just smiled and said not to worry about it. And I said, 'What happens when the police find out?' And he laughed and said, 'Arnold Rothstein *owns* the police.'"

Miss Dale frowned. "And then things just went totally downhill from there. I said some things I shouldn't have said, probably. Johnny said some things. I told him I would *not* go out with gangsters. He said, fine. He said no one was going to tell him who he could see and who he couldn't."

"And shortly after this," said Miss Lizzie, "you and John ended your relationship."

Another frown. "That nigger bitch again."

"Miss Dale?"

"Yes. All right—*yes*, damn it. But the thing is, I honestly wasn't trying to . . . control Johnny. I wasn't trying to run his life. I was worried. I was truly worried that he'd get hurt. Or get himself killed. And look. Look what happened. I was right."

Miss Lizzie nodded.

"If he'd listened to me . . ." She lowered her head once again, and for several moments she said nothing. Her shoulders shook once. When she looked back up, her face was streaked with mascara. "I really did care about him, you know. I loved him. I truly did love him."

She sniffled. "He was the most beautiful man I ever met. Oh, *shit*," she said. She gasped and then lowered her head once more. She raised her knees to her face and wrapped her arms over her head, as though trying to disappear, and then she began to sob—deep, heavy, coughing sobs that wracked her entire body.

Miss Lizzie and I sat there as the sound filled the room. I did not know what to say or do. I had not liked Miss Dale. She had said things about John today that would forever change the way I thought about him. She was shallow, she was petty, and she was a bigot. She dramatized herself so often and so easily that it was diffi-cult to know what, if anything, she was actually feeling. Perhaps she sometimes did not know herself. But at the moment, she seemed to be genuinely suffering.

Miss Lizzie said, "Miss Dale?"

Without looking up, her voice small and muffled, she said, "What?"

"Is there some place you can go? Out of the city?"

Miss Dale lifted her head and used the back of her hand to wipe at the black blotches beneath her eyes. "What?" She coughed.

"I believe that you should leave the city. The other day I men-tioned a friend of John's. Sybil Cartwright. You remember? She was murdered yesterday. Very likely she died because she knew some-thing about John. Perhaps the same things that you know."

"Murdered?"

"By the same person, I believe, who murdered John."

"Rothstein?"

"I don't know."

"But I . . . You think I'm in *danger*?"

"I believe that you could be. Is there some place you can go?"

She sniffled again. "I don't know. Maybe. Long Island. I know some people on Long Island. For how long?"

"I shouldn't think for very long. A few days, perhaps."

"But what about my work?"

"Bring it with you, of course."

"But it's so hard to *concentrate* when I'm with someone else."

Miss Lizzie nodded. "I'm sure. But it will be harder still when you're dead."

Miss Dale blinked at her. She sniffled once more and then wiped at her nose with the knuckle of her index finger. "Do you really think I should go away?"

"I do. As soon as possible. And now we must take our own leave. Thank you for your help."

Chapter Twenty-Five

"Where to?" said Mr. Cutter, after we had all climbed back into the Packard.

"A bar called the Spyglass," said Miss Lizzie. "Do you know it?"

"Over on the east side," he said. "Near Fulton Street."

"Yes."

He reached back, plucked his pistol from behind him, and leaned forward to slip it under the seat. "Who're we looking for?"

"A man named Joe Walters."

He turned the key in the ignition, revved the engine gently, and glanced in the rearview mirror. "Probably won't be there," he said and eased the car away from the curb.

"You know him?" asked Miss Lizzie.

"Used to work for Rothstein."

"He used to?"

"Rothstein dumped him."

"Why?"

"Turned into a doper. An addict. Rothstein didn't want him around."

"When did this happen?"

"Last year sometime."

"Do you know where we might find him?"

He shook his head. "Keeping low these days."

"Perhaps someone at the Spyglass can tell us."

"Maybe," he said. He did not sound convinced.

Miss Lizzie said to me, "Amanda?"

I was looking out the passenger window, watching the houses slip by. "Yes?"

"Are you all right?"

"Yes."

"You're very quiet."

For a moment I said nothing. "Mr. Liebowitz was right, wasn't he?"

"About what, dear?"

"When he said that we don't always know who people really are. Even if we know them for a long time."

"Well, yes," she said. "I'm afraid he was."

I felt at the moment rather as I had felt on Saturday, when I rode in the car with Lieutenant Becker. Back then—had it been only two days before?—it was New York that had changed. John's death had all at once transformed it from a wild, extravagant, welcoming metropolis, a city of infinite excitement and infinite possibility, to a gray, cramped, lonely, and frightening place.

Even though I had met him only days ago, he had become someone I admired and trusted. He had made me feel like an adult. Now, suddenly, he was a complete stranger. A bootlegger. A gangster. An opium eater. And God knows what else. I remembered him in the kitchen that Friday night, his tie loosened, his cuffs rolled back.

"I've got something for you," he said.

"For me?"

He smiled, stood up, put his glass on the table, and walked over to the icebox. He opened it, reached in, and pulled out a small square box of shiny golden cardboard, about six by six inches, tied with glossy black ribbon. He crossed the floor and handed it to me.

"What is it?" I asked him, taking it.

"Open it."

Inside, lying amid whispering white tissue paper, was an extravagant velvety orchid, creamy yellow and brilliant scarlet against a feathery spray of green.

I looked up at him.

He said, "Is it all right?"

I looked out the window at the houses flashing by. Blank, nondescript. But how many secrets, black and tawdry, crouched behind the clapboard and brick?

Miss Lizzie read my mind—which could not, I suppose, have been difficult. She said, "No matter what John did, Amanda, it doesn't change how he felt about you."

I continued to stare out the window.

"Do you remember what Mrs. Norman told you?" she said. "How excited he was about your coming? And what Mr. Cooper said? How fond he was of you?"

I swung around to face her. "Miss Lizzie, he was *lying* to me. He wasn't who he *pretended* to be."

Mr. Cutter glanced over in my direction, then looked back at the road.

"He never lied to you, dear," said Miss Lizzie. "He never said anything, one way or the other, about drugs, did he? He never said anything about Arnold Rothstein. And as for him pretending to be other than he was—we all do that, Amanda. I doubt that any of us could remain in this world if we didn't."

"He was breaking the law."

"So it seems. It might, however, be wisest to withhold judgment until you know the complete truth."

"But that's the whole point, isn't it? That's what Mr. Liebowitz said. We can't ever *know* the complete truth."

"Yes," she said and smiled. "That is indeed the whole point."

It was chaos. The odor of fish and ammonia filled the air. The streets were packed with large rumbling trucks, all of them, it seemed, frantically honking their horns. On the narrow sidewalks, seamen sauntered, businessmen bustled, drifters drifted. I saw no women.

I heard the sound of a ship's horn, from far off on the river, distant and removed.

But at that point, a kind of numbness had settled over me, and everything seemed distant and removed.

Mr. Cutter turned the car to the right, down a narrow street

not much wider than an alleyway. We passed a series of small, con-
stricted, forlorn-looking shops, all their windows fogged with dust:
a chandlery, a laundry, and a produce market. Then, on our right,
we saw the bar we wanted. It was advertised by a swinging wooden
sign, the paint chipped and faded, hanging slightly askew over the
narrow entranceway. On it, below the name, was the silhouette of a
black spyglass.

There were fewer people here. Mr. Cutter drove the Packard
some thirty or forty feet beyond the bar and then gently eased the
car up onto the sidewalk, the right wheels coming to a stop only
two feet from a sooty brick wall.

He turned off the ignition. "Okay," he said. "Be best if you two
stay in the car."

He leaned forward, tugged the pistol from beneath the seat, and
slipped it behind his back. He turned to face Miss Lizzie. "You have
any cash, Miss Borden?"

"How much do you need?"

"Couple of twenties."

"Of course." She opened her purse, took out her wallet, opened
it, peeled out two twenty-dollar bills, and handed them to him.

He tucked them into the breast pocket of his coat. "You have a
watch?"

"Yes. Do you need that as well?"

"You do. Can you drive a car?"

"Yes."

"The key's in the ignition. If I'm not back in ten minutes, you
get behind the wheel and you take off."

"You are alarming me, Mr. Cutter."

"Go to the Plaza, then call Morrie Lipkind. He'll send Robert
over."

"Yes. Very well."

"Lock your door." He turned back to me, his curl of black hair
swaying. "Yours, too. And mine. And roll up your window."

I nodded.

He opened the door and stepped out. Mechanically, I locked my door, slid over, locked his, slid back, and rolled my window up. In the rear seat, Miss Lizzie locked her door then shifted over to her left and locked the other.

I looked at her. "Is this a good idea?"

She was peering down at her watch. She looked up at me. "Mr. Cutter must know what he's doing."

"Are you sure?"

She smiled. "I am, let us say, hopeful."

We sat there. Waiting. Waiting some more.

"How much time?" I asked her.

"He's been gone for five minutes."

We sat.

I said, "Do you think that John really gave her an emerald necklace?"

"Miss Dale, you mean?"

"Yes."

"I don't know. I could've asked her, I suppose. But I was happy to leave when we did. I didn't find her an altogether—"

From behind us came an abrupt, muffled *pop*, like a car backfiring.

"—admirable person," she finished. She turned around to look through the rear window.

I was looking through it too. "Was that a gun?" I said.

"I hope not."

I saw a figure coming toward us, from behind, moving swiftly. "Is that . . ."

"Yes," she said. "Quickly, Amanda. Unlock his door."

I pushed myself over, unlocked the door, and pushed myself back.

Mr. Cutter swung the door open, flung himself in, turned the ignition, revved the engine, and jerked the wheel to the left. The car jounced off the sidewalk, shuddered, and then went shooting forward. Coming off him, I could smell the same acrid odor of gunpowder that I noticed in the park.

With his right hand, he pulled the pistol from behind him and shoved it under the seat.

"Okay," he said and ran his hand back through his hair.

"A problem?" said Miss Lizzie.

He shook his head. "I got his address."

"Was that a gunshot?" she asked him.

"Mine."

"It was necessary, I presume."

"Seemed to be."

Chapter Twenty-Six

The week previous, when I had been wandering, enraptured, through the city, I had made a brief foray into Chinatown. For a while, I had been captivated by the unfamiliar people pattering and chattering down the busy streets, all of them looking small and sturdy and self-contained. I had been fascinated by the incomprehensible ideograms emblazoned across the windows, and by the tiny smoke-filled shops and the bizarre foodstuffs crammed onto the counters within or hanging from the walls: vegetables I had never seen, orange-stained ducks and chickens, unidentifiable rusty slabs of meat.

But after a few moments, the foreignness began to unsettle me. I was an outsider, an alien here, and as often happens, uneasiness began to feed upon itself. Scenes from half-remembered stories rose up, unbidden, and hovered between the streets I walked and me. Vicious tong wars. Suffocating opium dens. White slavers snatching up naive young girls . . .

It was absurd, of course, and my response was deplorable, for I quickly reversed my steps and returned to Little Italy, where the language spoken was not quite so alien and the people seemed more familiar.

Now I was back in Chinatown. It was still alien and still unsettling.

Mr. Cutter drove through the dark, narrow streets, easing his way past the people hustling across them. We went by jewelry stores, more food shops, a tailor that offered "Ladies Dresses Made to Order in Chinese Styles," and countless tiny emporiums whose windows were cluttered with paper fans, paper kites, jade and ivory figurines, and precarious pyramids of wooden boxes, lacquered red and black.

He turned onto Pell Street, drove for a block, and then rolled the car up against the curb and stopped. He reached down and plucked the gun from beneath the seat, leaned forward, and shoved it behind his back.

"Twenty minutes," he said. "Keys are in the ignition."

Miss Lizzie said, "Should we lock the doors?"

"Couldn't hurt," he said.

Chinese people scuttled past the car, all of them ignoring it and us.

Amid the crowd, I saw a thin, beautiful young girl, perhaps my age, float by in a long red dress with a high collar, her hair spread like a shiny black cape across her delicate square shoulders. She held her head high, and she seemed utterly remote, utterly untouchable. My envy of her, of her impregnable self-assurance, was almost painful.

I asked over my shoulder, "Did you ever go to China, Miss Lizzie?"

"No," she said. "I should have. I always wanted to see it. Siam, as well, and Japan."

"Why?"

"Being in a foreign country, it seems to me, is one of the best ways to discover who you are. And the more foreign the country, the more compelling the discovery."

Over the years, in various parts of the world, I have remembered those words.

Now I said, "But you never went."

"No. A failure of nerve, perhaps."

I turned toward her. I could not imagine her nerve ever failing.

She smiled at me. "Or perhaps I simply reached a stage at which I wanted to discover no more about myself. Which amounts to the same thing, of course."

We talked for a bit longer, idly, about life, about families, about the police in New York City. She held her watch in her lap and glanced down at it every so often. After a while, she began to glance down at it more frequently.

Abruptly, someone rapped at the driver's window, startling me.

It was Mr. Cutter holding onto the arm of someone, or something, in a ragged black topcoat.

I leaned over and unlocked the door. He heaved it open, reached in his hand, unlocked the rear door, then heaved that open. I heard him say, "*In*," and the ragged topcoat, like a bundle of dirty laundry, toppled into the backseat.

With it, billowing across the car, came the foulest combination of smells I had ever experienced. The pungent stench of old sweat—sharper, even, than the peppery stench of Mrs. Hadley, the prison matron—was muddled with the penetrating acid reek of ancient urine and with something else, something dense and loathsome and fiercely dark. Reflexively, I coughed and looked away. I rolled down my window. I heard Miss Lizzie roll down hers. I sucked in some air.

Mr. Cutter swung into the car. "Sorry," he said, and pulled the door shut. He, too, rolled down his window. "He won't talk without an audience. Meet Joe Walters."

"I don't want no tricks," said the man in the ragged topcoat.

He was perhaps in his fifties; it was impossible to tell. Beneath that horrible coat he wore a tattered yellow sweater and a pair of stained, sagging black pants. His soiled gray socks were slumped down below his bruised ankles above a pair of dusty black pants. His thin gray hair barely covered a scabrous, purplish scalp. He had not shaved in several days, and his stubble was a dirty white. The rims of his pale brown eyes were inflamed.

Mrs. Norman had described Joe Walters as well dressed and clean. According to Miss Dale, he had been, only two years before, an associate of Arnold Rothstein's, and Mr. Rothstein, we were learning, was one of the major criminal powers in New York City. It seemed impossible to believe that the man sitting across from Miss Lizzie had ever been well dressed and clean, or that he had ever been connected to power of any sort.

"Get goin', get goin'," he said and flapped his hand at Mr. Cutter. "I don't want no one to see us."

Mr. Cutter started the car. "Where to?"

"I dunno. North. Outta here. Across Canal."

The car moved away from the curb.

The man turned to Miss Lizzie and bobbed his head. "Joe Walters."

"Elizabeth Cabot," she said. "My niece, Amanda."

"Yeah," he said. "Swell." He leaned toward Mr. Cutter, and a wave of stink surged over me. "Hurry up, will ya?"

"Calm down," said Mr. Cutter in his sandy whisper.

"Yeah, right," said Walters. "Ain't *your* balls on the line here."

He sat back, tugged the front of his topcoat together, held it there, leaned his stubbly chin down into his chest, and stared steadily down toward the floor of the car.

Mr. Cutter drove out of Chinatown, made a left on Canal, a right on Broadway, and followed that for some distance until he came to St. Mark's Place. He made another right there and then drove for three or four blocks until we came to a small park. He turned left at the park's east side and then drew up to the curb and stopped.

"Where are we?" asked Mr. Walters, looking around.

"Tompkins Square," said Mr. Cutter.

"Yeah. Okay." He turned to Miss Lizzie. "You got money?"

"Yes."

"I want a thousand."

"No," she said.

"You want Arnold Rothstein, I can give 'im to you. On a platter. Cost you a grand."

"I do not want Arnold Rothstein. I want information."

He shook his head. "One grand. That's the price."

"One hundred dollars," said Miss Lizzie. "In cash. Now."

"You know what happens, Rothstein tumbles to this? Me talkin' to you?"

"Mr. Rothstein will never learn that you spoke with us."

"He'll find out. And he'll gut me. He won't do it himself; he's too high and mighty for that. He'll send some muscle. But same deal—I'm gutted, and next thing I know I'm in the river feeding the fishes. You, too, lady. He'll send someone after you."

"Then there is really no point in your talking to us at all, even for a thousand dollars."

Mr. Walters sucked on a tooth for a moment. Then he said, "Nine hundred."

"One hundred dollars," she said.

"Jesus, lady. You got no heart at all?"

"I have one hundred dollars."

Mr. Cutter was partway turned in his seat, his arm along its back. "C-note buys a lot of H, Joe," he whispered.

Walters looked back at Miss Lizzie. "Five hundred."

"One hundred and fifty dollars. My final offer, Mr. Walters."

With his left hand, thoughtfully, he rubbed at the open sore on his forehead. Then he held out his right hand. "Money first."

"Half now," said Miss Lizzie. "Half when we finish."

He slapped the hand against the car seat. "Jesus!"

"Yes or no."

Walters looked around, out the window, and turned back. "Okay, okay. Half now." He held out the hand again.

Miss Lizzie opened her purse, took out her wallet, and opened it.

As she counted out the money, Walters watched her. Furtively, he glanced at Mr. Cutter. Mr. Cutter smiled. Walters blinked and looked back at Miss Lizzie's money.

Miss Lizzie held it out. He snatched it away and shoved it into the inside pocket of his topcoat.

"Okay," he said. "What you wanna know?"

"What was Mr. Rothstein's connection to John Burton?"

"Burton? Who gives a shit about Burton?"

"I do."

"He was a stuck-up society prick. An asshole."

I flinched. Even in my numbness, even after all that I had learned about John, it seemed impossible that anyone could feel so casually contemptuous of him.

"You do know," said Miss Lizzie, "that he is dead."

"Good riddance. A scumbag."

"Do you know why he was killed?"

"No idea. But probably Rothstein pulled his plug."

"Why would he do that?"

"Who knows. Burton crossed him, maybe."

"What was their connection?"

He shrugged. "Burton was Rothstein's guy in Europe. Used to go over there, arrange shipments."

"Shipments of liquor?"

Walters smiled slyly. "That what you think?"

"What I think is irrelevant. What is relevant, just now, is whether you want the rest of your money."

He scowled. "Drugs. Shipments of drugs."

"Drugs? What sort of drugs?"

"Everything. Heroin. Morphine. It's all still legal over there, see."

"Mr. Rothstein is importing drugs into this country?"

"See? That's the thing about Rothstein. He's a fuckin' genius. He's always about a hundred years ahead of everybody else. Prohibition—sooner or later that's over. They're gonna dump that amendment, the seventeenth—"

"The eighteenth," said Miss Lizzie.

"Yeah, right. They're gonna dump it, see. Too much trouble, Rothstein says. Too much crime, too much shit goin' on, the citizens are gettin' all pissed off. And when they dump it, make liquor kosher again, all the money's gonna dry up. So Rothstein, like I say, he's thinkin' ahead. He's plannin' things out, right? He's got the distribution already set up. The boats, the trucks, all that. So he just changes the stuff that gets distributed. It's simple, right? But it's fuckin' genius."

"At the moment, he's still importing liquor?"

"You don't get it, lady. Rothstein, see, he don't import nothin'. Not himself. What he does, he sets things up, you get me? He organizes things. He brings people together, he lends 'em money, he tells 'em how to do stuff. And then he sits back and collects his share. I mean, when Prohibition started, he put together a bunch of guys, Jews and Wops, to handle everything. Meyer Lansky, Benny Siegel, Carlo Gambino, Charlie Lucky. And look how good that worked out—money's still rollin' in, left and right. They're all over the fuckin' country. And now he's settin' up the drug stuff. And then later on, see, down the road, he'll be in the catbird seat."

"But surely the market for narcotics cannot be as profitable as the market for liquor."

"Are you nuts? It's a hundred times *better*. Pound of heroin costs you a few bucks in Germany. You bring it over here, you cut it, you sell a tiny little bag out on the street for a dollar. You make thousands. *Millions*. You're takin' the same risks, usin' the same trucks, same people, but the stuff you're pushing is a hundred times more valuable. Get it?"

"But there cannot be as many drug users, surely, as there are drinkers."

"Don't matter, don't matter. What's it's all about, see, like Rothstein says, is your margins. Your profit margins. With drugs, they're a hundred times higher."

"But to whom will the drugs be sold?"

"Anybody. Everybody. Way Rothstein puts it, people always want a little something makes 'em happy. Takes their mind off shit, you know? Heroin—you get some of that inside you and for a few hours everything is jake. Everything is peaches and cream."

Mr. Cutter said, "That the way it works for you, Joe?"

"Fu—" He cut himself off. He looked down then looked up. "Okay, yeah. I got a habit. I know that. But I dumped it before, and I can dump it again. All I need is a head start."

Mr. Cutter said nothing.

Miss Lizzie said, "I've read that other countries—Germany, France—will soon be changing their narcotic laws."

"Right," said Walters. "Right. Exactly. That's the beauty part. Because Rothstein, see, he's thinkin' ahead, like always. He's setting up things in *China*, so the raw stuff, the opium, gets shipped directly out. They got tons of opium in China—little fuckers over there, they don't know what to do with it. And Rothstein's got those Wops of his—Luciano and Gambino—and they're setting up places in Italy—factories, like—where they make it up into heroin. Presto chango, you got your product."

I remembered that John had been in China last year.

"Okay," said Walters. He looked out the back window then looked again at Miss Lizzie. "What else? You wanna know about Rothstein's frail? He's got a wife, but he got himself a sweet little piece of meat on the side also."

"I don't believe so, no," said Miss Lizzie.

"So what else you want?"

"The reason for John Burton's death."

"Like I tol' you, lady. I ain't got no idea. Yesterday I heard about it, and I said to myself, now what did that stuck-up prick do to get Rothstein so pissed off at him?"

"You're convinced that Mr. Rothstein was responsible."

"Hey. Don't you get it? He was Rothstein's *guy*. And no one's gonna hit Rothstein's guy without Rothstein sayin' it's okay. But if Rothstein wants someone dead, that person is dead."

Miss Lizzie glanced at me. I looked down.

Walters said, "What's the deal with Burton anyways? How come you wanna know so much about Burton?"

"Curiosity," said Miss Lizzie.

"Yeah, well. You know what curiosity did to the fuckin' cat, right?"

"I recall, yes." She opened her purse again, slipped out her wallet, and removed some more money. "Here you are. Thank you."

Walters seized the money and shoved it into his pocket with the rest. "One thing. You didn't hear none of this from me."

"No," she said.

"If I find out you talked . . ."

Mr. Cutter said, "You'll do what, Joe?"

Walters frowned, shook his head, and looked at Miss Lizzie. "Rothstein hears about this, and you're gutted, lady. You and the kid both. I mean that sincerely."

"Fine, Joe," said Mr. Cutter. "You take off now."

Walters turned. "I gotta *walk*?"

"Find a taxi."

Walters scowled again. "Yeah, a taxi, right." He grabbed at the door handle and turned back to Miss Lizzie. "You never heard it from me."

"No," she said.

He opened the door, stepped out, slammed it shut. The stink of him fluttered like an evil bat around the interior of the car.

Mr. Cutter said, "Where to?"

"The Plaza, please," Miss Lizzie said.

He turned around, started the car, and eased it out into the street.

I said to Miss Lizzie, "Is that what heroin does to people?"

"No. That is what Mr. Walters has done to himself."

"He's an addict, though, isn't he?"

"Yes, but at the turn of the century, Amanda, half the patent medicines in the United States contained heroin: cough syrup, stomach tonics, pain pills. I imagine that many people became addicted to their cough syrup. But there was never an epidemic of . . . creatures like Mr. Walters."

"But what happened to him?"

"He has been deliberately destroying himself for some time, I expect. I don't know why. Guilt, perhaps. Self-loathing, perhaps."

"But the heroin helps."

"I imagine it does, yes."

"And John was helping Mr. Rothstein bring heroin to America."

"Yes," she said. "So it seems."

Chapter Twenty-Seven

"Narcotics?" said Mr. Liebowitz.

"Yes," said Miss Lizzie. "John was apparently assisting Mr. Rothstein in arranging their importation. Morphine and heroin from Europe, opium from China."

He ran his hand over his slick white scalp and turned to me. His small, neat body seemed to have shrunk. "I'm sorry, Amanda."

The concern made my chest tighten. I inhaled, trying to loosen it. "I'm okay," I said. "Thank you."

"It must have been a shock for you—"

"I'm okay," I said. "Really."

"What did you learn at John's office?" Miss Lizzie asked him.

It was six thirty, and we were in her new suite at the Plaza. My own room was, once again, next door. The living room here was more luxurious than the one at the Algonquin: plush carpets, heavily padded furniture, framed landscapes on the wainscoted walls. Miss Lizzie and I sat on one of the two sofas, Mr. Liebowitz in one of the leather club chairs.

"Not a great deal," he said. "John Burton was well liked. He was respected. He did his job, in a manner of speaking."

"In what manner of speaking?"

"He didn't do it very often. He wasn't *there*, at the office, very often. He seems to have come and gone very much as he pleased."

"His trips to Europe, you mean."

"I mean in general. Throughout the year, throughout the week. He wandered in and out whenever he liked."

"How did he manage to remain employed?"

"For one thing, he brought in clients. He made the firm money. That's not difficult right now, of course, with the market climbing the way it is. But even so, it counts."

"'For one thing,' you said."

"Yes. For another, I got the impression that his employers had been encouraged to give him a certain amount of latitude."

"Encouraged."

"Yes."

"By whom?"

"I don't know."

"Mr. Rothstein, perhaps?"

"It's an old, established firm, Miss Borden. Not the kind of place, one would think, where a man like Rothstein would have any influence."

"I no longer know what to think, not when it comes to Mr. Rothstein and his influence."

"So far as I was able to determine, there's no link between the firm and Arnold Rothstein."

She nodded. "You were going to speak with John's lawyer."

"James McCready, yes. I did." He turned to me. "He wants to talk to your legal representative."

"Mine?"

"Yes. I told him that Morrie Lipkind would be in touch."

"But why?"

"He wouldn't say. But I'd guess that you've been named as one of John's beneficiaries."

"I don't want anything from John."

"It's only a guess, Amanda," he said.

"I don't *want* anything."

"Well, let's see what Morrie learns."

He turned to Miss Lizzie. "So, what do we do next?"

"I should think it obvious."

He smiled. "Obvious?"

"Yes. I shall have to speak with Arnold Rothstein."

His smile vanished. "You can't do that, Miss Borden."

"Indeed I can," she said.

They continued arguing. It was not dangerous, Miss Lizzie insisted. She would speak with Mr. Rothstein at Lindy's, a delicatessen, a public place where they would be surrounded by witnesses. He would not dare to harm her there.

Mr. Liebowitz pointed out that once Mr. Rothstein knew about her, about her interest in him, her life would be in jeopardy. Miss Lizzie pointed out, as she had to Mr. Cutter, that Mr. Rothstein almost certainly knew about her already.

"But what do you hope to gain?" he said.

"I hope to gain a confession," she said, "to the murder of John Burton." She smiled wryly. "But I admit that I am not entirely sanguine about my prospects."

"Then what's the point?"

"The point is that no one, not Mr. Rothstein, *no one*, can be allowed to kill another human being without being compelled, at the very least, to confront what he's already done."

He looked at her for a moment. Perhaps he was remembering that Miss Lizzie had herself been arrested and put on trial for the murder of her parents.

"That's a nice sentiment," he said, "but—"

"It is my sentiment, and I will not change it."

"You don't know that Rothstein killed him."

"I suspect that he didn't. Not with his own hands. From what we've heard, I suspect that he arranged for someone else to do it."

"He'll never admit that."

"Perhaps not."

"Definitely not."

"It still seems to me imperative that he be confronted."

"It's crazy."

"Perhaps." She smiled again. "But who knows? He may suffer an attack of whimsy and reveal everything."

"Yes, and then turn himself over to the police."

"Perhaps not that."

"I'm coming," I said.

"No," said Mr. Liebowitz.

"No," said Miss Lizzie, "you are not."

"If it's safe for you," I told her, "then it's safe for me."

She said, "Amanda—"

"Miss Lizzie," I said, "it was *my* uncle who got killed. *I'm* the one who found him. If Mr. Rothstein did it, then I want to meet him, face-to-face. Maybe John was a gangster and a drug dealer and whatever else. But he was still my uncle, and if Mr. Rothstein killed him, then I want to hear what he says."

"As I said, I don't believe that he actually—"

"Or *had* him killed," I said.

"No," she said. "It is absolutely out of the question."

"If I can't go with you, then I'll go on my own. I know where he'll be. He'll be at Lindy's, that delicatessen on Broadway. Seven nights a week, Miss Dale said. You can't stop me, not unless you tie me up and lock me in a room. And even if you do, I swear I'll get loose. I'll—"

"I have no intention," she said, "of tying you up and locking you in a room."

"Then I'm going."

"Miss Borden," began Mr. Liebowitz, leaning forward.

She held up her hand, quickly, imperiously. He sat back, frowning.

She looked at me, her gray eyes unblinking behind the pince-nez. She folded her hands together on her lap. "Amanda," she said, "you are a spoiled and willful child. I am quite certain that if you ever succeed in growing up, which seems increasingly less likely with every passing day, you will become a spoiled and willful woman."

"I'm going," I said.

She nodded. "On one condition."

"Miss *Borden*," said Mr. Liebowitz.

"What condition?" I asked her.

"That no matter what Mr. Rothstein says, no matter *what*, we will leave New York tomorrow morning, you and I. We will take the first train to Boston."

"Fine," I said.

"But Miss Borden," said Mr. Liebowitz.

She turned to him. "Do *you* want to tie her up?"

Chapter Twenty-Eight

Robert drove us.

He picked us up at nine thirty that night in front of the Plaza. Mr. Lipkind's Cadillac looked as though nothing had ever happened to it; the driver's side window had been replaced and the car had been washed and waxed. If there had been bullet holes in the metalwork—I had not thought, last night, to check—they were gone now.

Robert looked as he always had: tall and broad and handsome in his neatly tailored chauffeur's uniform.

"Robert?" said Miss Lizzie after we got into the car.

"Yes, ma'am?" he said, his deep voice rumbling.

"You and Mr. Liebowitz were both splendid last night."

"Thank you, ma'am. Like I told you, I'm glad I was there to help."

I asked him, "Where did you learn to shoot like that?"

"In the army, miss. In the war. I was with General Pershing."

"Was it bad, the war?" I realized, the moment that the words stumbled out of my mouth, how inane they were.

For a moment he said nothing, and I was beginning to believe that he had not, thank God, heard me. But then he said, "It was the worst thing that ever happened, miss. It changed everything. It changed everyone."

No one spoke. The silence expanded to fill the car. And then Robert said, "How is Mrs. Parker, ma'am?"

"She's well."

Miss Lizzie had called her before we ate our dinner at the Plaza.

Without mentioning where we were going tonight, she had told her that we would be leaving tomorrow morning. Mrs. Parker said that she would try to come over to the hotel to say goodbye.

"You know, Robert," she said now. "You were something of a disappointment to Mrs. Parker."

"Yes, ma'am, I know that. But it couldn't be helped."

"No, of course not. But you've been nothing like a disappointment to Amanda and me. I thank you, once again, for everything you've done."

"Me, too," I said.

We were telling him this, I suspect, because we still had an opportunity to do so. Despite Miss Lizzie's assurances, to me and to Mr. Liebowitz, and possibly to herself, we really had no idea what would happen when we confronted Arnold Rothstein. Perhaps, afterward, there would be no time for gratitude, no time for anything.

"You're welcome, ma'am," he said. "And you, too, miss."

All along Broadway, lights glittered and glared—from theater marquees, from restaurants and nightclubs, from the beams of the endless cars that swept up and down the busy street, their sleek sides darkly glistening beneath the streetlamps.

Lindy's Delicatessen was just south of Fiftieth. Above the wide window at the front was a long illuminated sign that read *World Famous Cheesecake*. Surely, with a sign like that outside, nothing unpleasant could happen inside.

Robert drove up to the curb, parked, stepped out, and came around to open the side door. I left the car, and then Miss Lizzie followed, using her walking stick to maneuver herself onto the sidewalk. People strode swiftly by, utterly indifferent to us—huddling couples, gawking families, predatory-looking young men, swaggering bands of well-dressed youths—all of them cocooned within their own dreams and debts and destinations.

"I'll keep circling, ma'am," Robert told her. "I'll be nearby when you come out."

"I know you will, Robert. Thank you."

"Are you sure you want to do this, ma'am?"

We had not mentioned Mr. Rothstein to him. Robert had obviously heard something from Mr. Lipkind, who had no doubt heard something from Mr. Liebowitz.

"I am quite sure, yes," said Miss Lizzie.

"Mr. Lipkind told me to ask you if maybe you'd reconsider, ma'am."

"I think not, Robert."

He smiled sadly. "Yes, ma'am. That's what he said you'd say. Good luck, ma'am. Miss Amanda." He tipped a finger against his cap, nodded gravely, then walked around the car, opened the door, and eased himself back in. We watched as he drove away, the Cadillac's red taillights smoothly swerving into that glistening, implacable river of traffic.

She turned to me. "Well," she said, "are we ready?"

I glanced through the passing pedestrians at the restaurant's window and peered inside. The place was packed: hundreds of customers and potential witnesses. Certainly, as Miss Lizzie had said, no one would dare harm us there.

I took a deep breath, inhaling that heady, urban nighttime air thick with automobile exhaust and frying food, laced with thin ribbons of perfume left lingering by the jostle of the crowd.

"Yes," I said. "I'm ready."

We walked over to the entrance, slipping past the people walking by, and I opened the door and held it for her. We stepped into blue cigarette smoke, glaring lights, and the rumble and drone of chatter.

The crowd was as Miss Dale had described it. Theater people, most of them laughing loudly. Clusters of men, some in checkered suits, some large and bulky like prizefighters. Young couples. A few vivid young women with tired eyes and tired mouths. All the tables appeared to be full.

A harried waiter, a sheaf of menus wedged beneath his arm, a pencil slotted behind his ear, scuttled up and told us breathlessly that seats would be available in only a few seconds.

"We shan't need them, thank you," said Miss Lizzie. "We're here to speak with Mr. Rothstein."

"Um . . ." he said. He blinked at her, in surprise or confusion. "Ah," he said.

"He's in the back, I believe," she said. "We'll find him ourselves. Thank you so much."

I followed in her wake as she limped, slow but inexorable, through the brightly lit dining area, through the clutters of conversation and raucous laughter. Her walking stick tapped lightly at the white tile floor.

At a corner in the rear was a kind of alcove. Two men were standing at its entrance smoking cigarettes and blocking my view of the booth inside. There was another booth adjoining it, beside us to the right, and that was empty.

One of the men—tall, lean, and dark, with a handsome, narrow face—saw us approach. He inhaled on his cigarette and held up his hand like a traffic policeman. "Sorry, ma'am," he told her and smiled pleasantly. "These seats are taken."

"Yes, I know," she said. "By Mr. Arnold Rothstein. I should like to speak with him, please."

At the mention of Rothstein's name, the two men turned toward the alcove. Now I could see into the booth. On the far side of it, sitting alone in the center of the red leather bench seat, was a tubby little man in thick-lensed horn-rimmed glasses and a lumpy black suit.

On the near side was another man, but only part of him was visible above the back of the bench—the shoulders of a white linen suit coat, and above those, a pair of slightly protuberant ears on a head of slicked-down, thinning black hair.

The tall man who had stopped Miss Lizzie now leaned toward this man and whispered something. The man in the booth whispered something back. The tall man turned back to Miss Lizzie. "Your name, ma'am?"

"Lizbeth Borden," she said. The tall man's eyes flickered once, very briefly, and then he leaned toward the man in the linen jacket and whispered again. The man in the jacket nodded, raised his left hand, pointed a finger at the tubby little man across from him, and jerked his thumb back toward the restaurant and us.

The tubby man nodded quickly, and then he shifted and bobbed his heavy body from the bench. Still nodding, he stepped between the two men standing guard and then scurried between Miss Lizzie and me. He seemed pleased to be leaving. A droplet of sweat fell from his round chin.

The tall man said to Miss Lizzie, "If you'll have a seat, ma'am. You, too, miss. Right in there." He nodded to the empty bench.

I slid in first. As Miss Lizzie eased herself in, I looked at Arnold Rothstein.

In his early forties, a few pounds overweight, he was smiling pleasantly at me, his pale, oval face looking open and friendly. His hair was combed back from a smooth, round forehead. His eyes were brown and alert, beaming with intelligence. There was a faint, self-indulgent puffiness around his cheeks, but his features were regular: a sharp nose, a small mouth, and a sharp chin. Beneath the linen jacket, he wore an off-white silk shirt and a sky-blue bow tie. On the table before him was a tall glass of milk, a small black leather notebook, and a Montblanc pen.

He did not look like the "Napoleon of Crime," like someone who could organize an international smuggling ring, like someone who could arrange a man's death. He looked like a very well-dressed bank clerk.

"Miss Borden," he said and smiled at her. His upper teeth, as Miss Dale had said, were false—brilliant white, slightly too large, slightly too even. "I've been expecting you."

"I assumed so," she said.

He turned to me. "And you must be Amanda." His face screwed up with concern. "Hey, listen, I'm really sorry about your uncle. He was a swell guy."

I said nothing.

He turned to the tall man. "Jack—"

The man stepped forward.

Rothstein looked back at Miss Lizzie. "Oh, sorry. This is a friend of mine. Jack Diamond. Jack, say hello to Lizzie Borden."

"Lizbeth," said Miss Lizzie. "Miss Lizbeth A. Borden."

Mr. Rothstein grinned. "Say hello to Miss Lizbeth A. Borden, Jack."

"Miss Borden," said Jack and nodded. No expression crossed his thin, dark face.

"How do you do?" she said.

"Okay, Jack," said Mr. Rothstein. "Herd 'em back for a while. Keep 'em there."

Jack nodded and stepped away.

Mr. Rothstein looked at Miss Lizzie. "You want anything? The cheesecake here is terrific."

"No, thank you."

"Amanda?"

"No. Thank you."

His hand dipped into the right pocket of his suit coat and emerged with a small white paper bag. He opened it and held it out to Miss Lizzie. "How about a fig? They're good for you."

Miss Lizzie shook her head. "Thank you, no."

"Amanda? Come on, try one. Look." He reached into the bag, plucked out a dried fig, popped it in his mouth, chewed, and swallowed. "Safe, see?"

"No, thank you," I said.

"Fine." He shrugged, a bit petulantly, I thought. "You don't want anything, you don't get anything." He closed the bag, slipped it back into his pocket, and put his hands together on the table, one atop the other. They were beautiful hands, nearly as white as the glass of milk, the fingers long and slim, the nails manicured. He looked at Miss Lizzie. "Okay," he said. "What can I do for you?"

"You can tell us why John Burton was killed."

He nodded. "You've been asking a lot of people the same question, I hear."

"We have, yes. And some of them have responded to it very badly."

"The circus in the park last night?" He nodded. "I heard about that, too." For an instant, contempt flashed across his face. "Pure stupidity."

"On our part or theirs?"

"Theirs. Someone got spooked, didn't think things through. They overreacted. Muscle over brains. Stupid."

"Whom do you suppose that might've been?"

He shrugged. "Lot of idiots out there."

"Well, then. Perhaps you can answer the question for us. Why was John Burton killed?"

He raised those graceful hands lightly off the table, palms toward us. "How would I know anything about it?"

"Wherever we inquire, Mr. Rothstein, everything seems to lead directly to you."

He smiled and let his hands fall to the table again. "That's flattering, naturally, but I've got to tell you, Miss Borden, you've been misinformed."

"Shall I tell *you* what we know?" she said.

"Sure," he said agreeably. He leaned back against the bench. "You do that."

"We know," she said, "that John Burton worked for you. We know that in the past he helped arrange deliveries of contraband liquor. We know that recently he was helping you arrange deliveries of contraband drugs: heroin and morphine from Europe and opium from China."

"Wow," he said, eyebrows raised. "That is really some kind of story." He grinned at me then at Miss Lizzie. "China, huh? Where'd you get all that?"

"What we don't know is why you had John Burton murdered."

"Oh, I was the one who did it, was I?"

"I believe so, yes. What we should like to know is why."

His face settled into seriousness, and he nodded. "Okay. Let me ask you this, Miss Borden."

She waited.

"Even if all that stuff was true," he said reasonably, "which it isn't, naturally, and even if I did have John Burton killed, which I didn't, naturally, because I personally liked the guy a lot, why would I tell you anything?"

"You've nothing to lose by telling us. You have my word that I won't go to the police."

He was amused. "Your word?"

She raised her head. "My word, yes. And consider that if I were to violate that, if I were to go to the police, of what use could my information possibly be? I've no proof of anything."

He smiled. "Okay," he said, "then tell me this. If you don't want to go to the police, how come you want to know all that"—he lightly waved a hand—"all that weird, fantastic stuff?"

"Amanda was fond of her uncle. She has a right to know why he was killed."

He glanced at me then looked back at Miss Lizzie and smiled. "Well, I'm a great believer in family, you know. I really am. But sometimes the best thing in a case like this is just to let it go. You know what I mean? You do your grieving, and you move on." He turned his cunning brown eyes to me. "Sometimes that's the best thing."

"All we want," said Miss Lizzie, "is to know why John was killed. And the name of the man who killed him."

He smiled. "And why d'you want the name?"

"So we will know."

He grinned. He was clearly enjoying himself. "You plan to whack him? The guy who whacked John?"

"No. We want only to know who he is."

"A little knowledge, you know, Miss Borden, that's a dangerous thing."

"Less of it, sometimes, can be still more dangerous."

He smiled. "Let me ask you this." He frowned abruptly. Shaking his head, he waved his hand. "Never mind. Forget it. It's kind of personal."

"What is it?" she said.

Another shrug. "Okay. Fair enough. You ask me a question, I ask you a question." He smiled again, his sharp brown eyes narrowing. He put his elbows on the table and clasped his hands together. "It's a famous case, isn't it? The trial of the century. I wasn't even alive when it happened, but I've heard about it. Everyone's heard about it. Forty whacks, right? It was a very big deal."

"What is your question?" said Miss Lizzie.

He leaned forward, his brown eyes looking shrewdly up at her from beneath his brow. "Okay, right, here it comes. You ready?"

"Yes."

"Did you kill 'em, Miss Borden? Did you whack 'em with a hatchet?"

Miss Lizzie sighed. "I was put on trial, as you may know," she said. "I was acquitted."

He sat back and spread his hands. "Acquitted, sure. But *not guilty*—that's not the same as *innocent*, is it?"

"I have answered your question."

He smiled again. "Well, now, you know, I was listening real close, Miss Borden, *real* close, and you know what? I didn't really hear an answer. I didn't hear a definite *yes* or a definite *no*."

She looked at him for a moment. He held his gaze, smiling easily.

At last she said, "I understand that you're a gambling man, Mr. Rothstein."

The smile didn't change. "I've been known to make a wager or two."

"Then permit me to propose something."

He waved the hand again. "Propose away."

"I propose that we play a game of poker. Not for money. For information. If I win, you will answer my questions. If you win, I shall answer yours."

His eyes were sparkling. "And what's going to keep us honest?"

"We shall be alone. Just you and I. No one will ever know the outcome."

"Still no guarantee."

"Are you a welsher, Mr. Rothstein?"

Flatly, he said, "Arnold Rothstein never welshes."

"I am prepared to take your word for it, then, that you'll be honest."

He smiled. "No offense, naturally, but how do I know *you'll* be honest?"

"I am no welsher myself."

He nodded. "You play much poker, Miss Borden?"

"Not recently," she said. "But I played rather a lot when I was younger. I should tell you that I was considered quite good, as it happens. Something of a 'shark.'"

He smiled again. He glanced over at me and then asked her, "One hand, one question?"

"Yes."

"Stud or draw?"

"I prefer draw. But I should like to be the one who provides the cards. If you don't mind."

"We play this game and then, tomorrow, you take off, both of you. Out of New York. No more questions, no more running around and bothering people."

"You have my word."

He grinned. "Okay," he said. "You're on."

"Very well. Shall I go purchase some cards? There must be somewhere nearby that—"

He laughed. "Hey," he said. "Not here. Not in Lindy's. Gambling is illegal in the state of New York—you didn't know that? Lindeman, the owner, he'd shoot me dead if I played in here."

"Where, then?"

He opened his leather notebook, flipped to the back, and tore out a blank page. He set that on the table, picked up his Montblanc, snapped off the cap, wrote something across the page, then pushed it across the table to Miss Lizzie.

"There," he said.

She lifted it and read it. "When?" she said.

"One o'clock. Tonight. Can you make that?"

"Yes," she said.

"Bring Amanda along," he said.

She shook her head. "You and I," she said. "Alone. That was the arrangement."

"Miss Borden, listen to me. I don't hurt young girls." He smiled. "And I don't hurt old women, either. What are you to me, you and Amanda? What kind of threat? None at all. Like you say, you can't give the cops anything, even if you *had* anything. I hurt you, what's the percentage in it for me? None at all."

"She is not coming," she said.

He shrugged. "Fine. Then no game."

Miss Lizzie looked down at the sheet of paper then looked up at him. "Why do you want her there?"

He glanced at me again before answering her. "Because," he said, "I want her to see it." He narrowed those brown eyes once more, and once more he smiled. The smile now was cruel, like the grin of Lieutenant Becker. It was in this moment, for the first time, that I truly believed that Arnold Rothstein was an evil man. "And because I want her to hear you say it."

Miss Lizzie was silent.

I turned to her. "I want to come with you."

He held out his hand as though offering me, like a gift, over to her. "There you are. So what is it? Do we play or not?"

Miss Lizzie looked at me. I nodded. She turned back to Mr. Rothstein. "We play."

Chapter Twenty-Nine

Forty-two Pearl Street, the address on Arnold Rothstein's piece of paper, was a small office building. A lamp above the double door burned brightly. I stood beside Miss Lizzie on the stoop as she opened her purse and found the key that Mr. Rothstein had given her. She slipped it in the lock and turned it. The door opened. We stepped inside and closed the doors behind us. Miss Lizzie flipped the knob that threw the deadbolt.

The lights were on in here, too, glowing softly inside glass fixtures overhead. The walls were green, the linoleum floor was yellow, the ceiling was white. There were eight offices on this floor, four on each side.

There is something disquieting about an office building at night. You know that the emptiness is only temporary, that tomorrow morning people will be making vastly important deals behind closed doors, buying and selling, winning and losing. Muffled voices will rise and fall, someone will cough, someone will laugh, and a distant drawer will slam shut.

But at night, with everyone snatched away, hauled up by some huge deep-sea dredge, the hallways seem almost spectral. The sound of your feet on the hallway floor is not only too loud, is it too corporeal, too much an intrusion of the real into the dream left behind by the people of the day.

And, in our case, we could not be certain that the offices behind those doors were, in fact, empty. Mr. Rothstein might have sent someone ahead of us.

At the end of the hallway was a stairway. We climbed it, Miss Lizzie in the lead. At the second floor, as we came around the corner, we saw a hallway identical to the one below. Eight offices. On the frosted glass of the second office to the right, in neat block letters, were the words *Redstone Enterprises.*

"Redstone," said Miss Lizzie. "Rothstein. The same name, essentially."

She put the key in the lock, turned it, opened the door, and flipped on the light.

Inside was a small room starkly painted white. There was no window, and the air smelled of dust and disuse. On the far side, opposite the door, were a wooden rolltop desk and a swivel chair. Atop the desk sat a banker's table lamp. Beside it was a narrow door. On the right and left walls stood rows of gray metal filing cabinets. In the center of the room was a rectangular wooden table, its top covered with green felt. Six wooden chairs surrounded it, two on each side and one at each end.

"Have a seat, Amanda. I shall take a quick look around."

I sat down at the table in one of the two seats facing the door.

Her purse hanging from her left arm, Miss Lizzie went hobbling about the room, opening cabinets and drawers. "Nothing," she said. "Nothing." She pushed up the rolling top of the desk, fiddled around inside for a moment, then carefully drew the top back down. "Mr. Rothstein," she said, lightly clapping her hands twice, "has evidently had everything removed from here some time ago. The dust is a quarter of an inch thick."

"Is that good or bad?"

"I couldn't say."

She limped to the door by the filing cabinet, opened it, and pulled the string hanging overhead. A light flashed on inside. She pulled the string again, and the light disappeared. "A water closet," she said as she closed the door. "It wants a bit of cleaning."

She came over to the table and sat down to my left, setting her purse on her lap and putting her hands neatly atop it as though she were awaiting a train.

I looked at my wristwatch. One o'clock.

Miss Lizzie reached into the pocket of her skirt, removed her own watch, and glared for a moment at its face. "Mr. Rothstein is late," she said. She laid the watch on the table.

"Yes," I said. "He's probably scared silly."

She laughed. Once again, it was a good, easy, up-from-the-stomach laugh. Hearing it, one would never guess that we were awaiting the arrival of a man who could, without a flicker of hesitation, order us killed.

Or perhaps kill us himself.

"Yes," she said, "I'm quite sure you're right."

For a few moments, we sat there.

After a while, I said, "Miss Lizzie?"

"Yes, dear?"

"I just want to say that if things don't go the way they're supposed to . . . well, I just want you to know that I think you've been a good friend. A really good friend." I felt my throat thicken and my eyes begin to sting. "And I'm really grateful for everything you've done." One more word and I would start melting away.

Smiling, she reached out and gently touched me once on the cheek. "I thank you for that, Amanda." Her hand fell to her lap. "And permit me to say that you've been a good friend, too. An excellent friend. I've been extremely grateful for your company these past few days."

"I know I'm a pain in the neck. I know I'm stubborn . . ."

Smiling, she said, "But think how tiresome things would be if you weren't. I regret none of it, dear. Truly. None of what's happened. I regret only the circumstances in which we came together again."

"Do you think—"

The front door opened, and Arnold Rothstein stepped in, grinning. "Hello, ladies. Guess you found the place all right?" He shut the door, and the sounds of wood meeting wood, of the metal latch catching in its metal slot, were somehow final and irrevocable.

"Your directions were perfectly accurate, Mr. Rothstein," said Miss Lizzie.

"Glad to hear it." He stepped over to the opposite side of the table, slipped the paper bag of figs from his jacket pocket and plopped it onto the table. He took off the jacket and hung it over the back of a chair. He pulled out the chair, sat down, and slid it a bit closer to the table. He untied the bow at his neck, letting the ends hang loose, and unbuttoned his collar. He slipped a flat, round, gold cufflink from his left cuff, set the link on the table, and rolled his cuff back. On his thin, pale wrist was a gold watch with an alligator leather band.

"Nice watch," he said, nodding toward Miss Lizzie's.

"Thank you."

He slipped the cufflink from his right cuff and dropped it beside the other. "My father had a watch like that."

"Did he?"

He rolled up the cuff. "Used to keep it hidden in a drawer in his bedroom."

"Not hidden terribly well, it would seem."

He smiled. "I used to snatch it once or twice a week, pawn it, and use the money to play cards."

She nodded. "As you said, Mr. Rothstein, you are a great believer in family."

The smile became a grin. "I redeemed it, every time, and put it back in the drawer before he got home. He never knew. And I made a nice little profit of the deal. Every time."

"Very enterprising of you."

The smile faded. He glanced at his watch. "Okay," he said, "you've got the cards?"

Miss Lizzie opened her purse and took out two decks of Bicycle brand playing cards. "A red one," she said, "and a blue one. Have you a preference?"

"I don't care." He reached into the bag and pulled out a fig.

"Shall I choose, then?"

"Fine." He popped the fig into his mouth.

"Then I choose . . ." She held the red package in one hand, the blue package in the other, as though weighing them. "I choose blue. Is that acceptable to you?"

He swallowed. "Fine."

She tucked the red package back into her purse, leaned over, and set the purse on the floor. She was about to open the blue package when Mr. Rothstein said, "Hold on."

"Yes?" said Miss Lizzie.

"You want to, we stop this right now. You forget the game. You forget your questions. You leave. You get out of the city, you go home. Both of you. No one'll stop you."

She smiled. "Well," she said, "that's very kind of you, Mr. Rothstein, but if we did that, then we should never have our questions answered, should we?"

He nodded. "Okay." He shrugged and gently waved his manicured hand. "Okay. Whatever you want."

Miss Lizzie tugged at the cellophane strip at the top of the package. It tore off before it finished its circle. "Drat," she said. She knifed her thumbnail along the wrapper, working it.

Mr. Rothstein smiled. "Need some help?"

"I am perfectly capable, thank you."

At last she peeled away the clear wrapper. She balled it up in her left hand and looked around for a place to deposit it.

"Toss it on the floor," said Mr. Rothstein. "Someone'll get it in the morning."

"That seems rather cavalier."

"I own the place. Someone'll get it. Toss it on the floor."

"Well," she said reluctantly, "if you say so." She opened her hand and let the wrapper fall to the wooden floor.

She pushed back the lid of the package and pried out the deck. One of the cards, a seven of clubs, skittered loose and tumbled to the green felt of the table. She set down the empty package, picked up the seven, slotted it back into the deck, and began a clumsy overhand shuffle.

"If you don't mind," she said to Mr. Rothstein, "I feel that I should deal first. I am, after all, the visitor."

He shrugged.

Looking down, watching her hands, she split the deck and did a slow riffle shuffle. Toward the end of it, the topmost cards snagged together and stood upright, creating a small, stiff, triangular tent.

"Oh dear," she said. Carefully she straightened them out, aligned the deck, split it again, then did another riffle shuffle, more successfully this time.

She looked up at Mr. Rothstein and smiled proudly. "Rather like riding a bicycle, isn't it?"

He nodded. "How about an ante?"

She frowned. "But we're not playing for money."

"Just to make it interesting."

"I brought no money with me."

"The watch. You put in the watch; I put in my cufflinks." He scooped them up and rolled them like a pair of dice into the center of the table.

"This watch," said Miss Lizzie, "was my mother's."

"You take it off her body?"

Miss Lizzie stared at him.

He waved his hand. "Never mind. Bad joke. The cufflinks are genuine gold coins. From ancient Rome. Ante or not?"

Holding the cards in her left hand, she took the watch in her right, moved it to the center of the table, and placed it beside the cufflinks. She sat back and shuffled the cards again, overhand.

"I think they're plenty shuffled," said Mr. Rothstein.

She set them on the table, using both hands to arrange them neatly, and then sat back. "Cut them, please," she said.

He reached out, tapped the deck, and smiled. "I trust you," he said.

"How nice for me," she said and picked up the deck. Slowly, carefully, she dealt five cards to each of them, leaning over and placing his directly before him, one atop the other: *snap, snap, snap, snap, snap.* Mr. Rothstein waited. When she finished and put down the deck, he picked up his cards and fanned them, tightly, only enough for him to see a sliver of each upper right-hand corner.

Miss Lizzie picked up hers, fanned them much more broadly, and said, "Oh, Amanda, *look!*" She showed me her hand: three queens, the ace of diamonds, and the four of clubs.

"*Hey*," said Mr. Rothstein. "You can't do that."

She looked across the table, puzzled. "Amanda has as much interest in the outcome as I do."

"You just can't *do* that, lady."

"You cannot seriously object to her seeing my cards. What harm does it do?"

He looked between us, back and forth, and finally sighed. "Forget it." He picked up his hand, plucked out a pair of cards, and placed them face down on the table. "I'll take two," he said.

She laid down her hand then slowly and meticulously dealt him two cards. She returned the deck to the table, lifted her hand, and studied it thoroughly. "Hmm," she said.

Mr. Rothstein hooked his fingers into the paper bag, pulled out another fig, poked it into his mouth, and chewed.

"Hmm," said Miss Lizzie. "Yes. I shall take . . . no . . . *yes*. I shall take one." She removed the four of clubs, laid it face down, carefully placed her cards on the table, picked up the deck, and dealt a single card neatly on top of her four. She picked up the hand, looked at it, showed it to me, and then asked him, "What do you have, Mr. Rothstein?"

"Two pair," he said and spread them along the table. He smiled. "Kings and jacks."

"A full house," said Miss Lizzie and spread out her own hand. She had picked up another ace, the club.

Mr. Rothstein looked down at her cards. He leaned back and crossed his arms over his chest. "One hand, one question."

"Yes," she said. "Was John Burton helping you bring drugs into this country?"

"Only one question, and that's the one you want to ask?"

"It is, yes, the one I wish to ask."

"Yeah," he said. "He was." He gathered up the cards. "My deal." Smoothly, he shuffled overhand, split the deck and riffled it once, twice, again, then put it in the center of the table. "Cut," he said.

Demurely, precisely, taking her time and using both hands, she cut the cards.

"Ante?" he said.

"Ante what?" she asked him.

He unbuckled the strap of his watch and laid the watch in the center of the table.

Miss Lizzie pushed his two cufflinks forward.

"That's a *Cartier*," he said. "You know how much it cost?"

"Those are genuine gold coins," she said. "From ancient Rome."

He stared at her.

"But," she said, "if you choose not to ante . . ." She reached for the cufflinks.

"Leave 'em there," he said, and then, his fingers a blur, he swiftly dealt out the cards, each of Miss Lizzie's clumping with the others into a small, trim group directly in front of her. He dropped the deck, picked up his hand, and fanned it.

Once again, Miss Lizzie showed me her hand: three of clubs, five of diamonds, two of hearts, jack of spades, and ace of spades.

"How many?" Mr. Rothstein asked her.

"Two, I think. No. Sorry. Three." She removed three of her cards, including the ace, and tabled them.

"One for me," he said. He exchanged one of his cards, picked up his hand again, glanced down at it, and looked over at Miss Lizzie. "What've you got?"

"Four aces," she said and spread them out along the green felt.

Chapter Thirty

Once again, for a moment, Mr. Rothstein stared down at her cards. Then he flipped his own onto the table and put his arms along the arm of the chair. "What's the question?"

"Mr. Rothstein," she said almost formally, "did you order the murder of John Burton?"

"Yeah," he said. "I did. Your deal."

"Excuse me," I said.

He turned to me. "*What*?"

"May I use the toilet?"

He waved dismissively. "Yeah, yeah." He looked at Miss Lizzie. "Your deal."

As Miss Lizzie collected the cards, I got up and walked over to the water closet. I opened the door, jerked the string that turned on the light, closed the door, and leaned against the wall, my arms crossed. I was short of breath.

I had come in here for two reasons. First, my heart was slapping so loudly against my chest that I was afraid Mr. Rothstein would hear it. He had confessed. He had *admitted* that he had been responsible for the death of my uncle.

We knew now. Or, rather, we knew part of it. We did not yet know why.

My second reason for coming, of course, had been to distract him briefly while Miss Lizzie palmed and disposed of her winning hand. It would not please him to discover that the deck held an extra four aces.

Miss Lizzie had not asked for my help, and she probably did not need it. But friendship, as she said, carries with it concern.

I lowered the toilet seat and flushed.

I washed my hands then dried them with the towel hanging on the rack at the door.

My mouth was dry. There was a small tumbler on the sink, but it was filthy. I ran the water, cupped my hands beneath it, and drank. I dried my hands again, opened the door, pulled the light's string, and went back into the room.

Mr. Rothstein was saying, ". . . family probably came over on the Mayflower, am I right?"

"Not quite so early as that," said Miss Lizzie.

Each of them held five cards. In the center of the table, next to Mr. Rothstein's watch, was a heavy gold money clip. Along its gleaming front sparkled a horseshoe made of diamonds and gold.

As I sat down, Miss Lizzie showed me her hand.

A four-card flush: hearts and a queen of clubs.

"You know when my family came over here?" Mr. Rothstein said.

"No," she said. "When was that?"

"Less than a hundred years ago. You know what happened to the Jews in Europe?"

"I've read about it, yes. They were very badly mistreated. They still are. Did you want any cards?"

"One." He spun a card forward.

Carefully, *snap*, she dealt him a new one.

He left it lying there. "And they ran away. The ones who didn't get killed in the pogroms. You know about the pogroms?"

"Yes. They were horrible. I shall take one card as well." She laid down her hand, picked up the deck, and carefully dealt herself a card.

"The Jews all ran away," he said. "None of them had the gumption to fight back."

She picked up her cards. "Against insurmountable odds? Gumption, in such a case, would seem rather foolhardy."

"It won't happen again," he said. "Not here. Things are different now."

"I am sure they are. Do you wish to play this hand or not?"

He snatched up the new card, tucked it into the cards in his hand, looked down at them, and then, with a grin, slapped all five cards onto the table. "Beat that if you can."

A high straight: ten, jack, queen, king, and ace.

Peering at him over her cards, Miss Lizzie smiled. "I can, actually." She laid out her hand on the table. She had completed her flush.

Mr. Rothstein sat back and blew some air from between his pursed lips. He said nothing.

"Mr. Rothstein?"

He looked up. "What's the question?"

"Why did you order Jack Burton killed?"

"He was shorting me. My deal."

He reached out for the cards, but Miss Lizzie held onto hers. "In what way was he shorting you?"

Still leaning forward, elbows on the table, hands hovering over the cards, he said, "One hand, one answer."

"That is not an answer. It requires clarification."

He sat back. "Clarification."

"Yes."

"This is the last time I clarify."

"I accept that."

"I found out he was making deals on the side. Using my money. My product."

I said, "How did you find out?"

He turned to me. "You playing in this game?"

"No, but—"

"Then shut up." He turned to Miss Lizzie. "My deal."

She pushed all the cards across the table, then drew in the Cartier watch and the money clip and set them beside the cufflinks.

Now as Mr. Rothstein shuffled, he examined the cards. Not obviously—just a casual glance at their backs as he shuffled overhand, to see if they were marked. He split them, reversed the two portions, melded them, then casually ran his fingers along the edges to see if they were stripped. He split them again, riffle shuffled, laid them down. "Cut."

Miss Lizzie cut them. "Shall we ante?" she asked.

He reached into his left pants pocket and slipped out a large roll of cash. It seemed to consist entirely of five-hundred-dollar bills. He counted out twenty of these—ten thousand dollars—picked them up, and smacked them onto the felt. "Against everything you've got," he told Miss Lizzie. He shoved the roll back into his pocket.

"Against the watch and the cufflinks," she said.

"All of it," he said, "or nothing."

"Ah, well." She pushed everything into the center. "You drive a hard bargain, Mr. Rothstein."

I reached toward the bills. He glanced at me. I said, "May I look?"

Impatiently, he waved a hand: Go ahead.

I picked one up and examined it. In the center was a portrait of President McKinley. I had never seen the bill before, and I thought it astonishing that such a flimsy piece of paper could represent so much money. A single one of those bills would buy an automobile.

"Okay, okay," he said and pointed at the stack. I returned the bill.

He dealt the ten cards. Miss Lizzie discarded three then took three more. He discarded one then took another.

His three jacks lost to her straight.

He threw in his cards and sat back. "Cards are going your way," he said.

Miss Lizzie smiled. "Lady Luck. It *is* early yet, however."

"Not that early. What's the question?"

"How did you learn that John was cheating you?"

He looked at me and sighed. He turned back to Miss Lizzie. "Owney Madden," he said. "He figured it out. Come on. Deal."

Miss Lizzie collected the cards and, again, meticulously shuffled them. An overhand. A riffle. Another overhand. Another riffle.

Owney Madden. He seemed to genuinely like John. I had genuinely liked him. The world was, once again, not the place that I had imagined it to be.

Mr. Rothstein plucked a fig from his bag and put it in his mouth. Another overhand. Another riffle.

"All right already," said Mr. Rothstein.

Gently, she set the deck on the table. "Your cut."

He cut the deck, reached back into his pocket, and took out the roll. I counted as he quickly stripped bills from it. Forty of them. Twenty thousand dollars. He returned the roll to his pocket, straightened out the bills, lifted them, and put them in the center of the table. "Against everything," he said.

Miss Lizzie moved all her winnings to the center, beside the huddle of currency.

He folded his arms over his chest. Once again, she dealt out each card carefully, one exactly atop the other. She set down the deck, picked up her hand, and held it over for me to see. Nothing. The only decent card was the ace of spades.

Mr. Rothstein picked up his hand and looked at it. "Three," he said and tossed in the cards.

She dealt them. One. Two. Three.

"And I shall take three, as well," she said.

She discarded three, put down the hand, lifted the deck, and dealt herself the cards. One. Two. Three. She lifted the hand and looked over it at Mr. Rothstein. "What do you have?"

He blew out some more air, disgusted, then pitched the cards onto the table. "King high."

"Ace high," she said, showing him the hand.

"*Shit*," he said. His face red, he swept up the paper bag of figs and hurled it across the room. It banged against a filing cabinet and bounced to the floor.

Miss Lizzie put her hand to her breast. "Mr. Rothstein!"

"*What's the fucking question?*"

"Who actually killed John Burton?"

His eyes narrowed into slits, and he spat out the name—and

the anger I felt when I heard it was blunted by a sad sense of inevitability.

"*Shit,*" he said to Miss Lizzie. "That moron Fay was right. Sending those schmucks after you last night. I reamed his ass for it, but goddamn it, he was *right.*"

Then, abruptly, he stopped. He took a deep shuddering breath. "That's enough," he said. I believe that he was talking to himself, ordering himself to stop. Slowly, stiffly, as though following instructions, he began to roll down his left cuff.

"Pardon me?" said Miss Lizzie.

He glared at her. "You really thought you could pull this off? You really thought I'd spill all this shit and let you walk away?"

"But we had an arrangement. You said—"

"You were a *sap.*" He leaned forward, his hands on the edge of the table. "There's no way in the world you walk out of here." His face was red again. "You're dead meat." He sat back, pointed to his cufflinks, and turned over his hand, palm upward. "Gimme," he said.

"But I won them," she said. "Fair and square."

"Fuck," he said. "*Gimme.*"

"No."

He winced with scorn. "Oh, for Christ's sake." He turned toward the door. "Jack?" he called out. "Get in here!"

I looked at Miss Lizzie. She looked at me.

Mr. Rothstein called out, "*Jack?*"

The doorknob turned and the door swung open. Mr. Cutter stood there, dressed all in black again, his pistol held down at his side. He smiled. "Jack sends his regards," he said.

Chapter Thirty-One

"Holy shit," said Mrs. Parker. She inhaled on her cigarette. "You played poker with Arnold *Rothstein*?"

"Yes," said Miss Lizzie.

Miss Lizzie and I had not taken the first train for Boston, which had left that morning at five o'clock. It was now ten o'clock, and everyone was gathered in a large conference room down the hall from Mr. Lipkind's law office.

We sat in big, thickly padded chairs around a broad circular mahogany desk as flat and shiny as a roller rink. I was sitting in the chair nearest the door, with Miss Lizzie settled to my right. To her right sat Mrs. Parker, wearing a very smart summer dress of pale blue linen. Then came the rough and rugged Lieutenant Becker in a nicely cut gray suit. After an empty seat, almost directly across from me, came Albert, looking exactly like Albert in a three-piece suit that was just a shade too small for his big square body. Next, to Albert's right, were Mr. Liebowitz, Mr. Lipkind, and handsome Robert (extremely dashing in a black three-piece suit). And finally Mr. Cutter, sitting to my left in his usual uniform of crisply ironed midnight black.

Mrs. Parker said, "And he *told* you what you wanted to know? He actually told you?"

"Yes," said Miss Lizzie.

"But what happens now? What if he changes his mind?" She put her cigarette between her lips and inhaled deeply.

"And decides to kill me?"

"For example," said Mrs. Parker, and exhaled a cone of smoke.

Miss Lizzie nodded. "Once I knew where Mr. Rothstein wished to meet with us—an office he owned on Pearl Street—I telephoned Mr. Liebowitz. He came here, to this building, and borrowed Mr. Lipkind's wire recorder. Long before we arrived at the rendezvous, Mr. Liebowitz broke into the office. There is a rolltop desk there, and that is where Mr. Liebowitz concealed the wire recorder and the microphone."

While Miss Lizzie and I were in that office, we had never once mentioned the recorder. Any of Mr. Rothstein's people might have been lurking somewhere near.

Now she smiled across the circular table at Mr. Liebowitz. She said, "I confess that I was very pleased to see that machine."

Smiling back, he canted his head briefly toward her. His bald scalp glinted. "I was very pleased to leave it there," he told her.

Lieutenant Becker was stroking the sides of his jaw with his finger and thumb. He said, "You got everything on a wire?"

"Yes," said Miss Lizzie. "Technology is a marvelous thing."

"That's police evidence," said Becker.

"No," she said. "It is *my* evidence."

Becker frowned. "I can—"

"You can do nothing," said Miss Lizzie, "for the reasons we discussed before, and for several others, which I shall soon explain. Besides, the wire is no longer in New York City. I have had it sent elsewhere."

This was not true. The wire was in Mr. Lipkind's office, in a safe, along with Mr. Rothstein's gold cufflinks, which were the only things she had won last night that Miss Lizzie had insisted on keeping. Mr. Rothstein had worn them habitually; they were well-known, and she had decided it would be a good idea to have access to them.

Everything else, except for Miss Lizzie's gold pocket watch but including all the money Mr. Rothstein had put on the table, she had told him he could keep.

For some reason, he still hadn't seemed very satisfied with the way his poker game had turned out.

Now Mrs. Parker said, "But Rothstein could have sent someone up there, to that rendezvous of yours. He could've set up an ambush." She used the ashtray in front of her to stub out her cigarette.

"He did," said Miss Lizzie. "He sent a man named Diamond." She turned to Mr. Lipkind. "What do they call him?"

"Legs," he said.

"Of course, yes," she said. "Legs." She turned back to Mrs. Parker. "He's evidently a very good dancer. In any event, it was he that Rothstein sent. But, you see, both Mr. Cutter and Robert"—she nodded to each of them—"were good enough to make an appearance of their own. And Mr. Cutter prevailed upon Mr. Diamond to change his mind."

Mrs. Parker looked from Miss Lizzie to Mr. Cutter and then back to Miss Lizzie. "Prevailed upon. Gotcha. But, in the end, why would Rothstein tell you anything? He didn't *have* to."

"Have to, no. But, for one thing, he believed that Amanda and I would never walk out of that room alive. He could say whatever he wished, or so he thought. For another, he wanted a piece of information from me. He believed that sooner or later I would tell him what he wished to know."

"And what was that?"

"It is irrelevant now."

Mrs. Parker looked at her for a moment and then said, "Son of a bitch. You've actually got Arnold Rothstein on a wire admitting that he ordered the killing of John Burton."

He had also admitted to an involvement with both Owney Madden and Larry Fay, neither of whom would be pleased with Mr. Rothstein should the contents of the wire be made public.

"Yes," said Miss Lizzie. "And he knows that if anything happens to me, or to Amanda, the wire will be released."

"Why not just release it anyway? It'd serve Rothstein right."

"I gave him my word."

"He gave you *his* word," said Mrs. Parker, "and his word wasn't worth shit."

"But mine is."

What Miss Lizzie did not say was this: She didn't believe that the New York police would act effectively against Rothstein, even if the wire were released. But she did believe—and, as it happened, she was correct—that she and I were both safe. Mr. Rothstein, she felt, would not risk his own life on the possibility that police corruption might save him. And, even had the police let him alone, there were still Owney Madden and Larry Fay for him to consider.

"And did he tell you who killed Amanda's uncle?" asked Mrs. Parker.

"Yes," she said. "Of course he did."

Mrs. Parker frowned. "But won't he warn the man? Won't he tell him that you know who he is?"

Miss Lizzie shook her head. "Mr. Rothstein knows what would happen if he did that."

"But who?" said Mrs. Parker. She looked around the table then back at Miss Lizzie. "Who was it?"

Slowly, Miss Lizzie turned from Mrs. Parker, sitting next to her on her right, to look at Albert, who sat two chairs farther down, just beyond the empty chair. She smiled at Albert—a brief, brittle smile—and said, "Why do you suppose, Mr. Cooper, that we invited you here?"

Albert had his hands folded together on the table. He was looking at Miss Lizzie, and his square, broad face was as empty as it had seemed back on the very first day I met him, weeks ago, when he arrived with my uncle at Grand Central Station. Now he smiled faintly at Miss Lizzie, and then he shrugged—shrugged exactly as he did back then, as though he had virtually no idea how he could properly answer her question.

"We do know," said Miss Lizzie, "that you killed him, Mr. Cooper."

Albert's heavy eyebrows slightly furrowed with puzzlement.

"Under orders from Arnold Rothstein," she said.

He looked from Miss Lizzie to Mr. Liebowitz, then to Mr. Lipkind, and then directly across the table at me, still apparently confused.

He said nothing—not to Miss Lizzie, not to me.

I wondered why he wasn't speaking.

Miss Lizzie continued, "What we don't know is when it was that you started working with Mr. Rothstein."

Albert turned to her, his face blank again.

"Probably even before the war," she said. "You were Rothstein's creature. Likely you have always been Rothstein's creature—his safeguard, keeping an eye on John for him."

Mr. Lipkind, sitting two chairs away from Albert, spoke up now. "John probably never knew that you were reporting to Rothstein," he said. "But he was careful. He kept all his private business hidden—the drug deals, the money. He hid all of it from everyone. Including you."

Albert looked at him blankly.

And now Mr. Liebowitz, sitting to Albert's immediate right, joined in. "But somehow you found out. Found out that he was stealing Rothstein's money. And you told Rothstein. Rothstein didn't like that."

Albert produced a small frown just then as though realizing he was under attack from essentially everyone in the room, which is very much how we had rehearsed all this.

We had no proof of anything other than Rothstein's word. The only way for us to get Albert to admit to the crime was to force him, or trick him, into the confession. All of us working together, pressuring him, effectively surrounding him.

So far, however, the results were less than spectacular. Albert remained silent. He steadfastly held his folded hands together on the table.

I think that he was deliberately refusing to speak because his silence gave him some level of control over what was happening. We could all gang up on him and we could all attack him, but if he refused to respond, our efforts seemed simply futile. And the longer his silence stretched, the more futile they seemed.

I remember thinking, too, that waiting through his silence made us desperate to hear anything that he was willing to say. I recall telling myself that when he spoke, if he did ever begin to speak, we needed to be very careful not to let him expand his control.

Miss Lizzie spoke, and again Albert lifted his eyes and stared across the table at her. "And you used a hatchet to kill him," she told him, "because at some point, John had told you about Amanda's history—about the hatchet used in a murder three years ago, in Massachusetts. John was in contact with Amanda's parents, and at some point, presumably, they told him the whole story."

Mr. Lipkind spoke up. "Maybe John found the story amusing," he said, and Albert turned to him. "You, Mr. Cooper, found it merely convenient. Of all the people involved in this, you were the only one who *could* have known about Amanda, and about the hatchet."

This was not true, of course. John might also have told Daphne Dale, or indeed anyone else. But Daphne Dale wasn't here, and we weren't trying to coerce anyone else into a confession.

Miss Lizzie's face was grim. She said, "You deliberately arranged things such that Amanda would be blamed for the murder. That was, of course, utterly despicable.

"And then," she said, "you made a pretense of helping us. You gave us Sybil Cartwright's name, but only because you knew that sooner or later we would discover it on our own. We already knew about Daphne Dale, but you believed that Miss Dale was no danger to you or Rothstein; her relationship with John had ended some time ago."

"Miss Cartwright," said Mr. Lipkind, "was a more recent relationship. And maybe she knew what John was up to. And so, while Miss Borden and Amanda were busy with Miss Dale, you went to Miss Cartwright's hotel, killed the desk clerk, and then you killed her."

Mr. Liebowitz cleared his throat, leaned forward, and said, "Lieutenant Becker here went over to Queens this morning, to talk to your friend Mrs. Hannesty."

Albert glanced at Lieutenant Becker, sitting slumped back in his chair, who grinned and cheerfully saluted him with two fingers.

Mr. Liebowitz said, "You may be interested in learning that Mrs. Hannesty has changed her testimony somewhat. According to what she told the lieutenant, it had slipped her mind that you weren't actually her guest on the night that John Burton was killed."

Albert looked at Becker, his face expressionless. If he knew anything about Becker, he knew that the lieutenant was perfectly capable of forcing other people to say whatever he wanted them to say. True or not.

For a moment, no one around the table spoke.

Then Mrs. Parker turned to Miss Lizzie and said, "What do we do now?"

That was the line Mrs. Parker had insisted on delivering. She said that it took full advantage of her "bright-eyed gamine" quality.

Miss Lizzie said, "That is up to Amanda."

Without a word, Mr. Cutter, sitting beside me, reached his right hand behind his back and pulled out a Colt semiautomatic M1911 from beneath his belt. He eased back into the chair a bit, held the weapon in front of him, jerked the slide with his left hand, and let it snap forward. Then, silently, he handed it to me.

Around the table, everyone was absolutely still.

I took the pistol in both hands. It was very heavy. I rested the base of its grip on the wood surface before me, and I aimed its barrel down the table. At this distance, and despite my basic ballistic ignorance at the time, I didn't need to sight along the top of the barrel to know that it was pointed directly at Albert.

We had rehearsed this several times, Mr. Cutter, Mr. Liebowitz, Miss Lizzie, and I. There had been only one bullet in the magazine before Mr. Cutter cocked the weapon. Now that bullet was nestled in the chamber. If Albert refused to talk, I was to fire it up into the ceiling, to demonstrate my seriousness. (We were, fortunately for this piece of theatre, on the top floor of the building.)

Lieutenant Becker said to me, "Hold on there, now."

"Back off," said Mr. Cutter in that whisper of his. Whisper or not, it shot across the table to Lieutenant Becker like a thrown knife.

Becker glared at him, glanced at me, glanced at Albert, and then sat back, frowning. He crossed his arms over his chest.

Albert was staring directly at the muzzle of the pistol. He looked up into my eyes.

"You killed my uncle," I said. "Why, Albert?"

My uncle had been a cheat and a drug dealer. He had—despite what Miss Lizzie said—lied to me by pretending to be someone other than he was. But he had been kind to me, too, and he had been generous. He had been charming and thoughtful and funny. He had made me feel, for the first time in my life, like I was a grown-up.

Albert—a man he called his friend—had taken advantage of him, of their relationship. Albert had walked up to him late on a Friday night, as he had on many nights and days before, but this time, he had reached out and slammed him with a hatchet. And then he had hacked him with that horrible thing, brutally, again and again, smashing away his life.

He had done this knowing that I was asleep not fifty feet away, knowing that I would be accused of the crime.

This whole thing—the table, the witnesses, the dialogue—everything here might have been a fine display of stagecraft. But at that moment, at the very center of my heart, I knew with absolute conviction that if it would help me get to the truth, I would pull the trigger of that Colt, without any hesitation at all, and I would shoot Albert.

I think that Albert, looking into my eyes, saw this.

He stared down for a moment at his folded hands then looked back up at me.

"Okay," he said. He nodded a few times. "Okay. I get it. You love the guy. This I totally get, miss. This I totally understand. He is a guy that people just naturally love. Everybody. Men and women. Kids. With this guy, you could not help yourself."

No one at the table moved. No one spoke. Everyone was leaning slightly forward now, listening to Albert.

Albert didn't look around the table. He continued to look at me and cleared his throat. "He is very smart. But you know that, right?" He smiled quickly. "And you know he is smooth, like silk from China. And he is brave, miss. You never see that part of it, but he is totally, one hundred percent brave in every situation. Brave like an archangel. And in a really sour situation, when things are going bad on you right and left, this is a guy who can save your bacon. Always. In France once—and this is a totally true story, miss—he saves my actual life."

He moved his body slightly toward me and lowered his head a notch as though he were about to confide a secret. He said, "He is the Golden Boy, see. The Golden Boy. That's what he is from the very beginning. The Golden Boy, miss."

He cleared his throat again. "That's why I am there. Like she says." He nodded toward Miss Lizzie. "To keep an eye on him. To make sure he is okay. And I did. I saw to it. I did my job. I took care of him."

He paused and looked down at his folded hands then back up at me. "But see, the thing is, miss, he is a guy who is missing something. Missing a part, you know? A piece of the equipment. It's the part that tells you, 'No.' It's the part that says, 'No, you cannot do that.' It says, 'No, right here is where you got to draw a line. Right here is where you got to quit.'" Albert shook his head sadly. "He doesn't have that part, miss. He never had that part."

He took a deep breath, puffed up his cheeks, and blew out the air slowly from his pursed mouth as he let himself slowly fall back against his chair, his hands sliding along the table and stopping atop the wooden chair's arms.

He looked defeated. Deflated. As though he had been tossed there by the tide.

Glancing over at me, almost wearily, he said, "A few months ago, I hear there is a problem. A chunk of money is missing." He sighed. "A very big chunk of money is missing. It is suggested to me, see, that I find out where it is disappearing into."

He glanced at Mr. Liebowitz then looked back at me. "They come to me, see. I don't go to them."

"I understand," I said.

For a moment or two, he looked straight ahead, not at me, but beside me, past me, into some hidden piece of private history.

He sighed again, and then he swung his eyes back toward me. "I find out, okay? No big surprise. He is smart, and he has been around the block a few times, but I been around that block, too, miss. I know how people hide money. And so I find it. I know where it is. But I inform no one, see. No one. Instead I go to a guy I know, and I say to him, 'Look, there's a guy at the Dakota. I want you to go to him and tell him this. I want you to tell him that Mr. Rothstein knows about the money. You tell him he's got to make things right, or Mr. Rothstein will make them right himself, the way Mr. Rothstein makes things right.'"

As I said, the Colt that I was holding was heavy. Now its barrel swayed a bit to the right and then to the left. I took a deep breath, tightened my grip, raised the barrel, and brought the weapon back to bear on Albert.

Albert ignored the gun. He said, "You know what he does then, miss?"

"No," I said. "What did he do?"

"He laughs. Can you imagine this? He laughs when the guy tells him. You get it? This is what I mean about missing a part. Who could laugh in that situation?"

Albert lowered his head. I waited. When he raised it again, he said, "Okay. There's a phone call I get. Last week this is. I am informed that two people are proceeding to the apartment, to deal with the money problem. I say, 'No. No two people. I will deal with this problem myself,' I say. They ask me am I sure? 'Yes,' I say, 'I am sure.' See, miss, I owe him that. It should not be other people. It should be me."

He looked at me carefully, as though studying me. "It is okay, miss. He never knows what is happening. I hit him from behind, just a tap, and he is out like a light. No pain, no trouble. He does not suffer, miss. I promise you this. Using the hatchet, that is only to make the cops confused for a while. I know I will fix things for you later, see. For sure I will. And, listen, before I forget, there was something that he wanted you to have."

He reached slowly into the front of his coat, the left-hand side.

An interesting thing happened at this point. Despite my earlier warning to myself, I had been lulled by Albert's voice and by the story he was telling. When he reached into his coat, I was genuinely curious about whatever it was that he might be bringing out. And I think that by this point, most of the people sitting around the table felt the same way.

But another part of my mind, one over which I had little or no real control, noticed instantly, as Albert's hand began to emerge from the jacket, that what Albert held in his hand was the brown wooden grip of a revolver. Without thinking about it at all, without debating it, that part of my mind immediately made me pull the trigger of the big Colt pistol.

At the same time, it seemed, Mr. Liebowitz was leaping up out of his chair, next to Albert, firing a small automatic down at the man, firing again and again and again.

Albert's hand flopped down, empty, from his suit coat as his body jerked and twitched and bounced, and then he lay slumped in the chair, his mouth awry, his head lolled to the side. His eyes stared up at the ceiling.

"Jesus H. Christ," said Lieutenant Becker and pushed himself away from the table.

The room stank of gunpowder.

I was still staring at Albert. I looked around the table. Mrs. Parker, her face pale, was staring at him, too. Without looking away, she opened her purse and fumbled inside it. Mr. Lipkind was staring at me then frowned and looked down. Miss Lizzie leaned toward me and put her hand on my arm.

Mr. Cutter was somehow standing behind me. Gently, he took the gun from my hand, shoved it behind his back, walked around me, bent over Albert's body, and examined it. He turned to me. "You missed," he whispered. He turned to Mr. Liebowitz. "You didn't." Curtly, he gestured with his hand: gimme. "The pistol," he said.

Mr. Liebowitz put his pistol on the polished mahogany table and slid it across. Beside him, Mrs. Parker had the lip of the upraised silver flask in her mouth.

Mr. Cutter snapped up the weapon. He asked Mr. Liebowitz, "Traceable?"

"No."

Mr. Cutter walked around my back, past Miss Lizzie and Mrs. Parker, and held out the automatic to Lieutenant Becker. "Yours."

"Fuck you," said Becker.

"You just solved the Burton case," said Mr. Cutter. "A clean kill."

Mr. Liebowitz said, "I'll back you, Becker. I was here. I saw it."

Becker looked back and forth between the two of them. He said to Mr. Cutter, "Gun's not mine."

"You found it," said Mr. Liebowitz.

"Where?"

"In the safe at Burton's apartment."

"What safe?"

"In the library," said Mr. Liebowitz. We went there this morning, you and I. We found it. I opened it for you. You asked Albert to come down here, to Morrie's office, to answer some questions. He confessed then tried to pull out a gun. You pulled out that one, and you killed him."

"Thin," said Becker.

"Thick enough," said Liebowitz. "You'll get a commendation."

Mr. Cutter said, "And your friend Rothstein will owe you."

Becker leaned forward and took the pistol from Mr. Cutter's hand then sat back and hefted the weapon in his right hand. He looked at Liebowitz. "How come I used this instead of my own pistol?" He jerked his thumb toward the left armpit of his rumpled suit coat.

"You had it in your coat pocket," said Liebowitz. "You didn't trust Cooper. As soon as he started talking, you slipped your hand, casual-like, into your pocket."

For a moment, Becker looked down at the gun again. Then he nodded. "That I can sell."

Mr. Cutter tugged a handkerchief from his rear pocket and handed it to Becker. "Wipe it. Don't forget the clip."

Mr. Liebowitz searched around near his chair and found the five spent cartridges he had fired. Using his own handkerchief, he wiped them clean and then tossed them back on the floor.

Mr. Lipkind stood up, his round face grim. "Okay," he said and looked around the table. "Okay. This never happened. Miss Borden, Mrs. Parker, Amanda—none of you were here. You got that? Miss Borden?"

"Yes."

"Mrs. Parker?"

"Jesus, yes. I've got it."

"Amanda?"

I was staring again at Albert. There was not much blood. His black vest seemed simply stained as though he had spilled coffee on it. He looked like someone merely feigning death, playing some morbid trick. In a moment, he would blink his eyes and sit up and smile at everyone.

"Amanda?" said Mr. Lipkind.

I turned to him. "Yes," I said. "I understand."

"Promise me," he said.

"I promise."

Chapter Thirty-Two

Mr. Cutter drove Mrs. Parker, Miss Lizzie, and me to Grand Central in the Packard. Along the way, we stopped at the Algonquin to pick up Woodrow, Mrs. Parker's dog. Mrs. Parker sat up front, the Boston terrier panting happily on her lap. Miss Lizzie and I sat in the rear.

None of us spoke much. But as we drove down Forty-Second Street from Fifth, Mrs. Parker turned to Mr. Cutter and said, "Do you have a first name, Mr. Cutter?"

"James," he said.

"James, that was very brave. Going to Mr. Rothstein's office that way."

"Robert came along."

"Yes, well, Robert was very brave, too, of course. But going up against a professional criminal, even with Robert there—it was still very brave, I think."

He turned to her and I could see his handsome face in profile. His shiny black forelock trembled. "It's my job, Mrs. Parker."

"Dorothy," she said.

He smiled. "Dorothy." And then he turned back to watch the traffic. I thought I heard Mrs. Parker sigh before she turned to look out her window. Over her shoulder, I could see the dog. He was staring straight ahead.

We had said our goodbyes in Mr. Lipkind's office. The farewell was a bit hurried; Lieutenant Becker was still in the conference room, waiting for the signal from Mr. Liebowitz to telephone headquarters.

"Look, Amanda," said Mr. Lipkind. "You just go back to Boston, and you forget all about this."

"I don't think I can," I told him. "Forget about it, I mean."

"You will," he said. "Sooner or later." He was wrong, of course.

"And don't you worry about your uncle's lawyer," he told me. "I'll be seeing that shyster tomorrow. I'll give you a jingle, let you know what happens."

"I don't want anything from John."

"Let's see what happens first. In the meantime, you have a safe trip back." He held out his hand.

I took it, and we shook.

I turned to Mr. Liebowitz and his round shiny head, and I held out my hand. "You were great," I said. "Thank you."

He took my hand between both of his and squeezed it. "My pleasure. I hope I see you again." He smiled. "But in different circumstances next time."

"I hope so," I said. He released my hand, and I turned to Robert. "You were great, too, Robert. Thank you." Again, I held out my hand.

Smiling, he took it. His big black hand was gentle, and his dark eyes were warm. "It's been good to know you, miss. You take care of yourself."

"You, too."

Miss Lizzie said her goodbyes, and then Mr. Lipkind said, "Now get out of here, both of you. Mrs. Parker's waiting."

Just before we left the office, Mr. Liebowitz said, "Amanda?"

I turned back. "Yes?"

"It's over," he said. "Cheer up."

I shook my head. "I keep thinking about Albert. About . . . you know. Firing that gun."

He shook his head. "You missed. I killed him."

"Yeah, but why did he reach for a gun? I was pointing that big pistol right at him. Maybe he wasn't too worried about me. But he had to know that Lieutenant Becker had a pistol, too. And he probably knew that you had one."

He stroked his shiny, bald scalp. "Well, I can think of two reasons."

"What two reasons?"

"First off, maybe he thought he could get away with it and escape."

"And second off?"

He smiled. "Second off, he knew he couldn't get away with it, but he knew he could end it right there."

"But why? Why end it?"

"Maybe he wasn't happy with what he'd done. And maybe he thought you were the only person who had a right to fix things."

"But why?"

"Well, maybe because he believed that you were the only person who loved John as much as he did."

For some reason, this hit me very hard. I felt a bit as though I had been kicked in the chest. I took a deep breath. "Oh," I said.

"You okay?"

"Yes. Yes, I think so." I took another deep breath. "Really? You really think that's what happened?"

"I don't know, Amanda. None of us will probably ever know." He smiled. "Go," he said. "Get to the station."

The Grand Central Terminal was the same bright, bustling cavern it had been when I first arrived. People still scurried back and forth, striding with determination across that huge marble floor. But now I wondered whether all of them knew where they were going, knew what might meet them when they arrived.

The train would be leaving in fifteen minutes. Miss Lizzie bought tickets, and Mr. Cutter found a porter for our bags.

Mrs. Parker embraced Miss Lizzie and then turned to me. "When you come back here," she told me, "you get in touch."

"I will."

She put out her hand and we shook. "I can't say it's been fun," she said, "but it's certainly been interesting."

I smiled and then turned to Mr. Cutter. "Can I talk to you for a minute?"

He nodded.

Miss Lizzie and Mrs. Parker watched as we stepped away from the counter, toward the information booth. I stopped about half-way there, amid the rush of people, and he stopped beside me.

"Mr. Cutter," I said.

His blue eyes looked into mine. "Yes?"

"Did I really miss Albert when I fired that gun?" I asked.

He smiled. "By a mile," he whispered.

Epilogue

And now the final summing up.

As I said in my earlier volume, Miss Lizbeth A. Borden died in 1927. On June 1, to be precise.

Arnold Rothstein died on November 6, 1928, two days after being shot in a cheap hotel on West Fifty-Sixth Street. He had been lured there by a man named George "Hump" McManus, with whom Rothstein had played a game of poker and lost, and to whom he still owed the money. For weeks, Rothstein had refused to pay. MacManus finally lost patience with him. And so, despite the millions of dollars he had accumulated—the millions he had invested in the drug trade—despite his reputation as one of the greatest gamblers in the history of New York City, Arnold Rothstein died because he welshed on a bet.

I, of course, was not surprised.

The American drug trade, the massive enterprise that he had personally organized, got along quite well without him. (But perhaps it wouldn't have got along quite so well if it hadn't been Mr. Rothstein who had organized it.)

I saw Mrs. Parker several times in New York, when I was attending Columbia Law School, and a few times in Los Angeles years later. She died in New York City on June 7, 1967. She bequeathed her entire estate to Dr. Martin Luther King Jr., whom she had never met.

As for the estate of John Burton, John had changed his will during the week I spent with him, and he had left everything to me. Everything, however, turned out to be only his apartment at the

Dakota. Although he was a broker himself, he owned no stocks or bonds, and somehow his bank account had been stripped on the Monday following his death, by whom, no one knew. The police, Mr. Lipkind told me, suspected Albert. But they suspected Albert, too, of emptying John's safe after he killed him, and if Albert had done so, he had left the ten thousand dollars inside it. Albert, of course, was not talking.

Mr. Lipkind came up to Boston, with Robert driving, to bring the ten thousand dollars and to argue with me about keeping the apartment. I told him I would never stay in it again. He suggested that I could rent it out and essentially live off the income. Finally, more to end the argument than for any other reason, I agreed to rent it, provided the rent money went into an account to which I would have limited and only occasional access. I felt that this was very noble of me. Over the years, however, I was—occasionally— very glad to have that access. I finally sold the apartment in September of 1960.

I did not really want the ten thousand dollars, either. But Mr. Lipkind was persuasive about that as well, and later—once again— I was thankful.

That September, before I signed the final papers, I went back to the apartment. It was empty—bare, stripped. I wandered through the rooms: the library, the living room, the bedrooms. Someone had left an old wooden crate in the kitchen. I sat down on it and remembered watching John sip King's Ransom Scotch, his vest open, his collar undone, his shirtsleeves rolled back, his smile flashing.

Sorrow does not ever really pass. It merely encysts itself until a memory blunders against it, and its bitter shell splits open.

My uncle had not been who he pretended to be, as I had said to Miss Lizzie. But, as she had said to me, few of us ever truly are. And it was he who had first handed me the city of New York in all its flash and dazzle, all its beauty and wonder.

Mr. Lipkind remained my lawyer until his death in 1948. I saw him and Robert several times. Mr. Liebowitz I saw occasionally, and then more frequently after I had entered into a line of work not unlike his own. My second husband and I became quite close friends with him. He died in 1965.

And then there is Mr. Cutter.

In 1932, after my first husband was murdered and I required some specialized help, I located him. He provided the help I needed, and we began an association that lasted for some thirty-five years.

Once, on Lamu, an island off the mainland coast of Kenya, we talked about Miss Lizzie. He said that he had never doubted for a moment that she had killed her parents.

"Why?" I asked him.

We were lying side by side on towels spread atop the hot white sand. The sunlight lay on our naked bodies like a weight. He rolled his head toward me, his forelock swaying. "I watched her," he said. "She got what she wanted. Every time. From you, from Rothstein, from everyone." He shrugged his brown shoulders. "If she wanted her parents dead, then pretty soon her parents would get dead."

I told him what she had said, years before, while she and I were sitting in that Packard in Chinatown waiting for him to bring back the scabrous Mr. Walters.

We were talking about the police, she and I—talking specifically about Lieutenant Becker and Commissioner Vandervalk.

"What they tried to do to you, Amanda," she had said, "make you say that your uncle had . . . violated you, that was entirely unforgivable."

"Like Mr. Lipkind said, they don't have anyone else."

"That doesn't matter," she said firmly. "There is no worse thing with which to charge someone. There is no worse thing that someone can do to a child."

She looked to her left, out the car window at the people scurrying across the street, at the passing cars, and then she closed her eyes. For a moment, she sat there silently, and then her body made a small, quick shudder.

On Lamu fourteen years later, the sun leaning down on us, James said to me, "You think that her father . . ."

"I don't know, not for sure."

"Why both of them?"

"I don't know."

A year ago, when his illness had become quite serious and we both knew that he did not have much time, he finally told me the truth about Albert Cooper.

We were still living in the house in Chartres, down by the river, where I have done most of my work. I was sitting beside him on the bed.

"Yeah," he said in his quiet whisper of a voice, looking up at me from the pillow. His hair was thinner now, and white.

"So I *did* hit him," I said.

"In the stomach. The exit wound was hidden by Albert's chair." He smiled wanly. "You were a real marksman, even back then."

"Everyone lied to me. *You* lied to me."

"You were a kid. No one wanted you to carry it around."

"But how did the police explain it—the other wound in Albert's body?"

He smiled. "That was a big surprise for Becker. But he was Vandervalk's boy, and Vandervalk wanted the case closed."

One more morsel of guilt for my collection. "So I was the one who killed him."

"Don't forget Liebowitz. He put five slugs into him. It's a toss-up, I'd say."

I looked off.

His frail hand slowly slid along the duvet until it found mine.

"Self-defense," he said.

I turned to him. "Did Miss Lizzie know?" I could not think of her by any other name.

"Liebowitz told her, before the two of you left for the train that day."

I shook my head. "The woman was impossible."

"She saved your ass."

"Several times."

"She loved you."

I looked at him. "I suppose she did."

His hand tightened briefly, gently, on mine. "So do I."

I smiled. "I know."

Everyone is gone now. Although my promise to Mr. Lipkind more or less expired back in the forties, when he did, I have kept it until now, and I have made arrangements that it be kept until long after I take my own leave.

By the time you read this, all of us will be only memories.

But there is something else that Miss Lizzie once said:

Perhaps being a memory is not a such bad thing after all.

Acknowledgments

I have stolen from the following books:

Michael and Ariane Batterberry. *On the Town in New York*. Routledge, 1999.

The Federal Writers Project. *The WPA Guide to New York City*. Pantheon Books, 1982.

Liza M. Greene. *New York for New Yorkers*. Norton, 2001.

Sanna Feirstein. *Naming New York: Manhattan Places & How They Got Their Names*. New York University Press, 2001.

The Historical Atlas of New York City, Eric Homberger, Owl Books, 1998.

Jim Haskins. The Cotton Club. Plume, 1984.

Robert E. Drenna, ed. *The Algonquin Wits*. Kensington, 2001.

Marion Meade. *Dorothy Parker: What Fresh Hell Is This?* Penguin Books, 1989.

Dorothy Parker. *The Portable Dorothy Parker*. Penguin Books, 1976.

Emily Wortis Leider. *Becoming Mae West*. Da Capo Press, 2000.

Jill Watts. *Mae West: An Icon in Black and White*. Oxford University Press, 2001.

Howard Teichmann. *George S. Kaufman, An Intimate Portrait*. Atheneum, 1972.

Lewis Yablonsky. *George Raft*. McGraw-Hill, 1974.

Frederick Lewis Allen. *Only Yesterday*. Perennial Library, 1964.

Edward Behr. *Prohibition: Thirteen Years that Changed America*. Arcade Publishing, 1996.

Polly Adler. *A House Is Not a Home.* Popular Library, 1955.

Michael Arlen. *The Green Hat.* Boydell Press, 1983.

T. S. Eliot. *The Waste Land and Other Poems.* Penguin Books, 1998.

David W. Maurer. *The Big Con.* Anchor Books, 1999.

Jimmy Breslin. *Damon Runyon: A Life.* Laurel, 1992.

Graham Nown. *The English Godfather.* Ward Lock, 1987.

Albert Fried. *The Rise and Fall of the Jewish Gangster in America.* Columbia University Press, 1999.

David Pietrusza. *Rothstein* Carroll and Graf, 2003.

Leo Katcher. *The Big Bankroll: The Life and Times of Arnold Rothstein.* Cardinal, 1960.

Jean Hugard, ed. *Encyclopedia of Card Tricks.* Dover, 1974.

John Scarne. *Scarne on Cards.* Signet, 1973.

About the Author

Walter Satterthwait is an author of mysteries and historical fiction. While working as a bartender in New York in the late 1970s, he wrote his first book: an adventure novel, *Cocaine Blues* (1979. After his second thriller, *The Aegean Affair* (1982), Satterthwait created his best-known character, Santa Fe private detective Joshua Croft. Beginning with *Wall of Glass* (1988), Satterthwait wrote five Croft novels, concluding the series with 1996's *Accustomed to the Dark*. In between Croft books, he wrote mysteries starring historical figures, including *Miss Lizzie* (1989), a novel about Lizzie Borden, and *Wilde West* (1991), a western mystery starring Oscar Wilde. *New York Nocturne* (2016) is his most recent novel.

WALTER SATTERTHWAIT

FROM MYSTERIOUSPRESS.COM
AND OPEN ROAD MEDIA

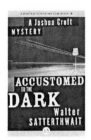
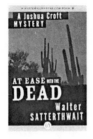
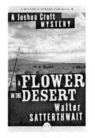

MYSTERIOUSPRESS.COM

OPEN ROAD
INTEGRATED MEDIA

MYSTERIOUSPRESS.COM

Otto Penzler, owner of the Mysterious Bookshop in Manhattan, founded the Mysterious Press in 1975. Penzler quickly became known for his outstanding selection of mystery, crime, and suspense books, both from his imprint and in his store. The imprint was devoted to printing the best books in these genres, using fine paper and top dust-jacket artists, as well as offering many limited, signed editions.

Now the Mysterious Press has gone digital, publishing ebooks through **MysteriousPress.com**.

MysteriousPress.com offers readers essential noir and suspense fiction, hard-boiled crime novels, and the latest thrillers from both debut authors and mystery masters. Discover classics and new voices, all from one legendary source.

FIND OUT MORE AT

WWW.MYSTERIOUSPRESS.COM

FOLLOW US:

@emysteries and Facebook.com/MysteriousPressCom

MysteriousPress.com is one of a select group of publishing partners of Open Road Integrated Media, Inc.

THE MYSTERIOUS BOOKSHOP, founded in 1979, is located in Manhattan's Tribeca neighborhood. It is the oldest and largest mystery-specialty bookstore in America.

The shop stocks the finest selection of new mystery hardcovers, paperbacks, and periodicals. It also features a superb collection of signed modern first editions, rare and collectable works, and Sherlock Holmes titles. The bookshop issues a free monthly newsletter highlighting its book clubs, new releases, events, and recently acquired books.

58 Warren Street
info@mysteriousbookshop.com
(212) 587-1011
Monday through Saturday
11:00 a.m. to 7:00 p.m.

FIND OUT MORE AT:

www.mysteriousbookshop.com

FOLLOW US:

@TheMysterious and Facebook.com/MysteriousBookshop

OPEN ROAD

INTEGRATED MEDIA

Find a full list of our authors and
titles at www.openroadmedia.com

FOLLOW US
@OpenRoadMedia